LANA KORTCHIK grew up in two opposite corners of the former Soviet Union – a snow-white Siberian town and the golden-domed capital of Ukraine. At the age of sixteen, she moved to Australia with her mother. Lana and her family live on the Central Coast of New South Wales, where it never snows and is always summer-warm. She loves books, martial arts, the ocean and Napoleonic history. Her short stories have appeared in many magazines and anthologies. She is the author of the *USA Today* bestselling *Sisters of War* and *Daughters of the Resistance*.

T0035119

Also by Lana Kortchik

Sisters of War
Daughters of the Resistance
The Countess of the Revolution

Sisters of the Sky

LANA KORTCHIK

ONE PLACE. MANY STORIES

HQ
An imprint of HarperCollinsPublishers Ltd
1 London Bridge Street
London SE1 9GF

www.harpercollins.co.uk

HarperCollinsPublishers
Macken House, 39/40 Mayor Street Upper,
Dublin 1 D01 C9W8
Ireland

This paperback edition 2024

1
First published in Great Britain by
HQ, an imprint of HarperCollinsPublishers Ltd 2023

ISBN: 9780008661250

Printed and Bound in the U.S.A. by Lake Book Manufacturing, LLC

*For Joel. What an adventure the last eleven years
have been. I love you!*

And endless battle! We only dream of peace
Through blood and dust . . .

Alexandr Blok

PART ONE

Chapter 1

Moscow, October 1941

In October 1941, the air in Moscow didn't smell of leaves and damp grass, like it normally would at this time of year. Instead, it smelt overpoweringly of fire and death, while the earth trembled and the sky overhead roared like a wounded animal. The explosions sounded like thunder, like an autumn storm that would soon pass, giving way to sunshine and calm; nothing but golden branches whispering quietly in the breeze – only it had been four months and this particular storm didn't show any signs of passing. The noise of battle had become the soundtrack to the lives of those who still remained in the city as they moved fearfully about with their heads low and eyes to the ground.

Nina Petrova was no longer afraid of the explosions. She no longer ran for shelter every time she heard the high-pitched shriek of the siren. And that was what scared her the most. War had become normal.

There was a time when she had taken peace for granted. The peaceful sky of her childhood wasn't something to treasure and be grateful for. It just *was*. Suddenly, without warning, one scorching day in June that started out just like any ordinary day, with no indication of the horror to come, the Germans invaded, selfishly snatching away the blue sky and Nina's future.

If she'd known this could happen, if she'd known happiness was such a fragile and fleeting thing, she would have cherished *everything*: every moment with friends, every ice cream on the banks of the Moskva River, every trip to the cinema and bike ride with her brother, every cup of tea in the morning and peaceful night with nothing to fear. She would have laughed louder, hugged her loved ones more often and breathed more deeply. She would have lived every day like it was her last. Perhaps then she would have fewer regrets as she stood in the middle of an airfield with tears in her eyes and her arms around her younger brother, who was going to war.

Trying to hide her tears from Vlad, she glanced at her watch. They didn't have much time.

'Don't look so glum,' said Vlad, pulling her hair. 'It's going to be all right.'

'Ouch!' she exclaimed. 'That hurt.' She pouted but not for long. She knew it was Vlad's way of showing affection.

'Finally, we get to show Hitler what we are made of. I can't wait to get inside my fighter plane and give him a taste of his own medicine.'

Nina's face fell. The thought of her little brother charging the Germans on his metal steed made her heart skip with pain. For a moment she couldn't talk, so she watched Vlad instead, trying to commit every detail of his face to memory. At eighteen, he looked so grown-up and was being so brave. How did that happen so quickly? Wasn't it only yesterday that he was a skinny eight-year-old, clinging to his older sister's skirt when their mother had died? Nina's eyes filled with tears.

Next to the two of them, Nina's best friend, Katya Bogdanova, was crying inconsolably, her eyes on her husband Anton, who held their three-year-old girl in his arms. And all around, other families were saying goodbye to their young men. Mothers and fathers hugging their sons, perhaps for the last time. Wives clinging to their husbands. Nothing but tears and miserable faces.

This was what war did. It took loved ones away in one soul-destroying, devastating instance. One moment they were there, the next they were gone. Nina knew all about it, having said goodbye to her father, uncle and three cousins in the space of three months.

The airfield was slush under her feet. Snow, water and mud mixed together to make walking difficult. The sky was grey, threatening snow. It felt right. Cheerful blue skies and bright sunshine would seem out of place on a day like this.

'Don't fret, girls. We have the most reliable planes in the world,' said Anton, holding his daughter close. 'Yak-1 is a marvel of Soviet engineering.'

'That's right,' said Vlad. 'We trained hard for this. We are ready. You have nothing to worry about.'

'You could be the best pilots in the world, in the most reliable planes, but if German fighter planes are firing at you, what difference does it make?' said Katya, a small woman with freckles and long red hair. Her hands were shaking. Her face seemed grey in the pale autumn light. She looked like any moment she was going to be sick.

'The war won't last long,' said Anton, kissing Katya on the corner of her lips. 'We'll be back before you know it.'

Nina lowered her head and said, 'We are facing an army of three million well-armed and well-trained soldiers, with tanks, guns and aircraft the likes of which we have never seen, on every inch of our border, burning, looting and bombing everything in their path, occupying thousands of kilometres of Soviet territory.' Three pairs of eyes watched her in silence. She added, 'What I'm saying is, I don't think this war will be over any time soon.'

Vlad said, 'They might have the tanks and the guns, but they have nothing like Yak-1.' There was pride in his voice as he glanced at the aircraft waiting across the airfield to take them away from their families, perhaps forever.

Katya exclaimed, clinging to Anton, 'We had so many happy memories on this airfield. It feels like a lifetime ago.'

Katya was right, Nina thought. It *was* a lifetime ago. Past life: careless hours of joy with friends, learning to glide through the air like birds without a care in the world, sunshine and songs and a bright future ahead of them. Current life: darkness with not a glimmer of hope because Hitler had come to the Soviet Union, bringing destruction in his wake. And her brother standing by her side, minutes away from getting inside a plane and leaving for the front.

Military training was compulsory for schoolchildren in the Soviet Union. All through school, they studied military history, met with veterans, learned to shoot and use a gas mask. In their spare time, they were required to do a sport or defence activity outside school. When the girls were sixteen, Katya had suggested a flying club. There were hundreds of them scattered around the country, run by Komsomol, the Communist League of Youth. Tuition was free and the clubs were open to boys and girls. To learn to fly was everyone's dream in the thirties, the golden age of Soviet aviation. 'We can be like Marina Raskova,' Katya had said one day, when school had broken up for the summer and the girls were at a loss with what to do with their time. Raskova had just set an international distance record of six thousand five hundred and forty kilometres, having flown a full day and night from Moscow to the far eastern reaches of Siberia, proving anything was possible.

Nina had reluctantly agreed, even though heights scared her. She followed her best friend to the aviation club like she had followed her to chess and skiing clubs when they were younger. The chess and the skiing didn't last but flying did. As Nina had soared in her open cockpit plane on her first solo flight, her heart caught in her throat – not from fear but from pure joy. She felt free as a bird and just as happy. She was hooked.

Here on this airfield, they had experienced so many firsts together. Her first time in the air. Her first time in the air alone, without an instructor. Bringing her younger brother with her for the first time and introducing him to this magical world of adventure. They had grown up on the airfield, coming here straight from school, bonding with their planes, learning about aviation and spending hours in the sky. Until recently, it had been a hobby. Now that the country was at war, it had become much more than that. After three months of intensive training on fighter planes, Anton and Vlad were about to fly to the front, like most boys from their club.

The familiar airfield Nina loved so much looked alien today; an enemy, not a friend. With a heavy heart she glanced at the aircraft lined up in the mud. They were not the open cockpit U-2s they had all trained in but Yak-1, the most advanced fighter plane the Soviet Union had ever produced. They were killing machines, equipped with three machine guns and capable of reaching speeds of up to six hundred and twenty kilometres per hour and an altitude of ten thousand metres. They were resilient, fast and reliable. Were they strong enough to protect her brother at war? Nina shuddered and looked away.

'I'm only sad because I'm jealous,' she said, forcing her lips to smile, putting on a brave face for Vlad. 'I wish I was going too.'

'Speak for yourself,' said Katya. 'I'm happy to stay behind and wait.'

Flicking her long blonde hair back, Nina said, 'Wait for what? I heard a female pilot from Leningrad took her plane and flew to the front, without permission.'

'Yes, they kept the plane and sent her back home,' said Vlad.

'War is not the place for women,' said Katya. 'We are supposed to stay home and look after our families. Take care of children.' She stroked her daughter Tonya's dark hair.

Anton nodded. 'Agreed. As a father and a husband, I would rather be the one doing the defending.'

'Exactly!' Katya placed her hand on his arm. 'I want to finish university. I want a normal life.'

'What normal life, Katya?' asked Nina. 'If the Nazis come here, there will be no normal life. There will be no university. Remember my friend Misha? He told me he saw a German motorcycle unit on Leningradka two days ago, followed by two armoured personnel carriers. Apparently, they made it all the way to the Severnyi Rechnoi Station.'

'And the Red Army quickly turned them back,' said Katya.

'They were the first. They won't be the last.'

The thought of the Nazis on the streets of Moscow filled Nina with rage, the likes of which she had never experienced before. How dare they come here, tearing people's lives apart? She thought of her darling father, forty-five years old and suffering from arthritis, risking his life at the front. He wasn't a fighter, he was an engineer, the kindest and most peaceful person she'd known. In all her life, she had never heard him raise his voice. They had had three letters from him since he left and then, silence. *The post is terrible*, she told herself. *Papa is fine. It's just the post.* Some days she believed it. Other days, she woke up in the morning and could barely breathe from fear.

Anton put a friendly arm around her and smiled. 'They are not here yet. Don't worry about something that hasn't happened or you will drive yourself crazy.'

Vlad nodded. 'And stay away from the front. Katya is right. It's not a place for women. Fortunately, they won't take you.'

They were quiet for a moment. Nina was trying hard not to cry. She didn't want to fall apart in front of her brother. She would wait until he was gone. Vlad stared into the distance, like he was already miles away.

'You have ten minutes,' an officer shouted.

Anton pressed his daughter closer, while his eyes remained on

Nina and Katya. 'Look after each other, girls. Make sure you get enough food. Promise to write.'

'We promise,' said Nina. Katya nodded, sniffling, her eyes and face red from tears.

'Take care of yourself. And don't let Anna get to you,' said Vlad.

'All right.' Nina's hands started to shake at the thought of facing her stepmother alone, without Vlad and without Papa. 'But only if you promise to take care of yourself.'

'I promise.'

For eighteen years, she had looked after her younger brother. She had rocked him in her arms when she was five and he was a newborn baby, held his hands when he was learning to walk, taught him how to ride a bicycle, wiped his tears when he fell and dealt with schoolyard bullies. Over the years, she had protected and taken care of him. When he was sad or hurt or afraid, it wasn't his parents but his big sister he had always run to. Nina was his first word when he was a baby. She remembered it like it was yesterday. His chubby cheeks moving, his mouth wide, making the first sounds with a huge effort, 'Na-na.' Who was going to protect him now, at the front? 'I don't think you've ever been away from home by yourself before,' she said quietly.

'I don't think I have.'

'Don't do anything dangerous. And be careful.'

Vlad saluted her, grinning. 'I'll be careful. And brave. I'll make you proud.'

'You don't need to go to the front to make me proud because I already am.'

The officer shouted that it was time. Nina wanted to scream at him to leave them alone. She wanted another five minutes with her brother, wanted to stop time and stay like this forever, in the middle of the airfield in wartime Moscow, with her arms around him, so she could keep him safe. Her heart aching, she hugged her brother tightly and then let him go, even though every fibre in her body was desperate to hold on. Her hand on her chest, she watched as he walked to his plane. When he was about to climb inside the cockpit, she shouted, 'Vlad!' When he turned around, she said, 'I love you!'

'I love you too.' Then he disappeared inside the plane and soon she could hear nothing but the sound of engines and a child's ear-piercing scream.

'Papa!' shouted Tonya as Anton attempted to walk away. 'No, Papa!' Nina turned around just in time to see Tonya wrestle out of Katya's arms and run across the airfield to Anton. Katya watched helplessly, her hands shaking, her face frozen, as if she were moments away from a breakdown. Anton opened his arms and Tonya jumped into them. 'Don't go, Papa.' He held her, stroking her hair and whispering something. Pressing her little body to him, Tonya placed her head on his shoulder. For a moment she was quiet. They remained like that, father and daughter, clinging to each other for dear life. Kissing her gently on the cheek, brushing her hair off her face, Anton carried the child back to Katya.

'Goodbye, little one. I love you more than anything in the world. Look after your mama for me.'

He tried to pry the little hands away when Tonya started screaming, choking on her tears and coughing. 'No! Papa, no!'

Katya put her arms around Tonya and for a moment they stood still, all three of them holding on to each other. 'Come, little one. Papa has to go. But he'll be back soon. He will bring you presents,' said Katya, her voice breaking.

'Don't want presents,' Tonya shouted, refusing to let go of her father. 'Want Papa.'

'I won't be gone for long. I'll be back before you even notice. I promise.'

'Time!' shouted the officer. How Nina hated him just then. She hated him like it was all his fault, like he was the reason they were saying goodbye to their loved ones this dreary morning.

With a superhuman effort, Katya wrestled the screaming child from Anton. Tonya became hysterical. Tears were streaming down

Anton's face. 'I love you so much,' he said, his voice thick with emotion. 'So much.' He kissed the little girl's face and hands, but on and on she screamed, trying to grab his neck.

When he walked away, turning around every few metres, he looked shattered, like every step brought unbearable pain. He tried to smile for his daughter but the smile came out twisted and sad. It was a ghost of a smile.

Then he was off, climbing inside the cockpit and starting the engine. Through a fuzzy screen of tears, Nina watched the planes take off one after another, becoming smaller and smaller, while her heart felt like it was growing bigger and heavier.

Now that her brother could no longer hear her, Nina was sobbing loudly, just like Katya and Tonya by her side. Their airfield, the place of so much joy, had suddenly become the place of heartbreak.

And all she could think was, *Will we ever see them again?*

Nina felt lost after Vlad had left. A few days without her brother, night after sleepless night, and she tried to go on as before, to pretend her life hadn't stopped on the day Hitler's hordes invaded her homeland. She cleaned and cooked and gazed out the window. Every morning, she woke up early and, ignoring the cold grip of fear inside her, walked to the university because trams were no longer running. But before the cleaning and the cooking and the studies, she would rush to the mailbox, praying for news. It had been three, four, five days without a word. Finally, a week had passed with no news from Vlad.

In a large auditorium, Nina sat next to Katya and listened to a substitute lecturer talk about the correct way to pronounce the English *th* sound, while somewhere on the outskirts of Moscow the Germans prepared for the final offensive on the capital.

As Nina looked at Katya's transfixed face whispering English words under her breath, she felt a strange sense of displacement, like she was in the wrong place at the wrong time. Hardly anyone

13

attended the lectures anymore. Most male students and staff had been drafted into the army and many women had evacuated east, away from the advancing Germans. The auditorium looked orphaned and abandoned. Just like all of Moscow, the university was a ghost of its former self.

Seeing it like this broke Nina's heart. All she had ever wanted was to become a journalist like her mama. The day she had been accepted to do her journalism degree at Moscow State University, her mother's *alma mater*, was one of the happiest of her life. The narrow corridors, the wide auditoriums and cobbled courtyards of the university held a special meaning for Nina. They represented a lifelong dream. Once upon a time, Mama had walked these corridors and sat inside these auditoriums. Now it was Nina's turn. The university was her home. When she was here, she felt closer to her mother than ever.

Just like Mama had done two decades earlier, Nina would sit under the domed ceiling of the university library and read Hugo and Voltaire in French, Remarque and Mann in German, Wilde and Austen in English, dreaming of a different life and glancing at the manicured lawn and poplars outside. There was a whole new world out there and the university was her ticket to discovering it. Her studies had been her life, until now.

'I'm going home,' whispered Nina, suddenly jumping to her feet.

'Why? Not feeling well?' Katya tore her gaze away from the blackboard and looked at Nina.

'I don't see the point in this. We can't stop the Germans by making the *th* sound.'

'This is important too. After the war is over, you'll be glad you continued your education!'

'I can't concentrate. All I can think of is Vlad, out there on his own, without me.'

'I know. All I can think about is Anton. I miss him so much. And . . .' Katya stopped talking and her eyes filled with tears.

14

'Honey, what's wrong?' asked Nina, taking Katya's hand. 'What happened?'

Katya looked up, dried her tears and took a deep breath. 'I got a letter from Anton.'

The familiar fear gripped Nina by the throat and for a moment she couldn't breathe. Here was Katya, crying after receiving a letter from Anton. What could possibly have happened?

'Don't worry, it's nothing bad,' Katya said quickly. 'They are fine. Still travelling to their posts. Still in the air for most of the day. Vlad is safe. You haven't heard from him, have you?'

Nina shook her head sadly.

A few people were throwing glances at the girls. The lecturer had stopped talking about the difference between past perfect and past continuous and was looking in their direction.

'Sorry,' Nina muttered, turning red. 'We were just leaving.' The girls put their coats and hats on and wrapped themselves in scarves. Although it was autumn, Nina could already feel winter's icy daggers in the air. This year, it seemed determined to lay its claim on Moscow early. Every night, it snowed, and every morning, as soon as the sun came up, the snow melted, leaving a slushy mess behind.

Nina and Katya walked outside and found a bench under a large oak tree overlooking the fountain. A golden carpet of leaves was under their feet, while branches still dressed in colour reached for them, as if trying to tell them something. The park was a sea of yellow and brown.

'I love it here,' said Nina with regret. 'Especially at this time of year.'

'I know. We had such happy times here, you, me and Anton.'

'Vlad was supposed to start next year. Now he's gone. It feels like our whole life is on hold.'

'It might be on hold but it's not over. Even though it feels like it,' said Katya, picking up a small branch and breaking it between her fingers. Just like Nina, she looked completely lost. 'Tonya asks for Anton every day. It breaks my heart. I don't know what to tell her. Yesterday she asked if he left because of me.' Katya sighed, wiping her tears away with the back of her hand.

Nina took Katya's hand. 'Why would she think that?'

'She heard us, Nina. She heard us arguing before he left. We've been doing that a lot lately.'

'Don't be too hard on yourself. All married couples argue.'

Katya dropped her head in her hands and sighed. 'I knew he was leaving the next day. Why did I have to say such horrible things to him? I told him I didn't ever want to see him again and Tonya heard me. Now he's gone.'

'He knows you didn't mean it. And you can explain it to Tonya. Tell her Mama and Papa love each other very much but sometimes grown-ups argue. What did you fight about anyway?'

Katya shrugged and looked at her feet. 'He wants us to move in with his mother. She's sick and alone. He doesn't want her to be on her own while he's at the front. I told him I could never leave my mama. She needs help with the boys. Besides, I can't stand his mother. She's a witch. Nothing I ever do is good enough for her. *I'm* not good enough for her precious son.'

'You didn't tell him that, did you?'

'I did. Ever since he told me he was leaving for the front, I haven't been myself. I've been so afraid. I haven't been sleeping or eating and I took it out on him. Now I wish I hadn't said anything.' Katya was silent for a moment. 'Nina, what if God has heard my words and decides to punish me by taking my husband from me? What if Anton never comes back?'

Nina pulled Katya into a hug and tried to smile. 'Of course, he'll come back. It's hard for everyone. We all worry too much. That's why you fought. The stress of it all. And Anton knows it. I bet he's forgotten all about it.'

'You think so?' Katya asked, looking at Nina with broken eyes.

'I know so.'

After the bell rang, Katya returned to the lecture theatre and

Nina walked home through the mud. The sky darkened and snow began to fall. On every street corner, there were placards depicting the Motherland, represented by a haggard woman with dull eyes, pointing an accusing finger at Nina, demanding that she volunteer for the front.

On Gorkogo Street, the shop windows were hidden behind bags of sand, while in the sky, giant airships drifted like clouds. There was not a person in the street. Moscow was a ghost town as it waited for the Nazis to arrive, unrecognisable even to Nina, who had lived here all her life. The Kremlin had been covered with wooden beams, made to look like a regular building to stop the Nazis from spotting it from above. A fake bridge had been built nearby to confuse the enemy. Roofs and walls of famous buildings had been painted a different colour. And red stars no longer adorned famous Moscow towers. All of the city's inhabitants were holding their breaths in fearful anticipation, prepared for the worst but hoping for the best because Comrade Stalin had told them he would never surrender the capital.

The air-raid siren sounded and Nina heard the roar of planes. For a moment, she stood in the middle of the street and watched them, her knees shaking. Instead of bombs, leaflets rained from the sky. She picked one up. 'You will go to sleep Soviet and wake up German,' she read, shuddering.

There were no bomb shelters in Moscow, so Nina went down to the metro station. Unlike the streets above, the station was crowded. People from all walks of life had made it their home and folding beds covered all available space on the rails and platforms. Children were shouting, running around and crying for food. Mothers held them close, singing soothing lullabies and hiding their tear-filled eyes because they had no food to give them. Nina's heart clenched with pity as she looked away from them to the beautiful mosaics on the walls.

When the all clear sounded, Nina climbed out of the station and continued on her way.

At home, on the third floor of a dilapidated building on Lenin Avenue, pandemonium reigned. A three-year-old was screaming hysterically, while a newborn baby wailed in her crib. Nina's stepmother, a sour woman in her early thirties called Anna, was rocking the crib, while trying to pull the toddler off the floor.

'Good, you're here,' she said to Nina, who could barely hear her over the noise. 'Lena needs a feed. Could you take Leo to my room and play with him?'

'Hello to you too, Anna,' Nina muttered under her breath, turning to the child, who had peeled himself off the floor and, his eyes still swimming in tears, ran to her side and hugged her knees. 'Nina, Nina!' He threw himself in her arms and she held him close. Leo's little face reminded her of Papa. He had the same upturned nose and dimples when he smiled. Her heart hurt a little every time she looked at him.

A moment later, Leo's smile disappeared, giving way to a demanding expression on his face. 'Read a book!'

'Of course, darling. What book would you like?'

'Catty!'

'His Cat Leopold book is on my bed,' barked Anna.

Nina took her shoes off and, still in her street clothes, followed Leo, who was pulling her in the direction of his mother's bedroom. Once there, he jumped on the bed and shouted, 'Read!'

Nina spotted the book on the bedside table, open to Leo's favourite page. Taking off her scarf and jacket, she reached for the book. Underneath was an envelope. Nina would have ignored it but out of the corner of her eye she saw that it was addressed to her. Picking it up, she turned it this way and that, puzzled. What was a letter meant for her doing in her stepmother's room? The envelope had already been opened. Nina recognised her brother's handwriting.

'Read now!' cried Leo and his face crumpled like a prune. Any time now it was going to dissolve into floods of tears.

'Of course, darling!' Nina placed the envelope in her pocket and opened the book. Leo sat in her lap while she read, her mind wandering away from Cat Leopold's adventures to her brother's letter. Once the little boy had enough of the book and moved on to his cars on the floor, she peered inside the envelope and pulled out a piece of paper, unfolding it with trembling hands.

My darling sister,

I hope you listened to me and are staying away from recruitment stations. I heard that fighting is terrible where we are headed. Not that we've seen any real fighting yet. We've been flying from airfield to airfield, making our slow way to the front. More often than not, we have to wait around for days. The waiting is excruciating. My Yak is an awesome machine though. I can't put into words what it's like to control it. Sometimes it feels like it can read my mind, others like it's got a mind of its own. That's how I think of it now. Like a living being. I know we can do great things together.

The whole country seems to be on the move, some evacuating away from the front, others going to fight. We know we are close because yesterday we heard explosions and felt the earth tremble.

Anton says hi. It's freezing cold and all they give us is barley. We don't complain. We know it's nothing compared to what's to come. I'm just glad that you are home safely.

With all my love,

Vlad

P.S. Don't let the witch get to you.

Anna was shouting for Nina to come out of her bedroom and take the baby, but Nina paid no attention. She pressed Vlad's letter to her chest, while tears streamed down her cheeks. Moments later, the door flung open. Anna stood in the doorway, baby Lena on her hip. As fast as she could, Nina hid the letter in her pocket.

'Are you deaf? I need help with the baby!'

'I was reading to Leo.'

Leo was on the floor, making car noises as he moved his toys around. Anna narrowed her eyes. 'I can't do everything around here. If I call you, drop whatever you are doing and come.'

'You don't do everything around here,' Nina muttered.

She knew Anna had heard because the expression on her face changed. Her eyes became slits and her mouth opened. 'What did you just say?' she bellowed.

Nina didn't feel up to a confrontation. She turned away.

Unfortunately, Anna was always up for an argument. She lived for conflict, feeding off it like a vampire off blood. She grabbed Nina's hand. 'How dare you answer back! We feed you, clothe you, give you a roof over your head and this is how you repay us?'

'This is my father's apartment,' said Nina quietly. They had this argument multiple times a week. Nothing she said ever made a difference.

'And I'm your father's wife. For years I have tried to be a mother to you but you make it very difficult.'

'You told me to start cooking my own meals when I was ten. To drop out of school at fifteen to get a job at a factory. To find my own place to live at sixteen. If my father didn't step in . . .'

'Yes, he seems to wear rose-coloured glasses when it comes to you. No matter what you do is fine by him. But he's not here now.'

'Oh, and does being a mother give you the right to open my letters? Were you even going to give this to me?'

Nina waved Vlad's letter in front of Anna, who looked flustered but only for a moment. 'I had to make sure your brother was safe. Of course, I was going to give it to you.'

'Why did you open it? It's not addressed to you.'

'I'm glad I opened it.' Anna leaned closer, her finger in Nina's face. 'Who is he calling a witch?'

Nina could smell alcohol on Anna's breath. She recoiled from her. 'Have you been drinking?'

'That's none of your business.'

'You know Papa doesn't like it when you drink. It's not good for the children to see you like this.'

Anna squared her shoulders and glared at Nina. 'There's a lot to be drinking about.'

'But you are breastfeeding. Papa said . . .'

'I don't care what he said. He's not here, is he? Not here to help us at all.'

'He's fighting. He has no choice. But you have a choice. The children need you.'

'Why don't you mind your own business?' Anna cried, storming off. Nina went to the kitchen, opened the cupboard and found Anna's bottle of vodka. Unscrewing the top, she poured it down the sink. Anna would be furious but she was doing it for Leo and Lena.

In bed that night, Nina repeated Vlad's words to herself. *Don't let the witch get to you.* It was easier said than done, in this small space she shared with Anna and the children, without Vlad or Papa to act as a buffer. Her brother had always been protective of her when it came to Anna, as if he were the older of the two. When Papa had first married Anna and she moved in, it felt like their world turned upside down. 'Everything will be all right,' their father had said to them. 'Anna is going to be like a mother to you.' Nina didn't think anyone could replace her mother, who they had lost so suddenly and devastatingly, within mere months of her falling ill. But she had believed her father. He had never lied to her before. A few weeks after she moved in, Anna had locked fifteen-year-old Nina in the bathroom for not eating the meal she'd cooked. Vlad, all eleven years of him, had stood up from the table, pushing his plate away. 'Can you blame her?' he had said. 'Your cooking is disgusting. And if you treat my sister like this again, you can go back to where you came from. You will never be part of our family.' Since that day, Anna hated them both and, when their father wasn't looking, went out of her way to make their lives hell. Because she didn't have a job, she had

21

plenty of time on her hands and a vivid imagination capable of devising various petty punishments for the two of them. The airfield became their escape.

As she was drifting off to sleep, Nina heard Leo crying softly next door. Where was Anna? Why wasn't she going to him? When the crying became more intense, Nina couldn't take it anymore. She didn't want to face Anna, but she couldn't leave her little brother so upset. She climbed out of bed, slipped her feet into her slippers and walked to the kitchen, where Leo was on the floor, kicking his little legs. 'What's wrong, little one? What's the matter? It's way past your bedtime.'

'Don't want to sleep by myself. Scared by myself.' The child hiccupped and stared at Nina with his big blue eyes.

'Where is Mama?'

'With baby.'

'You can come to bed with me for a little while. Would you like that?'

Leo's face lit up with joy, and he wrapped his chubby little arms around Nina's neck. But before Nina had a chance to take him to her room, Anna stormed in and, without a word, snatched Leo out of Nina's arms. Not looking at Nina, she left with the child. Nina and Anna were like strangers on a bus, not talking and avoiding eye contact. They were in fact strangers, despite seven years of living under the same roof. Anna didn't know her at all, Nina realised. And she didn't want to know her.

Anna's screaming woke Nina in the middle of the night. She pulled a pillow over her head and tried to go back to sleep. Moments later, Anna was in her room, shaking her. 'Did you hide my drink?'

Nina blinked. Anna's angry face looked fuzzy in the dark. 'I poured it down the sink.'

Anna became hysterical. 'What have you done? I won't be able to buy any more.'

Nina shrugged. 'Perhaps it's for the best.'

'Don't you understand? I could get some nice bread for us at the market for the vodka.'

'But you don't. You drink it. You drink the vodka you could have used to get bread for Leo.' Nina sighed. She was so tired. Why was Anna in her room? Why wasn't she leaving?

'Who are you to judge me, you leech? Get out, you spoilt brat! Pack your things and get out.' Anna pulled Nina out of bed and threw her on the floor. Nina cried out, rubbing her knee, while Anna pulled a suitcase out of the wardrobe and threw some clothes inside it. 'Now that your father is not here to step in, I can finally get rid of you. You are useless, good for nothing! Twenty-two years old and what have you done with your life? Just another mouth to feed. You don't contribute. I have my hands full trying to feed myself and the children. I am a nursing mother and I don't get enough food. And here you are, with your student ration, eating all our food.' Anna spat on the floor and glared at Nina with disgust.

Nina wanted to sweet-talk Anna, like she normally would. She didn't want an argument in front of Leo, who got upset by raised voices. But this time there was no appeasing her step-mother. She had been drinking and could only hear the sound of her own voice.

Anna went to slap Nina but she pushed her away, running out of the room, down the dark corridor and out of the apartment, closing the door quietly behind her because she didn't want to scare the children. Taking two steps at a time, she hobbled down-stairs, her knee hurting after her fall from the bed.

Once Nina was outside in the cold, with wet snow falling on her face, the cold biting the skin of her cheeks that were damp from tears, she paused for a moment. The truth was, she had nowhere to go. Her friends had evacuated or had problems of their own. She was all alone, with no roof over her head and no one to turn to, while the Germans were closing their circle around Moscow, burning and pillaging the countryside. All she could hear was Anna's voice, telling her she was useless and good for nothing. But Nina didn't cry for long. Since her mother had died, her life consisted of a series of injustices, great and small. This was just one of them, and if she stayed in that house, she knew it wouldn't be the last.

Suddenly, she knew exactly what she had to do.

Nina spent the night at a neighbour's apartment. In the morning, she stepped outside and couldn't believe her eyes. Fresh snow had fallen during the night, turning the streets of her childhood into a winter wonderland, hiding the bomb craters and the damaged buildings, making everything look fresh and beautiful, untouched by war. Speechless, she watched it all with awe, taking in short icy breaths.

But the awe didn't last. Two blocks away from her building, she stumbled on six dead bodies laid out on the street. When she turned the corner, she saw five more. She averted her eyes as she made her slow way through the snow, doing her best not to slip on the ice. Despite the virginal snow glistening in the morning sun, the familiar streets no longer looked like a fairy tale. Soon the snow would melt and turn into mud, and Moscow would once again look damaged and torn.

Nina stopped outside a sixteen-storey building that had been partially destroyed by a bomb. Taking a deep breath, she climbed the stairs to the second floor. The corridors were teeming with people. Soldiers in uniform and important-looking civilians rushed past Nina without a second glance. They all looked like they knew where they were going, like they had somewhere important to be, while she stepped from foot to foot uncertainly outside a wooden door with a little metal plaque that read, *Alexander Vladimirovich Andreev, Recruiting Officer.*

Before she completely lost her nerve and turned back, Nina knocked on the door and pushed it. The door gave way. The man sitting behind a desk was round and bald, hunched over his documents with a pen in his hand. His eyes looked tired. He seemed aged, not so much by years as his thoughts and worries. 'Can I help you?' he asked, putting a blank piece of paper over the documents, as if afraid Nina was going to steal the military secrets they contained.

'I would like to volunteer for the front.' She stood to attention like a soldier.

'You are in the wrong place, my dear. You have to go to a recruitment station.'

'They say they don't recruit women.'

'Then you have your answer. I don't see what else I can do.' He looked down at his documents, his eyes resting on the blank piece of paper.

'Please, help me. I have a valuable skill, you see. I'm a pilot. I've spent six years learning how to fly. It could be useful, for our country, I mean.' She rubbed her hands nervously and watched the man's face.

'Why don't you enlist as a nurse, like many other young women? I hear there's a shortage of nurses.'

They were the young generation growing up in a young country – the Soviet Union. Since childhood they had been told that men and women were equal. Women could do any job they wanted. A tractor driver? Why not? A mechanic? But of course. All over the country, girls joined aviation clubs to learn how to fly. Now that it was war and her country needed her, Nina was expecting the same equal treatment. But equality in theory didn't translate to equality in practice, during war. 'I want to defend my country. I want to do my duty, to honour my obligations . . .'

'Nursing is not honourable enough?' he interrupted.

'Certainly, but it's not for me. I want to do everything I can to stop the Nazis and I won't rest until I can do so.'

'You think you can stop the Nazis?' He looked like he was fighting a smile.

'I want to fly as a combat pilot, sir. I heard there's a shortage of pilots.'

'You heard wrong. Every second young man and woman in the country wants to be a combat pilot. We don't have enough planes for you all.'

Nina thought of her beloved U-2. Sometimes she could swear it was alive and could understand her. To Nina, it was more than an aircraft, it was a dear friend. 'I will bring my own plane.'

'You are eager to go to your death.' Alexander took off his glasses, cleaned them with a handkerchief and replaced them on his face. 'Why don't you sit down?' He pointed to a chair in front of him. 'I have a daughter a few years older than you. She enlisted as a nurse and left for the front three months ago. We haven't heard from her since.'

'The post is terrible. I'm sure you'll hear from her soon,' said Nina, perching on the edge of a chair.

'That's what I keep telling myself but . . .' He looked at her with a sad smile. 'Why are you so desperate to get to the front? It's not all the glory and adventure you young people seem to think it is. It's mind-boggling hard work, inhumane conditions, constant fear and death. It's not a place for a young girl.'

'I'm aware of that, sir.'

'Somehow, I don't think you are. You are all idolising this war, wanting to become heroes. A woman flying as a combat pilot. It's the most ridiculous thing I've ever heard.' He shook his head, like he was disappointed in Nina.

'With all due respect, why is it ridiculous, sir? Since we were children, we've been told that boys and girls are equal. Isn't it the cornerstone of the Communist doctrine? Women can do everything men can.'

'Not this.'

'How is this different?'

'It just is. Go home, dear. Go back to your family. What you are asking for, it's not going to happen. I wish I could help you. But if I do, I won't be able to live with myself. I'm not having this on my conscience.'

26

'You can tell your conscience you had no choice,' said Nina, getting comfortable in her chair.

'How so?'

'I am not leaving this office until you say yes.'

If Alexander was surprised by this declaration, he didn't show it. Lifting himself up, he said, 'Very well. I have a few errands to run and recruitment stations to visit. I probably won't be back today.'

'I'll be here when you return tomorrow.'

Alexander sighed. 'Don't you have somewhere better to be?'

Nina thought of Anna's twisted face as she threw Nina's clothes inside a suitcase. 'No, sir,' she replied.

Shaking his head, as if amazed by her, he said, 'By law, I am required to lock this door. Once I go, you will have to stay here all day and all night.'

'I will stay here as long as it takes.'

'Then I'll see you tomorrow. Should you get hungry, there are biscuits in the cupboard and some tea. Have a good day!'

He packed his documents away, locking them in a safe, then nodded to Nina and left.

When the door closed behind him, Nina paced around the office for a moment, then sat down once again and looked out the window at people rushing to the nearby train station like the devil himself was at their heels.

After half an hour in the uncomfortable chair, she moved to Alexander's soft leather armchair. She was glad she had her favourite book with her. For the next few hours, she lost herself in Jules Verne's incredible world of underwater adventures. It was the twentieth century, she thought. People had conquered air and sea. It was preposterous that she wasn't allowed to go to the front and fight for her country that was in dire need of help. How was it fair that men were allowed to fly in combat and she wasn't, when she had more experience and skill?

When it got dark in the room, she turned the lights on, opened the cupboard and helped herself to some biscuits and a hard-boiled candy. Then she sat back down and read Vlad's letter one more time, even though she knew it by heart.

She fell asleep with her head on the letter and didn't wake up until she heard a key in the lock. For a few moments, she didn't know where she was. The morning light was streaking through the curtains, playing on her face. She could hear the din of traffic outside and an occasional blast of a horn. Moscow sounded exactly the same as it always did. She could almost trick herself into believing that there was no war, if it wasn't for the occasional explosion somewhere on the outskirts of the city and the acrid smell of smoke.

The door opened and Alexander walked in. 'You are still here,' he said, sounding surprised.

Nina rose to her feet. 'Of course, I'm still here. You locked the door.'

'Now you are free to go.'

'Not unless it's to the front.'

He watched her for a moment in silence. Then he motioned for her to sit. 'Have you thought this through? Is it what you really want?'

'Yes, sir.'

'Have you discussed it with your parents? Your family?'

'I only have Papa and a younger brother, and they are both at the front.'

'And nothing I can say can change your mind?'

'How would it look if a recruitment officer stopped an eager volunteer from joining the army?'

'Very well.' Alexander sat down in his armchair, silently studying Nina for a moment. Finally, he said, 'Today is your lucky day. I got a call yesterday evening. Straight away I thought of you. Have you heard of Marina Raskova?'

'Hasn't everyone?' Nina perked up. Marina Raskova was her hero. Reading about her exploits as a pilot and navigator was what inspired her and Katya – and tens of thousands of other girls around the Soviet Union – to join a flying club and learn how to fly.

'Major Raskova has been entrusted by Comrade Stalin to create three female-only units of pilots and navigators. Does that sound like something you would be interested in?' Alexander rubbed his hands together, looking pleased with himself.

Nina leapt off her chair with excitement. Interested? Was he serious? 'It sounds perfect!' Her breath caught. 'Three units of women?'

'That's what they said. Personally, I think it's madness.'

Nina wanted to hug Alexander and dance with him around his tiny office. 'Thank you, sir! I won't forget it.'

'If I were you, I'd think about it carefully. I don't think you realise quite what you are signing up for.'

'I have thought about it and nothing else!'

'In that case, report to the assembly point at Zhukovsky Academy at four. Don't be late.'

'Thank you!' she exclaimed. 'I will be the best pilot this country has ever known, male or female.'

'You are definitely modest enough.'

'You won't regret it!'

'I'm regretting it already. Sending a young girl to a certain death. What is this world coming to?' He continued talking, but Nina was no longer listening. She was running down the stairs two steps at a time, her heart beating with joy.

The silver cupola of the Zhukovsky Academy shimmered in the late-afternoon sun. Nina paused to admire the tall brown building with its gilded columns and tall windows. Located in the former Petrovsky Palace, built by Catherine the Great to celebrate Russia's victory in the Russian-Turkish War, the academy had produced some of the best pilots in the country. It had produced heroes, explorers and adventurers. And here was Nina, standing outside with her hand on her heart, hoping to become one. As she crossed the courtyard towards the entrance, she had a clear image of herself in military uniform, behind the controls of a bomber or a fighter plane, releasing explosives over German infrastructure or attacking German aircraft. How satisfying would it be, to shoot down a plane that was bombing innocent Soviet civilians on the ground?

The large auditorium was filled with young women. A few wore military uniforms but most were dressed in air club uniforms or civilian clothes. Many had mud on their hands and stains on their clothes, having come straight from digging trenches. Some were holding their textbooks, while others had arrived with their possessions packed in a duffel bag, ready to set out at a moment's notice. They all had one thing in common, however. Their eyes were burning with passion and excitement.

As Nina pushed her way through the crowd, looking for a seat, snippets of conversations reached her.

'As soon as I heard, I came running. Raskova is my hero.'

'Mine too. I never thought I would meet her in person.'

'I've been turned away from every recruitment station in the city. I was ready to run off to the front when someone told me about this.'

Nina made her way to the back of the auditorium, hoping to hide behind the other girls, who seemed braver and looked like they belonged there. Nina, on the other hand, felt completely out of place. If only Katya was there. Nina wouldn't feel nervous if her best friend and partner in crime was by her side.

Someone called her name but she continued moving towards her seat, assuming they were after a different Nina. Suddenly, as she was about to sit down, she felt a tap on her shoulder. Spinning around, she found herself face to face with Katya.

'Are you deaf? I've been calling you for five minutes,' Katya said, grinning.

'Katya!' Nina could hardly believe her eyes. Forgetting all about her nerves, she hugged her friend. 'What are you doing here?'

The girls found two seats together and sat down, turning towards each other. 'The Komsomol organiser came to talk to us at the university this morning. Where were you, by the way?' Not waiting for Nina's reply, Katya continued, 'He told us about Marina Raskova and what she is trying to do. Then he asked for volunteers.'

Nina was twitching in her seat with excitement, looking this way and that, trying to spot Raskova. But the stage remained dark. 'Of course, you told him it wasn't a woman's job to defend her country?'

'I was going to. But then, every single girl raised her hand. How would it look if I was the only one to say no? I heard that some of the nurses who refused to go to the front have lost their rations. My little girl is already starving. I couldn't risk it.'

'They were looking for volunteers. They won't force us girls. Not like they do the men. Not yet, anyway.'

Katya shrugged. 'You never know. Besides, it's too dangerous in Moscow right now. The Nazis are almost here. They said something about six months to a year of training somewhere far from the front line. Away from Hitler. That sounds good, doesn't it? I'm going to take Tonya with me.'

'Who will look after her for you?'

'Maybe she could just wait for me while I study . . .'

'Wait for you where?' Nina felt sorry for her friend. She knew how afraid she was for her little girl and how hard she had tried to evacuate. Unfortunately, they couldn't get on the overcrowded trains which soon stopped running altogether. Even though they wanted to leave, they couldn't. They were trapped in the city.

Katya spoke very fast, her eyes flashing with fear. 'A friend of mine works at a factory making uniforms for the army. She leaves her two-year-old daughter alone in the room all day, with plates of porridge. When she comes home, the porridge is smeared all over the floor and the girl doesn't even cry. She doesn't talk either. She's always silent.'

31

'Tonya is better off with your mama, Katya. She will keep her safe.' The girls were quiet for a moment, lost in their sadness.

The stage lit up and a dark-haired woman appeared. She was wearing a uniform adorned with the golden star of the Hero of the Soviet Union award, the highest distinction in the country. On her head was a beret with a red star. Her shoulders and neck were straight, her long hair pulled back into a bun. Nina heard a gasp, a collective intake of air and then everyone fell quiet, as if the woman had waved a magic wand over her audience. Everyone recognised their hero, Major Marina Raskova, having seen her face in the papers many times. They had heard her voice on the radio as she spoke of her passion for aviation, the passion that had brought every single one of them here today. They had followed with trepidation as she set out on the famous flight on board the *Rodina*, where Marina, as part of a crew of three women, had set a world record for a straight-line long-distance flight. Marina Raskova had traversed their great country back and forth by air many times. She had flown the most advanced aircraft in the world. She had survived ten days lost in Taiga, without food or water. She had become the first female navigator in the Soviet Union. If anyone could help them get to the front, it was her.

And now here she was, standing in front of them, petite, fragile-looking and wide-eyed. When she began to speak, every single person inside the auditorium became transfixed.

'Dear sisters! I have a vision. I believe that women can fight in this war alongside men on the front lines and be as brave, as dedicated and as hard working. I believe that we have much to offer. And seeing so many of you here today, I know I'm right. Who wants to join me in my fight against Hitler?'

A forest of arms flew up in the air and the women shouted. Major Raskova raised her hand and, as if by magic, silence was restored.

'I knew it. You are already heroes because you have the heart and the desire to do your best for your country. I have good news for you. Comrade Stalin has entrusted me to form three all-female aviation regiments: night bombers, dive bombers and fighter pilots. Any woman in the Soviet Union who has experience or interest in planes can volunteer. Our homeland is in danger. Our children rely on us to protect them. The journey will not be easy. It will require strength and sacrifice. But I promise you that it will be worth it. I suggest you go home and think hard about what you are about to do. Talk to your parents. Ask their permission. And come back here tomorrow. I hope to see every single one of you.'

Raskova's speech was met with a standing ovation. Even Katya looked elated as she clapped.

'What do you think? Will you join Raskova with me?' Having been met with opposition every time she tried to volunteer for the front, having thought of nothing else since her brother had left and finally having heard Raskova speak straight to her heart, Nina knew this was the only path for her. It felt right. There was a sense of destiny in this, like she was meant to be here, in the dimly lit auditorium, facing the biggest decision of her life.

'What choice do I have? I had to write my name down at the entrance. What will happen if I don't come back?'

'You heard Raskova. They are only looking for volunteers.'

'That's what they always say.' Katya shrugged. 'If I join, I'll get to fly. I'll get to do what I love. Mama can look after Tonya. Leaving her will break my heart but it's only for a few months. How much longer can this war possibly last?'

Nina didn't just walk home that evening, she flew. All the weight she had carried on her shoulders in the last few months lifted as if by magic. For the first time in a long time, she felt lighthearted and happy. Not only was she joining the legendary Marina Raskova to fly at the front but Katya was coming with her. Together, what did they have to fear?

* * *

It took Nina a few moments to gather her courage to climb the stairs to her apartment and open the door. All the lights were out and she couldn't hear any voices. Everyone was in bed, it seemed, and Nina was relieved. Although she wanted to say goodbye to Leo and hold the baby one last time, she couldn't face Anna, not after what happened.

Quiet like a mouse, without taking her boots or coat off, Nina made her way down the long corridor to her room and closed the door. For a moment she stood still, taking it all in. She felt strangely out of place, as if the books she loved and her childhood toys and the posters on the wall no longer belonged to her. Ever since her mother had died and Anna moved in, Nina dreamt of leaving, of starting a new life away from here, of reinventing herself. Then why was her heart suddenly so heavy with regret? She remembered how her mother used to sit on the edge of her bed when she was a child and tell her she could be anything if only she put her mind to it. 'I will make you proud, Mama,' she whispered.

What would Vlad say if he could see her now? Nina knew he wouldn't approve but she hoped he would understand.

Wishing she could stay, wishing it wasn't war, wishing her family was still with her, Nina found a small backpack that Papa had brought from a business trip to Kiev. The same Kiev that was now in Hitler's clutches, destroyed by bombs and fire and living through its worst nightmare. In her bedside table she found some old black-and-white photographs, happy faces of people long gone – Mama, Grandmother and Grandfather. Papa, teaching her how to ride her bike at five, his cap askew as he chased her, wind in her hair. Ten-year-old Nina holding her childhood companion, a spaniel called Athos. How carefree she had been, unaware of any evil in the world. And finally, a photo of her and Vlad ice skating, her arms around him, trying to stop him from falling. She wished she could put her arms around him now and protect him from everything, like she had done her whole life. Tears in her eyes, she placed the photos inside her bag, then added some clothes.

Her gaze fell on a poster on her wall. 'Women – to the planes!' it proclaimed in large letters under a picture of a female pilot inside the cockpit of a U-2 biplane. Once it had meant so much to her, that she could follow her passion and be what she wanted to be. Now her passion was taking her to the front, to fight to the death. She placed a hand on the poster and took a deep breath.

On her bed was an old teddy bear her parents had given her when she won her first gymnastics competition. The bear had become her good luck charm over the years. She never went anywhere without it. Picking it up, she hid her face in its matted fur. 'Come on, Mishka, we are going to war,' she whispered, placing the toy in the bag.

When everything was ready, she tiptoed into Anna's room. Kissing the children's sleeping faces, Nina whispered her good-byes, then placed a short note to Anna on the bedside table and left, closing the door on her past, wondering what the future would bring.

As she was walking out of the apartment, she heard the radio in the kitchen come alive with the sound of static, followed by the grave voice of Vyacheslav Molotov, the People's Commissar for Foreign Affairs. The Germans had broken through the Red Army defence and were about to enter Moscow.

Darling Vlad,

I hope you are well and safe and not missing home too much because I don't want you to feel sad. I have some news and I know it's not what you want to hear but please try to understand. Moscow felt so empty without you and Papa, and with the Nazis at the gate, I couldn't stay home and do nothing. Just like everybody else, I'm praying for a miracle but these days prayers don't seem to be enough.

I'm sure you've heard of Marina Raskova. Well, Major Raskova is organising three female-only aviation units.

Imagine my joy when I found out! Katya and I decided to join. Please, don't try to talk me out of it. I've never been more excited about anything in my life. Katya says we are crazy for even contemplating this. What do you think?

I am on the train now and have a few precious minutes to myself, a luxury these days, so I'm writing to you. I can't help but feel that going to the front will bring me closer to you and Papa. It sounds silly but knowing we are all fighting for something we believe in warms my heart.

With the threat of the German invasion, we are on our way to Engels for our training. Our train hasn't moved in hours, stuck behind a long line of other trains, and Major Raskova, with her chief of staff Militsa Kazarinova, are right now crawling under the carriages to get to the station master to demand preferential treatment for us. At every station, she tells them we are travelling to fight the Nazis. Isn't everyone? they say to her. Somehow she convinces them. We are almost in Engels. With a commander like this, anything is possible. We are all so happy to be doing this with her.

God willing, we'll complete our training soon and then we'll be posted to the front.

Please, keep yourself safe. Write and tell me how you are. I miss you!

Love always,
Nina

Chapter 2

Engels, November – December 1941

In a small provincial town on the Volga River, eight hundred kilometres south-east of Moscow, on an airfield belonging to the most prestigious military flight school in the country, in the middle of the night, a hundred women were marching side by side, breathing heavily in the icy air. Wet late-autumn snow fell on the ground, on the shoulders of the women around her, on Nina's face, running down her cheeks like tears. She thought with envy of the other nine hundred women who were at that precise moment peacefully sleeping inside the dormitory. She told herself their turn would come tomorrow or the next day, while Nina would stay in bed but it didn't make her feel any better. She wanted to sleep *now*. She wanted to feel warm *now*. Not that it was much warmer inside their sleeping quarters where the temperature was only a few degrees higher than outside.

The girls looked like clowns, not soldiers, dressed in over-sized men's uniforms and marching out of time. The tunics were so long, they covered their knees. Trousers reached up to their breasts. As they moved, empty flasks jingled against their rucksacks. On their hips, they had empty revolver holsters and gas mask bags. No one was going to take them seriously, dressed like this, thought Nina. Every day, the men who shared their training facility laughed as they walked past. They rolled their eyes and pretended to cover their heads, shouting, 'Duck, run for your lives, it's the women pilots taking to the sky.'

'Ignore them, girls. It doesn't matter what they think. Soon the whole world will know what we are capable of,' Major Raskova told them.

But it was hard to ignore the men when they called them the death battalion and taunted them every time they saw them. The girls paid them back by teasing them mercilessly, to the fury of Major Raskova's chief of staff, Militsa Kazarinova, who frowned on any fraternising with the opposite sex.

Nina shivered. They were dressed warmly, in uniform lined with fur, thick woolly overalls, fur gloves and hats. They even had mole masks to protect their faces when they flew. But it didn't matter how warm the clothes were because, when the temperatures plummeted to -30° Celsius and they took to the sky in the open cockpits of their U-2 planes, nothing helped. Girls were often in hospital with frostbite. Once, a whole squadron was sick and the lessons had to be cancelled.

'Happy now?' grumbled Katya, who was marching next to Nina, barely keeping to the rhythm, looking like any moment she was going to fall asleep. 'Is this what we signed up for? To be dragged out of bed in the freezing cold, forced to march for hours, and for what? What's the point?'

Katya was not herself in Engels. She was grieving her life in Moscow. Despite the war, she wanted to go on as before, with her daughter safe in her arms and a peaceful sky over her head. But Nina enjoyed being here. She loved every minute of the vigorous training regime because it made her better, as a person and a future soldier. It made her a better pilot, even if every minute of every day was a struggle.

Ignoring Katya, Nina concentrated on marching. Left – right – left – right. If she broke the rhythm, she'd be told off. If she slipped on the ice and fell, she'd be told off. She rubbed her tired eyes. Here in Engels, she never got enough sleep. Order to get up sounded long before the sun rose over the frozen Volga. The minute she got comfortable and warm in bed, she would hear, 'Up!' A pair of strong arms would shake her like a rattle, and an angry voice would inquire if she needed a special invitation. She would get up, dizzy and confused, and reach towards the barely warm radiator, where her uniform was drying. All she would dream about all day was to go back to bed. That, and something warm to eat. 'I'm not complaining. We are learning something that is going to help us at the front,' she whispered to Katya.

'What? How to walk to a count? I don't understand why we always march. We march to the mess hall, to the airfield, even to the bathroom. Why can't we walk like normal people?'

Nina couldn't understand it either. Even at night she was marching in her dreams and hearing Kazarinova shouting the commands in her screeching, unfriendly voice. 'Yes, but also we are learning the principles of flight, navigation skills, mechanical instruction, weapons. It will all come in handy. It might even save our lives one day.'

'You know what else would have saved our lives? Not volunteering in the first place.'

'Be quiet, girls. Or we'll all be in trouble,' hissed Masha Stepanova, a broad-shouldered, fair-haired girl who was marching next to them. 'You should be grateful. At least you are going to have breakfast this morning. Not everyone is so lucky.' Nina knew Masha had been flying supply missions in and out of Leningrad before joining Raskova's regiment. She had seen hunger first-hand.

'You call it breakfast? One hundred grams of oats soaked in water.'

'Ungrateful,' muttered Masha, turning away. Nina thought of Masha's stories of starving children who couldn't walk to freedom as they were evacuated from blockaded Leningrad on Ladoga ice. She shuddered.

Nina was surprised by how small and provincial Engels was. There were only four tall structures in the centre of town: three official buildings and a cinema. Nina looked at the cinema with longing every time she passed it. She loved movies. Unfortunately, the entrance was boarded up and no films were playing. And even if they were, she could never get the leave to watch one. A couple of recruits had sneaked out of the base without permission to see an operetta one day and were dismissed instantly.

Most other buildings in Engels were small, old and made of clay, often leaning to one side, looking like all they needed was the smallest push to slide to the ground. There were no shops where they could buy anything, not that Nina had any money. But the small town was a perfect place to train pilots. It lay among flat steppes, one big airfield as far as the eye could see. They could land anywhere in their U-2s, even on ice that covered the mighty Volga. And the front was still far.

'Attention,' shouted Captain Kazarinova. 'Right face!' The regiment turned right, out of time. Empty flasks clanked. A weak yellow sun appeared from behind the trees and shone its pale light on the girls, their faces red from the cold. For a few moments Kazarinova walked up and down the formation in silence, examining the women as they stood in front of her in petrified silence. Nina tried very hard not to fidget under the commander's gaze.

'At ease. Bogdanova, what's the matter with your boots?' Kazarinova stopped next to Katya. Everyone looked at her boots, which were still facing in the direction they had been marching, even though Katya, like the rest of the girls, was facing forward.

The girls laughed. Katya looked at the ground, turning red. 'They are too big, Mam. If we had shoes that fit instead of men's boots . . .' She hesitated, coughing and clearing her throat.

'Take a step forward.' Captain Kazarinova stared at Katya as she adjusted her boots and shuffled forward, her eyes darting from side to side.

'Wrapping your feet with cloth was the first thing you girls learnt when you got here. Siniza, take this recruit and show her one more time how to do it properly.'

'Yes, Mam!' Small and nervous, Yulia Siniza jumped to attention. Kazarinova was about to walk away when something caught her attention. She turned back to Katya. 'What is that you are wearing? That's not regulation.' She pointed at Katya's neck, where a snow-white scarf was tied in a fetching bow.

'It's only a scarf.' Katya stammered, her hand on her neck. 'Doesn't it suit me?'

The whole regiment exploded with laughter. 'Silence,' Kazarinova shouted, looking angry enough to strike someone. Instantly the laughter stopped. A hundred pairs of eyes watched the commander. 'And what did you use to make this scarf?'

Katya opened her mouth and closed it. Her hands shook.

'Answer me.'

Nina took a step forward, coming to Katya's rescue. 'We took the little silk parachutes off unused flares,' she muttered.

'You both made it?' The commander's eyes narrowed on Nina.

Nina didn't know what to do. To tell the truth and say no, she had nothing to do with it, would be to betray her friend. To lie and say yes was to risk Kazarinova's wrath. But at least it would be directed at both of them. 'Yes, Mam.' She stood still, squeezing her fists tight, ready for Kazarinova to unleash her temper on her and Katya.

'The two of you will report to the headquarters before navigation skills this morning.' Kazarinova turned away and addressed the whole regiment. 'Attention, forward!'

They marched forward. 'Thank you,' whispered Katya, squeezing Nina's hand.

The girls around Katya and Nina giggled. 'Who are you trying to impress? If it's the pilots from across the hall, we are not allowed to even look at them. Kazarinova thinks we could fall pregnant just by looking,' said Yulia Siniza.

'Not trying to impress anyone. Just wanted to look nice,' Katya muttered, her face red.

'It's war, girls. It no longer matters what we look like,' said Masha.

'Of course, it matters. Our lives didn't just stop the moment the Nazis invaded.'

'What, you think the Nazis care what you look like? You think they won't shoot you if you have a nice scarf around your neck?' Masha laughed gravely, levelling her disapproving eyes on Katya.

'Silence,' barked Kazarinova. The regiment marched on in silence but there was a smile on every face except Katya's and Nina's.

The girls sat on the edge of Katya's bunk bed in the large gymnasium of the Red Army Officers' House that had been turned into a dormitory where a thousand women slept. In the corner was a room Major Raskova shared with her chief of staff. When they had first arrived, she was offered the room all to herself, with a double bed, a red carpet and a bouquet of flowers. Offended, she ordered the bed be replaced with bunk beds, saying she wanted to be like the rest of the girls. The bouquet she placed in the hall, so all the girls could enjoy it.

'Let me show you how it's done,' said Yulia, leaning forward. 'It's not rocket science, really. You wrap your feet in cloth, like this. You want your feet nice and warm.'

'And bigger, to fill the boots,' said Katya, her hands still shaking after the confrontation with Kazarinova.

'That's right. Then you make a ball out of newspaper like this. And stuff the ball inside the boots. This way, they won't fall off.'

Katya took some newspaper, crumpled it into a ball and threw it under someone's bed. 'You know what happened to me yesterday during parachute jumping?'

'Your boots fell off and nearly hit Kazarinova on the nose. The whole regiment was talking about it,' said Yulia.

'I hate parachute jumping. And I hate these boots. Why can't they give us boots that fit? Not only are they size 40, but one is bigger than the other.' Katya put them on, stood up and walked a few steps. Her feet made a metallic sound on the floor of the dormitory. 'It's uncomfortable.'

'If you want comfort, go back home. It's war, not your parents' dacha in Kolomenskoe.'

Yulia was small and freckly, with blonde curls and a cheeky smile. She had cried the hardest when Kazarinova ordered the girls to cut off their hair. The war surprised Yulia as she was studying at the Vaganova Ballet Academy, destined to dance on the biggest stages in the world. Instead, she pirouetted down the corridor as they walked to their practicals, which they all loved, and twirled on the way to theory, which they hated. Occasionally, she taught the girls how to waltz or tango. Foxtrot was everybody's favourite because it was so simple. They all took turns to do the man's steps and always ended up laughing so hard their tummies ached. Sometimes Yulia played the old piano in the hall for the girls and sang old romance ballads. Katya said it was almost like being back home and listening to her mama sing and play the piano. Every time she said it, she had tears in her eyes.

Now Yulia picked up a guitar and strummed. Her voice was unlike any voice Nina had ever heard before. It had volume, it rose and fell and filled her heart with longing.

'Why did you volunteer, Siniza?' asked Katya, stuffing more newspaper inside her boots. 'You are a musician and a dancer, not a fighter.'

'I volunteered to become a soldier. To kill the hated Nazis.' Everyone watched Yulia, who was so petite, she looked like she was gliding on air when she walked, graceful and light, almost transparent with her lithe limbs and pale skin, but who could do two hundred push-ups in a row and run one hundred metres faster than anyone in the regiment. Even in her oversized men's uniform she managed to look feminine and soft, her legs and neck long like a heron's. 'I lie awake at night and imagine dropping bombs on their heads. I imagine screams of pain. Blood everywhere. I don't want them to die instantly. I want them to suffer. I want to hurt them.' Seeing the stunned expression on the girls' faces, she added, 'They killed my family. My aunt and uncle and three of my cousins in Ukraine.'

'They killed my parents,' said Masha, coming into the dormitory. 'Starved them to death in Leningrad.'

If Yulia was a dancer, Masha was an athlete. The male uniform actually fit her, with her tall frame, broad shoulders and manly build. Besides flying, Masha's interests included horse riding and Sambo, the deadly Russian martial art. She taught all the girls how to throw each other on the ground and protect themselves from punches and kicks. Nina didn't enjoy these lessons as much as Yulia's. She wanted to dance. She didn't like to be thrown around in aggression. Most girls felt the same way and in what little free time they had, they gravitated towards Yulia. 'If one day you have to fight a Nazi, what are you going to do, dance around him in circles until he gets dizzy and falls?' grumbled Masha. Katya would reply, 'I will just shoot him with my machine gun or drop a bomb on his head from my plane, thank you very much.' Katya was good at shooting, even though she hated it. Almost every day she set the highest score at target practice.

'Raskova and Kazarinova will see you now,' Masha said to Nina and Katya.

'How did they seem? Are they upset? Angry?' asked Katya, her fingers fidgeting with her boots.

'They are beside themselves. As they should be. We are here to fight the Nazis and you waste your time on frivolous things like scarves. You should be ashamed of yourselves. Some people don't take this war seriously.'

Nina didn't think Katya had done anything wrong. Not something to be punished for, anyway. Back home, Katya sewed all her clothes. She had learnt from her mother, who was a seamstress. Even though they were poor and sometimes couldn't afford food, Katya always had new dresses and her clothes always had ribbons in them. Just because they were off to war, didn't mean she had to change who she was. Nina glared at Masha and the two girls walked towards the headquarters, where Raskova and Kazarinova were waiting for them.

Katya said, her voice high-pitched and shaky, 'Kazarinova hates me. She's always looking for an excuse to do something nasty to me. I can see it in her eyes. Have you noticed them? They are like a wild animal's. I pity the poor Nazis who cross her path.'

Kazarinova did have scary eyes. They instilled fear in everyone who came in contact with her. Clearing her throat, Nina said, 'Don't worry, I'll tell her it was my idea.'

Katya stopped and turned around to face Nina. 'But it wasn't your idea. Why would you lie?'

'Kazarinova likes me. She always tells me how well I'm doing.'

'I know. She never stops talking about you. "Why can't you all be more like Petrova?"' Katya did her best to imitate Kazarinova's nasally voice.

Nina giggled, even though she felt like crying. 'See, it's better if she thinks it was me.'

Katya shook her head. 'I can't let you take the blame for this.'

'What is the worst that could happen? It's only a silly scarf.'

The headquarters was a small room with a desk and some chairs. When the girls arrived, Major Raskova was behind the desk, looking through documents. Her hair was short like all the other girls, her eyes dark from exhaustion. She looked at Nina and Katya's white petrified faces and smiled encouragingly. Nina felt a little better.

Captain Kazarinova stood in the corner, looking out the window at the airfield with a mournful expression on her face.

'Why don't you sit down?' she said to the girls. She no longer looked angry, just tired.

The girls sat down. Nina hid her trembling hands in her lap.

'What were you girls thinking?' Kazarinova asked quietly. 'To destroy government property when the government is at war, to cut parachutes meant for training purposes, to make a scarf. Wasting your time and mine, when all your thoughts, all your actions must be towards our common goal.'

Nina and Katya lowered their heads in shame. Katya said, 'We just wanted to feel attractive. You cut our hair and put us in oversized men's uniforms. I feel like I'm not myself anymore. Like I lost a part of myself that I liked the most. Even at a time like this, I want to remain a woman.'

'We are at war. You must learn to behave like soldiers. When the war is over, you will have the rest of your lives to be women.'

'And what if the war is never over?'

'That's our job, mine and yours, to make sure that it is. I want the two of you to think long and hard about what you've done.' She pointed at Katya's neck with disdain. 'It's not only frivolous, it's criminal. If it becomes known outside of this training facility, you two could face serious consequences. I know people who got ten years of hard labour for less than this.'

Nina felt blood rush to her face. She glanced at Raskova, who didn't raise her head from the documents and appeared to pay no attention to the conversation.

'You two will be dismissed from the regiment. We are an elite aviation division and will not abide such behaviour. Our girls must be an example to every young lady in the country.'

Katya didn't say anything. Was it Nina's imagination or did she look relieved? Heart beating fast with trepidation, Nina exclaimed, 'Please, Mam. It will never happen again. From now on we will become exemplary. We will be the best pilots you've ever had. We want to stay and fight. Please don't send us back.' She couldn't continue talking and turned away from Kazarinova.

To be dismissed over a scarf, after all the effort and sacrifice, the long days, the sleepless nights, the early mornings, the hunger and exhaustion and trying to be the best they could! The injustice of it made her chest ache.

'Please, no crying. You are soldiers. Already they are not taking us seriously, just because we are women. They think we don't belong at the front. Don't give them an excuse to say we told you so. We must prove them wrong.'

Nina dried her tears with the back of her hand. 'Please, if you let us stay, we will do our best to prove them wrong.'

'I'm sorry. My decision is final.'

Nina looked at Katya, who was staring at the floor in silence.

Raskova cleared her throat and said, 'I'm not one to question your authority, Captain, but please allow me to speak up for the girls.' Kazarinova nodded. Nina held her breath. Raskova rose to her feet. 'With all due respect, you expect too much from them. It will take time to make soldiers out of young girls who until recently were told that they would get married, have children and live their lives like women. Overnight, it seems, everything has changed. And these girls are ready to sacrifice themselves to stop Hitler. Let's take that into account.'

'They have committed a transgression. They must be punished.'

'Their crime is wanting to remain women. Even now, even at war. Surely you can sympathise with that?' Raskova smiled at Nina and Katya. 'Don't worry, girls. You are already the most beautiful women in the world because of what's in your hearts. You are here to do amazing things. By coming here, you have proven how brave and selfless you are.' She turned to Kazarinova. 'Everyone makes mistakes. I'm sure you'll agree, Captain? We don't want to deprive ourselves of such fine aviators over something so minor. I've been watching you two. Both of you make me proud. What do you say, Captain? Can we give them another chance?'

To Nina's relief, Kazarinova nodded. 'Very well. But consider this your last warning.'

Nina felt like jumping on the spot. She wanted to run to Raskova and hug her. 'Thank you so much. You won't regret it.'

Kazarinova glared at them. 'Don't think you are getting away with it. Your punishment is one night outside cleaning the outhouse. You are free to go.'

Katya opened her mouth to argue but Nina elbowed her in the arm and Katya remained silent. Back in their quarters, she was fuming. 'A night outside in the freezing cold, cleaning the outhouse. I'd rather be dismissed and go home.'

'Quiet,' whispered Nina. 'Don't let anyone hear you talk like that!'

But Nina shouldn't have worried. The other girls were too busy getting ready for a dance held in the hall that night.

'I hope Oleg Nikolaev is there. I've never seen anyone so handsome,' said Yulia. She held a box containing a dark concoction in her hands and was applying it with a small brush to her long eyelashes, then using a needle to separate them.

'He has a sweetheart waiting for him at home,' said Zhenya Timofeeva, a tall fragile-looking girl with sad eyes. She was a little older than the rest of them, with a husband at the front and two children she had left with her mother in a town that was now under German control. Sometimes at night Nina heard her cry and every time she wanted to put her arms around her. Because of her extensive flying experience, Zhenya was Raskova's deputy commander but she was so easy-going and fun, the girls thought of her as a friend rather than their commanding officer. They knew they could tell her anything and it would remain between them. Zhenya would never run to Kazarinova and betray the girls' secrets.

'So what? She's miles away and I'm right here!'

'I thought we weren't allowed to attend the dance? They want to make soldiers out of us, not frivolous young women who flirt and giggle with men. Or make scarves out of parachutes.' Nina did her best to imitate Kazarinova's grouchy voice.

'We are not allowed to go to the dance hall. But once the lights are out, who is to stop us from crossing the corridor and peeking through the door? If we're lucky, we can even hear the music,' said Zhenya.

'We can dance.' Yulia stretched her arms out dreamily and performed a pirouette.

'Wow, Yulia, do that again, that looked amazing,' cried Zhenya, trying to imitate Yulia and falling. 'Ouch.' She got up, rubbing her back.

'Shame on you,' said Masha, shaking her head. 'There's a war on and you are thinking about dances and men. No wonder no one is taking us seriously.'

'Just because there's a war on, doesn't mean our lives are over, silly,' said Yulia.

'The war *is* our life. Why did you even join? You should have stayed in the rear where you can dance and flirt while people are killed for their country.'

'Why can't we fight the enemy and still have fun? We are not all robots like you. We have feelings,' said Yulia. 'Maybe if you complained less and concentrated on your training, you wouldn't be so bad at target practice.'

Nina knew Masha wasn't a robot and she did have feelings but she had seen things, horrifying things, that made dances and entertainment seem frivolous and wrong. Every time she asked Masha about Leningrad, the girl clammed up. It wasn't that she didn't want to talk about it, Nina realised. She couldn't.

Masha glared at Yulia. 'Look who's talking. Like you even care about your studies. Where did you get that mascara? I couldn't buy any even before the war.'

'We made it,' said Yulia proudly, studying her reflection in the mirror. 'Would you like some?'

'Made it out of what?'

'Some soot.' Satisfied with her eyelashes, Yulia started brushing her short hair. She had once told the girls if they brushed their locks a hundred times before bed, their hair would grow back in no time.

'Don't let Kazarinova see you,' said Katya bitterly. 'Ten years of hard labour and instant dismissal for wanting to remain women.'

Masha shook her head. 'In the last week alone, the Soviet Union has lost ninety planes. That's ninety pilots like you and I who didn't come back from their missions. The Nazis are advancing on all fronts, while our army is suffering tremendous losses. And in the midst of this destruction, all you are thinking of is how long your eyelashes are or what to put around your necks to make yourselves more attractive.' Masha turned away in disgust. 'We should be at the front, flying combat missions against the Nazis. Instead, we are stuck in the rear, marching like we are training for a military parade. At this rate, the war will be over and we won't have time to fight.'

'Don't worry. This war won't be over any time soon,' said Katya reassuringly. 'But if you want to be a real soldier and do something important, why don't you join us tonight as we clean the outhouse?'

'I would rather go to the dance,' said Masha, wrinkling her nose, making both activities sound like pure torture.

The outhouse was a wooden structure across a small field from their building. While the other girls were dancing in the dark corridor, hoping Kazarinova wouldn't catch them, or studying or sleeping on their bunk beds, Nina and Katya, armed with large chisels, attacked the smelly mess that was frozen solid. Frustrated, Katya threw her chisel on the ground. Putting her head in her hands, she cried. 'I can't do this anymore. I just can't. It's too much.'

Nina put her chisel down and drew Katya into a hug. For a moment, they stood still without saying a word. 'Don't cry, honey,' said Nina. 'It could have been worse. They could have dismissed us.'

Katya looked up. Her eyes glistened in the dim light of a kerosene lamp. 'But that's all I want. To go back home. To see Tonya.

She's all I can think about. I wish I could pick her up and hold her and feel her weight in my arms. It's been weeks since I've done that. I feel like a part of me is missing. When Kazarinova said we were being dismissed, my heart soared with joy. I thought making that scarf was the best thing I have ever done.'

'I know, darling.' Nina missed Leo and baby Lena terribly, and they weren't even hers. She couldn't imagine what it was like for Katya. A part of her felt guilty for standing up to Kazarinova and asking to stay at the regiment.

'I didn't even tell Tonya I was going. Remember how she was when Anton was leaving? I couldn't put her through that again. I just held her all night and then slipped away in the morning without saying goodbye. It took me half an hour just to walk through the door. I couldn't take my eyes off her sleeping face. I'm trying not to think of how much she must have cried when she realised I was gone. All I can hear is her little voice inside my head, calling Mama.'

'You are doing it for her. So that she can grow up and live her life in a free world. And your mama is there. She'll take good care of Tonya for you.'

Katya shook her head, emitting a sob. 'I worry about her so much.'

'The Red Army pushed the Nazis away from Moscow. Even Comrade Stalin is still there. He didn't leave the capital. If there was any danger, he would have. Tonya is safe.'

'I thank God for that every single day. But I can't stop terrible thoughts inside my head. What if she's not getting enough food? What if there is a bombing one day and they don't make it to safety in time? What if she runs out onto the road and there's a car? Mama is too slow to run after her. This fear for her is killing me.'

'Why don't you go back? Tell Raskova you've made a mistake and go back to Moscow.'

'How can I? I don't want to be a deserter. You know what the punishment for that is in the Soviet Union.'

Gently, Nina wiped the tears off Katya's face. 'You volunteered. You won't be a deserter.'

'You don't know anything about it. Besides, I don't want Raskova to be disappointed in me. I don't want to let anyone down. You heard what she said. She's proud of us for doing this. She won't be proud if I leave.' Katya looked into her gloved hands. 'I have to stay, even though I hate it here. The only thing keeping me sane is flying. Knowing I'll be a pilot one day.' Katya half sobbed, half sighed. 'Why is everything so hard?'

Nina nodded in agreement. It was hard to get up at six in the morning, when all she wanted was to stay in her warm bed. It was hard to study for hours on an empty stomach, to march and do push-ups and pull-ups like men, while being shouted at by Kazarinova. The shooting practice was the hardest. The cold, the hunger, the uncertainty. 'Don't worry, we won't stay here for long. Soon we'll be at the front.'

'Is that supposed to make me feel better?' Katya sniffled.

'You have four younger brothers. This should be like a holiday for you.'

Katya smiled through her tears. 'It was definitely as smelly.' She glanced at the outhouse with disgust. 'I miss them all so much. I finally wrote to Mama and told her where I was. All this time she thought I was digging trenches on the other side of Moscow. It breaks my heart to think how much she worries about me.'

Nina smiled for her friend's sake, even though she didn't feel like smiling. 'I bet she's so proud of you.'

'I bet she'll kill me next time she sees me, if the Nazis don't. Thank God the boys are still too small to join up. She couldn't bear it if they left for the front.'

'Don't worry. The Red Army will push the Nazis away. Before you know it, the war will be over. Maybe even before we complete our training.' Nina winked.

'Don't tell Masha that. She'll be crushed.' The girls laughed. 'When did you last hear from Vlad?'

'A few days ago.'

'I got a letter from Anton. Would you like to read it?'

'Yes, of course.' In the light of the kerosene lamp, rubbing her hands together to stay warm, Nina read Anton's letter to Katya.

My beloved Katyusha,

I wish I could hold you and Tonya and see your beautiful faces. I miss you both so much. It breaks my heart to think of our little girl without her mama and papa but I understand why you decided to join Raskova. First, we fight and stop this evil and then we can hope to live a normal life. I am so proud of you. It's all I talk about. The men are sick of hearing about it.

We finally made it to the front. What can I say, it's nothing like we expected. But the planes we are flying are quite something. Yak-1 is a magnificent fighter plane. Everyone thinks so. We are lucky. There is a shortage of planes in the army. The other day I left my plane and walked to the mess tent to have something to eat. When I came back, two officers were inside, trying to start the engine. I was furious and chased the intruders away. Before they left, they told me I was being unpatriotic because they had an important mission. Don't we all, I said to them. We are constantly changing bases. Every week, it's a new airfield. We cover the retreating Soviet troops and try to stop German planes from harassing them. We are staying in civilian houses. My bedroom has pink curtains with flowers and a teddy bear on the bed. What a contrast between this peaceful home and hell outside.

There are fires everywhere. Sometimes I'm in the air and all I can see is red. We have not a minute to rest, to contemplate, to think about what we've seen, and I'm grateful for that. When the war is over, we will have nothing but time to think about it all. The thought scares me. They feed us pilots well here at the front, but strangely I don't seem to have any appetite.

Please do your best to keep yourself alive. Learn as best you can. Make sure you get enough sleep and food. I am counting the days until I see you again.

Vlad sends his love to Nina. I hope you girls are doing well. God keep you.

Yours always,
Anton

The girls did their best to keep themselves alive. They learnt as best they could, preparing physically and emotionally for the front. But no matter what they did, they couldn't get enough sleep or food. Some days Nina would take a piece of bread to the plane and it would freeze solid in her pocket. She would chew on it during the day, feeling a little less hungry, a little less lightheaded. And through it all, she thought of her brother. His letters were upbeat and optimistic. Everything was great at the front, according to Vlad. The food was great, the work was what he had always wanted to do, his quarters were great and his plane was the greatest. He never mentioned the danger or the fear. Nina knew he didn't want her to worry. But all she could see before she fell asleep at night was Vlad's plane engulfed in flames, hurtling towards the ground at great speed, carrying her brother to his death. She would wake up screaming, disoriented for a moment, and then thank God it was only a dream.

While Marina Raskova's aviators were waiting for the planes that their commander had chosen for them, they trained in U-2s, open cockpit biplanes that Nina and Katya were already familiar with from their days at the air club. The U-2 aircraft were used extensively at the front. Although they were defenceless against the Nazi fighter planes and could be knocked out with just a machine gun, they were light, cheap to make, manoeuvrable and didn't require a runway. They were perfect for carrying the wounded, delivering provisions and ammunition and were even used as a bomber, with explosives attached under their wings.

Something happened to Nina when she was flying. She became one with her plane until it anticipated her every wish. When she was up in the air, she forgot about everything, soaring through the sky, while underneath, as far as the eye could see, were trees and small clay buildings, like toys scattered around the snow-bound fields. Up there, all by herself, with the Germans a thousand kilometres away, Nina could almost forget about the war.

Sometimes she felt afraid but never in the air. She felt fear before she stepped inside the plane, on the ground, before take off. But when she was flying, there was nothing but joy and hope and light. She was free like a bird, from thoughts, from doubt, from death; her heart was bursting with happiness.

The airfield where they trained was in the middle of an empty plain, offering no protection from the bitter wind, but even the extreme cold that was felt so intensely at high altitudes didn't bother Nina. She put on her mask made of mole fur, which did nothing to protect her from frostbite, and entrusted her life to the flimsy machine made of tarpaulin and wood. Even though the smallest mistake could plunge her out of the sky towards earth, killing her instantly, she had never felt more alive.

But even the joy of flying high in the clouds, while her heart was trembling in wonder, didn't last. As days turned into weeks and weeks turned into months, as the girls learnt how to become something they had never thought they needed to become – soldiers trained to kill – all Nina's thoughts turned to her brother. Every day, when the postman delivered letters to their training facility, the girls would run to the hall and search through them. And every day, their hearts would break a little bit more because there were no more letters from Vlad and Anton.

Chapter 3

One Year Later

December 1942–January 1943

Two hundred women gathered on the airfield, talking in soft voices, their eyes on their beloved leader, Major Marina Raskova, who was standing in front of them, small, feminine, her dark hair trying to escape from under her cap, her eyes sparkling. All of her sparkling. Nina had never seen her this animated and happy. It filled her own heart with longing and made her a little less afraid. Fresh snow fell on the airfield, the buildings and the airplanes, making everything look festive, like it was a celebration. And in a way, it was. Finally, after fourteen months of training, the dive bomber regiment was going to the front.

'My dear girls, my sisters! We have waited for this day since the war started. We have worked hard for this. Words cannot express how proud I am of every single one of you for making it this far. This is what we live for. This is our purpose. I personally cannot wait!' Marina fell quiet, looking at the elated women in front of her with pride.

'Finally,' whispered Masha, standing next to Nina with tears in her eyes.

Marina took off her cap and pressed it to her chest. When she spoke again, her voice quivered. 'We've been assigned to fight on the Don Front, defending Stalingrad. Our mission will be to bomb the German troops by day. At the front, I know you will continue to make me proud, every single day. Stalingrad needs our help. If the Germans take the city, we will lose the war. Our communication with the Volga region will be cut. We cannot allow the enemy to take the city that carries our illustrious leader's name. Let's show them what we are made of. Let's show them that we can do anything. This is our chance to prove ourselves as soldiers and aviators.'

Stalingrad! Nina could barely breathe when she thought about what this word represented. She was besides herself with joy one moment and filled with paralysing fear the next. Would they come back from Stalingrad alive?

One after another, they had watched their sister regiments fly off to war. In March, the 588th Regiment, the night bombers, left in their flimsy open cockpit U-2s. For the last nine months, they had been harassing the Nazis at night, making their lives difficult, not letting them have a moment of rest and earning the nickname of Night Witches.

In May, the 586th Regiment of fighter pilots followed, defending strategic positions in their dangerous Yak fighter planes, attacking the Nazis heroically at Stalingrad. Rumour had it, one German pilot was so overwhelmed he had been shot down by a woman pilot, after he parachuted out and was captured, he offered her his golden watch as a present. The woman declined, horrified. Her name was Lilya Litvyak. All of the Soviet Union knew her. Newspapers and magazines were filled with stories of the women's heroic exploits. In their short time at the front, they had become heroes and every young girl in the country wanted to be like them.

While their comrades fought heroically, the 587th Dive Bomber Regiment, which Nina and Katya were part of, had to stay behind and learn how to operate a new aircraft. After training in a U-2 and then a Su-2, which they hated, they had finally received the planes Major Raskova had carefully chosen for them, the powerful Pe-2, one of the most sophisticated Soviet aircraft. They couldn't leave for the front until they mastered the difficult machine. The Pe-2 had twin tails and twin engines, one on each wing. The girls had to learn to fly on two engines, to balance them, to land out of balance on just one, in case the other one failed. The plane could carry one and a half tonnes of explosives and reach the speed of up to five hundred and forty kilometres an hour. Oh, to fly through the sky faster than a word, every day bringing victory closer! Nina couldn't wait. Equipped with five machine guns, bombing gear and bombsights, what havoc their Pe-2s would cause the Nazis. It was a challenging machine but the girls were up to the challenge.

A team of three operated the Pe-2. Nina was the pilot. Katya was the navigator. Olga Antonova, a tall and stocky girl with dark hair and an open smile, was their tail gunner. Short of women to operate the Pe-2s, Marina Raskova had recruited tail gunners from other regiments. Most of them were men because it took a lot of strength to recharge the heavy machine guns that jammed often. It took nerves of steel to climb into the tail gunner cockpit of a Pe-2, exposed to the enemy fire. Although the 587th was no longer an all-female regiment, all their pilots and navigators were female, and the girls were proud of it.

Nina and Katya were the only crew who had a female tail gunner. Olga not only possessed nerves of steel but also the upper body strength required to perform her duties. She grew up on a farm and was accustomed to hard labour, was a superb horse rider and could lift heavy rocks better than any man. When the war had started, she was working on construction sites all over Moscow. Her dream was to study geology. 'But I don't mind doing this for a while, at least until the war is over,' she had confided to the girls. 'The aeroplane is one of the most important technological advances of the twentieth century. It's good to be part of it.'

Nina was thrilled that Katya was her navigator but she knew Katya felt differently. All she wanted was to fly her own plane. She was devastated when she found out she was going to be a navigator and not a pilot.

'You should be proud of yourself,' Nina said to her distraught best friend on the day they were assigned to their posts. 'They chose you for your superior shooting skills. They only made me pilot because I can't shoot to save my life.' The navigator was responsible for dropping the bombs and operating a machine gun. She had to know how to shoot. And Katya could do it better than anyone.

'I don't even want to be here,' said Katya, her eyes red from crying. 'And now I don't get to be a pilot. I didn't leave my little girl to sit in a navigator's seat with a pile of maps on my lap.'

'Don't worry,' said Masha. 'It's war. Pilots don't last long in war. Before you know it, you'll have a chance to fly.'

That only made Katya cry harder.

Nina was disappointed she had been assigned to the dive bomber regiment. She wanted to fly a fighter plane like Anton and Vlad, to duel with the Luftwaffe planes in the sky, to be like the famous Lilya Litvyak, a hero to millions of Soviet girls. To soar through the sky in her shiny and splendid Yak-1, bringing terror and death to the Nazis. Instead, her job was to drop bombs on Nazi infrastructure and avoid direct combat with German fighters at all costs.

'You are so lucky,' said a girl called Alisa, who had volunteered to be a pilot but was stuck with the role of a parachute packer. 'I would fly a broomstick if it meant I could fight.'

Nina knew Alisa was right. So many women had been disappointed with their assignments, there had been queues outside Raskova's door for weeks. Suddenly, their beloved commander had a mutiny on her hands. In her usual level-headed manner, Raskova reminded the girls that they were fighting a war. Every role was essential and had to be filled. Besides, they were soldiers and orders were not up for a debate. The decision was final.

During long months of hard work in Engels, Nina often felt like they were never going to leave. She couldn't imagine a life other than the one they were living, waking up before dawn, hours of theory followed by hours of flying, marching everywhere and feeling hungry and cold. As she stood on the airfield next to Katya, waiting for the order to set off, Nina wondered what their life at the front would be like. She couldn't help but think of another cold day in Moscow in October 1941, when they watched Vlad and Anton fly off to war.

It was fourteen months since Nina had last seen her brother. Twelve months since his last letter. Fifty-two weeks of not knowing if he was still breathing. Her heart hurt from fear and uncertainty as she studied and flew her beloved plane and tossed and turned at night. If he was alive, wouldn't he write to her? A few lines in response to her own letters, each more frantic than the last. But if the unthinkable had happened, wouldn't someone notify them?

'To planes,' came the long-anticipated order. It was no longer snowing, which was a relief, because the Pe-2 was a dangerous aircraft to fly in bad weather. As soon as they heard the words, the exhilarated crews – pilots, navigators and tail gunners – rushed across the airfield towards their planes, laughing and pushing each other out of the way, a year of marching lessons flying out of their heads without as much as a goodbye. Kazarinova wouldn't approve, thought Nina. But Kazarinova wasn't there to see them. She was commanding the night bombers at the front, a thousand kilometres away.

Inside her cockpit, Nina watched as one after another the planes took off in an orderly manner, with Marina Raskova as their leader, growing smaller and smaller until they disappeared altogether.

'We are so lucky to have Raskova. I feel like nothing bad could happen to us while she's with us,' she said to Katya as they waited their turn.

'We are going to the front. Anything could happen,' replied Katya grimly.

'The other regiments would kill to have Raskova lead them. She is our lucky charm.'

Katya was the only one, it seemed, who wasn't happy about going to the front. When Nina asked her about it, she replied, 'You want me to be excited about getting myself killed? I'm not crazy like the rest of you.'

The girls sat in tense silence, staring straight ahead at the runway and the planes ahead of them. How many times had they taken off from this runway in the last year and two months? Nina had lost count. After all this time, it had become second nature. Yet, there was a big difference between flying in training and flying to the front. Her throat was dry and her hands were shaking. Her eyes felt like they were filled with sharp glass because she had not had a minute of sleep the night before. The sun was shining and the sky was blue for the first time in weeks. What a beautiful day to fly to war.

Finally, the signal came for their crew to move. Nina took a sharp breath. It was time.

'Ready? Here we go,' cried Katya, pushing on Nina's back, so that she could in turn push the heavy control stick to get the tail up for take off. Nina's arms and legs were too short to reach the controls in an aircraft designed for men. She had three pillows folded behind her but even that was not enough. She needed Katya's help to get the plane off the ground.

The engine growled like a discontented dog, its familiar sound a song to Nina's ears. The plane shook and began to move down the runway, faster and faster, gaining speed.

Finally, after fourteen months of depriving themselves of everything, of marching when they wanted to sleep, flying when they wanted to eat, parachute jumping and shooting and throwing training bombs when they should have been wearing pretty scarves and dresses, attending university and laughing with friends, the girls were off to war.

Under her wings, Nina could see the familiar airfield where they had spent many hours every day learning how to be aviators. Beyond the airfield was Engels with its short clay buildings hidden under fresh snow. In the last year and a bit, the town had become their home. The girls she had met had become family. Would she ever see Engels again? Flying to the front seemed so final, a monumental moment in time that was going to divide her life into two halves, into *before* and *after*. Nina didn't know what to expect, but she suspected that after today her life would never be the same again.

They were in the air for ten minutes when Nina realised something was wrong. The controls under her hands felt heavier than usual. One of the engines coughed and spluttered and finally went quiet. The plane pulled to one side.

Nina heard Katya's voice inside her headset. 'What is happening?'

It took all of Nina's strength to keep the plane straight. 'Engine trouble. We'll have to turn back. We can't make it all the way to the front on one engine.'

She willed herself to remain calm. This wasn't the first time she had flown on one engine. Going to the front, she knew it wouldn't be the last. Nina glanced at the neat formation of planes with regret, waved her wings in goodbye and turned back. She wished their planes were equipped with radios, like some of the fighter planes, so she could let Raskova and the others know they had to return to Engels.

When they reached the airfield, Nina guided the plane to an emergency landing, in her mind thanking Raskova for hours of training that had prepared her for this.

The mechanics told Nina, Katya and Olga it would take a few days to repair the engine. The girls would have to wait until then and find their way to the front on their own. They trudged back to their quarters in silence. It was a strange feeling, walking through the Officers' House without the other girls there. The place that had once been filled with voices and laughter was now silent like a ghost.

The girls sat in the empty mess hall, opened their rucksacks and unwrapped their bread.

'We'll be late for the front,' said Olga sadly.

'I have a feeling the front is not going anywhere,' said Nina, taking a bite of her bread. In all the excitement of this morning, she had barely touched her breakfast. Now she realised how hungry she was.

'And if we are late, is that such a bad thing?' asked Katya.

'I don't want to miss the action,' said Olga. 'I want to make them pay. For what they did to my family.'

'Don't you girls believe in signs?' asked Katya, staring at the bread in her hands, not looking at Nina and Olga.

'Signs?' Nina had already finished her bread and was wishing there was something else to eat.

'When the universe is trying to tell you something.'

'I suppose. Why?'

'It's like something is telling us not to go to the front.'

'The plane is broken. It's not a big cosmic sign. The engine failed,' said Olga, gazing out the window at the abandoned airfield.

'If we don't listen to the universe, something bad is going to happen.'

'Like what?'

Katya shrugged.

'Are you thinking of Anton?' asked Nina. She knew that look on her friend's face.

'Why have they stopped writing, Nina? If they are still alive, why haven't we heard from them?'

Nina closed her eyes and thought about her brother. There was an emptiness inside her because he was no longer around. His silence left her short of breath and heartbroken, no matter what she did, no matter how hard she tried to fill her time with tasks and her mind with the theory of aviation. She tried to feel him out there, to sense if he was still alive. She remembered his laughing baby face when she played peekaboo with him, remembered pushing him in his pram, thought of his chubby cheeks and tiny feet, his blond curls that stuck out in every direction, making him look like an elated hedgehog. The concentration on his face when she taught him to play chess at seven. How he jumped for joy when he beat her in a race for the first time. He was ten and she was fourteen, and losing interest in racing. Her brother had always been by her side. If he was gone, what would become of her?

'Don't worry,' said Olga, placing one arm over Nina's shoulder and another over Katya's, bringing them closer together, so that their heads almost touched. 'A friend of mine didn't have any news from her brothers for ten months. Then a few weeks ago she received fifteen letters all at once.'

'How wonderful,' said Nina. All she wanted was one line to let her know Vlad was safe. To get all his letters at once would be like a dream come true.

'Unfortunately, one of the letters was her older brother telling her their younger brother was killed at Stalingrad.'

Nina paled. She couldn't look at Katya, couldn't see the dread on her best friend's face.

It took three days for their plane to be repaired and another three days of waiting for the weather to clear. Nina wondered how the rest of the girls were doing. Had they reached the front? And what was it like? 'Unfortunately, we'll soon find out for ourselves,' Katya said.

And then it was time to go, flying during the day, unfamiliar airfields by night. In a village called Lopatkino, to their extreme joy, they found Zhenya, Masha and their tail gunner Igor, who were also waiting for their plane to be fixed. Not only that, but their commander Major Raskova had remained behind, to make sure the stragglers arrived at the front safely. As Nina landed, she saw a group of people waving and running to the aircraft. When she recognised them, her heart filled with so much joy, she thought it was going to burst. She felt like she was coming home to her family.

'Speaking of signs,' she told Katya. 'Doesn't it feel like it was meant to be?'

Katya scoffed.

It was New Year's Eve and they celebrated with their guitars and a little bit of vodka. The terrible year of 1942 was over. What would 1943 bring them? With all her heart, Nina hoped it would bring the end of war. They lifted their glasses to the new year and their future as soldiers. The men from Raskova's crew drank most of the vodka, while the girls only took a couple of sips. Tail gunner Nikolai Erofeev flirted with the girls, mechanic Vladimir Kruglov became sombre and quiet, while navigator Kirill Khil sang loudly and told jokes. It was a night filled with joy at being alive, at looking forward to the future, at being young. They were on the brink of something incredible, a new page in their lives, and most of them couldn't wait.

'What is it like?' Katya asked Masha, who was nursing a small glass of vodka in her hands, staring into the distance. 'Life at the front.'

Masha shrugged. 'People think it's one heroic exploit after another. It's not. Mostly it's just hard work. Exhausting and never-ending, day after day, with no end in sight.'

'Were you scared?' Katya wanted to know, curling up into a pretzel on her chair. On the table in front of her was a photograph of her little girl. Katya wanted to feel closer to Tonya as she welcomed the new year.

'Every moment. You wouldn't be human if you weren't scared. But you still get up, get ready and go out there, every single day. And that's what makes you a hero.'

'Was it hard?'

'Of course. But everything worth doing is hard. Before the war, I was working on construction sites, building metro stations all over Moscow, and I thought it was the hardest thing in the world. But what a feeling it was when in February 1935 we saw the first train running through the city. How we celebrated, how we danced! We had created something special. It made all the hard work worth it. You know what I mean?' The girls nodded. Masha smiled. 'When I was digging the metro, practically living underground like a mole, all I dreamt of was to fly high in the sky. Even though it's war, I feel like I'm living my dream. I wouldn't want to be anywhere else.'

Katya shrugged. 'It all feels so pointless. How can we win? Look how far the Germans were able to advance. The Information Bureau can't keep up with them!'

'That's the spirit,' said Masha.

'They made it all the way to the outskirts of Moscow. They are starving Leningrad to death. The Baltic states, Belorussia, Ukraine, Crimea, Voronezh, Rostov are occupied. Soon all of the Soviet Union will follow. We are fighting a losing battle. We are risking our lives for nothing.'

'Don't let anyone hear you talk like that. It almost sounds like treason,' whispered Masha.

'Treason? My heart is breaking,' said Katya, turning away from Masha and taking a sip of her tea.

Nina squeezed Katya and ruffled her hair. 'The enemy couldn't take Moscow or Leningrad. They are not as strong as they want us to believe.'

When the food and the vodka were gone, everyone sat in a circle around Major Raskova, who played her favourite tunes on the piano and sang her favourite songs. Her fingers ran over the keys cheerfully and fast at first, and then slower. The music became melancholy and sad. As her head nodded in time with the melody, Nina watched the tense faces around her. They had worked hard for this. They were ready. It didn't mean they were not afraid.

When the music fell quiet, Nina said, 'That was amazing. Where did you learn to play the piano and sing like this?'

'Music was supposed to be my future,' replied Raskova. 'My parents are musicians. I was planning to apply to the Moscow Conservatory to study music when fate intervened. I got sick and it affected my voice, so I had to choose my other passion, chemistry.'

'How did you become an aviator?' asked Katya. The girls were watching their hero, their faces flushed with admiration.

'I got a job as an assistant at the Aero Navigation Laboratory of the Zhukovsky Air Force Engineering Academy. While I drafted drawings of flight instruments, I fell in love with aviation. The rest is history.'

'We wanted to thank you for getting us this far, Major Raskova. If it wasn't for you, we would never have made it,' said Zhenya, who was quiet that evening, her eyes sad, as if on the brink of going to the front she was mourning her pre-war self.

'You are welcome, Lieutenant Timofeeva,' Raskova replied. 'You can call me Marina when we are off-duty.' She looked at the girls and smiled. 'I know how tough it is for us women. I was turned away from every conscription point in Moscow myself.'

'Even though you have the Hero of the Soviet Union medal? Even though you are famous?' Nina found it hard to believe.

'Hardly famous.'

'After the flight of the *Rodina*, everyone in the country knows your name.'

'It might be so but they sent me to teach male pilots because of my extensive experience. And I said to them, if I am good enough to teach the new recruits, how come they are the ones going to the front and not me?'

'What did they say?'

'They said there were no female regiments. So I decided to create some.'

'You refused to give up,' whispered Nina.

'By that point, I was receiving thousands of letters from young women like yourselves, begging me to help them get to war. And here I was, unable to help even myself. So I gathered all the letters together and marched into the Defence Ministry.'

'Were you scared?' asked Katya.

'Petrified. At first, they told me in no uncertain terms what I was suggesting was lunacy. They told me future generations would not forgive us for sacrificing young girls. But I pointed out the girls were already taking matters into their own hands, running off to the front, stealing airplanes and getting themselves killed. It was our job to help them, organise them, train them and keep them as safe as possible. They needed direction. They needed leadership. Then Stalin intervened personally and I got my wish.'

'I want to be you when I grow up,' said Nina quietly. She was grateful for the twist of fate that allowed her to cross paths with this astonishing woman.

'Me too,' said Masha. Zhenya nodded.

'You'll be better than that. You'll be *you*. And you'll make our country proud,' replied Marina. 'We are making history, girls. The Soviet Union is the only country in the world that allows women to fly in combat. And we are the ones who made it happen.'

'I hope we get a chance to fight. Now that America is in the war, what if we don't?' asked Masha. 'What if the war is over before we even get to the front?'

'Don't worry, girls. There will be plenty of fighting for all of us. Be patient,' said Raskova. 'And if the war is over soon, thank God for that. I live for the day when I can hug my little girl again. Everything I do, I do for her.'

'She must be so proud of her mama,' said Katya, her eyes glistening. Nina knew she was thinking of her own little girl, waiting for her mother in Moscow.

Marina nodded. 'Tanya wants to be just like me. I hope with all my heart that, when she grows up, there will be peace in the

Soviet Union and she won't have to be like me at all. I want her to live a normal life. To be happy. That's what I'm fighting for.'

'I'm scared,' whispered Nina. She couldn't believe she was saying it out loud, to their commander of all people. She had only ever admitted it to herself in the dark of the night. But she felt like she could tell Marina anything. She knew she would understand. 'What if I'm not good enough?'

'Don't be scared,' said Marina. 'Remember, we can do anything. And as long as you do your best, you are good enough. You came this far. That's outstanding. When I first thought of female-only regiments, I couldn't even imagine how many talented and brave young women would join. Thanks to you, my dream has become a reality.'

Marina turned to her piano and played a tune. Zhenya joined in with her guitar and they all sang their commander's favourite song, while outside snow fell in a white curtain, hiding the ugly bomb craters and destroyed village huts, making everything look breathtakingly beautiful.

A fire's aflame in the shore,
Teardrops of pitch on the logs.
The accordion sings in the dugout
To me of your smile and your love.
It was a new year, a new beginning.

The snowstorm cleared the next day and the three planes were gliding in the direction of Saratov, carrying Nina and her comrades to the front. The sky over their heads was pure azure, with a tinge of purple from the rising sun. There was not a cloud as far as the eye could see, and Nina wondered if this was the last time she would fly through a peaceful sky, fly without having to fear for her life, without explosions and gunshots and anti-aircraft guns determined to take her little aircraft out, without the enemy fighter planes on the warpath, hunting just for her. What would it be like, to fly in combat? And did she have what it took?

When she started thinking about it, her hands began to tremble so much the plane she was controlling trembled too. She tried to focus instead on the miniature houses, cars and people scattered underneath, and then nothing but a white sea of snow and bare trees swaying in the wind. Somewhere west of here was Moscow. And somewhere further west still were her father and brother. She would fly on her trusted Pe-2 to the end of the world if it meant she could lay her eyes on them one more time. She would give anything to see them again.

Marina's plane was ahead of Nina, leading the way. Zhenya and Masha were behind her. The small formation was flying in a textbook fashion, like they were still in Engels on a practical exercise. Nina felt an overwhelming sense of pride for the other girls, for being a small part of this regiment that was ready to lay down their lives to bring Hitler down. They were sisters, with a common goal and determination. Thanks to Marina, they had almost made it.

Inside the plane, Nina could sense Katya's dark presence behind her. The other girls were elated about flying to war. Not Katya. Nina wondered if she would feel the same if she had a child waiting for her at home. Or would she want to fight even more because she had someone to protect?

It all happened in a blink of an eye. One moment Nina was coasting along, thinking what a nice day it was and how lucky they had been to be entrusted with such a difficult but reliable and sophisticated aircraft. After months of training in Engels, she had grown to love her Pe-2. It had become a loyal friend. The sun was bright above them, unusual for this time of year. Underneath, snow glittered like diamonds. The next thing she knew, Katya was saying, 'I don't like the look of those clouds.'

'What clouds?' asked Nina. A moment later she saw them. There was an ominously dark mass in the distance, and Nina knew right away that a storm was coming. What felt like seconds later, the sky was no longer blue but dark grey. The wind picked

70

up. Nina watched Marina's wings tremble in the fog as she dived in and out of clouds. Snow enveloped the little plane like a heavy blanket and soon Nina couldn't see anything at all, not even the wings of her own plane, as if by some dark magic day had given way to night and she was flying in the dark.

Katya's faint voice sounded inside Nina's headset, barely distinguishable over the howling of the wind, 'We need to find a place to land.'

It was easier said than done. Their sister regiment, the night bombers, had done plenty of night-time practice. They could perform miracles, locating their targets in the dark and landing blindly. As a dive bomber, destined to fly during the day, Nina had no such experience. Nor did her plane possess equipment that would allow her to navigate in the dark. Her heart thumping heavily inside her chest, she glanced down. All she could see was the milky fog. Muttering a prayer under her breath, she pointed the plane in the direction of where she thought the land was. She saw something black approaching fast and pulled the stick but it was too late, it was already upon them, whatever it was. Nina shrieked, preparing for impact, but nothing happened. It was only a cloud.

She had to get a grip on her emotions. Two other lives depended on her. She needed to keep a cool head if they were to survive.

A few seconds passed and another dark shape appeared. Nina pulled the plane up to avoid it, realising at the last moment that the object was a bush. They were hurtling full speed towards the land and didn't even know it. Taking a deep breath and trying to steady her hands, she focussed on the dark shadow underneath. Having spotted the bush moments earlier, she knew vaguely where the land was. Holding her breath, she prayed she was correct.

They landed safely. When the Pe-2 came to a stop, Nina closed her eyes and remained motionless, stunned by this close brush with death, thanking God for putting the bush in her way, because it had saved their lives.

'We made it!' cried Katya. 'I can't believe we made it.'

Inside her headset, Nina could hear Olga's voice. 'You saved our lives. Well done, Lieutenant Petrova. What a landing!'

With her eyes still closed, Nina could hear the two girls squealing with relief. Unlike Katya and Olga, all Nina felt was a paralysing fear. She didn't want to tell the girls how close they had come to a certain death. They were not even at the front yet. It was the first of many close calls. Suddenly, she remembered Kazarinova's words. When she wanted the girls to perform miracles at training, she told them most new pilots never made it out alive of their first battle. Until now, Nina tried not to think about it, telling herself it couldn't possibly happen to her. After nearly crashing her plane moments after leaving for the front, she realised anything could happen.

She felt Katya's hand on her shoulder. 'Are you all right? Why are you so quiet?'

'I'm fine,' Nina tried to smile. 'What's that noise?'

'I think it's Olga.'

Katya was right. Olga was knocking on the divider and shouting, 'I'm stuck. Let me out!'

Together they pulled the lever, opened the hatch and let Olga out of the tail gunner cockpit. 'Thank you. I think the lock jammed.' Olga rubbed her eyes as if she had just woken from a bad dream. 'What a day to be flying.'

'Have you seen what happened to the others?' Nina's voice quivered.

The girls looked at the angry dark sky. 'Zhenya and Marina are experienced pilots. They'll be fine. They have flown in bad weather before,' said Katya reassuringly.

'That's right. The girls are wizards in the air. If anyone can survive the storm, it's them,' said Olga. Neither of them sounded convinced.

'If my calculations are correct, we are right here.' Katya pointed at a dot on her map. 'There is a small village nearby, called

Razboishina. If the other crews made it, that's where they'll go.' Katya looked at her compass. 'We'll have to walk *that* way.'

Nina looked in the direction where Katya was pointing. All she could see was a wall of snow. In the distance, there were shadows that looked like trees. A small road twisted its way through the snowfield and disappeared behind the horizon. It was barely visible, hidden under a thick layer of snow.

Katya added, 'We could wait for the storm to pass or we could start walking and, with luck, we'll get there in an hour or so.'

'There's no point waiting,' said Nina. 'We could be here forever.' The storm showed no signs of slowing down.

'Let's walk,' said Olga. 'I'm not afraid of a bit of snow. But I am afraid of wolves. I don't like the wilderness.'

'What makes you think there are wolves here?' asked Nina.

'Can't you hear them?'

'I thought it was the wind.' With trembling hands, Nina felt for her gun.

They gathered their belongings and, throwing one regretful glance at their plane that looked sad and lost in the storm, in silence walked three kilometres to the village. Even if they wanted to talk, they wouldn't be able to hear each other over the wind. And Nina didn't feel like talking. It took all her strength to make her way through the snow, falling down to her waist, pulling herself out, step after excruciating step. The journey that would normally take forty minutes took four hours.

Nina was ready to collapse from exhaustion when they saw the first buildings, white and narrow, like ghouls in the far distance, partly obscured by the falling snow. 'It's lucky you know how to read the map and the compass,' she said to Katya. 'Or we'd really be in trouble.'

'I wouldn't make a good navigator if I didn't.'

They walked past a school and a village library, and knocked on the door of the first house that they saw.

The chain attached to the doghouse rattled. A large dog barked aggressively and the girls recoiled, startled. It barked again and again, but its tail wagged in greeting.

What felt like an eternity later, they heard a grouchy voice, followed by heavy footsteps. 'Who could it be in this weather?'

The door opened. On the doorstep stood an old woman.

Her name was Mira. She fussed over the aircrew like a mother hen, shepherding them inside, giving them the best room in the house, with a large soft bed and goose feather pillows. In the kitchen, she pointed at some fried potato skins on the stove. 'We ate the potatoes yesterday. These skins are all I have. I'm sorry I can't offer you anything else. The Red Army took it all,' she croaked, waving through the window in the direction of a chicken coop without the chickens and a pigsty without the pigs. 'I don't mind. Better our boys have it than the Nazis. When they come here, I'd rather not have anything at all.' She crossed herself and whispered something under her breath. Her wrinkled face looked grey with fear.

'It is our job to make sure they don't come here,' said Nina, reaching for a spoon. She realised how hungry she was. The potato skins didn't look particularly appetising but they were better than nothing.

The old woman burst into tears. It was a few minutes before she could talk again. 'It breaks my heart,' she said, sniffling, 'to see young girls like yourselves, wearing uniform, off to fight these monsters. I said goodbye to three sons and six grandsons a year and a half ago. God forbid my daughter and granddaughters decide to enlist. Then I'd have no one. It's not a woman's job to fight.'

'It's a job of all citizens to defend their country,' said Nina. She liked Mira. She reminded her of her grandmother, who had died when Nina was ten.

Mira shook her head. 'Look at the three of you. So pretty, so feminine. Why did you decide to go to the front?'

'We are going to drop bombs on the Nazis' heads. We can't wait,' said Olga through a mouthful of potato skins.

Once again Mira crossed herself. She muttered, 'What is the world coming to?'

Nina could barely keep her eyes open through dinner. When they finished eating and Mira showed them to their room, she fell into the soft bed and was asleep instantly. Her last thought was of the other crews. She could still hear the wind growling outside. She could see the snow, shimmering in the setting sun. It was a miracle the three of them had landed safely. What if the others hadn't been so lucky?

When Nina opened her eyes, she heard loud voices somewhere in the house. What time was it? It was still dark outside and felt like the middle of the night. Far from easing, the storm seemed to be getting worse. Nina glanced at her watch and saw that it was six in the morning. Katya's bed was empty. Nina couldn't believe it at first. Katya had never been a morning person. Kazarinova had to practically shoot her gun in the air to wake her in Engels. She was often in trouble because she was late.

Nina closed her eyes. She felt like she had barely slept. Her eyelids were heavy and her body sore. If the storm was still raging outside, there was no point getting out of bed. She was going to go back to sleep and catch up on much needed rest.

As she was drifting off to sleep, she heard Katya's voice. Was it her imagination or was Katya laughing? Another voice joined hers. Young, high-pitched and excited. Zhenya! Forgetting how tired she was, Nina jumped out of bed and rushed to the kitchen barefoot, still dressed in frilly white pyjamas Mira had given her the night before.

'We got here late last night. Imagine my relief when they told us there was another crew in the village already,' Nina heard Zhenya saying.

'And Raskova? Any news?' asked Katya.

'No. You haven't heard anything?'

'No.'

For a moment the girls were silent. When Nina walked into the kitchen and Zhenya and Masha saw her, they ran up to her and hugged her. Igor, their tail gunner, waved happily from the table, where he was busy eating left over potato skins and drinking black tea.

'Thank God you girls are safe,' cried Masha.

The three of them stood in the middle of the kitchen with their arms around each other. 'All day yesterday I thought we were the only ones to survive,' said Zhenya. 'What a terrible day it was.'

'What happened to you?' asked Nina, feeling lightheaded with joy.

'We landed five kilometres from here, by the forest. It was the forest that saved us. I could see the trees and knew the land must be close,' said Zhenya. 'Miraculously, our plane is undamaged. Took us a long time to walk here. It was hell outside. How about you?'

As Nina told them about their narrow escape, she glanced out the window. It was still snowing heavily. 'Marina and her crew should have been here by now,' she muttered.

'Don't worry,' said Olga, who was sitting at the table and chewing on a piece of brown bread. 'It's Marina Raskova we are talking about. She's survived bad weather before. She's survived running out of fuel, a week lost in the taiga without food or water and even being attacked by a bear. She'll survive this too. A bit of bad weather is nothing to someone like her.'

'I hope you are right,' whispered Nina. But Olga's words did nothing to calm her fears. 'When the weather clears, we can go out and look for them.'

'I bet by then they'll make their own way here,' said Zhenya.

Nina sat down at the table next to the other girls but couldn't even look at the food. All she could think of was Marina. Their beloved commander was one of a kind, a visionary, a woman who endeavoured to change the way things had been for generations and succeeded. She was kind, selfless and down to earth. She always put her girls first. They could come to her with anything.

Nothing was too trivial or unimportant. To Marina, they were women first, soldiers second. Their feelings mattered.

When in January 1942 the thousand women had been separated into three regiments and assigned their roles, once Katya had come to terms with the fact she couldn't be a pilot and Nina accepted that she wouldn't be flying a fighter plane, the only thing the two girls had wanted was to fly together. They were a team. It only made sense that they flew together as pilot and navigator.

Unfortunately, to Captain Kazarinova it made no sense. 'You know each other too well,' she had said. 'It's important to train with an unfamiliar pilot or navigator, to learn to work with different skillsets and personalities. You can't fly together. Too much idle chit-chat, you won't be able to focus on your work.' No matter how much the girls had pleaded, no matter how much they swore there wasn't going to be any chit-chat, Kazarinova wouldn't relent. Nina and Katya would not be flying together.

The girls had spent a few days sulking and in shock. They flew with other people and hated it. They only saw each other for a short time in the mess, long enough to eat their meals. Finally, they had gone to Raskova and told her everything. 'We are stronger together than we are apart,' they had said. 'We complement each other. We've known each other for as long as we can remember.'

Raskova had listened to them for five minutes, then called in Kazarinova and asked if she would reconsider. 'Female friendship is the most precious thing in the world,' she had said. 'It brings out the best in us. We can't get in the way of something like that.' She hadn't exactly ordered Kazarinova to put the girls together but she made it very difficult for her to say no. And she hadn't said no. The next day, the girls were flying together again. Nina loved Raskova for that. For her diplomatic manner, her kindness and understanding. For always being there for them.

Marina Raskova always found a way to help them. It broke Nina's heart that they couldn't do the same for her, to come to her rescue, wherever she was. Her helplessness was killing her as days went by and all she could do was watch the road outside, with no sign of Marina and her crew.

A week later, the snow stopped and the wind quietened, and still they couldn't go out in a truck to look for the missing crew because all the roads had been snowed in. They spent hours every day walking around the village, looking for clues. It was like searching for a needle in a haystack.

To take their minds off their fears, the girls kept busy, helping Mira around the house, clearing the snow that was up to their waists in places, washing floors, fixing broken gates, even building an outhouse. The temperature fell to below -40° Celsius but it didn't stop the girls who were accustomed to flying at high altitudes in extreme weather. By the end of every day, after hours of sawing and hammering, her face flushed from the cold, Nina's shoulders hurt and she was ready to fall into bed. For a few hours, she tried to forget about everything by losing herself in hard work and banter with friends. It didn't help. All she could think of was the gaping hole in the middle of their lives. Out there somewhere, their beloved commander Major Marina Raskova was lost without a trace. And in a small village not far from Saratov, the two crews were lost without her.

Raskova was the only one who knew where they were headed and what their orders were. What were they going to do without her? Eventually they would have to make their way to the front. How long did they wait? When did they decide that it was time to go without Marina? The girls couldn't even talk about it. Leaving without their commander was inconceivable.

With every day that passed their hope dwindled until it turned to despair. If Marina and her crew had made it out of the storm alive, wouldn't they be here by now? This was the only village around. There was nowhere else for them to go.

'She has a daughter,' Nina said. 'What if something happened to her? What will it do to her little girl?'

'You can't think like that,' Katya said. 'You can't give up on them.'

Ten days after their arrival, they were helping Mira clear snow in the garden when they saw two small boys sprinting down the road, waving and shouting, their faces flushed from excitement, from running too fast for too long.

'What is it?' asked Katya. 'What are they saying? It sounds like—'

'Plane,' said Nina, her heart dropping. 'Something about a plane!'

The boys got closer. 'Wreckage! We found the wreckage!' they cried.

For a few moments no one spoke. Nina watched the boys' red faces and her heart trembled. 'Plane wreckage?' she managed finally.

The boys nodded. 'On the riverbank. We can show you.'

'And the crew?'

The boys looked at one another before shrugging. 'We didn't see anyone. We noticed the plane from the road and came straight here.'

On the walk to the river, Nina felt numb inside. She couldn't speak as they made their slow way through snowbound roads. The village soon gave way to a forest, a white kingdom of pines and birches, their barren branches reaching for the sky as if in prayer. It felt like the forest would never end, when, finally, they came to an open space and Nina saw the river, hidden beneath a thick layer of ice.

'The boys didn't find the bodies. There's still hope,' whispered Katya.

Nina clung to those words with everything she had. Every bit of her wanted to hope. And yet, every bit of her was breaking down with trepidation.

* * *

The left bank of the Volga River, not far from the village of Razboishina, was a mix of soil and rock, a steep wall jutting out above the ice. As the girls stood mutely, looking at the blackened remains of the plane, Nina wondered if Marina Raskova had seen the riverbank in the dark and had mistaken it for a cloud, crashing right into it. Nina's legs became weak and she began to slide to the ground. Olga helped her up and Nina noticed that her hands were shaking. Katya was crying silently. Zhenya said, 'They parachuted out. I know they did. We just need to find them.'

'If they parachuted out, why didn't they make their way to the village? What's taking them so long?' asked Nina. Seeing the wreckage made it real. Until now, she couldn't admit to herself that Raskova was gone. Now that she saw the mangled plane, she knew it was a possibility.

'They didn't have their maps on them. They went the wrong way. They will be in the forest, walking in circles, looking for a way out. The forest looks deep enough for three people to be lost for a week. They'll be fine. Freezing cold and exhausted but fine. They can melt snow and drink it. They can eat bark.' Zhenya was talking fast, a machine-gun fire of words to hide her heartbreak.

For a few moments, they stood with their heads down, without moving or looking at each other. No one dared approach the plane. No one spoke. Nina was petrified of what they might find inside the smashed cockpit. She wanted to turn around and run. Taking the few steps to the aircraft required more strength than she possessed, and so she remained motionless next to her comrades, clinging to the last remnants of hope.

Finally, Igor said, shuffling forward, 'I think I can get down this slope. I can help you girls down.'

Olga scoffed. 'We don't need your help, thank you very much.'

'Speak for yourself,' said Katya, giving Igor her hand.

It took them twenty minutes of clinging to the slope and trying not to fall. Nina was grateful for the delay. She needed to gather her courage for what lay ahead. When she saw the plane up close, her eyes filled with tears. She couldn't bear looking at it. She turned away. The plane had been completely destroyed. A rock had pierced the cockpit in two.

When she lifted her head, forcing herself to look, she saw her beloved Marina Raskova. 'No,' she whispered. 'No, no!' Their commander's head was split by the rock, while the metal back of the pilot's seat had beheaded Marina's navigator, Kirill. Nina wanted to turn back time and go back to the moment when she still had hope. She wanted to unsee the scene before her. Major Raskova couldn't be dead. She was immortal, like the wind, like the sun. She was a force of nature. She couldn't have fallen so close to reaching her goal. It wasn't fair.

Slowly Nina sank to her knees and cried. By her side, the other girls were sobbing. Igor took off his hat, his face damp with tears. 'She died instantly. She didn't suffer. She died doing what she loved,' he said. No one heard him. The girls were inconsolable.

It took a long time for them to calm down enough to look for the rest of the crew. They found the mechanic Vladimir and the tail gunner Nikolai still at their posts.

'They look like they don't have any injuries,' whispered Katya.

'You don't suppose they froze to death?' Nina's insides were chilled with horror.

'If only we had found them sooner, we could have saved them,' said Zhenya.

That helplessness again, and the guilt. They tore at Nina's insides, making her want to scream in pain, to howl like an animal, like the storm that had killed Marina. She felt guilty because Marina was gone and she was still alive. Marina was a better pilot, a better navigator and a superb commander. Had she lived, she would have achieved amazing things. She would have made a difference. Much more of a difference than Nina could ever make. Why was she still here, while Marina Raskova was gone? Where was the justice in that?

As Nina stood next to Marina's crushed body, she didn't see her as she was *now*, defeated and broken, so close to having her dreams realised. She saw Marina alive, her face flushed with passion, hair wild and eyes sparkling. She had led them and taught them and encouraged them, she inspired them and made them better every day. She had been their superior but treated them like equals, with respect. At thirty-one, she was only a decade or so older than most of them, but they loved her like a mother. Because that was what she had been. A mother to every single one of them.

The sun played on bridal-white snow, making it sparkle. Somewhere west from here, the world was being torn apart by Hitler and his troops. There was chaos and death and not a glimmer of hope as he made his way deeper and deeper into the country, killing and burning and destroying everyone and everything that stood in his way. But the village of Razboishina was peaceful and quiet, seemingly untouched by war.

Except, the war was already here. It was in the hunger and fear on everybody's faces. It was in the heartbreak of the local women, who had said goodbye to their husbands and sons and didn't know if they would ever see them again. It was in the horror plane wreckage on the left bank of the Volga and the lifeless bodies of Marina and her crew. Nina knew the Nazis didn't kill Marina but she blamed them nonetheless. If they hadn't come to the Soviet Union, bringing misery and despair in their wake, Marina would still be alive.

Nina gritted her teeth with hatred as she cleared the snow off her Pe-2 in the village square. Nearby, Zhenya and Masha worked on their plane, their eyes red from tears.

Four days earlier, Marina's body had been taken to Moscow. She was to be given the Soviet Union's first state funeral of the war, with a thundering salute of guns and an air force flyover. Soviet state officials were going to attend. The same officials she had fought tooth and nail to establish the first female aviation regiment in the world. She was to be given a hero's farewell, just like she deserved.

The girls sleepwalked through their days, shell-shocked and mute, like earthquake survivors. No one knew what to do next, so they did nothing.

They were Raskova's regiment. Without her, what was going to happen to them?

'Nothing,' grumbled Masha. 'Nothing is going to happen to us. We are going to be disbanded and sent home. Our planes will be given to a male regiment. I hear there's a shortage.'

Even Katya didn't seem happy at that.

Zhenya nodded. 'The war has been going on for a year and a half now and we still haven't dropped a single bomb. We haven't proven ourselves, yet. And now with Marina gone, we might never get a chance.'

Nina said, 'Remember what Marina used to say? We can do anything. Our sister regiments have been fighting for months. We have completed a gruelling training regime. If they want to send us home, we'll fight it. Although why would they send away capable pilots who are already here and trained and battle ready? We can do this, for Marina. We can make her proud.'

They had telegraphed for orders as soon as they found out about Raskova but hadn't heard anything yet. They had no idea where the rest of the regiment was. Every day was just like the one before. They got up with the sun, although Katya preferred to sleep late. They had their breakfast of oats soaked in water and a stale piece of bread if they were lucky, then they rushed to the village square and cleared snow off their planes, polishing them until they shined, longing to soar in the skies, to find their purpose once again. They returned home around nine in the morning, by which point Katya sauntered in from the bedroom, still in her pyjamas. 'I could get used to this,' she would say.

'Then stay here,' Mira would reply. 'Stay as long as you want. Wait out the war.'

'We can't stay here until the war is over,' said Nina. 'But we'll stay until we have our orders.'

Mira shook her head. 'Orders, orders. Only a heartless monster could order young girls to war to be killed.'

'Not to be killed. To help. To make a difference.'

But Mira continued to shake her head with disapproval.

In return for her hospitality, the girls repaired everything in the house and the garden that needed fixing. They painted the walls and replaced the old wallpaper for Mira and her neighbours. As they worked, they sang Marina's favourite songs and talked about their commander. In the evening, Zhenya played her guitar. After two weeks of this, the little village began to feel like home and the villagers had become family.

The sky was peaceful and the days stretched in front of them with nothing to do but help the villagers, who brought them presents every day to thank them. Nina had a collection of books, a string of onions and a dress from the village women. The dress was stunning, blue like the sky, reaching just below her knees. When she twirled, it flew up like a parachute. How she longed for peace, for summer, for a balmy night of carefree dancing, so she could wear the dress and feel beautiful.

How long could they go on like this, suspended in time and space, and not knowing what to do next?

The news finally arrived when they had lost all hope and were contemplating going back to Moscow. A young man came running in as they were finishing their breakfast. 'Is there anyone called Zhenya Timofeeva here?'

Zhenya stood up. 'That's me.'

'There is a telephone call for you at the village council building.'

The girls watched as Zhenya followed the man. They waited in tense silence, not touching their food.

When Zhenya reappeared at the end of the road, Nina knew

instantly it was bad news. Zhenya's head was bent as if in mourning. She walked slowly towards them as if dreading to tell them what had happened.

'What is it? What did they say?' asked Masha.

Zhenya watched them for a moment without saying a word.

'Are they taking our planes? Are they sending us back?' asked Nina, her heart sinking.

'Cheer up, girls. We are going home,' said Katya. 'We'll see our families again. We've done our duty. Our conscience is clear.'

'Speak for yourself,' said Masha. 'We've worked hard for a chance to make a difference. I will not let them take it away from me.'

Zhenya said quietly, 'They are not sending us home.'

'Then why do you look like you are about to cry?' asked Nina.

Zhenya sighed. 'They want me to assume temporary command. We are to join the rest of our regiment and proceed to the Stalingrad front. I am to lead you girls in our first bombing missions.'

The girls cheered. Everyone except Katya and Zhenya, who looked white like snow.

Nina took Zhenya's hand. 'What's wrong, honey? Why are you so sad? You should be celebrating.'

Zhenya shook her head. 'They want me to replace Raskova. How could I do it? What if I'm not good enough?' In frustration she pulled at the few strands of hair that were peeking from under her hat. 'Of course, I'm not good enough. How could I compare to her? Will the girls even listen to me?'

'You make a good point. Your voice is too low. You speak quietly, like a mouse. No one will listen to you because they won't be able to hear you.' Katya giggled and tickled Zhenya, who looked like she was about to burst into tears. 'If you want to be a leader, you need to learn to speak like a leader.'

Nina pushed Katya out of the way. 'Of course, we will listen to you. Everyone will listen to you. And you don't have to be like Marina. You can be yourself.'

'I don't understand. Why did they choose me? Out of all the girls, why me?' Zhenya's eyes were two round saucers of fear in her pale face.

'Maybe because you are the most capable. And the most experienced,' said Nina. 'You can do it, Zhenya. I know you can.'

'I could never lead all those girls to a certain death and tell everyone what to do. I want someone to tell me what to do.'

'We all want someone to tell us what to do. A grown-up to come and make everything better. Someone like Marina. But she is gone. We have to accept that.'

Zhenya shook her head. 'I will telegraph and tell them I decline. I'll tell them I'm not the right person for the job.'

Nina grabbed her hand. 'If they didn't think you were capable, they wouldn't have chosen you. You received an order. You can't decline. You have no choice but do as they say. And you will be fantastic.'

'If you decline, they will send us home,' said Masha. 'It will all be in vain. The last year, all the training we've done, all for nothing.'

'And we'll be here for you, helping you every step of the way,' said Nina.

'I suppose you are right. This is what Marina would have wanted,' said Zhenya.

'You will do it?'

'I will do it.'

The girls spent the rest of the day cleaning the planes, checking and re-checking every little detail. Olga found some red paint and brushes in the village and they painted 'For Marina Raskova' in bright big letters on their wings.

'That will show them,' said Masha. 'Let the Nazis be the ones who are afraid. Let them pay . . . for everything.'

The whole village gathered to say goodbye. Everyone brought something for the girls. One woman had a small wooden icon. She handed it to Nina. 'Place it in your pocket and never go anywhere without it. It will protect you.'

A man brought a screwdriver. 'It's my good luck charm. I can fix anything with it. But you need it more than I do.'

The other villagers brought what little food they could spare, old potatoes and beetroot, a stale piece of bread, some raw barley in a cup.

Mira cried as she hugged the girls. 'The Nazis killed my husband. They took my sons and grandsons away. Make them pay for everything they've done.'

Nina had tears in her eyes as she climbed into the cockpit. It felt like she was saying goodbye to her family.

Zhenya's plane began to move. Nina followed. Soon they were in the air and the village became smaller and smaller until it disappeared altogether. All Nina could see in front of her was the white field stretching as far as the eye could see, all the way to hell on earth that was the Stalingrad front in January 1943.

Chapter 4

January 1943

Nina knew they were almost there because of a low rumbling noise she could hear. At first, she thought it was the sound of an engine, perhaps another plane. As they got closer, the sound became louder. It felt like the air around her was vibrating as if it was alive, an invisible volcano about to erupt. As they approached the Stalingrad front, all she could see was fire. The countryside was no longer an unblemished white under her wings. It was black and red, angry, torn and bleeding. Seeing the Russian land burning made Nina's heart ache. In her mind she could still see Mira's face, aged before her time with grief, asking the girls to avenge her husband, to make the Nazis pay. And there was so much to make them pay for, thought Nina as she watched the flames devouring everything in sight.

After receiving their orders, the two crews had been reunited with the rest of the regiment. The other girls welcomed them with joy. They hadn't expected to ever see them again. But the joy was only brief. A cloud of mourning hung over the regiment. Everyone walked around like they were asleep, like they expected any moment to wake up and find that it had all been a terrible nightmare, that Major Raskova was still with them.

Zhenya shouldn't have worried. Two hundred women of the 587th Dive Bomber Aviation Regiment were overjoyed to have her as their commander. She took charge like she had been born to it. It wasn't the same Zhenya that had left the little village. She looked more confident and sounded louder. She did what Nina had told her to do and found her own way. Raskova was like a mother to the girls. Zhenya became an older sister. And now she had passed her first test as their leader. She had brought the girls to the front.

In a perfect formation the planes circled the airfield. Nearby was a small village that looked abandoned; bombed-out huts, destroyed barns, burnt-out cars scattered under their wings. The winter sun reflected from a church spire and off the tiles of every roof. Below, Nina could see a handful of people waving at the formation. Here it was, the moment they had all been fighting for since that day at the Zhukovsky Academy when they first heard Major Raskova speak of a greater purpose, of conquering the sky and the prejudice, of standing up tall and facing the evil with weapons in their hands. As soon as their wheels touched the ground, their lives would change forever. From then on, they were at war.

Nina was about to commence her descent towards the little airfield when something in the atmosphere changed. There was a tension in the air, as if a thunderstorm was coming. She could sense danger, could hear a new, unfamiliar sound, of aircraft engines that were hostile and loud. Were they the promised Soviet fighter planes that were supposed to escort them to the front but had never turned up?

And then she saw them. One, two, three dots in the sky that grew gradually until they became the German fighter planes, the dreaded Messerschmitt.

'Are you serious? We only just got here,' Katya muttered. She was saying something else, but Nina could no longer hear her over the machine-gun fire; short and angry, like dogs barking.

Seconds later, the perfect formation broke up. Like pins in a bowling alley, the Pe-2s scattered in every direction. Although they were equipped with machine guns, the Soviet bombers were no match for the German fighters. The Nazi planes did a quick loop and turned around, clearly intent on pursuing them. They looked determined, like eagles that had no intention of letting their prey get away. Nina's heart was beating violently and her throat was dry. It was her first taste of war and she didn't like it. She wished she could be anywhere but here, exposed and vulnerable, like a mouse caught in a trap in front of the Luftwaffe pilots who wanted to kill her. It felt unnatural, against the order of things. She had done nothing wrong. She didn't want to die and didn't deserve to.

One of the enemy fighters was coming closer. She could see the pilot's face as he stared straight at her. It was the face of a machine, with not a trace of human emotion. Nina dropped altitude to get out of the fighter's way but felt that it was too late. She squeezed her hands tight over the controls, preparing for a sudden impact.

All that training in Engels and they didn't even touch down at the front, she thought. As they neared Stalingrad under a direct attack by German fighter planes, Nina wanted to live so desperately, it made her chest hurt. There was so much she hadn't done. She hadn't finished her education. She hadn't found her brother and father. She had never been in love or had children.

Suddenly, as if out of nowhere, two Yak-1s appeared. Seeing red stars on their wings filled Nina's heart with hope.

She felt the controls tremble in her hands. Her whole body was shaking and it felt as if the plane was shaking too. Nothing she had done in Engels had prepared her for this. In Engels, they shot at targets that never shot back. They threw practice bombs at pretend infrastructure that hadn't been defended with anti-aircraft guns. They performed their manoeuvres expertly without fear for their lives.

Nina could no longer think straight. Her head was spinning and her vision became blurry. What to do? Were the German planes still there, intent on destroying her and her friends inside their little aircraft? She gasped for air, taking short shallow breaths that didn't fill her lungs with enough oxygen. She wanted to shut her eyes and scream but knew she had to land the plane or the Germans might as well have won. She had to get herself together, for Katya and Olga, who entrusted their lives to her every time they stepped inside the cockpit.

Trying to calm herself by slowing her breathing, in and out, in and out, while her heart slammed against her ribcage, Nina sighted the airfield and aimed for it. Slowly, gracefully, she landed her plane, as if she was in an exam and Major Raskova was watching her from the ground, a scorecard in her hands. When the plane came to a stop, she sat for a few moments without moving. Katya's hand on her shoulder brought her back to reality. 'Nice welcome to the front,' she said, shaking her head as if chasing away a bad dream.

'What did you expect? A three-gun salute?'

'If it wasn't for those Soviet fighters . . .' Katya looked up in the sky where the Yaks had disappeared, chasing the German planes away. One by one, the other Pe-2 aircraft landed. The girls emerged, looking worse for wear, their eyes darting around fearfully.

'I felt so helpless out there. I honestly thought this was it for us. I don't know if I can do this,' said Katya.

'This is what we've been training for.' Nina didn't want to admit that she had felt helpless too. It was a terrible feeling, her blood running cold, her hands shaking, her body refusing to do what it was supposed to do to survive. 'We might as well get used to this.'

'How do we do that?' Katya looked like she was about to be sick. 'How do we get used to something like this? How do we survive? You saw what we are up against. It's a matter of when, not if.'

Olga emerged from the tail gunner cockpit. 'That's the spirit, Katya. Well done, Nina. Your courage and cool head saved our lives. Again.'

Nina didn't want to tell the girls that she hadn't been cool-headed or courageous at all. Up there when the fighters had appeared, she felt afraid and small and ready to give up.

Was Katya right? Was it only a matter of time? Today they had been spared. What about tomorrow?

White-faced and shaking, the women of the 587th sat in the mess tent not far from Stalingrad, bowls of barley in front of them. Even though it had been hours since she had last eaten, Nina couldn't even look at food. She felt she was going to be sick. They had dreamt of this moment for so long. All they wanted was to come here, to make a difference, to fight for their country. Now, as she watched the grim and disillusioned faces around her, she realised that the recruitment officer had been right all along. They had romanticised the front. The reality of it was very different. Nina wasn't prepared for the raw animal fear inside that paralysed her and refused to let go.

The girls couldn't talk or look at each other. The men from the 10th Leningrad Regiment, who were to share the airfield with them from now on, were a different story, however. They were having a great time at the women's expense, cheering and teasing, their voices loud and rowdy inside the dark tent. 'Into the dugouts, everyone! Helmets on your heads. The women are taking to the air!' shouted a short young man, almost a boy, with a thin moustache and pimples over his pink face. There was an expression of pure panic in his eyes as he ran in a circle with his hands covering his head.

'Nice performance,' shouted Masha. 'You should be a clown instead of a pilot.'

'Forget about the Germans. There is a new danger in the air. Women pilots,' shouted another man, tall and broad, with a wide smile on his face.

'Ignore them, girls,' said Zhenya, her face red. 'They are just boys. It must be hard for them too, living in this hell. Before you know it, we will prove them wrong. We will prove everybody wrong.'

The men continued to laugh at the girls, at their ill-fitting uniforms, at the fear on their faces.

'Why aren't you eating?' Katya asked Nina. 'You need your strength.' She had already finished her barley and her bread, and was busy throwing angry glances at the men.

Nina concentrated on her food, on picking up handfuls of watery barley with her fingers, because there were no spoons, on placing them in her mouth. She didn't want to think about what had happened in the air earlier, but all she could see in her mind was the German pilot's face, emotionless as he was about to shoot her down.

She closed her eyes and imagined six-year-old Vlad, ice skates on his feet, shouting, 'Nina, look at me, look what I can do!' His little body spinning, spinning, spinning – and falling on the ice. Her heart falling too, bracing herself for the inevitable tears, only no tears came. A moment later, he was back on his feet, shouting, 'Look at me!' Mama clapping her hands, her face flushed with happiness, and ten-year-old Nina, skates on her own feet, saying, 'Let me show you how it's done.' Spinning on the ice – faster, faster, faster – until she was dizzy, much like now, except now she was dizzy with exhaustion and fear instead of exhilaration and joy. Catching up to her brother and skating slowly, holding his frozen hand in hers, teaching him how to skate backwards, laughing together and falling on the ice.

Her eyelids heavy, she felt herself drifting off, right at the table in front of the mocking men.

'It's a shame you ladies didn't arrive in summer,' the pink-faced boy exclaimed, sniggering. 'We would have decorated your dugouts with flowers. Pretty flowers for pretty ladies. We would put flowers on your planes. The Nazis would see them and not shoot you. They are a chivalrous nation that respects women.'

'That's enough, Lieutenant Korolin.'

Nina heard the words and thought she was dreaming. One moment she was thinking of young Vlad and falling asleep at the table, the next she was hearing his voice. It was part of the dream, that was all.

'May I remind you that after your first mission to Stalingrad you were throwing up by the side of the road. The whole regiment saw you. Kindly leave the brave ladies alone.'

Nina opened her eyes and blinked. In front of her stood Vlad. Anton was by his side, smiling. She blinked again, waiting for her brother to disappear, as dreams often do. Moments passed and he was still there. 'Vlad,' she whispered, blinking fast, head spinning, confused. Her eyes filled with tears. Vlad's smiling face became fuzzy. She wiped her eyes and reached out her hand to him.

Katya cried out and jumped to her feet, pushing her chair away, pushing the table away, ignoring the astonished exclamations of the other girls. She ran as fast as she could through the mess tent, shoving people out of the way, apologising and without a glance continuing on her way. Moments later, she was in Anton's arms.

Lieutenant Korolin hiccupped with laughter. 'Meet your knights in shining armour. The pilots who came to your rescue.'

Nina got up slowly, her eyes on her brother. A little over a year ago, she had said goodbye to a boy. Now she was greeted by a man. Vlad seemed taller, stockier and more mature. Fourteen months at the front had aged him. She wanted to follow Katya, to run to Vlad and take him in her arms but her knees were shaking too much. She couldn't move. It was Vlad who crossed the mess tent and pulled her into a hug. 'Didn't I tell you to stay away from the front?' he said. His eyes twinkled.

'Vlad,' she whispered, touching his face. 'I can't believe I'm seeing you.'

'I can't believe I'm seeing *you*, here in Stalingrad.'

She wanted to jump up and down with joy and sing at the top of her voice. She wanted to spin him around, like a lifetime ago on the ice. Forgetting instantly about the Nazi planes and her brush with death, she pinched his cheek and tousled his hair, marvelling at his familiar cheeky grin that she loved so much. So relieved was she to see him, she laughed.

The four of them found a small table away from the others. Katya looked like she would have preferred to be alone with Anton. She couldn't tear herself away from him. Nina knew exactly how she felt. She couldn't take her eyes off her brother.

'How is Tonya?' Anton asked.

'Tonya is well. Missing her parents. Mama says she loves drawing and cats. All she does all day is draw cats!'

'We are missing out on so much.'

'Mama includes a cat drawing in every letter. Here, I'll show you.' Katya fumbled in her pocket and pulled out a bunch of letters.

'Letters,' Nina said to her brother, pointing at the envelopes in Katya's lap. 'Do you know what those are? They are words on paper that you send to your loved ones to let them know you are still alive.' She pinched Vlad's elbow. 'Maybe later we can show you how a pen works.'

'I wrote to you almost every day. If you don't believe me, ask Anton,' said Vlad.

Anton nodded. 'He was always writing. It was his way of getting out of chores.'

'We haven't had a word from you for a year. Twelve months of not knowing where you were.' If just one of his letters had got through, she wouldn't have lived the way she had, not knowing if she should be mourning her brother, her heart frozen with fear. Seeing him in front of her, seeing his wonderful smile melted this fear a little, but most of it still remained, in the pit of her stomach, making her lightheaded and short of breath.

'What a wonderful coincidence, finding you here,' said Katya, her lips in Anton's hair, her hand in his.

'Not a coincidence,' said Anton. 'Unlike you, we received some of your letters. We knew what regiment you were with and where you were posted.'

'We volunteered for the Stalingrad front, so we could keep an eye on you girls. They took us, without a question. There's a shortage of pilots here,' said Vlad.

'A shortage? Really?'

'Many come here. But not many last,' said Anton, not meeting the girls' eyes.

Vlad asked, 'How are you girls feeling? A bit of a shock for you this afternoon.'

'My hands are still shaking,' said Nina. 'I'm surprised I was able to land that plane.'

'A true professional, keeping calm under pressure,' said Anton.

Nina shrugged. She didn't feel like a professional at all. Despite long months of training in Engels, despite early starts and hours of practice, despite the exhaustion and the sacrifices, she felt unprepared and out of place.

'Is it normal? Does it happen a lot?' asked Katya.

Anton said, 'You are at the front. The Germans are only thirty kilometres away. It happens.' The girls waited for him to say more but he didn't. Nina remembered Kazarinova's words. Most new pilots didn't survive their first flight. She shuddered.

The four of them couldn't stop talking. The girls told the men all about training in Engels, their journey to the front and the heart-break of losing their commander. 'Without Marina, we don't know who we are anymore. We have lost our identity,' concluded Nina.

'You made it here. You are ready to fight. You are bringing Marina's vision to life. She would have been so proud,' said Anton.

And they spoke about life at the front and what it had been like for the men – a new airfield every few days, early starts and long days; risking their lives on barely any sleep and seeing everyone close to them die.

Vlad said, 'Last week alone, the 8th Air Army defending Stalingrad lost two hundred planes.'

'At this rate, soon we'll have no planes left,' said Anton. 'But the tide is turning. After months in Stalingrad, we finally managed to get the Germans surrounded. Now our job is to shoot down transport planes that bring them food.'

'You are starving them?' asked Nina.

Anton nodded. 'It won't take long. The Battle of Stalingrad will be over before you know it.'

'But at what cost. Death is all around us,' said Vlad. 'Sooner or later, you get used to it and that's the scariest thing of all; to get used to death.'

'How do you do it? How do you keep going, knowing what's waiting for you out there?' Katya wanted to know.

'We try not to think about it. It's the only way. We take it one moment at a time because it might be all we have. We focus on why we are doing this. To get the cursed Nazis out of the Soviet Union, so that our children can live. It makes all the sacrifices worth it,' said Anton.

'Don't worry, Katya. With the boys by our side, we have nothing to worry about,' said Nina. 'They saved our lives today. They will keep us safe.'

'Yes, but who is going to keep *them* safe?' grumbled Katya.

For their first missions at the front, they were to fly with a convoy of Yak-1 fighter planes. Knowing the men would be by their side, protecting them as they bombed German strategic objects, brought comfort.

The flight crews of the 587th were stationed in a village three kilometres from base. The house where the girls were to sleep had been abandoned and one of the walls was missing. It was just as cold inside as it was outside, but Nina didn't care. She was so tired she fell into bed in her uniform and closed her eyes. Her last thought was of Vlad's beloved face. Despite her fear and uncertainty, despite what had happened in the air that day, she fell asleep with a smile on her face. They were both here, as if it was meant to be. They would look out for each other. She was going to do her best to protect him, like she had done her whole life. And he would protect her. Her heart felt a little lighter because she had found her brother.

Nina awoke to a sound of someone crying next to her. She sat up in bed, confused; for a few bleary-eyed moments, she was not sure where she was. And then she remembered. What time was it? It was pitch dark outside, but she could see the first glimpses of winter sun peeking through the clouds, signalling the start of the day that was going to change their lives forever. The day of their very first combat mission.

The soft crying noises were coming from the bed across the room, where Katya was curled up in a ball, sobbing, once in a while shuddering like she was having a nightmare.

'Are you all right, honey? What's wrong?' asked Nina, perching next to her.

Katya sat up and wiped her face. 'I don't think I can go out there. After what happened yesterday, after what the boys told us . . .' She was quiet for a moment, trembling in Nina's arms. 'Nina, I don't want to die.'

'You are not going to die,' Nina said, pressing Katya's hand.

'How do you know that? You've seen first-hand what we are up against.'

Brushing her own fears aside, Nina smiled. 'Remember what Anton always says? Don't worry about something that hasn't happened yet. We are here. We are alive. God will protect us out there.'

Katya's eyes grew large. 'God? What are you talking about? Our whole lives we've been told there is no God.'

It was true. The Soviet Union was a secular state because Stalin wanted his people to be devoted only to him, not God. Hence, there was no place for religion in the country. 'I don't know about that. My grandmother was religious. She lived in a village and sometimes she took me to church with her. Have you ever been to one before?'

'Once. It had been turned into a science museum by the Bolsheviks and it had a fantastic display of early cars and airplanes.'

'Well, my grandmother's village had a real church with a real priest, and I don't know how to describe it, but when I was inside, I felt like my soul was singing. I felt . . .' She searched for the right word. 'Happy and less afraid, do you know what I mean?'

Katya shook her head.

'My grandmother taught me a prayer. Whenever I'm in doubt, I repeat it to myself.'

'Does it help?'

'Sometimes. Would you like to try?'

Katya nodded, and the girls put their hands together under their chins, whispering, 'Our Father who art in heaven, hallowed be thy name.'

Nina didn't know if repeating the words had a calming effect on them or the prayer worked but Katya stopped crying and Nina's heart no longer felt like it might burst. Soon the sun was up, illuminating the threadbare carpet, the old wallpaper and Katya's face that was red from tears. Katya blinked, shielding her eyes. While the other girls woke up and got ready, while Katya brushed her short hair in silence, looking at herself in the mirror, Nina wrote in her diary, '28th of January 1943. Our first mission.'

Even Masha, who wanted nothing more than to be at the front, didn't say a word that morning. In silence they walked three kilometres to the airfield. Zhenya was in front of them, walking with her back turned to protect her face from the wind, breaking the snow that reached almost to her waist. The day before, Nina had been in such a shock, she hadn't had a good look at the base. Now she could see a white airfield, a long runway, a taxiway and three dugouts, one of them the mess where they had their dinner the night before.

Although she had no appetite that morning, Nina forced herself to eat her porridge and drink her tea that had no milk or sugar but was strong and hot and warmed her from the inside. After breakfast, she walked on shaking legs across the airfield. Katya's face was white like the snow under their feet, and her hands trembled as she organised her maps and notes but she was no longer crying. They watched in silence as the mechanic checked their plane one final time and the armourers attached the bombs.

'Be careful out there,' said Zhenya to a group of women standing in front of her, their faces tense but resolute. 'Fly well and show them we can do this. Most importantly, keep yourselves alive. I will see you on the ground, safe and sound.'

Once they were inside the cockpit, Olga said, 'I have something for you both. Mama sent me a package.' She showed Nina and Katya two white scarves. 'Something to remind us of home and peace.' She winked at Katya. 'I know you like scarves.'

Katya stroked the scarf with awe. 'It's beautiful. But we can't wear them. It's not regulation.'

'Fortunately, Kazarinova is not here to see us. Wear it at night. No one can stop us from being women at night.'

Nina said, 'I will wear mine now, inside the plane. It will bring me luck.'

The girls put their scarves on and took their positions. Nina watched as Zhenya waved to the rest of the regiment, threw her machine gun into the cockpit and climbed inside her plane, joining Masha and Igor.

'How did that prayer go again?' asked Katya, her voice breaking.

That day, they flew in formation with ten other Pe-2s of the 587th Regiment and seven Pe-2s operated by male pilots from the 10th Leningrad Regiment, with Zhenya Timofeeva as their leader. Their goal was to bomb enemy defences north-east of Stalingrad, near a tractor factory. As soon as Nina felt the familiar rumbling of her plane and the controls shaking under her fingertips in anticipation, as if by magic, her nerves settled. She had no time to be afraid. She had a job to do.

When they were in the air, Nina watched the land under her

wings, hidden behind the frosty mist. As the mist cleared, the ruins of Stalingrad became visible. Nina found it hard to believe that human beings were capable of this level of destruction. Once, this was one of the greatest cities in the Soviet Union. Now the city was all but gone and only a pile of rubble remained. Her heart clenched with sorrow as she watched the bombed-out buildings and railroads, burnt-out cars and destroyed factories floating underneath. Seeing the dark ribbon of the Volga River made her think of their commander, Marina Raskova. Would she feel proud if she could see them now? There were dark clouds above the river, moving fast and changing shape. When they got closer, Nina heard a loud noise and realised they were not clouds at all but explosions of anti-aircraft artillery shells as the German troops fired at the Soviet planes overhead. Fired at her and Katya and Olga. Nina shuddered, grabbing the controls tighter in her stiff fingers.

Katya touched Nina's shoulder and without a word pointed downwards. Nina saw a road winding its way past the river and an outline of destroyed buildings. It was their target, the tractor factory.

Machine guns were firing from the ground, long angry bursts that made Nina clench her fists in fear. Occasionally, the deep baritone of anti-aircraft guns joined in. What would Mama say if she was still alive and could see her now? Mama, who was so protective over Nina and Vlad, didn't want them to learn to ski or ice skate or fly. She was petrified something bad would happen to them. When Papa had bought a bicycle for the two of them to share, Mama refused to let them go on it. Nina was eight, Vlad had just turned four. *Please, Mama*, the two of them had pleaded. The shiny blue bicycle was the best thing they had ever seen. It was everything they had ever wanted. 'Absolutely not,' had been their mother's reply. Nina could still feel her longing for that bike, could taste her disappointment. 'Don't be ridiculous, Zoya,' Papa had said. 'You can't wrap the children in cotton wool. They need to experience life, to learn from their mistakes. They are human beings, not porcelain dolls.'

And here Nina was, experiencing life at its most horrifying. How she wished Mama was here to wrap her in cotton wool like a porcelain doll, to protect her from the evil around her. But she knew no one could protect her. She could only rely on herself, the skills she had learnt in Engels and the aircraft that was keeping her alive in the air.

All around her, the artillery bursts looked like a forest of giant daisies. *All it takes is one second*, she thought. In one second, a shell could hit her plane and all would be over.

They were two thousand metres up in the sky that was cobalt blue as far as the eye could see, with not a cloud, not a blemish in sight. On their first combat mission they got lucky with the weather. Had the weather been like this the day they had set out for Saratov, Marina Raskova would still be alive. Such a small thing, and yet it had cost a life. How fleeting it all was, how fragile, Nina thought as she glided through the hostile Stalingrad sky.

'Watch Zhenya's bomb bay doors,' said Katya. 'When they release the bombs, so do we.'

Nina made the aircraft freeze for three seconds, bobbing like an air balloon, so that Katya could take aim. Three seconds without movement while the plane became an excellent target for the Nazi soldiers below. They were the longest three seconds of Nina's life.

Finally, she saw bomb bay doors opening on Zhenya's aircraft. She was about to tell Katya but there was no need – a moment later she felt the bomb bay doors screeching open on their plane. Zhenya's aircraft descended straight into the artillery cloud. Holding her breath, Nina followed. Masha, Zhenya's navigator, released the bombs and a second later Nina felt Katya do the same. Another second, and they heard a deafening explosion below, followed by two more.

'We did it!' Katya shouted triumphantly. She was no longer the crying trembling mess she had been in the morning. 'That's our bombs exploding underneath! Can you believe it? How do you like it, Nazi pigs?'

On the ground, the girls were jumping up and down and high-fiving one another. Zhenya hugged each and every one of them. 'Congratulations on your first mission,' she said. 'You made me proud. You made Major Raskova proud. This was what we have worked so hard for. Today we have proven we deserve to be here.'

Anton and Vlad were waiting for them in the mess. They brought dehydrated eggs, some fish and a little bit of vodka. All pilots received one hundred grams of vodka with each meal. In the morning, Nina, who didn't drink, managed to exchange hers for an extra piece of bread.

'We watched you girls from the ground. You were magnificent,' said Vlad.

'So magnificent, my heart nearly stopped,' admitted Anton. 'I don't like this feeling. I wish you were still safely in Moscow.'

'So do I,' said Katya.

'I'm proud of you, though.' Anton pulled Katya closer and she put her head on his shoulder, smiling happily. They sat on a piece of tarpaulin under the wing of their plane. The girls barely touched their food, while the boys talked about their day. Suddenly, Anton said, 'Why are you both looking so glum? You are supposed to be celebrating.'

'I'm tired,' said Nina.

'My back is sore,' grumbled Katya. 'My bed was uncomfortable last night.' The men laughed like it was the funniest thing they had heard all day. 'What? What did I say?'

'You are at the front now. You are lucky to even have a bed,' said Vlad.

Nina felt deflated and empty inside. All her life had been leading up to this moment. A year of training, hours of hard work with not a moment of rest, day after day. Anton was right. She should be celebrating. But all she felt was an overwhelming sadness and all she could think of were the people inside the tractor factory. Even though they were German, they were human beings who had lost their lives because Katya had pressed the release catch. Nina couldn't keep her hands steady, couldn't even look at the food. 'We killed someone today,' she said grimly.

'Yes, a Nazi someone,' said Vlad. 'That's what we are here for.'

Nina shook her head. 'People who have families, wives and children, mothers and fathers, waiting for them to come back home. Because of us, they never will.'

'They chose to leave their families behind, to come here and kill ours. They deserve everything they get,' said Anton.

'Did they have a choice? Or were they just following orders? What would have happened to them and their families if they refused to come here?' asked Nina.

'Who cares why they are here? If it wasn't for them, I would be home with Tonya right now,' said Katya. 'And my husband would be with us.' She glanced at Anton, who smiled at her with affection.

'You can't do that to yourself. You can't think of them as people or you'll drive yourself crazy,' said Anton. 'You won't be able to do your job. You won't be able to live with yourself. Think of what they are doing to us. Instead of their loved ones, think of ours.'

'Think of Tanya Raskova, who will never see her mother again,' said Katya grimly.

Vlad nodded. 'Or our papa, who is fighting somewhere instead of working as an engineer at his beloved factory. We don't even know if he's still alive.' He lowered his head. When he spoke again, his voice trembled. 'When we first arrived at the front, we had a young pilot with us. Ivan Grishko, barely sixteen, funny and friendly, always telling jokes and playing his guitar. He got shot down and parachuted out into enemy territory a week after he arrived at the front. When the Germans retreated, we found him.'

'Alive?'

Vlad shook his head. 'They'd tortured him. He was missing his limbs; his face was barely recognisable, and all his teeth were gone.'

'They are not human. They are monsters,' concluded Anton.

Nina was shaking. She was cold and even the hot tea in her flask couldn't warm her.

Vlad said, 'Ivan had a mother who sent him socks and books. He loved to read. He had a sweetheart at home and was planning to marry her as soon as the war was over. Every time I'm in the air, I hope to do as much damage as possible. Every day I do my best . . . for Ivan.'

Nina thought of the land burning under her Pe-2 as far as the eye could see. She thought of her father's tense face when he was leaving for the front and of Mira's empty eyes as she implored them to take revenge on the Nazis. Of Marina's ravaged body. And still, when she closed her eyes, the shapeless ghosts of the people they had bombed that day pursued her. 'Does it ever get easier?'

'It does,' said Anton. 'You will soon get used to it.'

That was the problem, right there. Nina didn't want to get used to it.

Soon it got dark outside and Vlad returned to his quarters because he had an early start the next day. Nina was so tired, she felt herself drifting off on her uncomfortable chair, when she heard Katya and Anton whispering to each other.

'You shouldn't have come here,' said Anton. 'It's not safe.'

'Like I had a choice.'

'Of course, you had a choice. Raskova's regiment is made up of volunteers. I don't understand. Why would you volunteer for this, when we have a child at home?'

'When a recruitment officer came to the university and asked for volunteers, everyone said yes. How would it have looked if I was the only one who refused? I didn't want to put our family at risk.'

'Nothing would have happened, Katya. You should have stayed with Tonya. Our daughter needs you. You don't want her to grow up without her mother.'

Nina heard anger in Katya's response. She raised her voice.

105

'Are you saying I'm a bad mother?' Nina wished she wasn't there to overhear the private conversation. Eavesdropping on an argument between a married couple made her feel embarrassed.

Anton sighed. 'That's not what I'm saying at all. I'm worried about you. I want you to be safe. Maybe it's not too late. Maybe you could still go home. Be with our daughter.'

'How can I do it now, when they have invested a year of training in me? How would it look?'

'I don't care how it looks. I want our daughter to have a mother. I want to have a wife waiting for me when I return. I want you to survive the war.'

'What about you? You don't think I worry about you?'

'That's different. I'm a man. I don't have a choice.'

'I thought you said you were proud of me. Were you lying?'

'Of course, I'm proud of you. But . . .'

Katya interrupted. 'You think I want to be here? Don't you think I'd rather be home, with Tonya? You make it sound like it's all my fault. Like I'm being selfish, like I have abandoned my child on a whim. You are being hurtful and I don't deserve that.'

'It wasn't my intention to hurt your feelings . . .'

'All I want is to go back home, to Tonya. But it's impossible.' Katya started to cry.

'I don't want to fight. This is not a good time for arguments. We risk our lives every minute of every day. This could be the last conversation we ever have. I don't want to waste our precious moments on anger.'

'If you don't want to fight, then why do you?' Katya's voice wasn't as loud as before but it was just as angry.

'I'm sorry.'

'No, you're not,' said Katya, jumping to her feet. 'Leaving Tonya broke my heart. I'm devastated and I feel guilty every single day. Instead of supporting me, you are making me feel worse. I'm going to bed.' Without a glance at Anton's stricken face, she stormed off.

'Katya, wait,' cried Anton.

Her heart breaking for the two of them, Nina listened to Katya's angry footsteps as she walked away.

'I don't seem to say or do anything right,' muttered Anton.

'She's dealing with a lot,' said Nina, opening her eyes. Her eyelids felt heavy, like someone had filled them with broken glass. Her arms and legs weighed a ton. She would have to sleep here, at the table, she thought, because she didn't have the energy to move. 'Do you want to talk about it?'

He looked away from her, like he was embarrassed. 'Not really. You have your own problems. I don't want to burden you with mine.'

'What problems do I have?' Nina laughed, even though she felt like crying. 'You can tell me anything, you know that. You and Katya are my best friends. I care about you.'

Anton took a deep breath. 'I know she's dealing with a lot. But so is everybody else. Everything I say seems to upset her. She takes everything the wrong way.'

'It's war. She's exhausted and scared. I'm sure she didn't mean to snap.'

'War has nothing to do with it. She's been like this ever since Tonya was born. I don't think she's said one kind word to me in the last three years. I feel like I'm walking on eggshells all the time. It's exhausting.'

'It's the stress,' said Nina, trying to defend her friend's behaviour, even though she didn't understand it.

Anton rubbed his hands together to warm up and attempted to smile. 'Remember when the three of us first met? That summer we caught the train to the village where your grandparents used to live?'

'How could I forget?' The memory of that summer, of long balmy nights in front of the fire, of days spent swimming, gathering wild blueberries and rowing on the lake, filled her heart with warmth.

'Remember sitting outside all night, talking for hours? I miss that. Katya and I don't talk anymore.'

'I remember Katya challenging me to a race across the lake. I jumped in and swam as hard as I could, expecting her to follow. It took me forever to cross the lake and I was exhausted at the end. And when I finally got to the other side and turned around to see if she was swimming behind me, she was still on the other bank, laughing.'

'That's Katya. She loved playing pranks. I miss that. How carefree we used to be. I want my wife back.'

Nina put her arm around Anton. 'It will get better. The war will be over soon. Things will become easier and you'll have Katya back, just like before.'

In the following days, the girls flew ten more missions over the city of Stalingrad, which was bleeding to death in front of their eyes. Nina wished she could turn away from it all, so she wouldn't see the destruction at the Don Front in 1943. She knew what she'd seen would haunt her for the rest of her life. Even the knowledge that, for the first time in the war, the Soviet forces were advancing, having surrounded the Germans, didn't make it better. Even seeing the Soviet air and ground forces flatten the last German troops outside the city didn't make it better. In her worst nightmares, Nina couldn't imagine so much human misery everywhere she turned.

On the 1st February, the regiment released the last bombs over Stalingrad. On the 2nd February, they flew over the quietened city. There was no more fighting. The six-month-long battle, the most bloody and terrifying in history, was finally over. General Paulus surrendered on the day he received a promotion from Hitler, making history as the first German field marshal to ever concede to the enemy. It was the first Soviet victory of the war and Hitler's first defeat.

The 587th Dive Bomber Aviation Regiment drove their trucks into Stalingrad, and for the first time, the girls saw the destruction not from two thousand metres in the air but up close.

Nina wished she had stayed behind. She couldn't believe her eyes. Not a single building in the city was left standing. The streets were disfigured by bomb craters and barricades. Every tree, every structure they had come across had been damaged by fire. What was left of the German troops marched through the bleeding streets, past the women of the 587th, to a POW camp. Malnourished and barely able to walk, the German soldiers were a sorry sight. As they put one foot in front of the other with great difficulty, the Soviet soldiers hurried them along with their whips, while women and children threw stones at their emaciated bodies and spat in their faces.

'I bet my Leningrad is the same,' Masha said sadly. 'Bleeding to death.'

Zhenya said, 'It's too soon to celebrate. Mark my words, Hitler is not done with us yet.'

Nina knew Zhenya was right. Two million people had perished in the Battle of Stalingrad. What a bittersweet victory it was, she thought with tears in her eyes, while thousands of starved enemy soldiers stumbled past, while Hitler continued to plunge Europe into misery for his personal ambition, which Nina could never understand.

Chapter 5

February 1943

As the women of the 587th Dive Bomber Aviation Regiment celebrated the victory at Stalingrad, the war raged on. The front moved constantly and the regiment moved with it. Nina's days became a blur of nights filled with terror and long days of getting up before dawn, sleepwalking through breakfast and flying up to six missions a day, unleashing havoc on the German troops from her trusted Pe-2. Sometimes, in the evening, she didn't have the energy to climb out of the cockpit of her plane. Some nights she didn't sleep at all, her fears and the horror of what she had seen keeping her up. Some nights she got lucky and her body gave in to exhaustion, letting her have a few precious hours of much needed rest.

One evening, two weeks after they had arrived at the front, the four of them were sitting in the mess tent.

'I'm going to ask Zhenya to make me a pilot,' said Katya, not looking up from her plate, her eyes dark and tired. 'I never signed up to be a navigator, to sit behind and stare at maps. If I'm going to fight in a war, I might as well be doing something I enjoy.'

'That's great, Katya,' said Nina. 'I will miss you as my navigator but I want you to be happy.'

'I want you to be happy too,' said Anton. 'But most of all, I want you to be safe. I don't think it's a good idea.'

'What do you mean?' asked Katya, moving slightly away from him.

'I think it will be safer for you if you continue to fly as a navigator.'

Katya was silent for a few seconds, staring at Anton in disbelief. Then she said, 'You mean, I'll be safer with Nina flying me? You think she's a better pilot than me? You don't think I'm good enough?'

'That's not what I meant.' Anton sighed. Suddenly he looked so tired, Nina felt sorry for him. While their mission was to bomb the German infrastructure, Anton and Vlad actively engaged the German fighter planes. Every morning they climbed inside their cockpits and flew to fight a deadly duel, challenging Luftwaffe pilots who were some of the best trained in the world. From dawn to dusk, the men were under tremendous pressure, emotionally and physically. 'Nina spent the last year training as a pilot. You spent the last year training as a navigator. She has more experience, that's all.'

'What about what I want? Doesn't it mean anything to you?'

'Of course, it does. But I want you to remember that you have a family. We need you.'

'You can't tell me what to do. I'm not a child.' Katya shot up in her chair. 'Let's go, Nina. I want to talk to Zhenya.'

Katya walked away, not waiting for Nina to follow and not looking at Anton. 'Sorry,' Nina whispered, before running off to join Katya.

She caught up to her friend at the entrance to the mess tent. 'I hate that he talks down to me like I don't know what I'm doing. Like I shouldn't be here at all,' said Katya, her eyes flashing.

'He just loves you and is being protective. He wants to keep you safe and he feels helpless because he doesn't know how. I know exactly how he feels.'

111

Katya turned around and glared at Nina. 'Whose side are you on?'

'I'm not on anybody's side. But I can understand where he's coming from. Seeing Vlad get inside his fighter plane breaks my heart every time. I say goodbye to him every morning and spend the day wondering if I'm going to see him again. It's hell. I wouldn't wish it on anyone. It's hard for Anton, having you here.'

'It's hard for me too. But, for better or worse, we *are* here and there's nothing we can do about it. He needs to accept it and start treating me like a grown-up.'

They found Zhenya inside her dugout, sitting on her bunk bed, her arms around her knees, eyes damp with tears.

'Is something wrong?' asked Nina, climbing on the bed next to her.

'Everything is fine.' Zhenya shook her head and forced her lips into a sad smile that made her look like a lost child. She was about to say something else when Katya interrupted.

'I was wondering if I could fly as a pilot instead of a navigator. As our commander, you will help me, won't you?'

'I'm not your commander anymore,' Zhenya said quietly.

Nina thought she misheard. 'What? Since when?'

'I received a telegram twenty minutes ago. They are replacing me. Our new commander will arrive tomorrow.'

'I guess I'll be a navigator forever,' Katya muttered unhappily. 'That will make Anton happy.'

Nina took Zhenya's hand. 'We don't want another commander. We will tell them you are the only one for us.'

'I don't think it's up for debate. After all, they made it clear from day one this was only temporary. A regiment of skilled aviators needs an experienced leader.' Zhenya shook her head sadly. 'A part of me is relieved. It's a huge weight on my shoulders, being responsible for so many lives. What if something happens to the girls on my watch? I couldn't live with myself.'

'It's war. Even if something happens, it won't be your fault,' said Nina.

'I keep telling myself that but I can't sleep, I can't eat, I worry about every single one of you. At the same time, I care about you all. I know you well. I know what's best for you. I have your best interests at heart. I want to stay your commander so that I can look after you.'

'Why don't you tell them that?' asked Nina. The thought of someone new leading them into battle filled her with dread. After they arrived at the front, she had heard rumours about the 586th Regiment of fighter pilots and the problems they were having with their commander. They didn't respect her because she didn't fly. They thought she was a coward and a bully. Because of her, a gifted pilot committed suicide and the whole regiment was up in arms. Nina didn't want that to happen to them. They were sisters. They supported one another. After losing Marina Raskova, they needed someone they respected and loved to lead them to great things. Someone like Zhenya.

'They give the orders. It's not my place to question them,' said Zhenya.

Nina knew there was little they could do. Unfortunately, they didn't get to choose their commander. The choice was forced upon them. 'You are the best person we could wish for. You healed the regiment after Marina's death broke us apart. No matter who they send, she won't be as good as you.'

'I hope it's not Kazarinova,' said Katya, her eyes wide.

'Lucky for us, Kazarinova is busy leading the night bombers,' said Nina.

'That's a relief,' said Katya. 'But if not Kazarinova, then who?'

His name was Major Valentin Markov. He was a balding man in his thirties with suspicious eyes and large facial features, and as he paced in front of them, looking them up and down, a shocked hush fell over the line of women.

Nina heard subdued whispers around her. 'It's a man!'

'What were they thinking?'

'We are a female regiment. They couldn't find an experienced female pilot to lead us?'

On Major Markov's face Nina could see everything the women were feeling – surprise, disappointment and incomprehension.

'What do you think, sir?' asked Zhenya, taking a step forward.

Markov glanced at the girls, who were lined up in front of him, looking at the ground. Nina tried to see them through his eyes. They were dressed in oversized male uniforms that didn't fit. Their boots were too big. Their line was uneven. Their hair was growing out, peeking from under their caps and covering their eyes. They couldn't stand still under Markov's gaze, twitching and jolting. Markov's face was sour like an unripe grape as he observed his new regiment. 'Very impressive,' he said finally.

'Sure,' whispered Katya. 'He looks impressed.'

'He looks stunned. Was he expecting a regiment of men?'

'Of course, he was. Whoever heard of women flying in combat?' Nina made her best impression of all the recruitment officers she had ever spoken to.

'Look at his face. It's got *Why me?* and *What did I do to deserve this?* written all over it. He doesn't think women can be soldiers.'

'We'll just have to prove him wrong.'

Markov stopped next to Katya. Instantly she fell quiet. 'No talking in line,' he barked. 'I am your new commander, whether you like it or not. I warn you I am going to expect a lot from you. Don't count on any allowances just because you are women. And don't expect any special treatment.' He continued walking, looking straight at them, as if daring them to argue. No one said a word. 'We are united in one common goal – beating the Nazis. Forget anything else. Forget your own needs. Let that be your only driving force. Everything else can wait until the war is over.'

'Yes, sir,' said Zhenya. 'We are ready for today's mission, sir.'

'No more missions until you can prove to me that you are prepared. The last thing we want is fatalities because you haven't been fully trained. We start a rigorous training regime this morning. We will practice high-altitude flying and precision dive bombing. There will be night-time drills to get you used to the combat conditions.'

Zhenya pulled her shoulders back, instantly appearing taller than she was. 'With all due respect, sir, we have just completed a year of training in Engels. We are ready to fight. In the last two weeks, we've been flying combat missions every day.'

'Engels was child's play. This is the real deal. You are at the front now.' As Markov walked past Katya, he stopped. Katya fidgeted under his gaze. He pointed and said, 'Your uniform is covered in grease.'

'Radiator liquid, sir,' said Katya, flinching.

'Unacceptable. You are women, after all, not scarecrows in the middle of a field of potatoes.'

'We are soldiers first. And it's war.'

'Being a soldier doesn't mean you have to look like you are homeless. Wash your uniform. I expect to see you clean and presentable every morning.'

'I'd love to wash my uniform, sir, but we have no soap. And nothing dries here. The clothes just freeze.'

'I don't need your excuses. Find a way.' He turned away from Katya. 'We will start with an exam. The men from the 10th Leningrad Regiment will assess your skills and report back to me. Be ready in five minutes.'

Markov walked away, glancing at his watch. The girls huddled on the airfield, talking in hushed voices. 'Find a way,' Katya mimicked. 'You are women, after all, not scarecrows. Who does he think he is?'

'Our new commander,' replied Nina. Her heart was aching. If only Marina was still alive, everything would be different.

'Who does he think we are? A group of naïve schoolgirls?' demanded Zhenya, who was pale with rage. 'The men from the 10th are going to conduct our exams? We have more experience in the air than all of them put together. We are a regiment of well-trained aviators who have already flown in combat under enemy fire. What makes them better than us?'

'They are men. To Markov, that makes them better, I suppose,' said Nina.

'I wish we had Kazarinova instead,' Katya whispered. 'She might be a witch but at least she takes us seriously.'

When the first shock subsided, the girls lined up on the airfield, waiting for their assessment to begin, looking bewildered and confused. They wanted to be out bombing the Nazis, not wasting their time on a pointless exercise designed to prove that they could fly, even though they were women. Markov walked in circles from one aircraft to the other, examining them in great detail. Nina felt her hands shaking. What if he told her to throw away her teddy bear that she kept on the controls? She couldn't fly without her teddy bear. It was her good luck charm. Not only did it remind her of home, she was convinced it kept her safe.

He stopped next to Zhenya's plane. 'Who is in charge of cleaning these machine guns?'

'I am, sir,' said Ilona, one of the armourers. She sounded high-pitched, like a mouse squeaking. She looked like a mouse too, small and fidgety and scared for her life.

Markov narrowed his eyes and looked down at her without saying a word. Ilona went white under his gaze. When he spoke, his voice was too loud for the quiet airfield. Everyone could hear him. And everyone felt sorry for Ilona. 'There are grease stains all over them. Not good enough. To keep the weapons in good condition, they need to be carefully maintained. And that means cleaning them properly. I thought you would have learnt that in Engels.'

Ilona opened her mouth to reply but clearly could think of nothing to say. Her eyes filled with tears. A moment later she was sobbing with her head in her hands. Markov backed away, an expression of pure horror on his face. 'Women,' he muttered.

'That's one way of getting him off our backs,' muttered Katya. 'He's not used to seeing his soldiers cry. It scares him.'

Nina put an arm around Ilona, trying to calm her. Ilona sniffled. 'No one has ever spoken to me like this. Major Raskova was always supportive and encouraging. She always told me how well I was doing.'

'He is not Raskova. That much is clear,' said Nina. 'And we have no choice but to accept it.'

'He's so stiff and proper. Like a bayonet,' said Zhenya with dislike.

Katya giggled. 'That's what we are going to call him from now on. Bayonet! It suits him! I hate him already and it's only been two hours. How long is he staying?'

'Girls, don't get in trouble with your commanding officer. We might have to go through the war with him as our leader. We need to find a way to live with him,' said Nina.

'Bayonet,' hissed Katya, glaring at Markov across the airfield.

Nina gritted her teeth as she climbed inside the cockpit. No matter how she felt about their new commander, she was going to prove she was worthy of being here. She was going to do her best today, just to show this man who he was dealing with. They might be women but it didn't mean they couldn't fly.

Today there was no Katya in the cockpit behind Nina. In her place was the pink-faced boy who had mocked them when they first arrived. His name was Tim. In his hands he held a notepad. As they taxied out, he said, 'I should have updated my will this morning. I'm in the plane with a woman pilot. Fifty-fifty chance I will make it back alive. What do you think?'

'I think the more you talk, the less your chances are,' said Nina, her voice icy cold. Although she was stuck with him for the duration of this ridiculous and unnecessary assessment, she didn't have to be polite. She had a job to do. Putting up with insults wasn't part of it.

She shouldn't have worried because that was the only mocking

117

comment Tim made. As soon as they took off, he stopped talking and watched in amazement. He made little scribbles in his notebook but mostly he observed as she flew. After twenty minutes, he said, 'Do you want to know what I think?'

'Not particularly,' Nina replied bitterly. She cared what Major Raskova had thought about her. She cared what Zhenya thought. She didn't give a damn about this boy, who looked young enough to still be in school.

'I think you are remarkable. One of the best pilots I have flown with. I hope Markov is watching this.' There was pride in his voice, as if her flying ability had something to do with him.

Despite her anger, she couldn't help but smile.

After the assessment was over, Markov gathered them together on the airfield. Something in his face had changed. He looked at them differently. When he spoke, there was a hint of warmth in his voice. 'I want to compliment you, girls. Major Raskova had done a splendid job. She had taught you well. Some of the most impressive flying I've seen in a long time. And I've seen it all. I am proud of every single one of you. Together, we will show the Nazis what we are made of. Personally, I can't wait.'

Nina felt a warmth spread through her. It was a great achievement, impressing Bayonet. Something told her he wasn't easily impressed.

For the next week, they trained under the watchful eye of Major Markov. Nina could barely keep her eyes open after night-time drills and training flights. A few times Markov had joined them in the sky and she had to admit he was a fantastic pilot. Perhaps they could learn a thing or two from their new commander after all. It would be an honour to have him as their leader on their missions against the Nazis.

But therein lay the problem. There *were* no missions against the Nazis. As the girls watched the men of the 10th leave every morning, while they were stuck on the airfield, everyone's morale tumbled to an all-time low. It was their fourth week at the front and they were still waiting for something.

'I'm exhausted,' Katya said after another gruelling day of training exercises. 'And this tea is cold. Why did you bring me cold tea?' Pouting, she shoved her flask into Anton's hands.

'I'm sorry,' said Anton. 'Would you like me to get you more tea?'

'Yes, please,' snapped Katya, barely glancing in his direction.

'What about you, Nina? Would you like some warm tea?'

'Sure. I'll walk with you,' said Nina. Anton's face looked thinner than she remembered and there were dark shadows under his eyes. During what little free time he had, he should be resting, not fetching tea. Nina wanted to tell Katya that but knew it wasn't her place.

'How are you holding up?' Anton asked as they made their way through the snow towards the mess tent.

'We are doing fine, just fine. Markov is going easy on us. Perhaps too easy.'

'That's good. For the time being, you girls are safe. I can relax a little and not worry too much.'

Nina shrugged. 'It's like being back in Engels,' she said sadly. 'He's not taking us seriously.'

'You are not happy with him?'

'He doesn't trust us or care about our skill and readiness. Typical man, he thinks our place is in the kitchen, not in the air. I'm surprised he hasn't ordered us to the mess tent to serve porridge to male pilots.'

'Give Markov a chance,' said Anton. 'He is a good regimental commander. He's known for taking care of his men.'

'Exactly, *men*. But we are women. He doesn't know what to do with us. He thinks it unmans him to lead a female regiment. He's angry and he's taking it out on us,' grumbled Nina.

'You dislike him because he is not Raskova. But no one is Raskova. She is gone. You have to accept it.'

'We were happy with Zhenya.'

119

'I've heard many good things about Markov. He has a solid reputation. I wouldn't worry too much if I were you.'

When they returned with the tea, Katya was asleep inside their plane. When she woke up an hour later, the tea was cold again.

After three more days of Markov's rigorous training regime, the girls had had enough. Zhenya confronted him on the way to the mess. She dragged Nina along for moral support.

'We've been training for ten days and are yet to see any action,' she said. 'When are we going to start flying combat missions? This is what we are here for after all. The girls are unhappy.'

There was a sadness in Markov's face Nina had never noticed before. Even his smile looked sad, as if he had seen things and they had laid a stamp on him. 'What's your rush, girls? Why are you in such a hurry to get yourselves killed?'

'We are here to fight, not sit back and watch. We trained hard for this. Why are you holding us back?'

'In my own way, I am trying to protect you. Who am I to sacrifice young girls?'

It was obvious how difficult it was for him. He was a traditional Soviet man. All his life he had been told that his job was to protect women. How could he send them to a certain death? Nina almost felt sorry for him. 'Sir, we are soldiers, like everybody else,' she said. 'We want to be treated equally.'

'But you are not like everybody else. What if the Germans find out we have young women flying for us? They'll think we have run out of men. And the tears . . . You girls are always crying.'

Zhenya lifted her head and said, 'Never mind the tears. We can cry and still do our jobs. Please, sir, give us a chance. You won't regret it.'

'Girls, girls. I can't bear seeing you at the front. It makes me feel like less of a man. It makes me feel ashamed, like I've let you down somehow.'

Zhenya said, 'It's everybody's job to fight the Nazis. We thought there was a shortage of pilots?'

'There is no shortage of pilots. There is a shortage of planes.'

'You are just afraid of us. You think we'll be better pilots than you. Better than anyone.'

Markov bowed his head. 'Not afraid *of* you. Afraid *for* you. Up there, how can I keep you safe?'

'This is not what Raskova had in mind for us. If only she was still alive, this would not be happening. Why are we even here? What's the point? We might as well go home. Keep our planes. That's all you care about anyway,' said Zhenya, turning around and storming off without a glance. With an uncertain smile and a wave of a hand, Nina followed.

As she sat at her table that morning, with watery porridge in front of her, she realised Anton was right. In his own way, Markov cared. And because he cared, he was reluctant to use his girls in combat.

The next morning, Markov stood in front of them, looking tired and drawn, like he hadn't slept at all that night. 'Training is cancelled this morning,' he said, his eyes running up and down the uneven line of his aviators.

The girls muttered unhappily. 'Why? What did we do wrong this time? Are our boots not shiny enough? Are our uniforms not up to standard?'

Markov didn't seem to hear. He smiled. 'Congratulations, soldiers. Today will be your first combat mission under my command. We are to bomb factories under German control. A straightforward operation, in and out. Take care of yourselves out there and make me proud. Come back alive. I will be in the air with you, watching over you.'

Unhappy whispers quietened down, giving way to a shocked silence and, finally, celebratory cheers. Nina felt her heart dive all the way to her feet. She felt elated and petrified, all at the same time. Around her, the girls were shouting 'Hooray!' and throwing their caps in the air.

Markov shook his head. 'Girls, girls. You are so eager to go to your deaths.'

'For the greater good, sir,' said Zhenya, beaming.

They flew in a formation of ten planes. Markov was in the rear, so that he could see all his pilots. Zhenya's aircraft was the leader, just like before, while Nina was behind her. Once again, she wished their planes were equipped with radios. She wanted to hear the other girls' voices. She wanted to hear Markov's voice, she realised with surprise. Shaking with nerves, she longed for his calm directions. Even though there were three of them inside the Pe-2, even though she could see the other planes around her, it was lonely in the pilot seat as she flew over the burning countryside.

They approached the target area.

'No one is shooting at us,' said Katya. 'Are they all asleep?'

'We are about to wake them up,' replied Nina, circling the target. The aircraft was heavy with bombs hanging beneath its wings. Nina couldn't wait to feel the weight drop off as the bombs flew to the ground. 'Now!' she shouted and felt Katya release the catch that held the bombs in place. Suddenly it was no longer quiet as the bombs exploded and Katya shouted triumphantly. Nina was right – the explosions startled the Germans out of their reverie and soon the anti-aircraft guns joined in, firing at the small planes.

'Let's get out of here,' said Nina, turning the plane around.

The sky was so dark with smoke, Nina couldn't see a patch of clear blue sky anywhere. Around them, shells exploded and bullets whizzed, the explosions throwing the aircraft around. Nina fought hard to stay in formation behind Zhenya's plane, finally climbing high to escape the battle. At four thousand five hundred metres, the air grew so thin it was difficult to breathe. She looked behind and saw that all ten planes were flying wing tip to wing tip, like in an air show. Her heart soared with pride for her sisters, the air women of her squadron, for completing their mission, for being brave and overcoming their fear and other people's doubts. *Raskova was right*, she thought. *We can do anything.*

One after another, the Pe-2s made their way back to the airfield, following Markov's plane as he circled before landing – a victory loop over the airfield; a tradition Markov had established. 'Those on the ground will know that we are coming home victorious,' he had said. It filled Nina's heart with joy to finally be able to do this, not in training but after a successful combat mission.

When the wheels touched the ground, she breathed freely for the first time that morning.

As they waited while their plane was refuelled and reloaded, Nina said, 'What a feeling, to drop a surprise on the German heads and see them all stirred up, firing back. It was incredible!'

'Incredibly scary, you mean?' said Katya.

'Bayonet looks happy,' whispered Nina. 'I think this is the first time I've seen him smile.'

'He is proud of us girls,' said Masha, who had flown as Markov's navigator that day.

'What was it like, flying with him?'

'He kept me busy. He wanted to know where everyone was at all time. He didn't care about the enemy or the targets. He kept asking, where is Petrova? Where is Timofeeva? How is Siniza doing? Over and over again.'

'Just like he promised. He kept an eye on us,' said Nina. Maybe things would work out after all. Maybe Major Markov was just what the regiment needed.

They flew five more missions that day, each one a success. The next day, when they were in the air once more, everything seemed easier. Yes, Nina was still nervous but the rawness of her emotion was no longer there. Her hands didn't shake as much and her throat wasn't as dry. They flew to target, they released the bombs, they flew back. Was Anton right? Was she getting used to it? Would it soon become routine, just a job she did every day? Would unleashing death become normal?

She didn't want to believe it.

That afternoon, eleven planes set out on their mission but only ten returned. They did their victory loop around the airfield, even though their hearts were heavy with fear. As soon as they landed, the girls jumped out of the cockpits, lining up on the airfield. Markov was in front of them, looking up into the clouds, his face as grim as the sky. And the sky remained clear. There was no sign of another plane.

'Who is it? Who is missing?' Nina wanted to know.

'Yulia Siniza, Ira and Andrei. They were behind us, then they fell back suddenly. We don't know what happened,' said Zhenya. All eyes were on the sky as the girls and Markov waited in tense silence. Nina could hear her own heartbeat.

Finally, a small dot appeared in the distance and the girls cheered but their voices soon fell quiet. It was clear there was something wrong with the plane. The dot grew bigger, zipping this way and that, suddenly losing altitude and climbing up again. The girls clucked like hens at the sight of the troubled Pe-2.

'They are flying erratically.'

'Have they been hit?'

'I think I can see smoke. Is the plane on fire?'

'I don't see any smoke. Are they having mechanical problems?'

'Come on, Siniza, you can do it.'

When the plane landed, bouncing off the runway like a tennis ball, the girls ran towards it as fast as their oversized boots allowed. Yulia and Ira climbed out, visibly shaken, followed by Andrei, who had an amused expression on his face. Nina could almost taste her relief. They were alive. They made it back safely. That was all that mattered.

'Have you been wounded?' Markov wanted to know. 'Is something wrong with the plane?'

Ira shook her head. Her hands were trembling.

Yulia was the first to regain her composure. 'No, sir. Everything is fine, sir.'

'You two don't look like everything is fine.' He turned to Andrei. 'What happened out there?'

'There was a mouse in the cockpit, sir.' Andrei fought to remain serious and failed, his face dissolving into the biggest smile.

'A mouse?' Markov rose his uncomprehending eyes to the pilot and navigator.

Yulia blushed. 'It ran over my foot.'

'It climbed up my chair and fell in my lap,' said Ira.

The airfield shook with laughter. The girls spoke all at once.

'A mouse in your plane!'

'Your first passenger.'

'I hope you charged it for a ticket.'

'Did you offer it tea and biscuits and ask it to fasten its seat belt?'

Markov watched the girls for a moment. Then he laughed. 'Are you telling me you just unleashed a hundred tonnes of explosives on the Nazis and you are afraid of a little mouse?'

'It made tiny squeaking noises!' Yulia did her best to imitate the mouse. A fresh burst of laughter resounded on the airfield. 'Laugh all you want. I'm not getting back inside that plane until the mouse is gone!'

'Women.' Markov shook his head but he didn't look upset. 'What am I going to do with you girls? You have one hour. Pull yourselves together. When your plane is ready, you are flying, mouse or no mouse!' His eyes twinkled with warmth and relief.

Chapter 6

In the middle of February, temperatures fell below -40° Celsius. It was so cold, water froze in a bucket before the girls finished washing. Sometimes Nina's hair froze to her makeshift bed inside the dugout where she slept. If she got up too quickly, the pain of her hair being pulled was so intense, it made her cry out. Markov no longer told them off if their uniforms were dirty. In these extreme conditions, wet clothes froze instantly and never dried. Once, Nina tried to dry her overalls by the fireplace and they caught on fire.

As the days went by, Nina felt herself slowing down. Every step she took, every motion of her body required tremendous amounts of energy. She was too cold to move at a normal speed and the frostbitten skin on her face cracked and peeled off, like it did once on a holiday on the Black Sea when she was five and got sunburnt, except then it was summer and warm, there was no war and she was happy. Her mother was alive, her father doted on them, Vlad was turning from a baby into a chubby toddler who laughed and babbled incessantly, and Nina's whole life stretched before her like the unblemished summer sky of the south of Russia.

Often her fingers stuck to the metal controls, and when she pulled she left patches of skin behind. After a while, her hands were in agony. Every mealtime for a week, she had poured the shot of vodka she received into a glass jar, finally exchanging it for a pair of men's gloves that looked giant on her. The other girls laughed at the sight of her but her fingers felt better. Soon, she noticed first Zhenya, then Masha and then the rest of the girls started wearing gloves too.

Her face was always red, windswept and achy. Her eyes were bleary from lack of sleep. The 587th Dive Bomber Aviation Regiment changed airfields often, sleeping at different quarters almost every day; an old shed or a dugout, occasionally someone's house. And sometimes they had to sleep under the open skies, in the freezing cold.

Now that he was finally using them in combat, Markov had set a punishing schedule for his aviators. Although the pilots were fed well, often Nina was too tired to make her way to the mess and have her meals. The weight was falling off her. She had always been thin but now her arms and legs looked like twigs. The uniform, too big for her to start with, was hanging off her. Katya, who had always been round like a bun, was losing weight too and hating it. 'You won't like me anymore, look how thin I've become,' she kept repeating to Anton.

'Yes, because that's what I care about. Not whether or not you are safe but how thin you look,' he would reply.

'You barely glance at me anymore. I don't feel like a woman anymore. I don't even look like a woman in this oversized uniform.'

Anton would hug her and say, 'You look beautiful, just like always.'

Even though their days were just as long and gruelling, if not more so, in the evenings Vlad and Anton started bringing food and warm drinks to the girls' plane after their last mission. They would sit under the wing of their Pe-2 in silence because they had no energy to talk. More often than not, Katya would lean her head on Anton's shoulder and fall asleep. Even if she was too tired to eat, Nina looked forward to completing their last mission and seeing her brother and Anton. It felt like coming home to a loving family after a long day.

Early in the morning from her plane, Nina could see the villagers who had lost their homes, huddled together for warmth as they tried to get some sleep under the open skies. Soon they would awake and continue to move further and further east, doing their best to escape the unspeakable horror that had befallen them. Old people with all their possessions on their backs. Mothers pressing their children close to protect them. Women with sad eyes, having said goodbye to their husbands and sons, making their way towards salvation on their own. With nowhere to go and no place to call their own, frozen, hungry and afraid, on and on they walked because their lives depended on it, while military vehicles, motorcycles and trucks drove slowly past. In February 1943, it seemed to Nina that the earth had been tilted to one side and everything was moving east, away from Hitler and his troops.

One day in the second week of February, as they glided above clouds, closer and closer towards their target and the German artillery, Katya was unusually quiet. All Nina could hear was the loud humming sound of the engine and the beating of her heart. She was nervous this morning and could feel her pulse quickening as her fingers grasped the controls. After all the devastation she had witnessed in the last few days, it would feel especially satisfying to drop their bombs on the Nazis. Then it was back to base for more fuel and explosives and they would be off again. Just like any other day.

Although the Nazis were no longer advancing at the same speed as before, and although the Red Army had taken its revenge for a year and a half of humiliation with its victory at Stalingrad, the enemy were still gaining ground. They had superior aviation, better trained pilots and more planes. In the last week alone, the 10th Leningrad Regiment had lost four fighter planes. Nina barely knew the pilots who didn't come back from combat but the losses had hit her hard. At the back of her mind, there was a terrifying thought. It could have been Vlad. And tomorrow it might be.

Katya said, 'When it's all over, I don't think I'll go back to university. I want to stay home with Tonya and Anton. Maybe have another baby.'

Olga replied, 'When it's all over, I don't want to see another plane for as long as I live. I'm done with flying.'

'I couldn't live without it,' Nina said. 'This feeling of soaring through the air, above the clouds, above the birds, the freedom that takes your breath away. Life seems larger here. There is nothing in the world like it.'

'Especially when you are being shot at from every direction. No, thank you. I would rather be on the firm ground, where I'm safe,' said Olga. 'I want to finish my degree and become a geologist. My first expedition was the happiest two months of my life. We were in the middle of nowhere, sleeping under the stars, working hard, staying up late, having the time of our lives. When we returned, we learnt that the war had started. We had been at war for two weeks and didn't even know it.'

Suddenly, Nina heard a new sound. A lower hum of an engine, a bass to her plane's baritone. A bigger aircraft. For a moment, there was a hope inside her that it was a Soviet plane. When she saw the dreaded swastika and the familiar shape of the Messerschmitt, this hope turned to horror.

'Quick!' shouted Katya. 'Let's go!'

But there was nowhere to go. Their Pe-2 could never outrun a German fighter. Where was the rest of the formation? Nina was in the rear this time. In her haste to get away from the enemy plane, she had fallen behind and could no longer see the others. She knew Major Markov would be frantically searching for them in the sky. She could imagine the frown on his face when he couldn't find them.

'Olga, open fire,' shouted Nina. Her hands began to shake.

'On it,' replied Olga. Her machine guns began to sing. Just like Katya, Olga was a superb shot, one of the best in the regiment, which was why Marina Raskova had selected her for the position of tail gunner.

The German fighter was firing at them too. Suddenly, Nina felt a sharp impact. The cockpit filled with smoke.

'The plane is on fire!' shouted Katya.

Nina's eyes ached so much, she could barely see. The plane was no longer running smoothly. With smoke coming out of its starboard engine, it began to glide downwards.

The Messerschmitt had no intention of letting its prey go. It circled like a falcon, showering the Pe-2 with bullets. Olga was no longer shooting back. Her machine guns were silent. 'Olga, what's wrong?' cried Nina. 'Have we run out of ammunition?'

There was no response.

'Olga?'

Nothing.

Nina's heart skipped with fear. 'There's something wrong with Olga,' she cried. She could hear Katya shouting and calling their friend.

The engine was trailing smoke. Nina knew she couldn't keep the plane in the air for much longer. 'You have to jump,' she said to Katya, willing herself to remain calm, counting inside her head to stop the panic from taking over.

'What?' cried Katya.

'You have to jump right now, before it's too late. We are losing altitude.'

'I can't jump. You know I can't. I hate parachutes.' Katya sounded hysterical, like she was on the verge of a breakdown. It was Nina's job as a pilot to make sure she remained calm.

'You can. You've done it before. Now go! Save your life.'

'What about you?'

'I'm going to try and land this thing.'

'Let's both jump. Forget about the plane. Your life is more important.'

'What about Olga? We can't leave her in the plane to die.'

'Yes, you're right. Then I'm staying too.'

Nina could see the open field below. There was plenty of space to land but with the Messerschmitt about and the plane on fire, she wasn't sure she could do it. She would do her best, for Olga. But first she had to make sure Katya was safe. 'As your pilot, I order you to jump. It's the safest thing to do right now. I need to know you are all right or I won't be able to land.'

'I'm not going without you. If we die, at least we'll be together.'

'You have a child to think about. Now go.'

Her heart in her throat, Nina watched as Katya jumped out of the burning plane and her parachute opened like a giant mushroom. It was gliding through the air when the hostile sound of the other engine increased in volume and Nina heard the loud pops of a machine gun. With horror, Nina realised the German pilot was shooting at her friend. Just before Katya landed, her parachute caught fire. 'Katya!' Nina shouted.

Had she made a mistake? Had she sent Katya to a certain death? Her eyes filled with tears. Her hands shook, and so did the controls, causing the damaged Pe-2 to twirl and nose-dive through the air. Emitting a short scream of despair, Nina pointed her burning plane at the field below. When the wheels touched the ground and the plane careened down its makeshift runway, her overalls caught on fire. Suffocating from the smoke, she jumped out of the plane and rolled around in snow until the fire was out.

Coughing and gasping, her eyes watering, Nina rushed back inside the burning plane. 'Please, God, don't let it be too late,' she muttered as she threw open the hatch to the tail gunner cockpit. Olga was still in her seat, her head leaning to one side.

Her eyes were closed. 'Olga!' Nina screamed. 'Olga, can you hear me?' She shook her friend by the shoulder, searching for her pulse and whispering that everything was going to be fine. But even as she was saying it, she knew that nothing was fine. A bullet had hit Olga in the forehead. She was gone.

Sobbing, Nina tried to pull Olga's body out of the aircraft, when the enemy fighter plane returned, opening fire. 'I'll come back for you,' Nina whispered, wiping her tears away with the back of her hand. Letting go of Olga, she climbed out of the plane and ran towards a small forest. Hiding under a tree and closing her eyes, she cried quietly, while the German fighter circled a few times and left.

She didn't know how long she stayed hidden. When she could no longer hear the Luftwaffe aircraft, she emerged from the forest into the open field and looked around. The sun disappeared behind a cloud and the sky over her head looked grey and mournful. Nina brushed the tears from her eyes and shivered in the breeze. Her head was throbbing and her stomach ached with hunger, a dull pain that left her lightheaded and confused. Her mouth was burning. She needed food and water but she couldn't think about it just yet. She had to get back to the girls. Katya and Olga needed her.

She ran through the snow, falling and cursing and getting up again. When she saw her plane, she cried out in horror. It had caught on fire and the flames were devouring what was left of the tail gunner cockpit. Nearby in the snow, something caught her eye. It was her teddy bear, black and barely recognisable. She clutched it to her chest and sank into the snow, shaking all over, her eyes on the inferno that had swallowed Olga.

Nina wanted to crawl under the tree and cry her heart out. Her eyes couldn't focus and her head was spinning. But she couldn't let herself fall apart just yet. She had to find Katya.

Clenching her fists, she waded through the snow that was knee-deep in places. Every step was a struggle. Where was Katya? The last she had seen of her, her parachute was on fire and the enemy plane was shooting at her. Could she have survived that fall?

Nina took stock of her situation. The burning plane was behind her. In her pocket she had a revolver, a compass, a small folding knife, special matches that could burn when wet, documents, her teddy bear and a small piece of chocolate. Shoving the chocolate and a handful of snow in her mouth, she continued walking. Her progress was agonisingly slow. Her trembling knees, her exhausted body slowed her down. To find Katya, she had to move faster. What if her friend needed help? Nina couldn't see anything beyond the snow that had just started falling like a sticky wall. She couldn't work out where she was. Where did Katya land? What if Nina was moving away from her? She called her friend's name, again and again. She had already lost Olga. She couldn't bear the thought of losing Katya too.

As she fought her way through the snow, all she could think was, *it's all my fault*. These girls had trusted her with their lives and she had let them down. Now they were gone.

Katya could be anywhere. Her broken body could be right next to Nina, concealed by the snow, and she wouldn't even know. Hour after hour she walked through the never-ending white fields, ready to faint from hunger, wincing from pain in her left shoulder. She knew she needed help, knew she had to get back to her regiment and return with a search party because she was unlikely to find Katya on her own. But she couldn't let go. In her heart she felt that the only chance of keeping her friend alive was if she found her *now*. Time was not their friend. 'She's going to be just fine. Katya will be fine,' she repeated to herself. She had to believe it. If she allowed herself to think that Katya was gone, Nina would have no strength to go on, to look for help, to return to the regiment. She would perish here, in the wilderness, in the spot where her friend had perished.

The clouds cleared and the sun above shone brightly and cheerfully, as if there was nothing wrong in the world. As if there was no war and no death and one of her friends hadn't burned to ashes, having been shot by the enemy first, while her other friend wasn't missing, having fallen to the ground under the canopy of fire. Snow glistened like diamonds, beckoning her. Nina couldn't walk any longer. She sank to the ground and closed her eyes, feeling herself drifting, her head spinning with exhaustion, the world flickering on and off before disappearing altogether. How comforting it would be, to fall into oblivion and not feel the pain and not have to think about anything.

How she wished Katya was by her side. Everything would be all right, if only Katya was with her. Together, they would find their way back to base. Nina forced her eyes open. She didn't want to die. Katya needed her.

With a superhuman effort, Nina got up and started walking. The sun hid behind the trees, sending a few cold rays her way, as if saying goodbye. She was moving in circles, she was certain of it. She could swear she had passed the same bent birch tree half a dozen times. Her stomach hurt from hunger. They had some food supplies on the plane but they were gone, consumed by flames. Most days she remembered to place a piece of bread in her pocket. She usually ate it after one of their missions, in the safety of the airfield. By then it was frozen solid and her mouth and teeth would feel cold as she nibbled on the bread but it would give her enough energy to go on for the rest of the day. Unfortunately, on the day when she needed it the most, she had forgotten to pack it.

In another hour it was going to get dark. The thought of being lost and alone in the wilderness, of spending the night in this treacherous place, freezing cold and surrounded by danger, made her tremble. She felt like she was spinning towards her own destruction, without a chance of finding her way. There was not a soul around and no one would ever find her. She would die here, in a snowfield that stretched as far as the eye could see, without a beginning or an end. She closed her eyes and saw her father's face, imagined her brother's tears when he realised she wasn't coming back. She increased her pace, even though her feet were killing her and she had no idea where she was going.

In the dim rays of the setting sun, Nina thought she saw something by the trees. She wasn't sure what it was, only that it didn't look like it belonged there, in the forest. Bending down, she took a closer look. A telephone cable! Her heart trembled with hope. If she followed it, it would lead somewhere. No more walking in circles. Gripping it tightly between her frozen fingers, she made her way through the snow, little by little, step by step, until an hour later she came to a road.

It wasn't a large road but it had fresh tire marks, which gave her hope. Taking deep breaths, in and out to calm her beating heart, Nina sat on a log and waited. She didn't have to wait long. A vehicle appeared, shining its headlights in her eyes. For a moment, she was blinded and disoriented. She knew she had to get their attention but something stopped her. She watched the car drive past, berating herself for her indecisiveness. What was she going to do, sit here for the rest of her life, hiding away from people who could help her? What if this was the only car that evening?

But what if it was an enemy vehicle? She had on her Red Army pilot's uniform. In her pocket was her ID. What would the Germans do to someone who unleashed death on their heads every single day? Nina had no idea how close they were to the enemy territory when they crashed. Unlike Katya, she was terrible at reading maps, not that she had one on her now. That was why Katya was a talented navigator and Nina was a pilot. If only Katya was here. She would know what to do.

Once, in their other, happier, peacetime life, Nina and Katya had decided to go to the river for a swim. It was summer and warm outside. They had their bathing suits under their dresses and enough money to buy an ice cream and a cold drink. They were sixteen, it was school holidays and the girls were giddy with freedom and youthful fun. 'Maybe we can even meet some boys,' said Katya. 'I'm not going back to school without having my first kiss.'

Nina didn't care about boys. It was hot and she wanted to feel water on her skin. She wanted a suntan and a glass of lemonade.

The trams were not running and Katya suggested hitchhiking to the river. Nina refused. Hitchhiking was dangerous. Papa always told her so. She wasn't about to get into a stranger's car, even if it got her closer to the river on a hot day. 'Don't be silly,' said Katya. 'What could possibly happen? I do it all the time.' Nina stifled her inner voice and followed Katya. Nothing happened to them that day. They got a lift to the river. Although they didn't meet any boys, they had a great time.

As Nina sat by the side of the road, feeling her body shutting down, she thought with longing of her friend and their carefree days that seemed gone forever. She was still young and yet, she felt old, as if a lifetime had passed between this moment and that happy day by the river. Nina knew what Katya would do. She would stop the next car and demand to be taken to a place where she could telegraph her regiment. Katya would take the risk. Nina felt for the revolver in her pocket and stood up.

How could she leave her friend behind? Getting into a car, driving to safety while Katya remained, perhaps in desperate need of help, felt like a betrayal. Here Nina was, saving her own life, abandoning Katya without a second thought. 'I will be back for you,' she whispered, as if Katya could hear her. 'I will go and get help. I promise, I'll be back.'

Another set of headlights appeared. Nina waved but the truck didn't slow down, zooming past at a great speed, slush shooting from under its tires. Despondent, Nina sat back down, rubbing her eyes, hiding her hands inside the sleeves of her uniform to warm up. Her fingers felt cold and unresponsive. She could barely move them. She wished she had had the foresight to bring her gloves.

When another truck appeared, Nina picked up her revolver and shot in the air. The shot rang out through the forest, making her ears ache. It worked – the truck slowed down and two Red Army officers jumped out. 'What do you think you are doing, shooting at innocent people?' cried the taller of the two, while his companion wrestled the revolver from Nina, who was too tired to struggle. They looked irritated and angry and didn't seem to care that they were dealing with a woman.

'Documents?' demanded the smaller of the two, whose bald head made him look like an egg. He pointed her own weapon at her.

Grateful that her documents were safely in her trouser pocket and not in the cockpit of her plane, where she usually kept them, she flashed her ID. 'And who are you?' she demanded.

The expression on their faces changed. 'A pilot from Markov's regiment? What are you doing here? Where is your plane? What happened to the rest of your crew?'

Nina opened her mouth to reply but couldn't get a sound out. Suddenly, the exhaustion of the day, the fear and the heartbreak got the better of her. She broke down in front of the two officers, sobbing into her hands.

They watched her with pity, then one of them placed his hand on her shoulder. He said gently, 'Don't cry, Lieutenant. We'll get you back to base. Here is your weapon. Just don't shoot us again. Promise?'

Sniffling and rubbing her eyes, she nodded.

In the truck, she slept. When she awoke, she saw her airfield. She felt lost without her plane and without Katya and Olga, like a part of her heart was missing. But she was home.

The girls ran out to meet her, hugging her. They had spent all day waiting for her plane to return, hoping for a miracle. Behind them, she could see Markov's pale face. She could see her brother, rushing in her direction, tears in his eyes.

'Thank God you are back. We didn't think we'd see you again,' said Zhenya. 'But where are the others?'

Nina couldn't speak. She collapsed into Vlad's arms and cried.

* * *

Nina was inside her dugout, on her cold and uncomfortable bed of straw, curled into a ball, staring into space. It was dark but for a small candle burning on the table. She could see the outline of Katya's bed and her overalls draped over a chair, as if she had stepped out for a moment and was coming back any minute now. In the corner were Olga's boots. The room felt smaller without Katya and Olga, and the silence was deafening.

Nina stood up and walked to Katya's bed. She placed her head on the pile of straw Katya used as a pillow. 'Where are you?' she whispered, closing her eyes and imagining her friend's happy, smiling, alive face. Then she thought of the burning parachute carrying Katya to the ground. She groaned out loud.

She must have fallen asleep on Katya's bed because next thing she knew, Anton was sitting by her side, his head in his hands. His eyes looked dark and his hair was messy. There was a slightly deranged expression on his face, like he didn't quite understand what was happening. Seeing him there, lost in grief, made her cry. 'I'm so sorry,' she repeated. 'I'm so sorry!' Her teeth were chattering from the cold and she couldn't stop shaking.

He moved closer to her. 'It's not your fault,' he said, his voice barely a whisper. 'You can't blame yourself.'

'Of course, it was my fault. I was flying that plane. It was my job to make sure the girls were safe.'

'It's war. You can't control what happens out there. No one can.'

'Olga is dead because of me. And I don't know where Katya is.' She looked away from him. His anxious face was too much for her to bear. She felt responsible for his heartbreak. She hadn't done enough to save Katya. And now this man was crying next to Nina, who was safe in her bed, while Katya was gone.

'Tell me what happened.' His eyes filled with pain and Nina knew he didn't want to hear what she had to say.

Little by little, fighting tears and stopping every couple of minutes, she told him everything. 'I ordered her to jump,' she concluded. 'I didn't think I could land the plane safely, so I told her to jump.'

'You did it because you wanted her to live. You did what you thought was right.'

'But I was wrong. Had I not done it, she *would* have been safe. I don't know if she survived that jump. Her parachute was on fire. The Nazi plane was shooting at her. I made a mistake and it might have cost her life. How can I live with myself?' She pushed her nails into the soft skin on the inside of her arm. It didn't hurt enough to take her mind off everything she was feeling.

Anton took her hand in his and pressed it gently. 'How could you possibly have known?'

'Back then, in that moment, with Olga not responding and the plane in flames, losing altitude, parachuting out seemed like a safer option. But it wasn't. I feel like I've failed her. Abandoned her to her fate. If only I stayed longer and looked for her. Instead, here I am, in bed, safe and sound, and she . . .' Nina covered her face with her hands. 'Will you ever forgive me?'

'There is nothing to forgive. You did the right thing. You went to get help. Together we stand a better chance of bringing her back. We will start tomorrow. We won't stop until we find her.'

Yes, Nina wanted to say, but will we find her alive? She couldn't say it to Anton because she could see in his face that he still believed. He was clinging to his hope like a life raft and it was the only thing that was keeping him sane. She wished she could hope the way he did but she had seen what he hadn't – bullets whizzing towards her friend and a fiery ball carrying her to a certain death.

Chapter 7

February 1943

Nina slept like she had never slept in her life. She closed her eyes and fell into a black abyss, without dreams, without light, like death. She awoke because the ground was vibrating, as if a giant hand had lifted the earth up in the air and shook it like a child's rattle. Her first impulse was to wake Katya and tell her what was happening. She even got up and crossed the small space that separated the two beds. Seeing Katya's bed empty broke her heart a little bit more. She breathed in sharply, as if someone had punched her in the stomach, and sank to the floor, hugging her knees. Then she heard it – the sound of explosions.

It was not unusual to hear explosions so early in the morning. They were at the front after all. But this time the deafening bursts were no longer distant. It felt like the Germans were bombing their airfield.

Nina threw what little belongings she had in her rucksack, then looked around. At first, she wasn't sure what it was she was looking for. Then she realised – she didn't want to leave Katya's things behind. When they found her, she would need them. Nina took some of Katya's clothes, her favourite hairbrush, a present from her mother for her sixteenth birthday, and her diary.

On the airfield, chaos reigned. Everyone was running somewhere, getting the planes ready, loading explosives, placing equipment on trucks. The Nazis were advancing, Markov told a dishevelled group of women. There was a chance the airfield could fall into German hands. Although he sounded calm, his hands were shaking. 'We need to leave, now. Another hour and it might be too late.' Despite Stalin's order to stand to the death, Markov reasoned it would be madness to remain in front of German tanks and lose his people and planes. Retreating would be treason according to Stalin's Order 270. Not a step back, demanded their leader from the relative safety of his cabinet in Moscow. But not to retreat in the face of such threat would be suicide.

As Nina watched the planes belonging to the 10th Leningrad Regiment take off, she fought a feeling of trepidation, a helplessness the likes of which she had never experienced before. They had worked so hard but despite their efforts, they were forced to give way to the advancing Germans. All their sacrifices had been in vain. Olga's death and Katya's disappearance had been in vain.

When the order 'To the planes' sounded, she approached Markov. 'I can't leave without Katya,' she said. 'She's out there somewhere and I would like to organise a search party.'

'I understand where you are coming from,' said Markov. 'And under normal circumstances, I would say, absolutely. I would supply trucks and people. But the Germans could be here any moment. I can't risk your safety like that.'

'What about Katya's safety? Her life depends on us.'

'I'm very sorry. I wish I could help you but I can't. The regiment is leaving.'

'I'm not leaving. Not until I find her,' said Nina, shaking her head. Quietly, she added, 'I failed her once. I can't fail her again.'

'You can't stay here. You would be throwing your life away.' Markov looked at her with sad eyes. He carried a lot on his shoulders and not once had he shown that the weight was bothering him. 'I'm ordering you to retreat.'

'I'm sorry, sir, but I can't obey this order.'

'Orders can't be disobeyed. You are a soldier in the Red Army.'

'She is like a sister to me. I couldn't live with myself if I left her behind. Especially now that the Germans are so close.'

'We will push the Germans back. We've done it before and we'll do it again. We just need time. When it's safe again, we will come back and search for Katya.'

'What if by then it's too late?' Nina looked him straight in the face. 'I'm not leaving, sir. Not until Katya is with us.'

With a pensive smile on his face, Markov said, 'There is no way I can talk you out of it, is there?'

Nina stood to attention. 'Not a chance, sir.'

'Very well. As long as you understand the risks.'

Nina leaped in the air. She felt like hugging Markov. 'Thank you, sir. I will never forget this, for as long as I live.'

An explosion was heard and the earth under their feet rumbled. 'That might not be very long, Lieutenant Petrova, because what you are contemplating is suicide, pure and simple.'

'I'm doing it for my friend. She would do the same for me.'

'I'm sure she would. You girls surprise me. Your bravery . . . It's like nothing I've ever seen before.' He shook his head as if he were deeply disappointed.

'That's a good thing, sir. Bravery is a virtue.'

'Not if it costs me the life of a good pilot. Be careful out there. Don't get yourself killed.'

'I promise.'

Anton and Vlad volunteered to join Nina, having first cleared it with their commander. Markov supplied them with a truck, some maps of the area and weapons. Before they set out, he told her one more time to be careful and return safely. 'And bring Katya back. The regiment needs you girls.'

Nina wished Katya was there to see it. *Look*, she wanted to tell her friend, *he's not as bad as we thought, that Bayonet*. Not that the girls called him that anymore. They called him *Batya*, which meant father in Russian, a nickname that clearly showed he had earned their love and respect. Yes, he was demanding and expected a lot from them. But he expected a lot from everyone, himself included. Unlike other commanders, he didn't just send them out there to do the hard work. He was in the air with them every single day, risking his life, setting an example, watching over them, doing everything in his power to bring them back alive. He wasn't Marina Raskova but, despite their initial reluctance to accept him, Major Markov had found his own way into the girls' hearts.

The truck moved slowly through roads that drowned in snow. Anton was in the driver's seat, his hands stiff on the steering wheel, his eyes red-rimmed and broken. Nina's heart squeezed with grief every time she looked at him. What if they didn't find Katya? Or worse, what if they found her but it was too late? While in her mind she urged the truck to move faster, in her heart she was petrified. She wanted to delay the inevitable. Until they found Katya, she still had hope.

Without a word, Nina sat with her hands in her lap, watching the snow outside, while next to her Vlad moved his finger on his map. 'From what you've described, this is where you crashed.'

Nina glanced at the map. 'Yes, that looks right. I was in such a shock I didn't know where I was.'

'If we follow this road, we'll be there in less than an hour.' Vlad glanced at the road ahead and a large line of vehicles in front of them. Everyone was trying to escape the Nazi advance. The cars were barely moving. 'Traffic permitting, of course.'

'Katya would know exactly where it was,' Nina said sadly. 'She was good at things like that. That's why she was such a great navigator. I mean, *is*. She *is* a great navigator.' Nina started to cry. 'Every time something happens, I want to tell her. Do you think she's still out there somewhere? Waiting for us to find her?'

'Of course, she is,' said Anton with conviction. And a little quieter, 'I have to have faith. For Tonya.' His face seemed calm but for a slight tremor of his lower lip.

Tonya! Nina groaned at the thought of her. What would it do to the beautiful little girl if she lost her mother at such an early age? Nina knew exactly what it would do. She'd been through it herself and she wouldn't wish it on her worst enemy. 'Katya never wanted to join, you know? Never wanted to come here in the first place. As if she knew . . .' Knew what? That she wouldn't survive four weeks at the front? Nina couldn't say it out loud. She couldn't even think it. 'She followed me here.'

'She seemed upset that morning,' said Anton. 'She said she didn't feel like going out. That she wanted to stay behind, that she was exhausted and couldn't take much more of this. That she didn't want to be here.'

Every time Nina closed her eyes, she heard her own voice, telling Katya to jump, sending her to her death. And all she could think of was, *if only*. If only she had let Katya stay on the plane. If only she hadn't encouraged her to join Raskova's regiment. If only it wasn't war.

If only Katya had lived to see her twenty-third birthday.

They were twenty minutes away from the crash site and Nina became fidgety with nerves. She couldn't bear seeing her burnt-out plane again and knowing that Olga was inside. Over and over in the past two days she kept coming back to that one moment. The Nazi bullets raining down on her. Promising to come back for Olga and returning to find the tail gunner cockpit burning. She was certain Olga had been dead by the time they crash-landed. But what if she wasn't? What if there was the slightest chance she was still alive? Had Nina abandoned her and run for cover, when she should have been helping her?

The sound of war was deafening all around them. Somewhere nearby a battle was underway. Nina ignored it. It was like background noise, ever-present and no longer terrifying. Was it her imagination or did the sound intensify, as if they were driving right into the epicentre of a volcano? She drummed her fingers on her knees. Markov was right, they needed to hurry or it would be too late.

Another noise made her look up and pay attention. A threatening noise of aircraft engines. 'What are the chances they are our planes?' asked Nina.

'Not a chance,' said Anton. 'Look up.'

She glanced out of the truck window and saw the swastika, counting four planes in the grey skies above them. The Nazi pilots saw them too and started to shoot at the line of cars underneath.

'What do we do?' cried Nina. There was nowhere to hide. The German pilots could pick the Soviet vehicles out one by one and not waste a single bullet.

Anton continued driving, his eyes on the road. 'Nothing to do but keep going and hope they'll go away.'

'They won't leave until every single one of us is dead.' Nina squeezed her eyes shut and placed her hands over her ears not to hear the regular popping sound of the machine guns. 'They are not bombing us.'

'Why would they waste their precious bombs? We are out in the open here. It's like target practice for them,' said Vlad. He shielded Nina with his body and she stayed in his arms, trembling. The truck shook as the bullets hit it. Finally, the engine coughed and fell quiet.

Perhaps the Germans thought they had done enough damage because the planes circled a few times and left. Only when she could no longer hear the engines did Nina breathe again. Vlad let go of her and looked up in the sky. 'Good news is, we are still alive. Bad news is, our truck is like a sieve, full of holes.'

The three of them climbed out. While Nina waited, Vlad and Anton opened the bonnet and looked inside. But even if they could get the engine started, Nina could see they wouldn't get very far. Three out of four tires were flat. She stood next to their belongings, waiting for the men to admit defeat. All around them, other damaged vehicles stopped by the side of the road, no longer able to continue on their way, while other men and women walked around their cars and trucks, shaking their heads, unsure what to do next.

Vlad peered over his map, marking the spot with his pen. 'We will come back for the truck or Markov will never forgive us.' He traced a line with his finger. 'It will take us two or three hours to walk. I suggest we set out now, before it gets dark.'

Nina wanted to stop and have something to eat first but the thought of the German planes overhead raining bullets on her, Vlad and Anton shocked her into moving. One after another, they trudged through the snow. The men were carrying most of their possessions and their two rifles. Nina was carrying a rucksack with Katya's things. It was heavy and soon her shoulders were aching.

'Would you like help with that?' asked Anton.

'No, I'm fine.' But she could feel herself slowing down, the rucksack dragging her behind.

'Here, let me.'

Anton took the rucksack. Nina smiled gratefully.

The fields stretched as far as the eye could see. She felt she'd seen them before but the truth was the fields went on and on for hundreds of kilometres, a white desert with no landmarks and no way of telling where they were. It was like being lost in the ocean.

'If my map is correct, the turn-off is coming up soon,' said Vlad, glancing first at the map and then at his compass. Five minutes later, they saw a path that was almost imperceptible under the snow.

A group of people ran past, their faces white, like they had seen unspeakable things and were in a rush to escape them. When Nina, Vlad and Anton turned onto the small road, an old man shouted, 'Where do you think you are going?'

'We are looking for a village called Smirnovo,' replied Vlad.

The man didn't stop. He barely slowed down. 'There is no Smirnovo!'

'What are you talking about? It's right here on my map.'

The man spread his hands wide, shaking his grey head. 'This morning there was a Smirnovo. And now it's gone. Razed to the ground. You better hurry away from here. We were lucky to get away with our lives.'

Nina, Vlad and Anton watched the old man's retreating back in helpless silence. More villagers wandered past; their bodies bent low under the weight of their possessions.

'What is that sound?' exclaimed Nina. She could feel the earth trembling under her feet and could barely stand straight. Her mouth opened in an astonished and frightened *Oh*.

'Tank units,' said Anton. He pulled Nina by the hand. When she didn't move, he pulled again. 'We can't stay here.'

'What about Katya?' she whispered. She couldn't see the tanks. All she could see was the snowbound fields that had swallowed her friend and Katya's excited face as she jumped up and down in excitement, what seemed like a lifetime ago, when they were young and carefree and had their whole lives ahead of them, repeating, 'He just asked me to marry him, can you believe it?'

Anton's face grew pale. He was silent for a moment, as if weighing up their options. Nina knew they only had one. To turn back and run. 'We have to go or in a minute we will be standing in front of German tanks,' said Anton.

'How can we leave her? How can I turn my back on her, again?' Nina was crying and rubbing her face with her gloved hands. She should have stayed and looked for Katya longer. Now it was too late.

'What else can we do?' asked Vlad, folding his map and placing it in his pocket.

They could no longer remain in the middle of the road, like shooting targets for the Germans. They had to walk away. They *ran* away, overtaking the old man and the other villagers, while the sound of battle felt closer and closer, as if the explosions were seeking them out. When they reached their truck, they glanced at it with regret and continued moving. Anton carried her rucksack and she carried his rifle. After walking for what seemed like hours in the snow, even that was too heavy for her. She slowed down.

'Are you alright?'

'I'm fine. I just need a minute!' What she needed was a lifetime to curl into a ball and cry for her friend.

'Why don't you have something to drink?' Anton reached into his pocket and gave her his metal flask. She took it, smiling with gratitude. After a few sips of water she felt better. Her head wasn't spinning as much and her mouth no longer felt dry, like it was filled with sand.

'Let's have something to eat,' Vlad suggested.

The three of them sat down on a log. While refugees from nearby villages ambled past, staring at them through unseeing eyes, Anton reached into his rucksack and pulled out a blanket, a loaf of bread, some pickled herring and a cucumber. He had even brought a fork.

'You've thought of everything,' Nina said.

'A part of me was hoping we would find Katya. I brought extra everything for her.'

'I don't want to eat Katya's food. What if . . .' She fell quiet. What could they possibly hope for?

'I feel so helpless right now.' Anton looked at his hands as if searching for answers. There were tears in his eyes. He didn't touch his food.

'I can't imagine her gone. When I think about her, I see her laughing and singing, talking about you or complaining about the war. I can't imagine her . . .' Nina hesitated. 'Not being there.'

'And yet you saw her parachute on fire.'

'She might have seen my plane on fire. She might be thinking the same thing about me. And yet, here I am, alive, looking for her.'

'If she survived the fall, I hope with all my heart she was well enough to escape before the Germans arrived.'

Nina shuddered. 'What would the Nazis do to her if they caught her?'

'What would they do to a navigator dropping bombs on them every single day? It's best not to think about it,' said Vlad.

Nina blinked. Despite the bright sunshine and the sapphire sky, the world dimmed and became dark like night.

Anton looked into the distance. For a long time they didn't speak. Finally, he said, 'I didn't want her to come here. I wanted her safe. But when she was finally here, I was so happy. She made this place feel a little like home for me. For the last couple of weeks, I thought that maybe it wasn't such a bad thing she was here after all. Now I feel so guilty. I should have insisted she return home.'

'You know she wouldn't have listened to you.' At the thought of her headstrong friend, Nina smiled with sadness. 'You have nothing to feel guilty about.'

Anton's voice caught when he said, 'What if the war is over and the years go by and we never find out what's happened to her? What do we do then?'

'Perhaps it's best not to know,' said Vlad, staring into the far distance, at the pines leaning their heads under heavy hats of snow.

'The uncertainty is killing me.'

They were finishing their lunch when they heard the hostile rumble of the engines and the cracking of the machine guns, like fireworks on New Year's Eve, pop-pop-pop.

Nina pushed her bread away. 'They are shooting the civilians,' she muttered. 'Innocent people walking down the road, trying to escape.'

'Why does that surprise you?' asked Anton.

'We need to take cover,' cried Vlad. But Nina couldn't. As if frozen to the spot, her legs refused to move and she was unable to run, to hide, to save her life. She remained sitting on the log, gawking at the planes. Anton pulled her to him and the three of them huddled under a fallen tree, their bodies pressed close together. She wished she didn't have to hear the shrieks of panic and pain as the refugees scrambled in every direction. She wished she could turn away from the sight of the poor villagers running and falling to the ground. She wanted to close her eyes but couldn't. All she could see was red on white.

The terrifying nightmare only lasted a few minutes but it felt like forever. When the planes were gone and nothing was heard but groans of the wounded, Nina, Vlad and Anton crawled out from under the tree.

'Help,' cried a man with a wound in his chest. 'Please, help me.' He was wheezing, barely able to breathe.

He closed his eyes. Did he faint or . . .? Nina felt her hands begin to tremble.

'He's still breathing,' said Anton. 'Barely.'

'Can we do anything for him? Can we help him?' she whispered.

'I have a medical kit in the rucksack. Some bandages.' Anton examined the man. 'I don't think it would make a difference.'

'He needs a doctor.'

'We can build a stretcher and take him with us,' suggested Vlad. 'When we get back to the regiment, the medic can take a look at him.'

With the inferno unfolding like a horror film before their eyes, the regiment seemed like a faraway dream – unreachable. Nina felt lost in these woods, with no hope of ever making it out alive.

In the forest nearby they found four long sticks and bound them together with rope that Anton carried in his rucksack. They added more sticks, enough to hold the weight of a man. When the stretcher was finished, they placed it next to the wounded man and prepared to lift him.

But it was too late. He was already dead.

Without a word, Anton covered the body with an oversized jacket he had found nearby. Once again, a feeling of helplessness washed over Nina like a wave. For a moment she struggled to breathe, as if the air no longer had oxygen in it.

'Don't cry. We couldn't help him. We tried,' said Vlad, holding her.

'I can't wait to go back, get into my plane and make the Nazis pay.' She was no longer crying but shaking with anger.

'We need to go,' said Anton. 'Before they're back.'

'What about the wounded?'

Anton glanced at the bodies by the side of the road. 'There are no wounded. They are all dead. We can check if you like.'

Her heart aching, Nina followed Anton and Vlad as they examined the people killed in the attack. There were twelve of them, six women and six old men. Finally, Anton stopped and shook his head. Nina nodded. 'Let's go!'

When they started walking, she thought she heard something. A tiny noise, like a kitten meowing. She stopped to listen. 'Don't you hear that?'

'What?'

There it was again, a low crying sound. Nina ran in the direction of the noise, across the road where a young woman lay dead, a bullet in her head. She unwrapped the scarf the woman was holding and found a newborn baby.

'Oh, no,' she whispered. 'What are you doing here? You poor little one!'

As soon as Nina took the infant out of the relative warmth of the scarf, he or she began to scream, red in the face, as if angry at the world. Nina's breath caught in her chest at the sight of the child and the mother, who would never hold her little one again. Nina suspected it was a boy because he was wrapped in a blue scarf. She pressed the child to her chest, rocking and singing softly. Instantly, he stopped crying and opened his eyes.

'You must be so scared,' she whispered. 'You poor thing. So small and you've already been through so much. Anton, Vlad, come and look at this. What are we going to do?'

'We can't leave the child here. We'll have to take him with us.' Just like her, Anton must have thought it was a boy because of the scarf.

'Yes, let's take him with us. But what will we do with him when we get back to the regiment?'

'We'll cross that bridge when we come to it.' Anton was looking somewhere above Nina's head and when she turned around to see what had caught his attention, she noticed black dots in the sky. The same instant, she heard the faint sound of the engines.

'They are back,' she whispered, pressing the child closer. As if sensing the seriousness of the situation, the little boy stopped crying and lay still in her arms.

There was no time to reach the trees. The enemy planes were here.

'Get down,' shouted Anton, just as the awful popping sound started. Nina threw herself on the ground, covering the child gently, making sure she didn't accidentally hurt him. Anton shielded her body with his, while Vlad found shelter under a fallen tree on the other side of the road. As if in a bad dream, Nina heard the machine guns and saw the snow around them rise like it was alive. The Germans were shooting right at them. Finally, what seemed like an eternity later, the planes moved on.

'Are you all right?' she whispered to Anton. He wasn't moving. Why wasn't he moving? 'Anton!' she cried. 'Can you hear me?'

'I can hear you. I'm fine,' he replied. 'And you?'

'Still in one piece. Where is Vlad?'

With relief, she saw Vlad running towards them. Slowly she rose to her feet and cradled the wailing baby. 'Shhh,' she whispered, rocking him. 'Shhh.' But she was as petrified as the tiny creature in her arms. For as long as she lived she knew she wouldn't forget this terrible day, when the sky showered them with bullets, when everyone around them was dying and they had no choice but to admit defeat and return to the regiment without Katya.

Anton dusted the snow off his tunic and reached inside his

pocket, pulling out a metal flask, holding it up with trembling hands. The flask had been bent by a bullet. 'It saved my life,' he said in wonder.

'And you saved mine,' Nina said quietly. The child squirmed in her arms, making little noises like a frightened mouse.

As they started up the hill, Nina carrying the baby, who was no longer crying but sleeping peacefully, Anton and Vlad carrying their weapons and belongings, they heard a shriek, like an animal in pain. Turning around, they saw an old woman who threw herself on the body of the unfortunate mother and wailed in grief.

'Varya! Varyusha! What have they done to you? And where is Timofei? Timosha! Timochka!' the woman called, searching through the empty scarf and looking in the grass and down the road, as if the infant could have run away. 'They took our baby boy. They took my grandson away. Tima! Where are you?' She wrung her hands, her face twisted with horror.

Nina walked towards the old woman. When she saw the baby, she jumped to her feet and with surprising agility ran to Nina's side. 'Tima, grandson!' Large tears were running down her wrinkled cheeks. Her hat fell on the snow and her hair was a matted mess of grey curls, like a halo around her face. 'Is he all right? Is he hurt?'

'He is perfectly fine,' Nina assured her, placing the child into her shaking arms. 'Don't worry.' She smiled at the expression of relief and joy on the woman's face as she held her grandson.

'Thank God!' she exclaimed, covering the sleeping child with kisses, crossing him with crooked fingers and muttering a prayer. 'I turned my back for a moment to talk to my cousin. Next thing I know, the Nazis . . . And my cousin dead in the snow. When it was safe again, I came running back and . . .' The old woman broke down, her shoulders bent as if by an unbearable weight, gazing at the baby's mother. 'Oh, Varya!'

'Your daughter?' asked Anton.

'Daughter-in-law. My son got married and then the war started and he left for the front. Timofei was born early. He's never met his father. Varya almost died giving birth to him. She was in hospital for weeks. A few days ago, she finally got better and returned home. We were so happy. My first grandson! And now this.' The old woman rubbed her eyes, leaving smudges of something dark over her face. 'I'm almost glad I don't know how to get in touch with my son. How can I write and tell him what happened?'

After a moment of silence, Vlad said they could no longer stay like this, rooted to the spot by grief and fear. They had to start moving. The German planes could come back any minute. 'Where are you headed? Is there anything we can do to help?' he asked.

'My sister lives in Prohorovo. I was hoping to get there by night-fall and the next morning continue east together. I'm Valentina, by the way.' After the three of them introduced themselves, she added, 'Varya has relatives in Novosibirsk.' For a moment the woman was unable to speak, sobbing into her grandson's fur hat. 'That's still far from the front, isn't it? Will we be safe there?'

'Yes, if you can make it to Novosibirsk, you will be safe,' said Anton.

'It's three thousand kilometres away. How can I walk three thousand kilometres with a newborn baby? Without Varya, how will I even find her relatives?' Valentina wailed. 'I have nowhere to go. Maybe my sister will think of something. Perhaps we can still go, even without Varya. I know her family's last name and the street they live on. They will be happy to see Timofei.'

'We'll take you to your sister,' said Anton.

'I can't go. I can't leave Varya behind.' The woman sank into the snow as if she had no strength to stand. She clasped Timofei to her chest and cried, her tears falling on his sleeping face. Nina couldn't hold back her own tears. She felt heartbreaking pity for the unfortunate grandmother and the tiny boy, who was sleeping peacefully, unaware that moments earlier he had lost the most precious person in his life, his mother.

Anton suggested they placed Varya's body on the stretcher

154

they had built earlier. Vlad and Anton carried the stretcher and a rucksack each behind their backs, while Nina struggled with the rest of their belongings and their rifles. Valentina carried Timofei, who woke up screaming. Nina suspected the boy was hungry. How far was Prohorovo?

'How will I feed little Timofei?' Valentina was saying. 'Maybe goat's milk will do. My sister has a goat. The Red Army took her cows and most of her chickens but left the goat behind. She is skin and bones but still gives milk. A miracle in times of war. I wonder if the goat can survive the trip to Novosibirsk. We could have milk on the road.'

'A goat can't walk three thousand kilometres,' said Vlad. 'It will only slow you down.'

'I will carry her all the way if I have to. As long as Timofei can have milk.'

The white desert stretched before them and the sad procession moved slowly through the countryside, next to other desperate people who had nowhere to go. Soon, the sun disappeared behind the shady woods. Although it was harder to walk at night, Nina was grateful for the cover of darkness. With luck, they would make it to Prohorovo in one piece. Her arms ached from the weight of everything she was carrying. Her stomach ached from hunger. Her face was sore from the tears and the cold wind. When she thought she couldn't walk another step, the road became wider and she saw narrow buildings made of wood and clay. 'Here it is,' said Valentina in a flat voice. 'Prohorovo.' Just like Nina, she looked ready to collapse. The baby was stirring in her arms, emitting hungry yelps.

Valentina's sister, Anya, was a smaller, younger version of Valentina. She fussed and cried when she saw them, welcoming them into her house, which was nothing more than a cabin in the woods, with a tiny garden, where a goat and a large dog competed for space. The sisters thanked Nina, Vlad and Anton with tears in their eyes.

'I wish I could offer you something to eat. But I have nothing. I ate my last potato yesterday. Short of killing the goat . . .'

'Don't kill the goat, you old fool. Instead go get some milk. Timofei is starving,' said Valentina.

Anya went out into the garden and soon returned with a jar of milk. Nina, Vlad and Anton shared their bread with the sisters. Nina had a few pieces of chocolate in her pocket. She offered them to Anya and Valentina and the old women cried. They hadn't seen chocolate since the war had started. Sated, Timofei slept on top of a blanket on the wooden floor. Anya said she would give up her bed for the brave and selfless woman pilot who risked her life to protect them from the Nazis. Nina refused, saying she would be happy to sleep on top of the stove, where it was warm and cosy. Anton and Vlad settled on the floor.

Before they said goodnight, Anya exclaimed, 'How can we ever thank you? I know!' She disappeared and returned a few minutes later with a bottle of vodka. 'For you,' she said, pushing the bottle towards Anton.

Anton refused. 'Thank you but I'm not much of a drinker. Vodka is a valuable commodity. Keep it. Exchange it for some food. You'll need it. It can buy you some bread and milk for Timofei on the road.'

Once again, the sisters cried, crossing themselves and thanking God for sending these strangers their way to save Timofei's life. Soon the little house settled down and all the noises subsided. All Nina could hear was the wind screeching outside and rattling the windows. Although she was exhausted after the nightmare they had just been through, she didn't go to bed right away, settling at the kitchen table by the burning candle long after the others had gone to sleep, staring at Katya's letter to her mother, the letter she was planning to send but never got the chance. Her hands trembling, Nina fiddled with the envelope, turning it this way and that, tracing the writing with her fingers. To read the letter felt like an invasion of privacy. To read it was to admit to herself that Katya wasn't coming back. Yet, she felt like she had no choice. In this surreal moment far from home, with the Nazis mere kilometres away, wrecking everything in their path with their fighter planes, machine guns and tanks, not knowing what the future would bring or if she even had a future, Nina needed to know what Katya was thinking in the last moments of her life. She wanted to feel closer to her best friend.

Dear Mama, Tonya and all the boys,

I wish I could find the words to describe how much I miss you. I think of you all the time and it makes my day a little brighter because I know the war will be over soon and I will hold you in my arms. Tonya, Mama loves you more than anything in the world, did you know that? You are the best thing that's ever happened to me. Every day without you feels like an eternity. I can't wait to see you again. That's all I live for – to see you again.

Mama, how are you all holding up? How is Nikolai's cough? Did you find a doctor to see him? What about Tom's guitar? Tell him I expect at least five new tunes when I come back. Remember, Tonya can't sleep without her teddy bear. If she falls asleep without it, she wakes up crying. How I wish I was there to tuck her in every evening.

Remember that summer day two years ago when we all went to the lake at our dacha? The boys jumped in the water, even Nikolai with his cough, and you shouted that it was too cold and told them to get out. They didn't listen, so you sent Papa to get them but instead he jumped in the water too and said it felt amazing and why don't we join them? And we did. Tonya had just turned one. We spent hours swimming and splashing and it was the happiest day. When the war is over, we'll have days like that again. I can't wait!

*Don't worry about me. It's not too bad here. It's not much
different from training in Engels. Sometimes they shoot at us
but because we fly so fast they always miss.*

I love you all so much.

Yours,

Katya

Nina folded the letter and put it in the envelope. Then she
pressed it to her heart, her tears falling on the wooden top of the
kitchen table. 'Don't cry,' said Anton, suddenly appearing behind
her and placing his hand on her shoulder. 'She would want us to
keep fighting. She would want us to stay strong.'

When she looked up, she saw that Anton was crying too. 'I
know. And we will,' she said. He sat down next to her. She pushed
Katya's letter closer to him. 'Would you like to read it?'

Anton nodded. She watched him as he read. His face looked
grey in the light of a candle.

'She saved my life once. Did you know that?' said Nina when
he was finished.

'I didn't know that.'

'We were fifteen. It was winter and we decided to go ice skating
on a lake not far from our house. The ice looked so strong and it
was freezing outside. We didn't think for a second that it might be
dangerous. We did it every year. I put my skates on quicker than
Katya and shouted that I would race her to the ice. She replied
that it wasn't fair but I didn't listen, I was already on the lake,
spinning in circles, happy, skating away from her. Wait for me,
she shouted. But I didn't wait. Suddenly, the ice started to crack
and I was trapped in the middle of the lake. I tried to make it
back to safety but it was too late. The ice underneath me crumbled and I fell right into the freezing water. My legs were in the
water but my upper body was still on the ice. I was holding on
for dear life but I could feel myself slipping. It was the scariest
moment of my life.'

'What did Katya do?'

'She was by my side instantly, despite the danger. While the ice was breaking around us, she pulled me by the arms until I was out and then helped me off the ice. By that point my legs were frozen and I could barely walk. I was sick with pneumonia for weeks afterwards. If it wasn't for her, I would have drowned in the freezing lake that day.' Nina dropped her head in the palms of her hands and cried. Moments passed before she could talk again. 'She didn't leave me behind, Anton. She didn't walk away from me to get help. She risked her life to save me and brought me home safely. But I couldn't bring her home safely.' Nina's voice faded to a whisper. 'What are we going to tell Tonya?'

Anton spoke slowly, like every word was agony. 'We will tell her it's war. We will tell her we did our best to find Mama. We will tell her Mama was a hero and she loved her very much, until the end.'

The candle crackled and died, plunging the kitchen into darkness. The two of them remained side by side, talking about Katya, and soon not talking at all but sitting in silence. Even though they didn't say a word, Anton's presence was a comfort to Nina. She felt like she wasn't alone, as if having him next to her made the weight of her grief a little lighter because she knew he felt it too.

PART TWO

Chapter 8

May 1943

Nina floated through the sky in her loyal Pe-2, above the birds and the clouds, close to the sun. Under her wings was the city of Krasnodar and the blue ribbon of the Kuban River as it made its twisted way towards the Black Sea, where Nina had spent some of the best summers of her childhood and where Hitler had been busy trouncing the Soviet navy. The ravaged city was surrounded by farms, like a sea of green that stretched in every direction, tended by women because most men were at the front, dying for their country. The fields reminded Nina of childhood, of running through the grass with Katya and Vlad, of sucking on clover and stuffing their mouths with raspberries, of endless summer. Every time she saw the emerald green below, Nina's heart soared alongside her plane. But occasionally, black ugly bomb craters scarred the perfect landscape, making Nina's chest ache.

Nina's new navigator, a young girl barely out of high school called Dasha, wore her hair in pigtails and never stopped laughing. Nina wondered what Dasha had to laugh about. They were living the same life, seeing death wherever they turned.

Nina never felt like laughing anymore, and yet here was Dasha, singing at the top of her voice as they flew over the war-torn countryside. The war had surprised Dasha as she was about to start university to study Russian literature. She possessed an encyclopedic knowledge of poems and songs, and talked non-stop. Nina didn't mind because Dasha's voice distracted her from the dark thoughts running through her head and made the missions go faster. Sometimes, in rare moments of silence, Nina would turn around in her pilot's seat and expect to see Katya behind her. Seeing Dasha's smiling face instead felt like her heart was stabbed repeatedly with a knife.

They were under fire from every possible direction today, or so it seemed. The anti-aircraft guns exploded in what, from the air, looked like giant horrifying daisies reaching for the sky. The ground artillery never stopped. Today, unlike most days, Dasha was quiet. Was she afraid?

'Why are you not talking this morning?' asked Nina. 'Tell me a story. Or sing a song. That new one you sang yesterday, what was it called? I liked that one. But don't forget to turn off the radio.' After months of waiting, their planes had finally been equipped with radios. Nina didn't want to get in trouble with Markov for chatting casually in the air.

But Dasha never got a chance to sing the song Nina liked. As soon as they approached the front line, they entered a wall of fire the likes of which Nina had never experienced. She could no longer see the peaceful green fields under her wings. All was angry red and orange, without an end in sight, or a break. The plane bounced and shook from the force of the explosions. Gritting her teeth, Nina followed Zhenya Timofeeva through a chaotic sky towards the target. When everybody dropped their bombs, the squadron turned around to fly back to base, still in tight formation. The clouds had become so thick the Pe-2s were forced to drop altitude to avoid them and were flying lower than they normally would. Nina's blood ran cold with trepidation. The closer they were to the ground, the easier they were to hit.

She could no longer see the Soviet fighter planes that were supposed to escort them that day. Without the men to cover them, the Pe-2s were open to an attack. Suddenly, the anti-aircraft guns stopped firing. For a moment, Nina could breathe again. Her fingers on the controls relaxed a little.

Dasha said, 'It's a bad sign. The German planes must be nearby.'

A moment later they heard them. Another moment, and they could see them. Luftwaffe fighters swooped down as if out of nowhere, determined to destroy the Soviet planes.

Nine Pe-2s huddled closer together, breaking the formation. Not because the pilots were afraid but because it was easier to defend themselves as a group. Apart, they were vulnerable. As a group, with pilots, navigators and tail gunners firing their guns and hurling grenades out of their cockpits, they stood a small chance against the German fighter planes.

Nina didn't even have time to get scared. One moment, they were flying back to base, having successfully accomplished their mission. The next, they were under attack. All it took was one second. One second was the difference between life and death.

Before she even had a chance to count the enemy planes, one of Nina's engines was hit and caught fire. In the Pe-2 behind her, Yulia's navigator and tail gunner blasted their machine guns at the German aircraft to give Nina a chance to escape. Nina's crew couldn't do the same. They had run out of ammunition. As their plane sank lower, one of the German fighters flew so close, Nina's heart nearly stopped. He hit their second engine and swooped away to line up for another hit. As he came in for the killer blow, the sky around them lit up with colour. It startled Nina and made her cry out.

'What was that?' shouted Nina, not sure Dasha could hear her over the noise of the battle.

'That was me, throwing signal flares at the Nazi pig,' said Dasha.

'Good thinking.' Nina liked Dasha. She might be young but she made up with intelligence what she lacked in experience.

'Beggars can't be choosers. Maybe it will scare him off.'

Miraculously, it did. The Nazi pilot turned around and fled.

'Good riddance,' muttered Nina. She was so tense, her shoulders and arms were aching as she fought to hold the damaged plane in the air. It was a battle she knew she was going to lose, sooner or later. The plane was flaming like a torch. If she didn't land it soon or order her crew to jump, they would all burn to death in an airborne inferno. 'I'm going to try and land this thing,' she said.

'Not yet,' replied Dasha. 'We are flying over Nazi territory.'

Landing in German-occupied territory was every pilot's worst nightmare. The Germans loved to make examples out of the pilots they captured. The punishments they inflicted on those who bombed them every day were horrifying.

'Please, please, please,' Nina whispered under her breath, biting her lip until it bled. She could feel the plane losing altitude and becoming harder and harder to control. She knew Dasha would be bending over her maps, trying to work out when it was safe to land.

'Now,' came Dasha's voice inside Nina's headset what felt like an eternity later.

'Finally,' whispered Nina, leaving the formation, her eyes searching for a safe place to land. The giant fields were like one big runway. Taking a deep breath to calm her nerves, Nina guided the aircraft to an emergency landing.

As soon as the wheels touched the ground and the Pe-2 stopped, the three of them scrambled out of the burning plane and ran. Once they were a safe distance away, they watched in horrified silence as the flames devoured the plane that had been their loyal friend for many months, that had carried them through hostile skies and shielded them from German bullets. '*Batya* will have to do without our traditional victory pass over the airfield today,' said Nina.

'He won't care, as long as everyone returns safely. After the horror flight we've just had, that would be a miracle,' said Dasha. 'I hope the others made it back.'

Dasha was right, it would be a miracle. In the first week of May alone, they had lost seven planes. Every day they had lost a crew. And every day, Nina's heart broke a little bit more until there was nothing left of it and it was but a shattered vase, full of scraps and pointy edges stabbing her from the inside.

'I keep wondering if I'm next,' said Dasha. Suddenly, the carefree girl Nina had grown to like was gone. She was replaced with a grim stranger who stared into the distance and didn't smile. 'I have so many plans. I want to get married and start a family. I want to finish my degree. What if it's all taken away from me?'

Nina patted Dasha's hand. 'When the war is over, you will do all those things.'

'But others won't. What if the war is over and we don't live to see it? I don't want to die, Nina. I am still so young.'

'We are not going to die,' said Nina, even though every day she believed it less and less. Death was all around them. Would they live long enough to see another sunset, let alone the end of war?

Nina had forgotten what it was like to sleep in a bed. The dugouts and abandoned houses of a couple of months ago were in the past. The 587th Dive Bomber Aviation Regiment flew so many missions every day and changed airfields so often, with the front moving and shifting in ways that were impossible to predict, she was lucky if she got a couple of hours of sleep in the grass or under the wing of her plane. It could have been worse, she told herself. At least it was warm. It would have been harder in winter, with sub-zero temperatures, fierce winds and snow making it impossible to get any rest.

It was a warm evening in the first week of May and Nina had no energy to walk back to her quarters after her last mission. All she could do was climb out of her cockpit. She felt herself drifting off on the grass by her plane when she heard footsteps. Not opening her eyes, she smiled. She knew it would be Vlad and Anton, who after a long day often brought her a cup of hot tea and something to eat, a bowl of barley or a piece of bread.

'Finished for the day?' asked Vlad.

She nodded, too tired to talk but happy to see them. Every morning, her heart stopped when she saw the two of them fly off to challenge the German fighters to a deadly duel. Seeing Vlad climb inside the cockpit of his plane, seeing his fighter plane taxying out towards death was a nightmare she could never get used to. Every time she heard the sound of fighter engines above her, she lifted her head and searched for Vlad's plane, searched for the white feather he had painted on its wings; for freedom, for hope, for peace. Every day she lived in fear. Every evening, when she laid her eyes on the two of them, she breathed again. With Anton and Vlad by her side, she felt at peace, even though she could barely move from exhaustion, even though the German anti-aircraft guns exploded in the distance, threatening to blow her little plane out of the sky, and her along with it.

'It's Katya's birthday today,' said Anton, sitting on the grass next to her. 'We brought something special, to remember her.'

They had a flask of tea and a sweet biscuit. Nina's eyes filled with tears. She reached for the biscuit. When she could speak again, she said, 'She would have been twenty-three today.'

'I can't accept that she's gone,' said Anton. 'Some days I'm convinced she's out there somewhere. Other days I know it's impossible. It's been three months.'

Vlad reached in his pocket. 'Look what I have.'

'A bottle of vodka? And three shot glasses!' exclaimed Nina. 'Where did you get that? You don't even drink.'

'I'll drink a little bit to Katya.'

'Me too,' said Nina. Anton nodded in agreement.

Vlad poured a small amount of vodka into each shot glass. Without a word, they touched their glasses together. Traditionally in the Soviet Union, they clinked glasses when drinking to some-one's health. They drank without clinking to someone who had died. Doing this with Anton and Vlad gave Nina hope, as if this simple gesture could keep Katya alive, wherever she was.

'When we were growing up, we always celebrated our birthdays together, remember, Vlad? For her birthday, we would go for a walk in the park. For my birthday in July, we would go to the river and swim. Katya loved swimming. She said the water took all her troubles away. Not that we had any troubles. We would sit side by side and plan the year ahead. Plan our whole lives. Talk about our hopes and dreams.'

'What did she dream about when she was a child?' asked Anton quietly.

'To meet a nice man. To have a family. A little girl to love and protect.'

'What did you dream about?'

'To become a writer.'

The two of them sat on the bank of Moskva River, their feet in the water, early morning sun in their eyes, making them squint. Their skin was golden after weeks of sunbathing. There were freckles on their faces and sand in their hair. It was Nina's sixteenth birthday. 'Another six weeks and we have to go back to school. Can you imagine?' said Katya, stretching and turning her back to the sun.

'I can't imagine it.' All Nina could think of was the here and now. The endless fun they were having in the sun. It was a particularly hot summer that year and she was loving it. Who wanted to think about school? 'Another few weeks and it will be cold again.'

'I want to do something special when school starts. I want to join the aviation club.'

'Isn't it for boys? Why don't we give dancing another go? Not ballet this time. Something modern.'

'It's not just for boys. Apparently forty per cent of those who join are girls. And even if it is for boys, so what? So much the better.

169

Every girl in our class is doing dancing. I want to be different. I want to be special. I want to learn how to fly.'

'Will your mama even let you go? Don't you have your hands full at home?' Katya's mother had just had another baby. Katya had four little brothers she was helping look after.

'All the more reason to be out of the house. Mama is cranky all the time. The boys are constantly screaming. I need to get away.'

'I'm sure you will enjoy learning how to fly. I'm doing a cooking class this year. Anna just told me I had to cook my own meals.'

'I'm not doing this without you.' Katya had the biggest smile on her face. A mysterious smile, like she had a secret she was dying to share with her friend.

'Why do you look like the cat that got the cream?'

Katya twitched with excitement. 'I met someone yesterday. His name is Anton and he's the most handsome boy I've ever seen. He told me about the aviation club. Apparently, they are looking for more people to join.'

'Are you joining to learn how to fly or to see Anton again?' Nina pinched Katya on her elbow and kicked water at her. Katya squealed and moved away. Nina added, 'And didn't you tell me a month ago Timur was the most handsome boy you've ever seen?'

'Forget about Timur. Wait till you see Anton.' Katya's eyes twinkled. They continued to sit side by side, splashing their feet in the water, talking about nothing and everything, on the brink of adulthood, their whole lives stretching in front of them.

When Anton and Vlad left, and Nina was alone again, too tired to walk back to her quarters but unable to sleep, she closed her eyes and thought of her friend, trying to feel for Katya out there. Was she still alive? The uncertainty left Nina with an emptiness inside she didn't know how to fill. What did they do about the giant twister inside their hearts that sucked all joy out until there was nothing left? Did they grieve? What if Katya was still alive? Did they hope? But for how long? And how did they know when to let the hope go?

Chapter 9

One balmy evening in the first week of June, after flying six successive missions, each more terrifying than the one before, Nina waited for Vlad and Anton. An hour passed and they weren't there. Her heart skipping with fear, she pulled her exhausted body out of the cockpit and trudged to the mess area where pilots and navigators of the 10th Leningrad Regiment were laughing and shouting, letting off steam after a long day. She looked for a face she recognised and spotted Tim Korolin, the boy with pimples who had laughed at them when they first arrived at the front. He no longer looked like he belonged at school. The last few months had aged him. Greeting Tim, Nina asked if he knew anything about Vlad and Anton.

'You are looking for Petrov? Join the club. Everyone is waiting for him.'

'What do you mean?' she felt the familiar grip of icy fear. Her hands began to shake. She could hardly breathe. The losses in the fighter pilot regiment had been immense, even more so than in the dive bomber regiment. Every day at least one plane didn't come back. Every day they mourned someone. Anton had told her that fighter pilots who had been at the front for three months were considered veterans. Three months!

But if her brother was missing or dead, Tim wouldn't be talking about him so casually, with a teasing smile on his face. Nina relaxed a little.

'Haven't you heard? He singlehandedly downed four enemy planes today. Everybody is talking about it.'

'He did?' Nina smiled happily, proud of her baby brother. 'And he's safe?'

'As far as I know.'

Still smiling, Nina sat down with a bowl of porridge. Miraculously, she even managed to find a spoon. The good news about her brother gave her an appetite and made her forget how tired she was. She was about to start eating when she heard a commotion behind her. She turned around.

'What do you mean, you ran out of porridge?' cried Inna, Nina's mechanic. She stood with an empty bowl in front of the cook, looking lost and sad, like a small cat abandoned in the rain.

'All we get is barley and stale bread,' joined in Lada, Nina's armourer. 'And now we don't even get that? You want us to go out there and work on empty stomachs?'

The cook shook her head and pointed helplessly at the empty pot. 'Sorry, girls. You should have come earlier. Now you have to wait till tomorrow.'

'We were working earlier,' said Inna.

'If they want us to work, they have to feed us,' exclaimed Lada.

'It's war,' said the cook. 'Food is scarce. There isn't enough for everyone. That's why you have to be quick. Come back tomorrow. I'll have something for you then.'

The girls moved away from the counter, their heads low. 'Come back tomorrow,' mimicked Lada. 'I have a ton of explosives to load before morning, for the pilots to fly. I can't do the heavy lifting when I'm about to faint from hunger.' She looked like she was about to burst into tears.

Nina felt sorry for the girls. The mechanics worked tirelessly around the clock, servicing the planes, making sure they were in working order and safe. The armourers lifted three tons of ammunition a day. Exhausting, never-ending toil. If anyone needed food, it was them. Unfortunately, those in command didn't see it that way. Mechanics and armourers received a soldier's ration, consisting of barley and bread, if they were lucky. Pilots and navigators got officer's ration that included vodka, tobacco and cigarettes, which they could exchange for eggs and milk in villages. Occasionally, they even got cheese or butter with their bread.

Nina waved to the girls, inviting them to join her at her table. 'You can have my porridge if you like. And my bread. And here is a slice of cheese.' She pushed her plate towards Inna and Lada.

'Cheese, what's that? I can't even remember.' Lada smiled happily at the sight of food.

'What about you?' asked Inna, a simple village girl who was built like an ox and had the biggest heart of anyone Nina knew. 'Don't you want your porridge?'

'I've eaten. I had some eggs and made a lovely omelette.' It was three days ago, but they didn't need to know that.

'You pilots are lucky. I should have learnt how to fly, if only for the food,' said Lada.

Inna replied, her mouth full, 'I did learn how to fly but didn't have enough flying hours. I begged Raskova to make me a pilot, but she told me every job is important and they need good mechanics at the regiment. She didn't say anything about the food situation.'

'Raskova was right,' said Nina. 'You save my life every day by keeping my plane running smoothly. If you are ever hungry, you come to me.'

'Thank you,' muttered Inna. The girls ate the porridge from the same bowl, taking turns to scoop it up with their hands.

'This cheese tastes like heaven,' said Inna. Nina glanced at the cheese before it disappeared. It had been a while since she'd had any and when the cook gave her a slice, she thought it was her lucky day. But the girls needed it more than she did. It would cheer them up. And they all needed some cheering up these days.

The expression on the girls' faces as they ate the cheese was priceless.

'Here comes the conquering hero,' they heard a voice behind them. Nina looked up. A few officers walked inside the mess tent, Vlad and Anton among them. She felt her shoulders relax at the sight of them. She waved. They waved back and made their way to the table.

Inna and Lada scooted to make room for the men. Inna said, 'I heard a reporter from *Pravda* is coming tomorrow.'

'Are they going to take photographs?' Lada exclaimed, her eyes like saucers. 'That's another reason I wish I was a pilot. No one ever makes a fuss of us, no matter how hard we work.'

Anton said, 'Vlad is going to be famous. Soon he'll stop talking to us mere mortals.'

Vlad turned bright red and looked at the ground. A few men came up, shook his hand and slapped him on the back, congratulating him. When they moved on, Nina asked, 'Is it true? Did you shoot down four planes today?'

He nodded, visibly pleased. 'I don't know how it happened. I got lucky, I guess.'

'Nonsense,' said Anton. 'Luck has nothing to do with it. It was pure skill and hard work. You were astonishing out there today.'

'Thank you,' said Vlad, looking ill at ease. 'Is there anything to eat? I'm starving. It's been a long day.'

'There is no porridge,' said Inna, scooping up what was left on her plate. 'Nothing left.'

As if by magic, bowls of porridge appeared in front of Vlad and Anton, who offered to share some with Nina, who happily agreed. Lada pouted. 'Do you see this? Can you believe it?' she said to Inna.

'I see it. I can't believe it.'

'No porridge for us but plenty for the pilots. How is this fair?'

'They have to fly the planes.'

'They wouldn't have any planes to fly if it wasn't for us.'

Nina pinched her brother teasingly as he ate. 'Look at you, the hero. Is the reporter really coming tomorrow? Everyone in the country will know your face. All the young boys will want to be like you. I'm so proud of you. Wait till Papa finds out. He'll be proud too.'

'I'm no hero,' said Vlad. 'Just doing my job. And I refused the interview and the photographs. Nobody is coming.'

'Don't be so shy. Who knows, you might inspire someone to become a pilot.'

'He's not shy. He's superstitious,' said Anton.

'Laugh all you want,' replied Vlad. 'Dmitri Kornilov was photographed for the newspaper two months ago. He was killed the next day. Alexei Voronov had an interview published. Next time he flew, his plane was hit by a shell. I'm not taking any chances.'

'You're right, don't,' said Nina. 'I would rather have my brother alive than famous.' She pulled Vlad closer and kissed him on the cheek. 'What is your secret? How do you do it?'

'I have learnt a few tricks in the last few months.'

'Tell me. I'm dying to know.'

Vlad sat up straight like he was at school answering a difficult lesson. In a serious voice, he talked about maintaining the height advantage, when to open fire and how important it was to make sure the sun was behind you, so that it blinded your opponent and not you.

'Told you. It's not luck but hard work, skill and determination,' said Anton. He turned to Nina. 'Thanks to your brother, our boys now believe they can beat the Nazis. They don't seem so unbeatable anymore.'

Chapter 10

July 1943

On the outskirts of Kursk, in the midst of a major battle in the middle of the night, Nina dreamed that the war was over, that Papa was back and Mama was still alive. She dreamed that Katya was drowning, her face twisted in panic as the water pulled her in. Katya's hands were reaching for Nina as she screamed for help. Rooted to the spot by fear and unable to move, Nina wanted desperately to run to her friend but couldn't. All she could do was watch helplessly as Katya disappeared in a whirlwind right in front of her eyes.

When Nina woke up, she could still hear the dripping and the rustling from her dream. Confused, she sat up in her makeshift bed of mud and straw and looked around but couldn't see much in the dark. When she jumped off the bed, she realised she was standing knee-deep in water. 'What is happening?' she cried.

'Rain,' said Zhenya, who was standing in the middle of the dugout, calmly lighting a candle. 'The dugout's flooded.'

All around them, the wooden chairs, their clothes and books were floating. 'What are we going to do?' asked Nina.

'I will go and tell the men to bring the truck with a pumping machine. Pump the water out. I doubt we'll get any more sleep tonight.' Zhenya yawned and made a few careful steps towards the entrance.

'You are going out like that?' asked Nina, her eyes wide. Zhenya had on a tiny robe and nothing else.

Zhenya shrugged. 'My clothes floated away. I'll find them later. I'm sure the men won't mind.' She laughed. 'We'll have to fly in wet uniforms today. Good thing it's so hot.'

Nina looked at her watch. It was three in the morning, two hours before they had to get up and start their day. Tonight was a good night. She got three hours of sleep. Swaying from exhaustion, she climbed out of the dugout into the rain that was coming down like a waterfall, soaking her instantly. Finding a piece of tarpaulin, she joined the other girls, who stretched under the wings of their planes, hoping to go back to sleep.

She remembered the last time they had slept under the pouring rain like this. It was a year ago, in Engels. Katya was alive and there was still hope. They still made plans for the future because they thought they had one. They believed the war would be over soon and that they would become heroes and make the Germans pay. None of them had been prepared for what the war would bring, Nina realised. After six months at the front, all she felt was a bitter emptiness inside.

Nina couldn't sleep and nor could the rest of the girls. They huddled together for warmth and clucked like hens, worrying about the weather, the Germans and flying in the rain. By the time they lined up on the airfield to start their day, they were a sorry sight. Thankfully, the rain had stopped. As they waited for Markov, Nina thought of her books, diary and letters that had been destroyed by water. She wanted to cry.

'Don't look so sad. The men pumped the water out. When we return, our dugout will be dry,' said Zhenya.

'Let's hope it doesn't rain again.' If it started raining as heavily while they were in the air in their little Pe-2s, flooded dugouts would be the least of their worries. They would be lucky to make it back to base alive.

'Remember last week you complained there was no water to wash with? You said you felt dirty. God heard your prayers.'

'I still feel dirty. And wet.'

Zhenya giggled. 'We all look like something a cat dragged in. Wait till *Batya* sees us. We'll never hear the end of it.'

When Markov appeared, however, he didn't seem to notice their bedraggled appearance. Pacing in front of them with the biggest smile on his face, he said, 'I received wonderful news this morning and I'm thrilled to share it with you. Thanks to our recent performance, we have been awarded a new name. We are now the 587th Raskova Bomber Aviation Regiment, in honour of Marina Raskova.'

Nina's heart swelled with joy. The girls cheered.

'To celebrate this occasion, we are going to start bombing early. To the airplanes, everyone.'

Nina had tears in her eyes as she walked to her plane.

Dasha asked, 'Why are you crying? It's exciting. Now we truly are Raskova's regiment.'

'I wish Katya was here. She would have been so happy. She loved Marina.'

In the evening, their eyes dim from exhaustion but smiles wide on their faces, the girls sat in a circle in the mess tent. Zhenya and Yulia cradled their guitars. Markov poured the girls some wine, a welcome change from vodka that no one liked. The music filled the tent and the girls sang their sad songs. Even though every day pushed them to breaking point, even though their hearts splintered every time they lost another comrade, even though everything out there was determined to kill them, they had much to be grateful for. They were still alive. They were fighting. They had become warriors, just like Major Raskova had predicted.

'I completely forgot,' said Zhenya, taking one hand off her

guitar. 'This arrived for you with the post this afternoon.' She held out a letter folded in two. It had Nina's name on it, written in careful, small handwriting.

'Thank you,' she exclaimed, eagerly reaching for the envelope. It was the first letter she had ever received at the front. She never even checked the post that arrived on the truck every few days because no one sent her anything. She recognised Anna's handwriting and hesitated for a moment. They had parted on bad terms. Why was the woman writing to her? Hands shaking, Nina tore the envelope apart and unfolded the letter.

> *Dear Nina and Vlad,*
>
> *I am sorry to be writing with bad news. I received the telegram yesterday. Your papa was killed under Kursk two weeks ago. He died a hero.*
>
> *After everything that happened, I can no longer stay in Moscow. I'm taking the children and joining my sister in Krasnoyarsk. I know that we didn't have the best relationship, but I needed to write to you and tell you that your father loved you very much and was proud of you both. You were the loves of his life. Don't you ever forget that.*
>
> *Take care and keep in touch.*
>
> *Anna*

Nina sat in shocked silence for a while, staring at the piece of paper that broke her heart. She could no longer see Anna's carefully written words, could barely hear the girls' voices. The writing became blurry and distorted and everything spun in front of her eyes, as if she was drunk or dangerously ill. Dropping the letter, she closed her eyes and felt her body sliding to one side. She wished she was alone, wished she could scream at the top of her voice and no one could hear her. And all the while, Zhenya's guitar cried in the night and the girls sang a popular war song.

And often in battle
Your face guides me
And I wonder
When I will see you again.

How did she get through the night? The dugout could have flooded again and she wouldn't have noticed. The Nazis could have razed the whole regiment to the ground and she wouldn't have noticed. Did she sleep? Did she dream of her father? She didn't know.

She tossed and turned and sobbed with her fist in her mouth, careful not to wake her comrades. Finally, she couldn't stay in bed any longer. Barefoot on damp earth, she walked out of the dugout and across the field, lay on her back in the overgrown grass and looked up. The dark sky was studded with diamonds. Nina had never seen anything like it. In Moscow, there were hardly any stars even when there was not a cloud overhead, but here, in Kursk, during the most terrible night of her life, a million festive lights sparkled at her with glee.

She remembered sitting like this with her father a week after her mother had died. They were at their dacha and she couldn't sleep. She was afraid of the dark and cried in her bed until her father came in and took her outside. Side by side they remained on the grass without saying a word, and the silence was comforting because she knew she was not alone in her grief.

Trembling from the cold, from the pain inside her chest, she had taken her father's hand. 'Do you think Mama is up there somewhere, looking down on us? Somewhere with the stars?'

'I don't know, darling. I hope so.'

Nina had turned away from the dull sky. 'Why did God take Mama?' She could barely speak. It hurt too much.

Papa had sighed. His eyes had flashed with sadness. 'I know it's a hard thing to accept, especially for someone so young, but we are not here forever. Nor are our loved ones.'

'It's not fair.' She had clasped her fists and tasted salt on her lips. She had been crying and hadn't even realised it.

'Sometimes, when I feel sad, I look at the stars. It puts things in perspective. Makes me feel so small. Makes my problems seem small.' Her father had pointed at the sky, whispering, 'Somehow, God has a plan for all of us. It will all work out for the best.'

Nina had always believed that everything happened for a reason because Papa told her so. But now he was gone, dead at forty-five, in the prime of his life, because of Hitler's bloodthirstiness, a stranger they had never met or wronged in any way. And as Nina looked up at the stars, five hundred kilometres away from home, alone and without her father, she realised she had lost her faith.

Bright in the sky, the stars twinkled like they had not a care in the world. In the morning, the sun would rise again and the morning breeze would rustle these fields and these trees, like everything was right in the world. The Nazis would continue to rip the Soviet Union apart, and Nina and Vlad would get inside their planes and fight. Life would go on like before, as if nothing had changed. How was it possible?

In the mess tent in the morning, Nina sobbed with her head on her brother's shoulder. Vlad was holding Anna's letter in his trembling hands. Neither of them spoke, while all around them soldiers and officers laughed and talked in loud voices. Spoons hit plates and outside the aircraft engines started and stopped as the mechanics performed last minute checks. Something exploded in the distance. Just like always.

They were huddled together at a table away from everybody else, their heads close together. Tim came up to them and asked if he could join them. 'Are you eating?' he demanded, glancing at the empty table. 'If not, move along and let others sit down. It's busy this morning.' They didn't even glance in his direction. Finally, he moved on.

Nina whispered, her fingers threaded through her brother's, her eyes aching, 'I always thought the war would be over and we would return home and see our papa. He was here in Kursk all this time and we didn't even know. I would give anything to have seen him one last time.'

'I hate the Nazis with everything I have. I will destroy them for killing our father,' cried Vlad, his face distorted in the dim light of the mess tent.

'Don't go out there and do something stupid. Papa wouldn't have wanted it. Don't risk your life for no reason. It won't bring him back.'

'I won't do anything stupid. You don't have to worry,' said Vlad. 'Wait here, I'll go and get you something to eat.'

'I can't even think of food right now.'

'Me neither.'

They sat in silence, lost in grief. The clock on the wall of the tent was ticking – ticktock, ticktock – almost as loud as the thoughts inside Nina's head. 'Do you remember Papa teaching me how to drive one summer?' she asked. 'He was patient and kind, even though I was a terrible pupil. I scratched the car on a metal pole at our dacha and thought, *oh no*. He was upset but tried not to show it. He didn't even tell me off.'

'I remember,' replied Vlad, tears in his eyes. 'It took him four years to save enough money to fix that scratch. And three months after he'd finally fixed it, he was teaching me to drive in the same spot and I scratched the car again on the same metal pole. The look on his face!'

'He loved that car like a baby. Washed it every Saturday and dried it with a cloth. I remember one day I was driving through a forest with him next to me. All of a sudden, there was a tree in front of us. I have no idea where it came from.'

'Well, you *were* in the forest. Forests have trees.'

'He cried out to me to slow down and I hit the gas in panic. I finally managed to stop, centimetres away from the tree.'

'I remember that day. He came home and said, "She can fly planes, but she's incapable of driving; how can that be?"'

'And I said to him, there are no trees around when I fly. I just need more practice, Papa. Tomorrow, I will drive better. "More practice in my car?" he replied. And his face went white.' She gasped for air, suddenly short of oxygen, tight-chested and dizzy.

'He was the best father a child could wish for. He told me I could be anything I wanted. If only I put my mind to it, I could achieve anything,' said Vlad.

'He told me to never stop following my dreams. To not let anything stand in my way.' When she was a child, her father was the one she turned to, whenever she felt sad or afraid or in need of encouragement. How she wished she could reach out and take Papa's hand and tell him everything she was feeling. He would find just the right words to comfort her. 'I miss him so much. He was all alone when he died. Do you think he was afraid?'

'You saw Anna's letter. He died a hero. He was brave until the end.'

'Both our parents are gone. We are orphans, all alone in the world.'

'Not alone. We still have each other.' Her baby brother pulled her close and they sat with their arms around each other, while all around them the airfield woke up and prepared for another long day.

'Please, don't leave me,' Nina whispered, touching his face. 'I couldn't take it if I lost you too.'

'I'm not going anywhere. I promise.'

That day, just like any other day, they climbed inside their cockpits, flew towards the front line and fought. They gave everything they had, for their father. As if on autopilot, Nina went through the motions of taxying out, guiding the plane towards the target, giving a signal to Dasha to release the bombs and taking them back to base safely. The satisfaction of hearing the explosions below took her breath away. The Nazis killed her father. Now she was making them pay.

That evening, Nina, Vlad and Anton drank a little bit of vodka to Papa. They didn't clink their glasses together, nor did they say anything. Everything that needed saying had already been said. Nina was no longer crying. She had no tears left. She was empty inside, a painful hollow feeling that scared her.

'It's a bad sign,' she whispered. 'Our papa is gone and no one is watching over us. Something bad is going to happen.'

In the second week of July, Major Markov was called away to Moscow for a few days. Nina wondered why he looked so reluctant to leave his girls, but when she saw who he was leaving in charge, she understood. Captain Bureev was tall, red-faced, bald and belligerent. He was known for his contempt towards his subordinates and doing all in his power to make his superiors notice him, often at the expense of others. The girls stood quietly as Bureev walked in front of them, staring them down.

'Fighters of the 587th Raskova Bomber Aviation Regiment,' he said with aplomb. 'You are doing great, for a regiment of women.' He sniggered, ignoring the disgruntled groans from the girls. 'Everyone is talking about your performance, but I think we can do even better. We can show them what we are truly capable of. I have a few suggestions on how to improve things while Major Markov is away.'

'If everyone is praising our performance, why do we need to improve?' asked Zhenya, who had recently been promoted to squadron commander. Once again, Nina reported to her, while Zhenya reported to Major Markov. 'We are already doing our best.' They worked ceaselessly through exhaustion, hunger and sleep deprivation. They had left their families behind to fight Hitler; elderly parents and children who might never see them again. They risked their lives every time they climbed inside their cockpits. And here was this newcomer, telling them they were not doing enough. Who did he think he was? He was no Markov, and he definitely wasn't Raskova. Nina stood in the sea of angry faces, not looking at Bureev. She didn't share the girls' anger.

Having lost Katya and her papa so recently, she didn't feel anything other than her all-encompassing grief.

'There is always room for improvement. We are fighting a war against the best-equipped enemy in the world. As a result, we need to do our best. A lot is at stake. We need to work more efficiently if we are to make a difference.'

Zhenya whispered to the girls, 'He's only here for a few days, and he wants to make changes to the way things are.' Louder, she asked, 'Are you saying there is something wrong with the way Major Markov runs things?'

'Absolutely not. But I thought of a few changes.'

'I can't wait to hear them,' Zhenya muttered.

Oblivious to the hostility in the air, Bureev continued, 'The Pe-2s will be able to carry a heavier load of bombs if the planes carry less fuel.'

There was a moment of stunned silence. The girls couldn't believe what they were hearing. 'With all due respect, sir, with less fuel, the planes won't be able to fly as far. That gives the pilots less time to complete their missions and return to base safely,' said Zoya Afanasyeva, the chief mechanic.

'Nonsense. We are soldiers fighting a war. Every once in a while we need to take risks to win.'

'If the planes carry more weight, they will use fuel less efficiently, and it will be more difficult to take off and control them, making it more dangerous . . .'

Bureev didn't let Zoya finish. 'Are you at the front fighting the Nazis or at a flying club flirting with your sweetheart? Are you combat pilots or a bunch of little girls in pigtails? Grow up, learn to take responsibility and stop moaning. While I'm here, this is how we are going to do things. It is not your place to question the decisions of your superior. When Major Markov returns, you can go back to the old way. However, once he sees how much more efficient our performance has become, I believe he will adopt the new way as well. You are dismissed.'

'What a bigoted fool,' muttered Zhenya as the girls walked to their planes.

'He is going to kill us all,' said Dasha.

'I hope *Batya* comes back soon,' said Masha. 'Wait till he hears about this. He would never compromise our safety like this.'

'With this pig in charge, we might not live long enough to see him come back,' said Zhenya, shaking with anger.

The girls watched in silence as the mechanics drained the fuel from the planes and loaded more explosives. As she lifted the bombs, Zoya muttered, 'This is suicide.'

As the plane took off, Nina knew straight away that Zoya was right. Overloaded and struggling, her beloved Pe-2 no longer obeyed her every thought but was rebelling against her, as if determined to punish her for what Bureev was doing. It was heavy and dragging them back to earth. How they managed to get it into the air, fly to their target, drop their bombs, return to base and land safely, Nina didn't know. Once they released the bombs, the plane became easier to control. Having shaken off the massive load, it spread its wings like a bird, and Nina felt a little more hopeful herself, even though she had never flown on so little fuel before.

As they landed, she let out a breath of relief, her heart racing. But the relief was short-lived. When they climbed out of the cockpit, they found the airfield in mourning. Two of their planes had crashed. One Pe-2 had run out of fuel on the way back to base. Another careened into a hangar and exploded because it was overloaded and failed to get enough height on takeoff.

Nina was speechless. She couldn't even cry. In the last few weeks, it seemed she had run out of tears, having used up a lifetime's supply. All she managed to say was, 'Who?'

'Luda, Polya and Timur. Nastya, Dina and Andrei,' listed Zhenya, her eyes dull.

Captain Bureev stood in the middle of the airfield with his head uncovered. 'Why do these things always happen on my watch?

I thought I was getting a regiment of professionals. Instead, they entrusted me with a bunch of amateurs,' he fumed.

The girls didn't reply. They were sobbing with their arms around each other.

Markov returned the next day, having received an urgent telegram from the regiment. As he stood before them, his face was dark, as if someone had hit a switch and a light had gone out. When he spoke to Bureev, his voice shook with barely contained emotion. 'You sacrificed our safety, the most important thing in the world, and for what?'

Bureev looked at his boots. He refused to lift his eyes to Markov. 'Efficiency, sir. We dropped a quarter more bombs in one mission.'

'You lost two crews and two planes. What you did was criminal negligence. You will be court-marshalled for this.'

That evening, the girls sat in the mess tent. No one was talking. No one was eating. It was dark inside the tent, and Nina could barely see the stricken faces of her comrades. She leaned back in her chair and felt herself drifting off to sleep when she felt a hand on her shoulder. With great effort she opened her eyes. 'Vlad, what are you doing here so late?'

'I had to make sure you were all right after what happened.'

The room was spinning, the walls of the tent performing a bizarre dance in the dark. Nina felt dizzy and unwell. 'I'm fine. Don't worry.'

'Have you eaten?'

She shook her head. 'I'm not hungry.' When was the last time she had eaten a proper meal? She couldn't remember. She had no energy or desire to eat.

'You need to look after yourself. You need your strength.'

'Don't have much strength left.'

'Stay here. I will get you some food. I have something to tell you. Something good.'

'Tell me now.' She was eager to hear what he had to say. It had been a while since she'd received good news.

'I'll get you something to eat first. I'm not telling you anything if you don't eat.'

'All right.'

Her eyes shut, she sensed Vlad come back with a bowl of something warm, felt his hand on her hand, her shoulder being shaken, heard his voice but couldn't make out the words. A moment later, she was sound asleep.

So much loss all around, so much death. What were they dying for? What were the Germans trying to achieve as they trampled cities and countryside and millions of lives under their boots and the wheels of their tanks? When Nina first arrived at the front, she was excited and ready for anything. She had wanted to prove herself, to become a hero, to make her father proud. To make Raskova proud. She was hungry for action. Her desire to fight had been so strong, she could almost taste it. Now, after losing so many people she loved, that desire was gone, leaving her disillusioned, deflated and empty inside. Faced with the realities of war, she had lost her purpose.

Every time she closed her eyes, Nina saw her father's face and the faces of her comrades, who had perished because of one man's ego and stupidity. Perished needlessly in an accident that could have been avoided, if only they had stood up to Bureev and disobeyed his order.

She was curled up under the wing of her plane, a piece of tarpaulin over her. The sun tinted the horizon pink and one after another the stars faded. The tops of the trees turned golden and the airfield began to stir. Nina heard voices and the sound of truck engines. And another, louder sound – fighter planes. She jumped to her feet and looked up. Who was in the air this early in the morning?

She watched with trepidation as two Soviet planes sped through the pink morning sky she had just been admiring. Suddenly, it didn't look so beautiful anymore. There were four small dots in the distance that soon grew in size. When she made out the dreaded shape of the German fighters, she shuddered. The enemy were circling, sniffing around like bloodhounds, having by some miracle found their small airfield, hidden away in the forest, almost imperceptible from the air. Outnumbered two to one, the Soviet fighters charged them.

As fast as she could, Nina ran through the grass, wondering who the brave pilots were. Across the airfield, she saw a small group of people watching the planes in the sky. With horror, she noticed a white feather painted on one of the plane's wings. Vlad! Her heart nearly stopped. Her hand flew to her mouth.

'Don't worry,' she heard a voice. 'Vlad will be fine. He's an expert at what he does.'

She turned around and saw Anton by her side, looking up with a tense smile on his tired face.

'Want to know what I heard?' he added. 'Rumour has it Vlad has been recommended for the Hero of the Soviet Union medal.'

'Really?' Her heart skipped. The Hero of the Soviet Union was the highest distinction in the country. Perhaps that was what Vlad was trying to tell her the night before. Her eyes wide with fear, she watched the battle unfolding over their heads.

Vlad was superb in the air. No wonder the Nazis were afraid of him. She had heard talk of Nazi pilots turning back and returning to their base at the sight of the famous white feather. But not these pilots. Either they had never heard of Vlad or they were brave enough to face him, but they showed no sign of hesitation, no desire to run. If she didn't know this was a fight to the death, if it wasn't for the machine guns barking with anger, it would look like the planes were playing some kind of a giddy game, rising higher and falling through the air, getting closer and separating, chasing each other and spinning in circles.

Nina turned away, fighting tears. This was the boy she had rocked in her arms when he was little. She had combed his hair and bandaged his grazed knees. She had helped Mama bathe him and kissed him goodnight every evening at eight o'clock sharp. What was he doing in the sky, trying to outsmart death?

She felt Anton's hand in hers, his fingers warm, giving her courage. In silence they watched the horror that was unfolding in the sky.

Vlad was doing so well. He was almost winning. The enemy plane had to weave and duck out of the way to avoid getting hit. 'Come on, Vlad, come on!' she whispered, jumping on the spot. She was ready to cry out in triumph when the sound died on her lips because suddenly it all went terribly wrong and she found herself living through her worst nightmare. Vlad's aircraft was no longer part of the game. Instead, it tilted to one side and began to fall, a funnel of black smoke coming from the engine. Someone was screaming. The sound pierced the air, making Nina's ears ache, making all the other sounds – the machine guns, the plane engines and the explosions – fade away.

'It's all right,' Anton said. 'It's all right.'

His fingers squeezed hers until it hurt. His face was distorted, like he was in pain.

She realised it was her who had been screaming. Her throat felt numb and she couldn't utter another sound, only watch in horror as the unthinkable was happening before her eyes. She had seen it before. How many times had she woken from this dream, from the vision of Vlad's plane falling into the void? How many times had she shot up in bed, shaking and crying, sweat and tears running down her face?

She was trembling and crying now and she waited impatiently to wake up. But this was not one of her nightmares. It was real.

'Come on,' said Anton, sounding desperate, almost angry. 'Come on, jump. Jump out of that plane. You can do it.'

Nina could barely stand. Any second now, she was going to fall. But she had to remain upright, for her brother. She had to be there for him when he landed. She stared at the falling plane and prayed. Any second now, a small figure would catapult out and a parachute would open, carrying Vlad to safety.

But it didn't happen. Nina watched in mute disbelief as her brother's aircraft crashed into the ground. All she could see were flames devouring the Yak-1 with her baby brother on board. And then she could no longer see anything at all. Everything faded until there was nothing left but the sharp pain in her heart.

She came to in Anton's arms. For a moment, she didn't know where she was or what had happened. Why was she on the ground? Why was Anton looking at her with tears in his eyes? Why were his hands shaking? And then she remembered. Her knees buckled under her and she would have collapsed again if it wasn't for Anton holding her to his chest, like she was a baby. She shook and screamed and sobbed, while he whispered something to her. 'What?' she wanted to say. 'What?' She couldn't make out the words. Was her brother all right? Was he asking for her? She had to go to him. She pulled away from Anton.

'I'm so sorry,' Anton was saying. 'I'm so sorry.'

'Please, let me go. Vlad needs me.'

'I'm sorry, honey.'

A small crowd of people gathered on the other side of the airfield where the plane had crashed but no one dared approach what was left of it. Nina could see Markov and Vlad's commander Major Popov, their faces long and mournful, watching the wreckage that was being consumed by fire. 'Please, let me go to him,' she pleaded.

'There is nothing we can do,' said Anton.

She fought against him and finally broke free. Faster than the wind, she ran the race of her life, across the airfield, past the crowd and towards the flames. She was almost there. Only a hundred metres to go. A few moments and she would reach him and she would help him. Her brother needed her and she would go to him even if it killed her.

When she was almost at the wreckage, Anton, who had been running after her, grabbed her hand. 'You can't go there. Any minute now, the whole thing is going to explode.'

'I don't care. My brother is inside that plane.'

Anton's face crumbled. 'It's too late now. It's too late.'

'No,' she whispered.

Anton held her close, not letting go. She fought him, spinning around, hitting out and twisting her hands. Moments later, a deafening explosion was heard. What was left of Vlad's plane disappeared in a ball of fire. Nina felt the power of the explosion, the heat on her face as the scorching wave hit her. She screamed at Anton, her hands clasped into fists. 'What have you done? I could have saved him. I could have still saved him.' Shaking, she collapsed on her knees and sobbed.

'I'm so sorry, Nina. I'm so sorry.'

Suddenly, she stopped crying. A calm descended on her, like a fog clearing. 'It wasn't Vlad in that plane. It was someone else. I know that. Sometimes other men from the regiment fly it. Just last week I thought it was Vlad in the air and I watched, but when the plane landed, his friend Tim came out.' She talked fast, a machine-gun fire of words to calm her aching heart. As she spoke, she felt better and better. Here she was, panicking too early. Of course, it was devastating and heartbreaking, seeing the plane explode like this. But it wasn't Vlad.

'It *was* Vlad. I'm sorry,' whispered Anton.

'No.'

She became hysterical, sobbing until her throat hurt. Through half-open eyes, like in a bad dream, she could see shadows of people moving past, felt someone lift her up and place her on a stretcher. A man in a medic's uniform leaned over her. She felt a sharp needle in her vein and everything went black. She slept.

When Nina woke up, she was lying on a bed made of straw inside a large dugout. Anton was sitting in a chair by her side. She felt groggy and confused. Her body hurt. Her throat felt sore.

When she tried to talk, she couldn't. She motioned to Anton to give her something to drink. He let her have a glass of water. She took a few sips.

'What's wrong with my voice?' she croaked. 'Why can't I talk?'

'You strained your voice.'

'Strained it? How?'

He looked away. She sensed he didn't want to tell her. 'Would you like something to eat?'

She looked around. There was a table right in front of her, covered with notepads, bandages and medical supplies. A kerosene lamp was burning brightly, throwing eerie shadows on the walls. To the right and left of her were beds, with people groaning, crying, asking for something or sleeping peacefully. 'Where am I?'

'You are at the field hospital. The nurses are looking after you.'

'What is wrong with me? Was I in an accident? What happened?'

He took her hand and squeezed it. 'You'll be good as new soon. You just need some rest.'

She sat up and looked Anton straight in the eye. When she spoke, her voice was barely a whisper. 'Anton, where is Vlad? Tell him I want to see him. I don't feel so good.'

Anton didn't reply. He looked shattered, like he had aged ten years since the last time she saw him. His eyes were dark with grief. What was that expression on his face? She had seen it before, earlier on the airfield, when the two of them stood side by side, watching her brother's plane as it plunged to the ground. 'No,' she whispered, 'no!' They were silent for a long time, her body twitching, tears falling on the white sheet she was lying on. 'I feel like it was me who died this morning,' she whispered.

Anton looked straight at her. So much intensity was in his gaze, so much heartbreak, she wanted to look away but couldn't. 'Nina, I'm so sorry,' he said. 'Do you hear me? I'm sorry it happened in front of you. I'm sorry you had to see it.'

'My brother is gone and I'm still here. I'm still breathing. How is it possible?'

Anton's hand pressed hers. 'I can't even imagine what you are feeling right now.'

'I'm glad I saw it. I'm glad I was there for him in his last moments. I wish I could hold him in my arms and tell him how much I love him.'

'He knows.' Anton brushed a strand of hair out of her eye. 'Vlad already knows you love him.'

'He must have been so scared.'

'Your brother? Scared? Never. He was a warrior, the bravest person I know.'

'We were the only two left,' she whispered. 'Vlad and I. Now I am all alone in the world.'

'I know it's not the same. But I'm here for you.'

When Anton left, she curled into a ball and remained like that, not moving or lifting her head. She didn't know how much time had passed. It could have been minutes or hours. She didn't sleep, but she wasn't awake either, her head spinning like she was drunk.

When Zhenya, Yulia and Masha came to see her, they found her in bed, her face in her hands. Pushing each other, they ran to her, hugging her, fussing over her, asking questions she didn't know how to answer. She said nothing, wishing she could remain curled up into a ball, alone with her heartbreak.

'We wanted you to know how sorry we are,' said Zhenya. 'We all loved Vlad.'

'We are here for you. You know that, don't you?' said Yulia.

Masha pulled Nina into a hug. 'If you need anything, anything at all, you tell us.'

The girls cried by her side, their arms around her, and all she wanted to do was put her hands over her ears and scream. She stared into the distance, past her friends and the pity on their faces, and waited for them to leave.

'Vlad was a hero. The bravest of men. You must be so proud of him,' said Zhenya, stroking Nina's fingers. Nina moved her hand away. Hearing the girls talk about her brother in the past tense made her heart shatter. It made the horror of what had just happened real.

'How I hate the Nazis!' exclaimed Masha, her little fists punching the sheet. 'Look what they are doing. We'll make them pay . . . for everything.'

But it won't bring Vlad back, Nina wanted to say but couldn't. She turned her head away and closed her eyes.

'Markov gave us all the afternoon off. He said we've been working too hard,' said Yulia. 'Others are playing basketball. It got quite competitive. But we came here. We love you and our hearts break for you. We wanted you to know that.'

A basketball game! Vlad would have enjoyed that. Nina groaned in pain because she suddenly realised that her brother would never play basketball again.

At the sight of Nina's face twisted in pain, the girls fell quiet. Nina knew what they wanted to do. They wanted to lure her away from the dark abyss with their kindness and their chatter. But there was no luring her away. As they tried to console her, as if that was even possible, as they fussed and clucked, she stared at a dark spot on the wall in silence. She wanted to say something, to thank them, to tell them she would be all right but couldn't. She didn't think she would ever be all right. Finally, thankfully, they got up and said their goodbyes, telling her they would see her tomorrow.

Nina thought she wanted to be alone but when the door closed behind them, she became afraid. The thoughts inside her head scared her. She was glad when a nurse came to see her.

'Would you like a drink? Something to eat?' the nurse asked. 'Have some nice buckwheat porridge, honey. You need your strength.'

'I want to see Anton. Could you find him for me, please?' One glimpse of his face and the weight pressing on her chest would lift, if only for a moment.

'I'll see what I can do. Why don't you sleep?'

Nina closed her eyes. Next thing she knew, Anton was by her side. He brought food, tea and vodka. He wanted her to drink to Vlad. She refused the food but took one sip of vodka and threw up over the side of her bed. When she was done, he washed her face and hands and brought her some water. He was talking about Vlad, but she couldn't focus on the words.

Finally, he got up to leave.

'Where are you going? Don't go,' she said. While he was by her side, she had something to focus on other than her grief. She didn't want him to leave. The dark abyss was terrifying to contemplate on her own.

'I'll be back soon. I'm going to tell Markov you can't fly tomorrow.'

'I'll be fine tomorrow.'

'You need time to grieve. You are not in the right state of mind to fly. I don't want you to put yourself at risk.'

She sat up straight. 'I need to fly. I need to make them pay for what they did to my brother. I want to make them suffer.'

'I don't think you should go out there. Give yourself one more day to recover.'

'I will never recover. Another day won't make a difference.'

Finally, she fell into an uneasy sleep, waking every now and then, her pillow wet with tears. Every time she opened her eyes, she saw Anton asleep on a small chair next to her bed and felt a little less lonely.

Chapter 11

July 1943

Nina put one foot in front of the other, slowly, painfully, like she was learning to walk all over again, like she was treading on broken glass. She would make it to her plane and she would fly, for Vlad. She wouldn't fall and she wouldn't crumble. For her brother, she needed to be strong.

When she stumbled and fell, a pair of strong hands pulled her back up, a pair of kind eyes watched her with concern. 'Are you sure you are up for it?' asked Zhenya.

'I'm up for it,' said Nina in a dull voice.

'We are right here if you need us. You are not alone.'

She might have said thank you, she might have nodded. She didn't know.

The only time Nina felt alive was when she was in the air, wreaking havoc on the Nazis. Every time the bombs dropped from her little plane, bringing death and destruction to the enemy, she whispered, 'This is for Vlad.' It was the only thing that got her through the day. It became her sole purpose.

From her first day at the front, she had one goal – to survive the war at all cost, to return home, to live a peaceful life with her father and brother by her side. Now that they were gone, what was going to become of her? Everyone she loved died. Katya, Papa, Vlad. *I'm next*, she thought as she lay awake at night, haunted by ghosts and nightmares. *I know I'm next because I don't see the reason to go on.*

The front moved and the regiment followed. Airfield after airfield, a new target to bomb every time they climbed inside their planes, but one thing remained the same – every day they risked being killed and every day they had to kill. It was what they did, the monotony of it turned it into a mundane, nothing-out-of-the-ordinary job. Some airfields were located near villages, and the crews could sleep in proper houses that had mostly been abandoned. Sometimes they slept in stables. Mostly they slept in hastily constructed dugouts or on the grass outside. Thankfully, it was warm. Nina felt the sun on her skin and remembered how much Vlad loved summer. She heard the birds chirping and thought of carefree summer days of their childhood, of nothing but games and joy, of swimming in the river with her brother, riding their bicycles, racing through the fields, of Vlad shouting, 'I told you, you could never catch me, I'm too fast for you!', of catching up to him and tickling each other and falling on the ground, laughing. Of growing up together. Now, as she stood on the airfield alone, away from the other girls, without her brother, nothing brought her joy, not even the warm breeze in her hair. She felt dead inside.

In the last week of July, in a village not far from Kursk, Nina had a little hut to herself. Late at night, after a day of avoiding death while bringing it to others, she sat on the porch and looked at the river, thinking how much Vlad would have liked this – balmy summer evenings and the river rustling nearby. She was glad she could be alone to think of her brother and mourn in peace, if only for a couple of nights. No need to smile politely to Dasha as she tried to engage her in conversation. No need to pretend she was fine when all she wanted to do was crawl into bed and howl in pain. Being on her own was just what she needed right now.

Nina sat on the porch for a long time, watching the deserted road, listening to the river, her heart beating, fast and painful, like a drum inside her chest. She was shaking and her teeth were chattering. She needed to do something about the cold. Feeling dizzy, swaying like she was ill, she made her way to the small woodburning stove in the corner, placed some wood inside and lit it. Then she fell into bed and closed her eyes.

A loud noise woke her. With great difficulty, she lifted her head. To her shock and surprise, sunlight filled the room. It felt like the middle of the day and she wondered if she was late. *Oh no*, she thought, *Batya is going to kill me.* That loud noise again – someone banging on the door. Hoping they would go away, she closed her eyes and turned to the wall. It felt like there was sand inside her eyelids and it made it difficult to stay awake. Her arms and legs weighed a ton. She couldn't move. It was suffocatingly hot in the house. She couldn't breathe. Opening her mouth, gulping for air, she pulled the sheet over her head. All she needed was sleep.

The banging became louder. Someone called her name. She thought she recognised Anton's voice. She wanted to call out to him but couldn't. Her throat was too dry. 'Anton,' she whispered. She heard the door breaking.

When she opened her eyes again, she saw Anton's face, fading in and out, flickering in front of her like a moving picture. She blinked, trying to focus.

He kept shaking her and saying her name. 'Nina, can you hear me?'

Next thing she knew, she was outside, lying on the grass. There was someone else with Anton. A man, tall and imposing, talking in a loud voice. 'Overheating. Not enough oxygen. Needs air and rest.'

She slept, dreaming of her brother running to her, his chubby toddler legs wobbly and unstable, his arms reaching. 'Lift me up, Nina. Lift me up.' She opened her eyes and reached out to lift her little brother up but he was no longer there.

Aching all over, she sat up. She was back on her bed, the medic was gone and it was just Anton sitting by her side. He took her hand. 'Why did you do a silly thing like that? You scared me half to death.'

'What did I do?' She rubbed her eyes. Her throat was burning. She touched it, wishing she had some water to drink. As if he could read her mind, he gave her his flask.

'Leaving the stove on all night. The medic said if I hadn't come to find you, you might not have woken up at all.'

Her eyes filled with tears. In her mind, she could see Vlad's plane, hurling through the air and finally hitting the ground. And there was nothing she could do to save him. Not a single thing. No, she shouted inside her head. No! 'Maybe it would have been for the best. I don't think I want to wake up.'

He held her. 'He would have wanted you to live,' he whispered. '*I* want you to live.'

His arms around her felt comforting and warm. She wanted to stay like this forever, safe in his embrace. 'Don't have anything left to live for.'

'One day you'll be glad you kept going. Time heals everything.'

'Not everything. Not this.' She couldn't imagine waking up one day and not feeling the overwhelming weight inside her heart. She didn't know how to go on when her brother was no longer with her. And she didn't want to.

Three weeks after Vlad was killed, Nina accepted the golden star of the Hero of the Soviet Union medal on his behalf. During the ceremony, her hands shook so badly she dropped the medal twice. When she thanked the general who had personally delivered the medal, her voice broke. She could barely get the words out. As she listened to the speeches praising her brother, listened to other people's accounts of him and learnt how many lives he had touched, tears ran down her face.

'You must be so proud of Vlad,' Anton whispered to her.

'I am,' she replied, clutching the precious wooden box containing the award. It was all she had left of her brother. 'But more than anything, I want him back. Maybe if he was less of a hero, he would still be alive.'

Nina was grateful there were no mirrors on the airfield. Since her brother died, she had lost so much weight, her uniform hung on her like she was made of sticks, like one of those scarecrows she often saw on the fields near their dacha as she and Vlad raced each other on their bicycles, their pockets filled with ripe strawberries they had just picked. Her cheeks felt gaunt to the touch. There was only one moment in her day when she felt like she was still living. When Anton came to see her after her last mission. Watching him walk towards her plane without Vlad by his side pierced her heart like a knife. But having him there made her feel warm inside.

'When Katya died, how did you go on? How did you find the strength?' she asked one evening. She could barely talk, so exhausted she was after five back-to-back missions. He looked tired too. His regiment had lost another plane.

'I had no choice. I had to keep going, for my daughter. I can't afford to make mistakes. I have to survive, for her. I don't want her to grow up without both of her parents. I want to be there for her, unlike my own father.'

'You never talk about him.'

'There's not much to say. He left when I was three.'

'Oh no.' She wanted to reach out and touch his hand. 'That must have been hard.'

He shrugged. 'I don't have many memories of him. Mama brought me up on her own. She worked three jobs just to put food on the table.'

'Did you miss him when you were a child?'

'I didn't know him. But I have spent my childhood wondering what I was missing. It was my best friend's father who taught me to ride a bicycle and climb trees, who took me fishing and mushroom picking. Mama was always too busy working to do anything with me. I never saw her.'

'She did the best she could.'

'I know. And I love her for that. But I've always wondered how different my childhood would have turned out had my father stayed. Maybe she wouldn't have had to work so much and I would have had a normal home. Now that I have a child of my own, I know I will never understand my father. Nothing could make me leave her. All I want is for this war to end so I can see her again.'

'It won't be long now,' Nina said, tears in her eyes. War would be over soon and Anton would hold his daughter in his arms but Nina would never see her father or brother again. They would never see Katya again. They sat in silence for a bit, lost in their sadness. Then she said, 'I remember the day Mama and Papa brought newborn Vlad from the hospital like it was yesterday. Katya was at our apartment. My grandmother was looking after us and we were playing with some dolls. When we heard the key in the door, we were so excited, we dropped the dolls on the floor and ran. I couldn't wait to see my new baby sister. I was convinced it was going to be a girl. Katya was going to be so jealous. She already had two younger siblings but they were boys and all she talked about was how annoying they were.'

Anton smiled. 'She loved her baby brothers so much.'

'I know. When I learnt Vlad was a boy, I refused to have anything to do with him. Mama asked if I wanted to hold the baby and I said no thank you, I will hold the next one but only if it's a girl. My parents laughed but I couldn't stop crying. I felt betrayed. I was expecting a new best friend. How could I be friends with a boy? I couldn't braid his hair or dress him in pretty dresses. I thought boys were silly.'

'How old were you?'

'Four.' She fell quiet, thinking of the excitement of that day, of the sinking feeling in the pit of her stomach, the sudden realisation that her life would never be the same again and from that moment on she would have to share her parents with this squirmy little creature who did nothing but scream and sleep.

'And then what happened?' Anton prodded.

'Vlad started crying. And crying and crying. No one could settle him, no matter what they did. They sang to him, he screamed louder. They offered him a feed, he screamed louder. Finally, I said, "Fine, give him to me." Carefully, they handed my baby brother to me, all wrapped up like a parcel, only his tiny face visible. The face was red and twisted and angry. He wailed so hard, my ears hurt. "What is it, little one?" I said to him. "Why are you so upset? Is it because you are a boy and not a girl? I'm upset too. But don't worry, it will be all right." Miraculously, he stopped crying and looked at me with his tiny blue eyes, like he was wondering who I was. The grown-ups were amazed I managed to calm him down. But I didn't care, I was too busy watching his little face, his open mouth, his eyes like buttons. I felt his weight in my arms and my heart melted. That was the moment I fell in love with him. He was the love of my life. He was the best boy.'

'And he grew up to be the best man. A hero.'

'He grew up to be my best friend.' Nina was sobbing, no longer able to talk, while Anton whispered that everything was going to be fine, that he was there for her, that he would always be there for her.

Chapter 12

August 1943

In an abandoned shed not far from their new airfield, Nina curled up on her bed of straw, clasping the wooden box that contained Vlad's Hero of the Soviet Union medal. She was afraid someone would steal it when she was asleep or away on a mission, so she started taking it everywhere with her. It was in bed with her as she tossed and turned through her sleepless nights. And it was in the cockpit next to her when she brought death to the Nazis. In the world where possessions no longer mattered, where she had nothing and cared for nothing, the box had become her only treasure, as if holding on to it meant she could hold on to her brother a little bit longer.

Nina hadn't seen Anton in a couple of days. They had been flying crazy hours, with not a moment to themselves, no time to rest and recover and remind themselves they were human beings and not machines destined to kill.

She missed seeing Anton's face. 'Maybe it's for the best,' she whispered to herself. Something strange happened to her whenever he was around. Her throat went dry and her heart accelerated. Despite the darkness of grief, she felt a sparkle of joy at the sight of him. And every time she saw him, she felt a stab of guilt. What was she doing? What was she even thinking? Anton was Katya's. He would never be hers.

The girls slept peacefully next to Nina. It felt like the middle of the night. Suddenly, the light of a torch broke through the darkness, blinding her. She blinked. There was a shadow behind the light and it looked like it was swaying or dancing on the spot. A loud whisper filled the stables. 'Girls, wake up! I need your help!'

When the torch moved sideways and the light was no longer in her eyes, Nina recognised Yulia Siniza. Her face was burning with unfamiliar passion and her cheeks were red. Nina had never seen her this animated.

The rest of the girls continued to sleep.

'You might want to speak louder if you want to wake them,' said Nina. 'Sometimes I have to shoot my weapon up in the air to force them to get up, especially Zhenya.'

Yulia shouted, 'Wake up! I have something to tell you.'

The girls groaned.

Yulia shook Zhenya, who swore under her breath and rolled over. Yulia shone the light in her face and shook her one more time. Then she shook the other girls. One by one, they began to stir, grumbling unhappily.

'What's happening?' Masha cried. 'Are the Germans attacking?' She jumped to her feet, reaching for her overalls.

'No, no, nothing like that. Don't worry, it's not an emergency,' said Yulia.

'If it's not an emergency, why are you waking us up so early?' Zhenya sat up and glared at Yulia. Her hair was a mess and her eyes were round. She glanced at her watch. 'What time is it? Four o'clock. I've only had two hours of sleep.' She rolled her eyes and lay down, covering herself with her shawl.

Yulia tap-danced on the spot. 'I just looked at the map . . .'

'In the middle of the night? Don't you have anything better to do?' asked Masha, throwing a handful of straw at Yulia.

'Yes, like sleep,' said Zhenya, stretching and closing her eyes.

'No, no, don't go back to sleep,' Yulia pleaded. 'Look!' She spread the map on the ground, twitching with excitement. The girls leaned closer to see better. 'We are here.' Yulia pointed with her finger. 'And this village here is Lomonosovo.'

'So what?' said Zhenya. 'What does Lomonosovo have to do with us?'

'If you let me finish, I'll tell you. Just before the Germans occupied Odessa, my parents moved east. I got one letter from them and the post stamp said Lomonosovo. My parents are only forty kilometres away. I could fly there and back in an hour. I could see my mama and papa.' Yulia wiped the tears of joy off her face. 'Can you imagine the look on Mama's face when she sees me standing on her porch? She will have the shock of her life.'

'Who is going to let you go?' asked Zhenya.

'That's why I need you. I want you to convince *Batya*.'

'We'll help you. But why couldn't it wait another hour, so we could get more sleep?' Zhenya complained. But even as she said it, she had the biggest smile on her face. One of the hardest things for these girls was being away from their families, without a word, without a sign, week after week, month after month as they went out every morning and cheated death. These women, who risked their lives every minute of every day, lived for the moment in the distant future when they would hold their parents, partners and children in their arms. Everything they did was to bring this moment closer. And not a single one of them knew if they would live long enough to see that day.

The girls found Markov in the mess tent, leaning over his maps, a spoon in one hand, a pen in the other. A plate of barley was in front of him. He saw the girls and smiled. 'Must be my lucky day. An actual spoon.' He lifted his hand and waved at them. Then he noticed the tense expression on their faces. 'You are up early. What can I do for you?'

206

The girls exchanged glances. Yulia blushed and stared at her feet. Zhenya said in her most serious and official tone, 'Sir, permission for First Lieutenant Siniza to fly to Lomonosovo, forty kilometres away, to visit her parents.'

Markov looked from Zhenya, who was watching him with an impatient expression on her face, to Yulia, who was red in the face and not meeting his gaze. 'I see.' He glanced at his map, as if searching for the tiny village of Lomonosovo.

Yulia jumped to attention. 'Please, sir. I will only be one hour, there and back. I want to hug my mama and papa, tell them I'm still alive, kiss them on the cheek. It's been two years since I've seen them.'

Markov shook his head. 'The Germans are too close. You'll be risking your life. You'll be risking the plane.'

'We risk our lives every time we get inside the cockpit. How would you feel if your parents were this close and you couldn't see them?'

'I would feel devastated.' Markov nodded and smiled. 'Very well. You have one hour. There and back.'

Yulia squealed with delight and jumped on Markov's neck, almost knocking him off his chair. 'Thank you, sir! I will never forget this, for as long as I live. Thank you for being so kind.'

Markov patted her on the back uncomfortably. His face was pink. 'Now, now,' he said.

Soon the word got out and everyone in the regiment turned up to see Yulia off. Some pilots brought chocolate from their precious supplies, others soap or bread. One male navigator from 10th Leningrad brought a soft bunny that had belonged to his niece. Another brought a book of his favourite poems. By the time Yulia was ready to fly, the cockpit was filled with presents for Yulia's parents.

Everyone had tears in their eyes when the plane was taxying out. 'Give our love to your parents,' they shouted. 'Tell them to hold on. We are fighting for them.'

'Thank you,' said Yulia, smiling. 'I can't wait to see them! Today is the happiest day of my life.'

Yulia's navigator, Ira, waved to the crowd. The regiment cheered. They knew they would remember this moment forever – watching one of their comrades fly off to embrace her family.

Nina completed four missions that day. It was almost evening but there was no sign of Yulia and Ira. Nina could see the tension on Markov's face as he looked up in the sky. 'I gave her an hour. What's taking them so long?' There was no anger in his voice, only concern.

Finally, a small dot of a plane appeared. By the sound of the engine Nina knew it was a Pe-2. Markov's face relaxed. As he watched the aircraft get closer, he smiled. 'Finally.'

When the plane landed, it was Ira who jumped out of the pilot's seat.

'What's wrong with Yulia? What happened?' asked Nina.

Ira shook her head, too upset to talk. When Yulia appeared, her face was red and her eyes damp. The girls rushed to her side.

'Oh, honey,' said Nina, hugging Yulia. 'Your parents weren't there? You couldn't find them?' Yulia collapsed in Nina's arms and started crying. *Oh no,* thought Nina. *Did Yulia just learn that her parents had died?* Her heart was breaking for her friend. She knew first-hand how much it hurt.

Ira said, 'We found her parents. They were overjoyed to see her. They kissed and hugged her for hours and refused to let her go. Everyone in the village came running to the plane. They were very grateful for the presents. Yulia's mother kept saying how happy she was. She didn't know if Yulia was alive, until now.'

In Nina's arms, Yulia became inconsolable. 'What's wrong, darling?' asked Nina. 'You saw your parents. They are well and alive. You are so lucky.'

Yulia rubbed her eyes until they looked raw. It took a few minutes before she calmed down enough to be able to talk. 'I couldn't bear to say goodbye to them. It killed me, having to say goodbye. I kept hugging my mama and papa and I didn't want to go. All I could think about was, what if it's the last time I see them?'

'Nonsense, Lieutenant Siniza,' said Markov. 'We are pushing the Germans on all fronts. Soon you will see your parents again.'

In the evening, Anton came to see her. 'How was your day? Here, I got you some tea.' He grinned and his eyes sparkled.

Nina couldn't look at his face. Staring at the buttons of his uniform, she pushed the flask away. 'My day was too long. I have no energy even for tea.'

'Would you like me to walk you to the dugout?' He offered her his hand.

'No, thank you. It's a warm night. I think I'll go to sleep right here, on this grass. We'll talk tomorrow, all right?'

'All right. Sleep well. Are you sure you don't need anything?'

'I'm sure.'

'Till tomorrow, then.'

But tomorrow was a blur of explosions and enemy fire under her wings, and after the sun went down, the girls asked Nina if she would like to join them for an evening of songs and guitar by the fire. She agreed, throwing one regretful glance at her plane where Anton would be looking for her. Later that evening, he came asking for her but she pretended she was asleep.

They had been friends for so many years. How could she find the words to explain to him why she couldn't see him anymore? How could she tell him that in the last couple of weeks everything had changed, that it all felt different, that something strange happened to her when he was around? An unfamiliar feeling grabbed her by the throat and wouldn't let go, wouldn't give her a moment of peace. She couldn't let this feeling take control. Katya was like a sister to her. Buried deep inside Nina's heart was a small hope that she was still alive. If there was even the slightest chance that her friend could return, however improbable, how could Nina claim Katya's husband for herself? Every time she glanced at Anton, every time he glanced at her, every time her heart beat faster at the sight of him, she felt like she was betraying her friend.

One morning she caught a glimpse of him in the mess, getting his porridge. She stood still for a moment, her hand on her mouth, and watched the back of his head and the familiar curve of his neck. He must have sensed her gaze because he turned around and waved. Uncertainly, she waved back.

'Nina! I haven't seen much of you in the last few days. How have you been?'

'Fine, fine. Busy. So tired.'

'I've been looking for you.'

'Yes, the girls told me. I was meaning to . . .' She looked at her hands, unable to continue.

He came closer, peering into her face. 'I've been worried about you.'

'Don't worry. I'm doing great. Markov keeps us busy. I have no energy for anything else. No energy to think. Thank God.' She took a step back, staring at the floor. 'I have to run. Our commander hates it when we are late.'

'I'll come and see you tonight. We can talk then.'

'I can't tonight. I promised the girls . . .'

'Tomorrow night?'

'Maybe.'

She was halfway across the mess tent when he called her. 'Nina?'

She didn't turn around because she didn't want him to see her tears. But she slowed down and said, 'Yes?'

'Have I done something? To upset you?'

'No, of course not.' She forced a smile, spun around and waved. 'I'll see you later.'

Another exhausting day, another empty evening without Anton. If only she could put one foot in front of the other, go through the motions without feeling, without thinking, survive another day, get through another night, bomb the Nazis and not betray Katya. If only she could stop her heart from breaking.

Chapter 13

August 1943

Nina was sitting with her back to her plane and her face to the road, thinking about Anton. Today was particularly tough, with the Germans determined to shoot her plane out of the sky. She had been avoiding Anton for a week and finally he had stopped looking for her, perhaps sensing that she needed some space. She missed seeing him like she would miss a limb.

Today especially she needed to talk to him. She had a dream about her mother and wanted to share it with someone. It was more than a dream, it was a memory, of Mama's kind face, her yellow dress flying up like a parachute as she spun, of little Vlad's voice shouting, 'More, more, more – don't stop spinning Mama,' and of Mama laughing and saying she was too dizzy to continue. 'Spin the other way,' pleaded Vlad, 'then you won't feel so dizzy anymore.' And Mama did.

A figure appeared across the clearing, walking fast. Nina beamed, lifting her hand in greeting, hoping it was Anton and instantly feeling guilty. She would have jumped to her feet, if only she had the energy. As the figure approached, her smile faded, her hand fell to her side and her heart filled with disappointment. The person running towards her wasn't as tall or broad-shouldered as Anton. It was someone else.

'Tim! What are you doing here?' She smiled at the pink-faced boy who once upon a time had made fun of them. Over the last few months, he had become a good friend.

'Looking for you.'

There was something in his face, a frown, a hesitation that she didn't like. Instantly, she tensed up. 'Did something happen?'

'I'm afraid I have bad news.'

Her heart sank. She had a bad feeling all day, and she had done her best to ignore it. 'What is it?'

'Two planes were shot down by the Germans this morning. One of them was Oleg's.' He paused as if he didn't want to continue.

Oleg was Anton's best friend. And Vlad's. 'Oleg's? Oh no! Is he . . .?' She couldn't continue.

Tim shook his head, his shoulders slumped. 'They found his body inside the cockpit.'

'Oh no.' She blinked fast to ward off tears. 'You said two planes. And the other?' She held her breath, waiting for the answer. Oleg usually flew in a pair with Anton. *Please God, no*, she thought.

'Anton's.' All air left her lungs. She couldn't breathe and couldn't say anything. Her face must have gone white because Tim pressed her hand and said, 'We don't know anything for sure. They haven't found him yet.'

Breathing hard, short desperate breaths that failed to fill her lungs with air, Nina looked away from Tim. She wanted to scream. 'How did it happen?'

'They were protecting the railroad station where the Red Army soldiers were boarding a train to the front when the Luftwaffe struck. There were forty of them. Forty against two. I'm very sorry.' Tim looked close to tears.

'You are right. We don't know anything yet. There's still hope.' She refused to believe Anton was gone too. He was the only one she had left.

213

'Of course.' In Tim's eyes she could see he didn't hold any illusions.

When Tim left, she remained in the grass, leaning on the wheel of her plane, staring into space. She didn't even try to sleep. When the girls found her in the morning, she was ready to pass out from exhaustion.

The controls shook in Nina's hands. The sirens were deafening. The gunfire, the shells, the explosions. They were all determined to disorient her, make her lose all senses, destroy her the way they had destroyed Katya, her father and brother. And now Anton. Every fibre of her body was screaming in pain. Every explosion made her heart burst, every flash of light made her cry out. As if through a storm she heard Dasha's shrieking. 'What are you doing? We are not flying straight!'

That wasn't surprising because Nina couldn't see straight. It was fortunate no German fighters crossed her path or she would have rammed them in her Pe-2, the rage inside her was so intense. The rage and the grief.

She had already lost everyone she loved. She couldn't bear to lose Anton.

Miraculously, they made it to the target and back safely. Nina flew eight missions that day but couldn't remember the details of a single one. It was all a blur. Afterwards, she heard there was a search mission going out to look for Anton and asked if she could join it. Five of them went in a truck, searching through the bombed-out countryside. In the soft light of the late afternoon sun, golden fields of wheat stretched in front of them as far as the eye could see. It looked peaceful and serene, if it wasn't for the occasional bomb crater or the sound of the siren or the noise of a distant battle. Nina didn't see or hear any of it. All she cared about was finding Anton. Finding him alive. What were the chances? If he was still breathing, wouldn't he have found a way to get in touch with the regiment by now?

They were about to turn back when the driver stopped the truck. 'There, under those trees,' he said. 'I can see something.'

Nina looked at the trees in the far distance. The sun was going down, its last rays reflecting off something metallic. A downed plane. Nina's heart nearly stopped. As the men ran towards the wreckage, she couldn't move. She stood with her hand on her heart for a few moments, delaying the inevitable. Then she started to run too, trying to catch up to the men.

The plane was a mess of mangled metal. No one could have survived the crash.

'Is it him? Is it Anton?' asked one of the men.

'It's him,' said Nina quietly. She could see the red letters on the plane: *For Katya!*

She closed her eyes and prayed, silent tears running down her face, the familiar dread spreading through her veins like poison. An image sprang to her mind, of his kind eyes as he held her in the field hospital after her brother had died, telling her he would always be there for her and would never leave her. Now she was truly alone in the world.

What was she even thinking, avoiding him these last few days, wasting the precious few moments they had together? It was war. The same rules didn't apply anymore because every minute could be their last.

'He's not in it,' she heard someone's voice that barely registered through the screaming inside her head.

With a shudder, she opened her eyes. 'What?'

'Anton is not in it. He must have parachuted out.'

'We need to find him. Search the area. He might be hurt,' she cried.

'It's getting dark. We'll have to come back tomorrow.'

'What if tomorrow is too late?' she whispered. But she knew the man was right. The chances of finding anyone in the dark were close to zero. Still, she refused to leave, forcing the men to continue searching, and together they walked blindly for an hour with their torches blazing, shouting Anton's name. They didn't find him.

Getting back inside that truck and driving away from him felt like a betrayal to Nina, like she was abandoning Anton to his fate and going back to safety, like she had once abandoned Katya. When they returned to base, she stumbled out of the truck and lay down on the grass. She didn't have the strength to move a muscle and didn't even stir when Dasha asked if she was all right or when Zhenya brought her a cup of tea. She didn't say a word when she heard Dasha tell the ground crew she hadn't been herself that day and needed to rest.

She didn't need to rest. She needed to know that Anton was safe.

Only when she heard Tim's voice did she open her eyes.

'Nina, can you hear me? I have good news.'

She sprang up with such force, she hurt her neck. 'What is it?'

'A telegram! Anton is in a field hospital in Bolotovo, five kilometres away.'

'Is he alive? Is he going to be alright?'

'He's alive. That's all I know. Wait, where are you going?'

'I'm going to see him!'

'You can't go now. You just flew for ten hours straight. I'm surprised you are still awake.'

'Try and stop me,' she cried, feeling suddenly like she had grown a pair of wings, like she had turned into her loyal Pe-2 and was flying with all her speed on the most important mission of her life.

It was dark in the makeshift hospital, as if not a glimmer of hope could get inside its flimsy walls of straw and mud. It was damp and cold, and dirt fell from the ceiling, landing on the men's faces. There were no windows and no clock, nothing to say what time of day it was. A lone candle trembled on a table strewn with dressings and syringes. A few beds had been placed close together. Nina wondered if it was enough for the stream of wounded coming here. She suspected it wasn't. On the beds, the men were groaning, calling for help, asking for a glass of water, something for the pain, a nurse to check on them or simply talk to them. Nina stopped at the entrance, overwhelmed. For a moment, she couldn't see anything while her eyes adjusted to darkness. And then she noticed him. He was lying on the bed in the far corner, his eyes closed, not groaning, nor asking for anything. He looked lost and pale. Her hands trembled at the sight of him.

Crossing the tent, she approached his bed, gently placing her hand on his. 'Anton,' she whispered. 'Are you awake?' He opened his eyes. Relief flooded through her. She could barely breathe. She thought she had lost him and here he was, smiling at her. She smiled back. 'What a fright you gave me. How are you feeling?'

'Amazed I'm still alive. A little sore.' He lifted himself up and groaned in pain. 'Happy to see you.'

'Don't move. You'll hurt yourself.'

'I couldn't move even if I wanted to. I feel like I'm a hundred years old. Everything hurts.'

'No wonder. They say you fought forty German fighter planes. Is that true?'

'Forty sounds about right. I didn't have time to count. Oleg was there too. Did he make it back?'

'He didn't make it. I'm sorry,' she said in her smallest voice. She wished she had better news for him. She couldn't bear to see him sad.

He closed his eyes. 'The last thing I remember is watching from the ground as Oleg was still fighting. Then I fainted. When I came to, I was here. Red Army soldiers picked me up.'

'Thank God you are alive. It's a miracle. God was looking out for you yesterday.'

'Yes, but not for Oleg.' Anton's voice trembled as he spoke. 'I saw the face of the German pilot who brought my plane down. He was only a young boy. When I jumped, I expected he would shoot my parachute down. But he didn't. He just turned around and left.'

'He spared your life. Why do you think he did that?'

Anton shrugged. 'Maybe he felt sorry for me. Not all of them are animals. They are just doing their job, like us.'

Nina's heart filled with gratitude to the unknown German pilot. 'Thank God,' she whispered, trying not to think of what could have been.

'I landed hard and hit my head. It's a miracle nothing is broken. I have concussion though.'

'You still remember everything. That's a good sign. You recognised me.' She winked, teasing him, longing to see his smile again.

'How could I not?' For a moment, he watched her in silence. 'Thank you for coming to see me.'

'How could I not?' She took his hand. 'I'm so glad you are all right. Who is going to bring me tea if anything happens to you?' Her heart was bursting with joy, at finding him alive, at being close to him again.

While he slept, she stayed by his side, looking at his face. Finally, she slept too, curled up in a chair by the side of his bed. When she woke up, he was still asleep but it was time for her to go. As she was walking away, she heard him say, 'Be safe out there. And come back to see me. I'll be waiting.'

She heard his words over and over inside her head that day, through German artillery fire and anti-aircraft guns, while Dasha sang in the cockpit behind her and the bomb release hatch screeched in triumph.

There was no more sleeping in the cockpit of her plane as soon as she finished her last mission. No matter how tired she was, she rushed to the field hospital to see him. He always had a smile on his face and a kind word for her, and she would forget about her exhaustion as she listened to him talk about his day. She brought him all her chocolate and he saved his tea for her. She drank it cold, even though she wasn't thirsty. Once, he had a surprise for her. 'Close your eyes,' he said. 'And open your mouth.'

218

'Why?'

'Just do it.'

She did as he asked, trying to spy on him through her eyelashes.

'No peeking,' he said, shaking his finger.

'If I don't peek, how do I know what you are going to do?'

'You just have to trust me.'

She closed her eyes and he placed something in her mouth. When she tasted it, her eyes filled with tears. The sweet taste brought so many happy childhood memories. 'Caramel! Where on earth did you get it?'

'A nice nurse called Klara gave it to me. She's taken a real shine to me.'

'Is she pretty?'

'She's gorgeous.'

'Really?' Nina frowned.

'Really.' Anton grinned. His eyes twinkled. 'Wait, are you jealous?'

'No, of course not.' She went bright red. She *was* jealous and the realisation took her by surprise.

'I think you are.'

She pinched him as hard as she could on his arm. The door opened and an elderly nurse walked in. She was short and round and her hair was grey and curly. 'How is my favourite patient this evening?' she asked.

'Marvellous, thank you, Klara,' Anton replied, smiling. 'Nina here is looking after me.'

The nurse checked his temperature, opened his chart and added a few notes. 'You are recovering fast. Miraculously so. You'll be back at the front in no time.'

When Klara was gone, he winked at Nina and said, 'Why the long face? What's wrong? Still jealous?'

'You are almost all better,' she whispered, suddenly unable to meet his eyes.

'And that makes you sad?'

'No, of course not. But once you get better, they will send you back to fight. I got used to having you here, looked after and safe.'

'I want to go back. I want to fly again. Are you worried?'

'Of course, I'm worried.'

'How do you think I feel, waiting here for you all day, knowing you are out there, in the air, under German fire?' He took her hand and brought it to his lips but stopped short of kissing it. Her heart felt like it would burst out of her ribcage. He pulled her closer. Any moment now his lips would touch hers. She closed her eyes, wanting it, longing for it, and yet, petrified of it. Petrified of what she was feeling.

Just like always, he knew exactly what was bothering her. 'Are you thinking about Katya? Don't. She would want us to be happy. She would want us to go on with our lives.'

Then he was kissing her and suddenly Nina could think of nothing but Anton.

Anton returned to the regiment a few days later. He walked with a slight limp and his shoulder was bothering him. Other than that, it was back to normal, flying from dawn to dusk, risking his life every moment that he was awake. Nina's heart broke a little every time she saw him climb into the cockpit of his fighter plane. She had to remind herself that they were soldiers, that this was what they did, that he worried about her just like she worried about him. One day it would all be over, she kept telling herself. One day they wouldn't have to wake up every morning, wondering if this day would be their last. One day, they would be able to live a normal life. And now she had something to fight for. She was no longer alone. She had Anton and her life had meaning.

One morning, on a rare day off for the regiment, caused by bad weather, Anton came to see her. He brought coffee. 'They ran out of tea,' he said.

'I can't drink that. I will never sleep again.' She never touched coffee, even though she knew it wasn't the caffeine that was keeping her up.

They sat next to each other on her bed. She was staying in a real house for the next few days, a nice change from the dugouts or hastily constructed huts or the damp grass by her plane. Her hostess was a small woman called Natasha, who offered her cut onion on a plate for dinner, saying it cured all ailments. Nina assured her she didn't suffer from any, saying no to the onion.

'I'm glad we are not out there in this weather,' she said. All she could hear was the sound of rain, like a wall of water crashing down. Better than the sound of explosions. 'I intend to stay in bed and not move for the rest of the day.'

'I have a better idea,' said Anton, beaming.

'What?'

'You can come with me in my truck.'

'Where are you going?'

'I'm going to town to pick up some spare parts.'

'You want me to go out in the rain? Absolutely not.' She beamed back. She knew in her heart that not the rain, nor even the Nazi bombs would stop her from joining Anton.

'And I'm going to look at some new planes for the regiment. They are giving us ten brand new Yaks. We waited a long time for this.'

'We need them.' For a few moments they didn't speak, each lost in thought. Nina wondered if Anton was thinking of his comrades who hadn't come back from their missions. Her heart was breaking as she thought of her brother who hadn't come back from his.

'If the weather clears, I'll even be able to fly one of these planes to see if they are as good as they keep promising us.' His eyes lit up like he was a little boy on his birthday, playing with a brand new train set.

His excitement was contagious. 'I would love to come with you. But who is going to let me go?'

221

'I already cleared it with your commander. You can help me with the boxes. Originally, Grinov was supposed to come. But . . .' He fell quiet. Lieutenant Grinov was one of Anton's closest friends in the regiment. A week ago, his plane had been blown up by the Nazis.

'I'm sorry. It's tough, isn't it? Losing so many people close to you.'

He nodded. 'It occurred to me a couple of days ago that I am the longest serving pilot in our regiment. Do you know what that means? Every pilot I started out with is gone. Every single one.'

'Oh no,' she whispered, wondering what it must feel like to be the only one left standing.

As soon as they stepped outside, they were soaked. Nina's boots filled with water. Her cap and uniform were wet. Even the hair under her cap was wet.

Anton took her hand. 'Sorry I dragged you out in this.'

'I don't mind, I . . .' But he didn't let her finish. A moment later, they were kissing in the rain, while thunder clapped overhead. Thunder or bombs? She didn't know and couldn't think straight.

'You look beautiful today, Lieutenant Petrova.'

'Me? I'm a wet rag. I'm wearing a uniform four sizes too big. My boots make my feet look huge.'

'I don't care about any of it.'

She didn't just walk to the truck, she flew. Since they had arrived at the front, her life had consisted of waking up before the sun, fighting hunger and exhaustion, fighting the Nazis, fighting herself and her exhaustion, maybe a few hours of sleep if she was lucky, and then doing it all over again the next day. Day after day, week after week, month after month of the same gruelling routine. A trip? Unheard of. A trip with him? She was so excited, she wanted to sing at the top of her voice. The thought of spending a whole day alone with him made her giddy, like she had drunk too much cheap wine and was dancing in the rain.

All around them was a sea of gold wheat, bowing to the wind. Gold flashes outside the truck window, like a reminder of a different time, a different summer. Occasionally, a black ugly bomb crater that looked out of place, a mangled car, a damaged building. Nina didn't want to see black. It made her heart hurt. Turning away from the window, she watched Anton's face instead as he concentrated on the road. Soon the movement of the truck soothed her and she slept. When she woke up, groggy and confused, she saw they had just arrived outside a grey industrial building that was partially destroyed by bombs.

'Where are we?' she wanted to know, pulling herself up in her seat and rubbing her eyes. She wished the trip would take longer. She had been so exhausted she could sleep for another year.

'The aviation factory.'

While she slept, the storm had passed. There was not a cloud in the sky. They jumped out of the truck onto a small airfield where ten brand new Yak-7 fighter planes were waiting, gleaming in the sun. 'Aren't they beautiful?' whispered Nina.

'And not a single bullet hole on them,' said Anton. His own plane looked like a sieve, with marks like scars telling stories of battles past.

'Not yet,' said Nina. The sun felt hot on her face and his hand felt warm in hers and suddenly all her troubles seemed far away, the gruelling hours of work, the exhaustion, the German bullets.

'Yak-7 are simpler and more powerful than our current Yak-1. More stable in the air and easier to control,' said Anton.

'You will be safer in it,' she said wistfully. There was something about seeing the planes that filled her heart with hope. They were shiny and new and unmarred by war.

A manager ran out of the factory doors to greet them, introducing himself as Vasili and inviting them to share a meal with him.

'Perhaps later,' said Anton. 'I'm eager to fly one of your new planes.'

'Your new planes, you mean? Choose one. Which is to your liking?'

Anton's eyes sparkled and he smiled. 'They all look beautiful. How about this one?' He pointed to the one nearest to them.

'Be my guest,' said the manager.

Anton walked to the aircraft, climbed inside the cockpit, put his headset on and waved. Nina waved back, her heart beating fast. She no longer felt nervous when she got inside her Pe-2. But watching Anton fly off on his fighter plane was a different story. Every time she saw him take off, she couldn't stop the flashes inside her head, the horrible images of her brother's plane hurtling towards the ground and bursting into flames. She told herself she had nothing to fear, not this time. Anton was an expert pilot and besides, he wasn't flying a combat mission today. There were no German planes nearby, ready to fight to the death. What could possibly go wrong?

There was something else she felt as she watched him start the engine and point the plane towards the long runway. Her heart was swelling with pride.

Anton flew in circles over the airfield, the grey factory building and the bombed-out streets. The plane was superb in the air. It handled beautifully and was a pleasure to look at, with its sleek lines and the red stars on its wings.

On the third circle, the plane began to sound differently. Instead of the regular noise of the engine, familiar to Nina like the sound of her own heartbeat, it spluttered and coughed. Nina's hand flew to her mouth. A moment later, she noticed smoke coming out of the engine. Like a wounded bird, the plane took a nose-dive and began to lose altitude. Nina shrieked. Petrified, frozen to the spot and unable to move, she watched as Anton brought the plane to a textbook emergency landing. Thank God the runway was long enough. The length of the runway and his incredible skill as a pilot saved Anton's life.

When the plane came to a stop, Nina ran faster than she'd ever run in her life. 'Are you all right?' she asked as soon as Anton emerged from the cockpit, looking slightly ill at ease.

'I'm fine. Are you all right? Your face is all white.'

She wanted to point out his own white face but she was too relieved, too shaken, too upset, too much of everything. She couldn't speak. She hugged him and pressed her face into his shoulder, fighting tears. For a few moments they stood in silence, in the middle of an unfamiliar airfield, in the middle of war, just the two of them.

Nina heard the manager's voice. 'I'm very sorry . . .'

She spun around. 'What do you think you are doing, comrade? One of our best pilots nearly killed himself on one of your planes. It's sabotage. When this becomes known . . .'

Anton's hand on her shoulder stopped her. 'Don't get angry. Wait till you meet the so-called saboteurs.' He chuckled. 'Take us to the mechanics,' he said to Vasili. 'If you could help me with these boxes, that would be great. I have presents for them.' The men picked up the boxes. Confused, Nina followed the two of them to the workshop, where small boys of nine or ten crouched on the ground. They looked malnourished and small, their faces dull, with circles under their eyes, like they hadn't slept in days.

These were the mechanics assembling fighter planes for the Red Army, Nina realised with shock.

'They are on their lunch break,' said the manager. 'Unfortunately, there's hardly any food for them today.'

'We can fix that,' said Anton, opening one of the boxes. Nina saw loaves of bread and tins of ham.

The boys cried out and ran to Anton. Tiny hands reached for the box, small mouths opened in anticipation, ten pairs of hungry eyes devoured the food Anton had brought them.

'Lieutenant Bogdanov almost killed himself on one of your planes,' said the manager sternly. The excitement vanished and the boys stood mutely, staring at their feet. They looked so pitiful; Nina wanted to cry.

'No harm done,' said Anton. 'I had a fright of my life but I'm still in one piece.' He took out a loaf of bread, broke it into big chunks and distributed it among the boys. Forgetting their embarrassment, they grabbed the bread and tucked in.

Only the smallest boy was too shy to come forward and help himself to the food. He couldn't have been older than five but his body was no bigger than Nina's three-year-old half-brother's. He looked a little like Leo, too, with his big blue eyes and blond hair. Her heart hurting, Nina took a bar of chocolate out of her pocket and approached him. 'Here. For you and your comrades.'

'What is it?' asked the boy suspiciously.

'It's chocolate. Haven't you had it before?'

The boy shook his head, not meeting her gaze.

Nina crouched on the floor next to him, so that her eyes would be level with his eyes. 'What's your name?'

'Sasha.'

She unwrapped the chocolate and broke off a small piece. 'Here, Sasha. Try it. I think you'll like it.'

The boy placed the chocolate in his mouth and closed his eyes. A moment later, his face lit up. He reached his hand out for another piece. Nina gave him the whole bar, wishing she had brought more.

Back in the car, Nina stared out the window. She couldn't talk. All she could see in her mind were the boys' exhausted faces, their empty eyes and skeletal bodies.

The truck was stuck in traffic. By the side of the road moved retreating army divisions. Next to them were the refugees, a never-ending stream of people trying to escape from Hitler and the horrors he brought in his wake. Everything – people, cars, trucks, motorcycles – was moving east, away from the front lines that were constantly shifting. Wounded soldiers staggered ahead, running away from bombed-out hospitals. They raised their crutches and waved their hands, asking for a lift. One after another they climbed into the back of their truck until there was no space to stand but the truck wasn't moving, so they climbed back down and limped away. Cows and horses ambled past, thin and ghoulish, barely able to put one foot in front of the other. Soldiers didn't raise their eyes off the ground as if they were embarrassed.

'Try to sleep,' Anton suggested. 'It's a long way back to base.'

But she couldn't sleep. 'Those poor boys. They should be at school.'

'Yes, in a perfect world, they should be at school. But this isn't a perfect world. There are no men left to operate the factories. All around the country, while their fathers are dying at the front, young boys work themselves to death in factories just like this one.'

Nina shuddered. 'Do they have a choice?'

'Not really. Usually, it's the mothers who bring them there. If they are at the factory, it's one less mouth to feed. They work eighteen hours a day, often without a break.'

Nina thought of her own childhood, of riding her bicycle with Papa and playing piano with Mama, of teaching Vlad how to skate, of ribbons, dance recitals and the smell of cake and cookies baking in their tiny kitchen. 'I can't even imagine what it must be like, growing up like this. Do they even feed them? They looked so hungry. And exhausted.'

'They get three hundred grams of bread a day, if they're lucky.'

'That's not enough for their growing bodies. Especially if they are working so hard.'

'That's why, while we've been stationed nearby, I've been bringing them something extra.'

'You've done this before?' She watched him with admiration, while he watched the road in front of them.

'A few times. When the army can't spare the food, I save half my ration and bring it here.'

'A grown man wouldn't last a week, working this hard on no food. And they are just children. No wonder they make mistakes. It's not a life for them.'

'It's not a life for anyone. It's war. They fall asleep at the machines. They maim themselves. They die from hunger and overwork. They run away to the front because they think it would be easier. And often it is.'

They were moving again through country roads, with fields overgrown and abandoned, villages quiet as if afraid to make a sound, buildings and people devastated and lost in the rain. When they reached a small forest, Anton made a sharp turn. A few minutes after driving down a muddy path under the leaning oak trees, he stopped and turned off the engine.

'Where are we?' asked Nina. 'Why did we stop?'

Anton had the biggest smile on his face. 'It's a surprise. Close your eyes and come out of the truck.'

'If I close my eyes, I won't be able to see where I'm going and then I'll fall.'

'Don't worry. If you fall, I'll catch you. Here, you can hold my hand. Now close your eyes.'

He helped her out of the truck and led her through the foliage to a clearing. She could feel small branches hitting her face and scratching her hands, the sun on her skin, his warm hand holding hers. She didn't know why but suddenly she felt nervous. 'Can I open my eyes now?'

'Yes.'

She looked around and squealed in excitement. 'A lake! You brought me to a lake!'

The lake wasn't large but it looked peaceful and inviting, the water clear like diamonds, as if there was no war raging mere kilometres away. Sunlight reflected off the surface and birch trees stretched their branches over the water in a perfect canopy. It looked so beautiful and serene, Nina thought she was dreaming. She wanted to pinch herself. All she had seen for the last year and a half was the dusty inside of her airplane cockpit, the devastated earth under her wings and death, everywhere she turned. It was hard to believe that this piece of paradise could exist in the midst of all the destruction. Instantly, she wanted to take her boots and clothes off and run to the water, to feel it on her feet and over her body. With the life they led, moving from airfield to airfield, in the air twelve hours a day, with barely time to eat or sleep, she had forgotten what it felt like to be clean.

'Didn't you tell me you couldn't wait for the pump truck to come in two weeks, so you could take a bath? I brought you here, so you wouldn't have to wait that long,' said Anton.

She was speechless as she looked from the lake to his smiling face. 'How do you even know about this place?'

'Unlike you, I don't have a navigator. It's just me in the cockpit. Once in a while, I have to look at my maps.'

Laughing, she threw off her overalls and, in her undergarments, ran to the water. 'I'll race you!' she shouted, jumping in, splashing water at him. 'I win!'

'That's not a fair race. You didn't give me warning. You didn't wait for me.'

'What kind of a race would it be if I waited for you?' She floated on her back, closing her eyes with pleasure. She loved the feeling of water on her skin. It made everything better. Suddenly she forgot about it all – their regiment, the gruelling routine, her fears, even the war. Real life seemed like a million miles away. Here by the lake, it was just Nina and Anton and not another soul around.

He stripped down to his long johns and jumped in. 'Be careful. It gets deep here.'

She stopped. 'How deep? I can't swim.'

'You seem to swim well enough to me.'

'That's because I can touch the bottom. I'm not really swimming, just walking around in water.'

'We used to swim across Moskva River growing up. It's easy.'

'Really? Race you to the other side.'

Moving her hands like pistons, she glided through the water like she was born to it. When she was on the other side, she turned around. He was right behind her, reaching for her, pulling her close. 'I thought you said you couldn't swim.' He ran his hands through her hair.

'I lied.' She grinned. 'I was the city champion at school. Two hundred metres backstroke.'

'Impressive. Any other hidden talents I should know about?'

He kissed her and they slid to the ground, still in the shallow water, waves lapping at her feet. He rose on his elbow, leaning over her and watching her face, as if memorising it like a poem.

'I've never met anyone like you,' he whispered.

Me neither, she wanted to say, if only she could get her breath back. She wanted to ask him about Katya but couldn't bring herself to say her name out loud, to break the magic spell between them. No matter what they did, when they were together under the wing of her plane, when she was thinking of him as she flew towards her target in her Pe-2, even now, alone with him under the brilliant summer sky, Katya was at the back of her mind. She wondered if she was at the back of Anton's mind. Then he kissed her and everything faded away, the lake, the sand they were lying on, the forest around them, Hitler's troops closing in on them, even Katya's disappointed face, it all ceased to exist. All she could see was him.

Afterwards, they lay side by side on the sand. It wasn't close enough. She climbed on his chest and listened for his heart. He threaded his fingers through hers. 'Your hand is tiny. Look how small it is.'

'It's not tiny. Yours is just too big,' she replied, looking at his hand holding hers, at the small scar on his arm, at his broad chest and wide shoulders.

'I can't believe someone so small and feminine can be so brave and selfless.'

'I'm not brave. I'm scared every day.'

'Just because you are scared, doesn't mean you aren't brave. Being scared and going out there anyway, that's real bravery. You girls are heroes. Look what you've achieved.'

'I'm not the hero. You are. I heard you are getting promoted.'

'Captain Bogdanov, at your service.' He laughed, happy and careless by the whispering lake, with Nina in his arms.

She pinched him. 'Is there anything else you are not telling me?'

'No, not at all.'

'Are you sure? I heard something about a medal . . .'

'Oh yes. Oleg and I have been awarded the Order of the Red Star.' He looked away from her, frowning, staring at the trees in the near distance. 'I wish he'd lived to see it.'

She didn't want him to be upset. Hugging him as hard as she could, she asked, 'How long do we have?'

He glanced at his watch. 'Twenty minutes.'

'For the next twenty minutes, let's not talk about the war. Let's not talk about anything sad at all. Instead, tell me your happiest memories.'

Anton wrinkled his nose in concentration. 'Let's see. I was nine. Mama came home from work one day with a puppy. She said she found him sitting in a puddle of water, lost and alone. She felt sorry for him and couldn't walk past. I still remember the feeling, seeing him for the first time, curled up in Mama's hands, squealing softly. My heart nearly burst out of my chest. That puppy became my best friend.'

'What did you name him?'

'Mars. Short for Marseilles. It was Mama's dream to see France. She knew she would never be able to go, of course. She collected stamps, coins, anything to do with France.'

'You miss her.'

He nodded. 'She writes to me every day. Only a few of her letters have reached me but I carry them with me everywhere I go, so that I can feel closer to her.' He patted his pocket. 'Your turn.'

She thought about her life before him. It seemed like a distant memory, fading away like a dream on a foggy morning. 'Flying for the first time. Feeling the controls under my hands, the plane responding to my every whim. Being able to command

231

this amazing machine, to feel this incredible power under my fingertips, to soar through the air, to feel free and light and above everything, even death. To feel immortal, like I'm going to live forever. I can't even put it into words, this feeling.'

He brushed a loose strand of hair out of her eyes. 'I know what you mean. I second that.'

'Your turn.'

He was quiet for a moment. 'Being accepted to university to study engineering. I was told I would never get in because the competition was so fierce. I worked hard for a year and I made it. That was a good feeling.'

'Is it something you still want to do after the war is over?'

Anton nodded. 'Absolutely. Engineering is my passion. I take after my grandfather. He built bridges and tunnels all over the Soviet Union. He was a genius.'

'You want to be like him when you grow up?' she asked, her eyes twinkling.

'I do.' His eyes twinkled back.

'My happy memory is every moment I spent with Katya. She was so much fun to be with. She always had an amazing ability to take my mind off what was happening at home. When Papa remarried, it was tough for me and Vlad. We tried to spend as little time at home as possible. Katya and I became inseparable.'

She fell silent, looking at the heavy clouds over their heads. It started raining again. She barely noticed. Anton said, 'My happiest memory is, you and I.'

Her heart catching, she stroked the palm of his hand. 'My happiest memory is . . . today!' She beamed.

'Mine too.'

Her voice barely a whisper, she said, 'Promise me something.'

'Of course. Anything.'

She watched him for a moment, her hand on his breathtaking face. 'Promise not to get yourself killed.'

'I can't make you a promise I'm not sure I can keep.'

'We've lost so many people we love. I couldn't bear it if I lost you too.'

He wiped the tears off her face and smiled. 'I promise to do my best to survive. And I thought we weren't talking about the war.'

'We are the only two left,' she whispered, her lips in his hair.

I've never felt like this before, she wanted to tell him. She wished she could stop time and stay like this forever, just the two of them, alive and happy and together. She didn't want to go back to the life where every moment could be their last.

Chapter 14

August 1943

It was dreary and wet, and although it was six in the morning, the sky over their heads was dark, threatening more rain. Nina rubbed her hands together. She thought with longing of the carefree day on the lake with Anton. A rare moment of joy in the horror of war, like a faraway dream that had never happened, only a week ago and yet so irretrievably in the past. Even though it was still summer, she was always cold. Maybe once the war was over, she could live somewhere warm. She made a note to herself to ask Anton when she saw him that evening. Would he like to live in the mountains of Caucasus where the sun was bright and winters mild, where the sun was scorching in summers and all around were water and mountains, like giants holding up the horizon?

The regiment was back in the same area where they had fought in July, with a big difference. In July, they were retreating. Now, they were gaining ground, pushing the Germans further west, away from Kursk. Nina's heart soared with every inch of earth they clawed back from the Nazis. They followed the front in their Pe-2s and everywhere they went, people welcomed them with tears of joy. They hugged and kissed them and were ready to give them their last bite to eat. Unfortunately, they didn't have much and often it was the pilots who shared their rations with the villagers.

Every evening after Nina's last mission, Anton was waiting for her, just like before. To the rest of the regiment, nothing had changed. But to the two of them, everything was different.

They were stationed in a village called Anisovskaya. Every morning, they waited outside an abandoned school for a truck to pick them up and take them to the airfield where another gruelling day of work would begin. Today, like most days, the truck was late.

Nina wished she was still in bed. All she wanted was to close her eyes and sleep and not wake up until the war ended. She often complained about the lack of sleep to Anton. 'We'll sleep when it's all over,' he told her. 'We'll do nothing but sleep.'

'*Nothing* but sleep?' she said, winking, tickling him.

'We'll never leave our bed.'

'I like the sound of that.'

She stared into the distance, hoping to see the headlights.

'Ten minutes late,' grumbled Zhenya, looking at her watch. '*Batya* will kill us. We should have walked there.'

'We'd still be walking an hour later,' said Nina. The airfield was five kilometres away. 'And look.'

Faint lights appeared in the distance.

'Great,' muttered Zhenya. 'Better late than never.'

The lights twinkled, disappearing behind a bend in the road, only to reappear moments later. Dark clouds moved swiftly over their heads, like they had a mind of their own, like they had somewhere important to be. Pine trees waved their bare branches in the wind, as if in greeting. Nina felt the first drops of rain on her face.

When the lights approached, Nina saw that it wasn't a truck at all but a small car, covered in dirt. It stopped next to the girls and a moment later a door opened. An expectant silence fell over the squadron.

A young girl jumped out. At first, Nina couldn't see her very well. The streetlights weren't working and the sun was just beginning to rise behind the clouds, throwing its silver rays over the few rickety buildings, the road and the women's faces. In this pale light Nina saw that the girl wore a large uniform that fit her poorly. Her hair was short. In her hands she held a small trunk. Was it a new recruit for the regiment? Nina blinked and saw the girl approach, slowly and uncertainly at first, as if she was lost and didn't know if she had come to the right place. And then she cried out, waved and started to walk faster, limping and wincing as if every step brought unbearable pain. There was something familiar about her. The way she held her head, the way she was moving. It couldn't be? Nina's hands began to shake.

'Katya!' someone shouted. 'Katya Bogdanova!'

Suddenly, every woman was running and Nina was running too, as fast as she could through the mud, her feet getting stuck. She was screaming Katya's name and pushing the others out of the way to hug her friend. Katya looked thinner than Nina had ever seen her. Her cheeks were hollow. Her eyes were dark but her smile was unmistakeably hers. It was the same smile Nina had grown to love when they were children aged four and five and six, playing together in the sandpit. Katya was there, in front of them, and she was alive. Nina's heart raced with joy at the sight of her face. She held her and tickled her, while Katya laughed and cried and hugged her.

'You are here,' exclaimed Nina, wanting to pinch herself and pinch Katya to make sure she was real. 'I can't believe it.'

'What took you so long?' asked Zhenya.

'We didn't think we'd see you again,' said Nina.

'I'm back! I can hardly believe it myself.' Katya's eyes were round like saucers as she looked at the girls and the village behind them.

When the first wave of greetings subsided, Katya pulled Nina aside and asked, 'And Anton? Is he all right?' She took a sharp breath, as if afraid to ask the question. 'Is he alive?' Her eager mouth remained open as she waited for Nina's reply.

All Nina could do was nod. Her joy deflated a little.

The truck appeared and the girls had to go. Nina watched through the dirty window as Katya stood in the rain, waving. A lone figure with a sad smile on her face.

PART THREE

Chapter 15

Nina and Katya sat side by side under the wing of Nina's Pe-2. Having lived through the last six months, having mourned for one hundred and eighty days and nights, having found the courage to say goodbye to her friend, finally convincing herself she was never coming back, having Katya in front of her now felt surreal to Nina, like she would wake up any moment and find that it was all a dream. After the day she had just had, everything looked blurry to her exhausted eyes and Katya's face faded in and out, like she was about to disappear. Nina didn't want her to disappear. She took her hand.

'I'm sorry about Vlad,' said Katya, stroking Nina's hair gently. It felt comforting, and suddenly, Nina wanted to cry. Katya put her arm over Nina's shoulders. 'And about your papa. I'm sorry I wasn't there for you when you needed me.'

An image sprung to mind, of her brother's plane hurtling to the ground in flames and her body collapsing in Anton's arms. Of screaming in pain in front of everybody, wailing in agony. Of still screaming in pain inside her head, every minute of every day and night, except when Anton held her. 'It's not your fault.

Tell me about yourself. I saw you jump out of the plane. Your parachute was on fire. What happened?'

'I had a bad fall but I was lucky. Some soldiers picked me up before the Nazis arrived. They took me to a field hospital. I had twenty broken bones in my feet.'

'I didn't know we had twenty bones in our feet.'

Katya chuckled. 'About that many. And every single one of them, broken. I will never walk without a limp again. I had first degree burns all over my arms.' She pulled the sleeve of her uniform up and showed the scars to Nina. 'These will never heal. I'll have them for the rest of my life, forever reminding me of that day.'

'How are you feeling now?'

'Not great. Don't tell anyone but I am not supposed to fly again,' said Katya. 'I have a certificate in my pocket stating I need further medical care.'

'If you are not well, you need to rest. Why didn't you go home?'

'I did. I spent two weeks with my family before returning to the front. The best two weeks of my life.'

'Was Tonya happy to see you?'

Katya's face lit up. 'So happy. When I held her in my arms, I could barely breathe. I knew this was where I belonged, with my little girl, looking after her. Not at the front fighting the Germans. She cried so much when we were saying goodbye, I thought my heart would burst. But I had to come back. I needed to know Anton was safe. I'm here because of him.'

Nina was quiet for a long time. Her chest ached. Finally, she said, 'Why didn't you write?'

'I did. You didn't get my letters? I wrote about a hundred. I even telegraphed.'

'We didn't receive any of it. We searched for you.' Nina thought of Nazi tanks making the earth move under their feet. She thought of Luftwaffe planes and German bullets raining on her, Vlad and Anton as they made their way through burning countryside, looking for Katya. Of dead bodies scattered on snow-white fields that were no longer pure but streaked with blood. Of a tiny baby crying on his dead mother's chest. She shuddered. 'We didn't think we would ever see you again.'

'What was it like after I was gone? Did Anton miss me?'

'Of course he missed you. He was heartbroken. The first couple of months were especially hard. I've never seen him like that.'

'I missed him too. I can't wait to see him again, to put my arms around him. Six months in hospital had been hell. Sometimes the only thing that kept me going was the thought of seeing him and Tonya again. I didn't know if I would find him alive. I worried about him constantly. I made a promise to myself. When I come back, it will be a new start for the two of us. No more arguments. Life is too short for that. Having survived a horrific fall, having found him alive, I feel like we've been given a second chance. It's a miracle.'

Unable to meet her friend's gaze, Nina stared at the trees swaying in the breeze. Katya leaned on her shoulder. Soon her breathing slowed down. She fell asleep.

Nina thought of the last time she had seen Anton. It was only yesterday but felt like a lifetime ago. They spoke about their future after the war, planning it in detail as if they knew for certain that they had a future. He said they would buy a house and live together, just the three of them. 'You don't mind if Tonya lives with us, do you?'

'Of course, I don't mind. I love Tonya like she is my own. She is the daughter of two of my favourite people in the world. Katya's, who is like a sister to me. And yours.'

As she listened to Katya's troubled breathing, she remembered Tonya's distraught face as she watched her father leaving for the front. Nina's future with Anton was forever gone, melted away like an illusion, like October snow in the morning sun. But Tonya would have her mother and father back.

It's all that matters, thought Nina, wiping her tears away. *It's all that matters.*

She saw his silhouette in the dark. His steps were heavy, his gaze down. Every moment of his day, he had to be alert and focussed as he fought his fearsome duels, like one of Dumas' musketeers on his faithful metal steed, riding out to gamble with death. And now that his day was finally over, he would barely have the energy to talk. Still, he came to see her every evening, instead of getting some rest. Every time she watched him walk to her, her heart raced inside her chest and her own hard day fell away. Seeing his face was the one ray of sunshine in her joyless existence. Every evening in his arms, all the tension left her body and she felt at peace. They had survived another day, despite the odds. One more day together. What a gift.

Sometimes she imagined they were an ordinary couple living an ordinary life. She waited for him to come home from work, while whistling a popular tune and cooking his favourite meal. He stepped through the door, put his briefcase down and said, 'Honey, I'm home!' And she ran to him, throwing herself in his arms, saying how much she had missed him. She had hoped that one day this dream would become a reality. She longed for the ordinary the way she had once longed for a life of adventure.

But now that Katya was back, everything was different. Nina would have to clench her fists, grit her teeth and say goodbye to the one who had kept her going these last few months through hell on earth. She didn't know how she was going to do it, didn't know how to go on without him. All she knew was that she would find a way, even if it broke her heart.

She watched him closely in the near darkness, watched his face melt into a smile. This moment was all they had. Any minute now he would see Katya and then he would never smile at Nina this way again.

'Hi, darling,' he said to her, his voice heavy with exhaustion, his eyes twinkling at the sight of her. 'Hi, Dasha.' He nodded to Katya, who was still leaning on Nina's shoulder.

'That's not . . .' Nina started saying but didn't have a chance to finish.

Katya opened her eyes and cried out at the sight of Anton. She leapt to her feet and ran to him, pushing Nina out of the way. Her arms went around Anton's neck. Her lips were on his lips. 'Anton!'

He caught her and held her close. On his face Nina saw surprise, confusion, joy and a trace of regret as he glanced in Nina's direction and quickly looked away. His face beaming, he said, 'I can't believe it. I just can't believe it. Let me look at you.'

Nina couldn't take it, she turned away from them. 'I will leave you two to catch up,' she said quietly. They didn't seem to hear her. She left them alone together, walking away from the airfield in the dark. Her heart hurting, she walked five kilometres back to their quarters and collapsed into her bed, exhausted but unable to sleep.

The regiment lined up on the airfield. The sun was rising, its shy light reflecting off the golden fields in the far distance. The rain was like tears on Nina's face. Katya was next to her, like a miracle, like living proof that God existed and He hadn't abandoned them in war. How many times had Nina stood alone in a crowd of women, on a battle-torn airfield somewhere, wishing Katya was still with her? How many times had she prayed for her return?

Somewhere on the other side of the airfield, the men were beginning their day too. If Nina turned to the right and stood on her tiptoes, she might spot Anton, his steps heavy in the mud as he walked to his brand new Yak-7 fighter plane, the plane he was so proud of and enamoured with, the plane that reminded her of their one day of bliss during war. Although Nina thought of him and nothing else, she didn't even glance his way because Katya was back.

Major Markov strolled in front of them with the biggest smile on his face. Nina stared. It had been a while since she had seen their commander smiling.

'Oh no,' whispered Katya. 'Bayonet is still here. I forgot all about him. Poor you, how did you survive eight months with him as your commander?'

'We don't call him Bayonet anymore,' said Nina, laughing at the old nickname.

'What do you call him?'

'*Batya*,' Nina said with respect. 'Once you get to know him better, you'll understand.'

Markov stopped in front of them. 'Today is a special day for our regiment. We have suffered many losses over the last couple of months but it's not every day that one of our comrades comes back to us. It is my pleasure to welcome Katya Bogdanova back to the regiment. Katya is an excellent navigator. She has already made our regiment proud. We are delighted to have you back.'

Katya beamed as the girls cheered and shouted. Her eyes scanned the crowd. 'So many new faces,' she whispered to Nina. 'So many people are gone. What happened to them?'

Nina didn't reply. She didn't have to. By the look on her face, Katya knew the answer. Her eyes dimmed a little.

They walked to the plane together, scrambling inside the cockpit and taking off, with Katya pushing on Nina's back, so she could reach the controls. Just like before. It was like the last eight months hadn't happened, as if it had all been a terrible dream. But not all of it had been terrible. As they glided through the air, Nina tried not to think of the way Anton's face lit up every time he saw her.

They had a perfect run that day. Everything went smoothly. No fighter planes bothered them. No anti-aircraft guns shot at them. Even the soldiers on the ground barely made an effort with their machine guns.

'It's a lot quieter than I remember,' said Katya as they completed their last mission of the day.

'If only it was always like that,' replied Nina, taking her headset off. 'The girls are planning a celebration in the mess. Zhenya is bringing her guitar. Everyone is delighted you're back.'

'A celebration with cake and champagne?'

'No, with barley and vodka.'

Katya wrinkled her nose. 'How I've missed this,' she said sarcastically.

But she had the biggest smile on her face when the girls gathered in the mess and Zhenya strummed her guitar.

'It's like coming home, isn't it?' said Katya. 'You girls are like family.'

Zhenya sang about lost love and tearful goodbyes, about the end of war and the beginning of the rest of their lives, about their beloved countryside and a peaceful sky over their heads. The whole regiment swayed in time to the songs with melancholy smiles on their faces. A few men joined them at the tables, Anton among them. It took all of Nina's self-control not to watch the two of them together, not to watch Katya's body as she leaned into Anton or the expression on her face.

It's as it should be, she repeated to herself. *It's as it should be.* Then why did it hurt so much?

Anton didn't look at Nina, but when Katya got up to get something from the kitchen, he tried to catch her gaze. Nina turned away, her heart hurting.

Even though they were at the front, risking their lives every moment of every day, the girls celebrated their friend's return with joy and laughter, like they didn't have a care in the world. Dasha told stories. Everyone cheered. A deck of cards appeared as if by magic and Tim shuffled and dealt. They were playing the Fool, a famous card game they all loved. It brought back memories for all of them, of a happier time with their families and friends, of long evenings in a different life, when explosives didn't drop from the sky.

Suddenly, they heard the sound of engines, loud and threatening in the quiet of the night.

'Who is flying at this time?' Zhenya wanted to know.

'It doesn't sound like our aircraft,' said Nina's mechanic Inna, who had an amazing ability to not only tell different types of planes apart by the sound of their engines but could determine which Pe-2 was coming back, whether it was Nina or Yulia or Zhenya in the air.

'The Nazis!' cried the girls.

How did the enemy find their little airfield, hidden away in the dense forest, barely visible from above? They had felt so safe here, so eager to celebrate Katya's return, they had forgotten to put the camouflage nets over their planes.

Moments later, the first explosion shook the airfield.

'They are bombing our planes on the ground,' Masha exclaimed with horror. There was a shortage of aircraft in the Soviet army. It was sad but true. The pilots were dispensable, while the planes were not.

The cards, the guitar, the food were forgotten on the tables. Ignoring the bombs, the girls ran across the airfield to their planes. In the dark, Nina didn't know how many enemy bombers were overhead. She could hear the whistling of the explosives before they hit the ground. She could feel the heat of the explosions. She was petrified, and yet, she had to save her aircraft at all cost.

Every minute felt like an eternity as they jumped inside the cockpits and took off, scuttling in every direction, while all around them the lightning and thunder of the bombing continued. Now that the planes were in the air, the German bombers could no longer target them. They circled for a while and disappeared.

It was almost midnight when all the planes returned. Miraculously, none had been damaged. Markov was waiting for them on the airfield. He thanked them for their quick thinking and bravery. Nina could barely stand straight while he talked to them. She was so exhausted, she was afraid she was going to fall asleep standing up, in front of her commander.

'I spoke too soon when I said how quiet it was,' said Katya, breathing heavily.

'Welcome back to the front,' said Nina. She wanted this day to be over.

The sky was crystal clear around them and the earth sparkled under their wings, and then suddenly, late in the evening, after all the horror of the day was finally behind them, the clouds sprang up as if out of nowhere and opened up in a flood of rain, pummelling the trees, the airfield, the ground, making everything appear blurry, like an old black and white photograph.

'Lucky this didn't happen while we were still in the air,' muttered Nina. 'Or we'd be in big trouble.' She took a deep breath, smelling fire and damp grass, grateful to find herself on firm ground as the weather worsened.

'Easy for you to say. I have night duty tonight. I'll be out all night in this,' said Katya.

Nina turned to her friend, away from the pouring rain. 'You can't do night duty. You can barely walk. I see you limping and crying out in pain. If you are on your feet all night, your bones won't heal properly.'

Katya shrugged like she didn't care. 'What choice do I have?'

'Talk to Markov. Tell him you need time to heal. He's a kind man. He'll understand.'

'The last thing I want is special treatment. Something happened to me at the hospital. Month after month in that bed, staring at the ceiling, doing nothing, and all I wanted was to come back to the front and fight. After the war is over, I'll have all the time in the world to heal.'

'By then it might be too late. Your body won't recover.'

Katya frowned. 'If Markov knows there is something wrong with me, he might not let me fly. He might send me back to the hospital and I couldn't take that. I couldn't be away from Anton.'

They found a free table at the mess tent and sat down, listening to the rain and looking inside their bowls of porridge. When they started eating, Markov came in and scanned the tent with his eyes, as if looking for someone. When he saw Nina, he motioned for her to come over and join him. 'I'll be right back,' Nina said to Katya.

Markov told her that, with the amount of losses the regiment was suffering, it was important to increase morale. And he had a brilliant idea how to do that: a regimental newspaper! 'You've always wanted to be a writer, did you not?'

'Yes, sir,' Nina replied.

'Wonderful,' he told her. She would write the articles herself and commission other girls to write them in their spare time. They needed stories of courage and heroism, to inspire the aviators. *What spare time?* she wanted to ask him. But she didn't. Maybe being in charge of a regimental newspaper was just what she needed to take her mind off Anton.

'I've been away for too long,' said Katya when Nina returned. 'I've forgotten how to eat with my hands. They always had spoons at the hospital, even though there was never any food.'

'Better food than spoons,' said Nina. 'You can't eat spoons.'

'What did Markov want?'

Nina opened her mouth to tell her friend about the newspaper. Then she changed her mind. Clearing her throat, her eyes darting away, she said, 'He told me the night duty has been cancelled.' Forcing herself to look her friend straight in the face, she tried her best not to blink. She had never been a good liar.

'Why didn't he tell *me*?'

Nina blushed. 'I don't know. He seemed in a hurry.'

'Why was it cancelled? Are the Nazis having a night off?'

'Who'd be out in this?' Nina pointed outside, where the wind was wailing like a wild dog.

Once Katya was asleep in the dugout the girls shared, Nina got dressed and reported for duty instead of her. Instantly, she was soaked to the bone. Even though it was still summer, the air had an icy feel to it, as if winter was letting them know it wasn't too far off. In the middle of the airfield, with not a soul around, Nina shivered and rubbed her hands together to get warm. She hated night duty. As a child, she had been afraid of the dark, of monsters lurking in the shadows, intent on causing her harm. When Anna came into their lives, Nina realised it wasn't the imaginary monsters she had to be afraid of. Here at the front, where the sky rained bullets and explosives, all her childhood fears came back.

As she stood under the pouring rain, trying to make out the outlines of the Pe-2s that kept them safe during the day, the wind whispering in her ear, she had never felt more alone. Even the mechanics weren't working in this weather. It was just her, in the middle of the night, within reach of the enemy, in a summer storm.

Every time she heard a noise, she jumped. Her heart was beating fast and her hands were shaking. She couldn't see much beyond darkness but she could hear trees groaning in the breeze like ghosts.

She tried to do what Dasha did to cheer herself up a little. She started talking to herself and then singing. But the sound of her voice scared her. It seemed alien, like it belonged to someone else.

She heard a twig break, followed by the sound of footsteps. *It's just the wind*, she told herself. *In a moment, it will be gone.* A moment later, she heard it again, closer this time. She shuddered. Someone was walking towards her in the dark and she had no idea who that someone was.

Taking a deep breath, she shouted, 'Who goes there?' Her voice came out high-pitched, petrified. Whoever the unseen person was, they would know instantly how afraid she was. 'Who goes there?' she repeated firmer. There was no reply. She could feel herself shaking. 'Respond or I will shoot. I'm very sorry but I'm going to shoot.' She didn't lift her rifle. It was one thing to drop bombs on the Nazis and never actually see the damage she inflicted. It was quite another to shoot a human being in cold blood. A few weeks ago, a male pilot had been standing guard and shot someone because they didn't answer his call. It had turned out to be another Soviet soldier, who hadn't responded because he forgot the password for the night. Luckily, the man had lived.

'For the last time, who goes there? Or I shoot.'

'Don't shoot. It's only me.'

She sighed with relief when she heard his voice. 'Anton? What are you doing here?' In a moment he was in front of her. For a long time she watched his dark silhouette in silence. And he watched her. Then she repeated, 'What are you doing here?'

'I wanted to talk to you.'

'Now, in the middle of the night? You have an early start tomorrow.'

'I wanted to talk to you without anyone around.' She couldn't see his face but she could hear the concern in his voice when he asked, 'How are you?'

'I'm fine. Absolutely fine.' Even though there were tears in her eyes, she forced her voice to sound strong. She was grateful for the darkness. With luck, he wouldn't notice how upset she really was. 'How did you know I was here?'

'You walked past me with your rifle. I called your name but you didn't hear me.' He reached out for her. The familiar emotions flooded her at the touch of his hand – affection, love, joy, and at the same instant, sadness and disappointment. She took her hand away. He added, 'It must be hard for you.'

'The night duty? I do it all the time. The hardest part is to stay awake or you could get in trouble with *Batya*. That's why I don't sit down. If I walk around all night, I can't fall asleep.'

'Not the night duty. Katya coming back.'

'Katya is alive. It's a miracle. I'm happy for her. And for you.' Nina tried her best not to sound bitter. After all, it was the truth. She was happy her best friend in the whole world was alive. She wouldn't be a very good friend if she wasn't.

'I've been thinking and thinking about it.'

'About what?'

'About the future. You and I. What to do next.'

'There is nothing to do. There is no you and I. Your wife is back. We need to forget about each other.'

252

'How do we do that?' he asked. She felt his presence next to her, the intensity of it. He didn't try to touch her again and she was grateful for that. 'How do we forget?'

Nina didn't know the answer to his question. She didn't know how to forget. All she knew was that they had to. Rain mixed with tears on her face. She wiped it with the back of her hand and said, 'We need to find a way . . . for Katya and Tonya. Your little girl deserves two parents who adore her and love each other.'

His silhouette quivered in the dark. Nervously he paced on the spot. 'I could never do to Tonya what my father did to me. I could never leave her. But I couldn't lie to Katya either. I have to tell her the truth.'

'No!' Nina exclaimed, horrified. 'No,' she said quieter but no less determined. 'She can never know. She'll be devastated. She will never forgive us.'

'She deserves to know.'

Nina reached out and touched his face. 'There is nothing to tell. We needed each other. We were there for one another. But now everything is different.'

He grabbed her hand and squeezed the tips of her fingers. 'What about us?'

She took a step back and another, so that he could no longer touch her. Her heart breaking, she moved away from him, when all she wanted was to feel him close. 'Katya is back. There is no us.' She shivered in the rain. 'Please, Anton. We shouldn't even be talking about it. You shouldn't be here with me because if Katya finds out, it will hurt her feelings. It's best if you go.' She gritted her teeth and clasped her fists, forcing herself to remain calm. She wasn't going to cry in front of him. She was going to wait till later. When he was gone, she would have the rest of the night to cry and scream and rage against her fate with not a soul around to overhear.

'I'll go if that's what you want,' he said quietly. *No*, she wanted to say. *That's not what I want.* But she didn't. He asked, 'Why are you here? Didn't you do night duty a few nights ago?'

'I took Katya's place. She's not well, Anton. She doesn't want anyone to know but she hasn't recovered yet. I see how much pain she is in. I hear her cry in the middle of the night. She needs rest. That's why you can't tell her. You are the only reason she came back to the front. If she knows that the two people she loves the most have betrayed her, it will destroy her.'

She heard him sigh, a short intake of breath, like he was frustrated or sad. After a short silence, he asked, 'Does Markov even know you are here? Are you supposed to fly tomorrow?'

'It doesn't matter. I can't sleep anyway.'

'If you are tired tomorrow, you will make mistakes. You will put yourself in danger.' He took her hand again and gently, lovingly stroked her fingers. She wanted to ask him to stop. If he didn't stop, she would break down right here, in front of him, in the middle of the night, in the rain. He touched her face. *Lucky it's raining*, she thought. *He won't know I'm crying.* He said, 'Why don't you go back to base and get some sleep? I'll stay here and watch over your planes.'

'What about you? Aren't you tired?'

'I'm fine.'

She shook her head. 'I can't let you do that. You are flying tomorrow too.'

'Then we both stay. I'm not letting you do this by yourself.'

All she wanted was to spend this night with him, not talking, not touching, just knowing he was next to her. But it was impossible. 'You can't stay here with me. We would have to lie to Katya again and it's not right. We shouldn't see each other anymore. You know that.'

'Then go. Don't worry about me.'

'But . . .'

'I insist.'

'You can't do this . . .'

He interrupted her. 'No matter what you say, I'm not going

254

anywhere. You might as well go and get some sleep.'

'Thank you for being so kind,' she whispered, pulling away from him, instantly feeling cold where his warm hand had been, longing to go back to him, to touch him one last time.

'You are welcome. Now go.'

She wished she could see his face in the dark. She had been so lonely, so afraid. She wanted to look him in the eye and tell him she loved him. More than anything, she longed to say out loud the words that had been running through her head long before she finally admitted it to herself. *You saved me*, she wanted to tell him. *I was lost and didn't know how to go on, then you burst into my heart and gave me a reason to keep going. You were my only light in the sea of darkness. Now that I've lost you, only the darkness remains. And once again, I don't know how to go on.*

She didn't say any of it. Instead, she turned around silently and walked away, back to her quarters, where she undressed and lay down with her eyes wide open, listening to Katya's heavy breathing.

They had been in the air for what seemed like forever. Nina couldn't wait to get back to base, so she could close her eyes and not open them again and not move until the next day. It felt like there were metal forceps around her temples, squeezing hard, like her head was about to explode. Her hands felt heavy and limp. Her eyes ached. *Maybe I'm coming down with something*, she thought to herself. *No wonder, in this weather.* She was always wet, cold and hungry. Every morning it took her longer to get up, to get ready, to make her way to the airfield. Yesterday, Markov had told her off in front of the entire regiment. This morning, she made an effort to be on time but she was still the last one to arrive. Nina could feel herself moving slower every day, as if her body was shutting down. On the plus side, she was no longer afraid as she took the controls in her hands. Most of the time, she was too exhausted to care what happened to her.

'Nina, what are you doing?' shouted Katya.

Nina shuddered as if woken from a nightmare. 'What?'

'The plane is nodding. Are you falling asleep?'

'No, no. I'm fine!' It was a lie, she wasn't fine. She forced herself to sit up straight. She could barely see ahead of her. The metal forceps dug in deeper. She wanted to put her hands around her head and scream.

It was getting dark. Pale searchlights flashed across the sky that was turning the colour of eggplant. Nina weaved. Katya shrieked. 'What are you doing?'

'Can't you see the German fighters? Six of them, right in front of us,' Nina said.

'What fighters? They are the anti-aircraft searchlights,' replied Katya.

Nina shook her head, her hands gripping the controls so hard, her fingers hurt. 'I'm telling you, I can see the headlights of German fighter planes.'

Their Pe-2 pivoted and dove and Katya shouted, 'There are no fighter planes. You are imagining them. Speed up or we are going to crash.'

'No,' Nina whispered, blinking fast. 'No.' There was something wrong with her eyes. She couldn't read the instruments. The little numbers danced together in front of her, fading in and out, mocking her. She would have to have a talk with her mechanic tomorrow. Inna was always meticulous but this morning she had clearly forgotten to clean the controls. Now Nina couldn't see. It was dangerous.

From the tail gunner cockpit, their tail gunner Igor shouted, 'Speed! Increase your speed!'

She didn't know how to increase her speed. She barely knew where she was. Her head was killing her and the cockpit was spinning in front of her eyes. Everything went dark and the last thing she knew was that her plane was in a dive, carrying them to a certain death, vibrating as it gained speed. 'I need to do something about that,' she thought. 'I need to fix it.' But before she could fix it, she fainted.

She came to on the ground. Katya was standing over her in the cockpit. 'Are you all right? Can you get up?' she asked, her eyes wide on her white face.

Nina blinked, trying to focus on Katya. Her face was fuzzy, as if hidden behind a screen. 'I'm all right. I can't get up.' Her body was hurting all over. Her head felt sore. 'What happened?'

'We nearly died is what happened.' Katya's face twisted. 'You knew you were tired. Why did you fly?'

'I thought I was fine. I thought . . .' Nina couldn't continue. Her teeth were chattering.

Katya placed the palm of her hand on Nina's forehead. 'Look at you. You are burning up. You need to see the medic.'

'Did you land the plane?'

'You fainted. I took over the controls.'

'But the plane was in a dive. The enemy fighters . . .'

'There were no fighters. I took care of the plane.'

'You saved our lives.' The enormity of what had just happened hit Nina and she groaned out loud. There had been no fighters. She was so tired, she was hallucinating. Katya was right. She shouldn't have flown. She was careless and because of her, the three of them nearly died. She couldn't talk anymore, couldn't take the expression of concern on Katya's pale face. In her mind, all she could see was the image of their Pe-2, twisted and broken on the ground, with their bodies still inside it.

Katya crouched by her side. 'Don't cry, honey. Nothing bad happened. We are safe and everything is all right. I'm sorry I was so harsh on you. It was the shock.'

'You weren't harsh. Just honest.'

'It's not your fault. All of us are under enormous pressure. No human being could handle this much. The exhaustion got the better of you, that's all.' She put her arms around Nina.

'I should have known better.' In Katya's arms, Nina felt a little less hopeless.

'It's going to be all right. We are human beings, not robots. Sometimes we need a break. Why don't you get some sleep? I can fly back to base. We are about half an hour away.'

Nina nodded, wiping her face.

On the way back, she closed her eyes but couldn't sleep. All she saw were the enemy fighters surrounding her and Anton's tormented face as he prepared to tell his wife they had been betraying her while they should have been mourning her.

She found him in the morning, when it was still dark, before their day began. He was at the mess area, waiting for porridge. And she couldn't even look at food.

'Nina? I was just coming to see you. I need to talk to you.'

'Don't. We shouldn't talk to each other anymore.'

'I just wanted to make sure you were all right. I heard about what happened . . .'

'I'm not all right.' She watched him with empty, broken eyes, unable to say more.

'I know,' he whispered. 'Come here.' He reached for her.

'We can't. I'm sorry.' He stood with his head low, not looking at her. She added, 'You have to promise me that you will never tell Katya about us.'

'I can't promise you that. I don't want to live a life of lies.'

She forced herself to get the words out, even though each one broke her heart a little bit more. 'You don't understand. Katya is like a sister to me. I've known her longer than I've known anyone. She was always a part of my life, for as long as I can remember. I could never do anything to hurt her.' She trembled. 'Major Raskova always told us that together we can do anything. We don't betray one another. We support and help each other. You and Katya have always been like family to me. You will forget me and the two of you will be happy again. Tonya will grow up with both parents.'

Anton shrugged, his eyes not leaving Nina's face. 'I can't even remember the last time Katya and I were happy. We can't be together for longer than five minutes without an argument. It just got so hard.'

'Marriage is hard. No one said it would be easy. You will make it work. For Tonya.'

'More than anything I want to make it work. But all I can think of when I close my eyes at night is your face by the lake that day. The way your eyes sparkled every evening when you saw me. When I woke up at the field hospital and saw you, I felt so grateful God had kept me alive. In the midst of all the destruction, suddenly I had something to live for.'

She shook. She could barely talk. 'You have something to live for. You have Katya and Tonya.'

'I love you, Nina.' He sounded hoarse, like he was coming down with a cold.

'If you love me, if I mean anything to you at all, promise me that Katya will never know.' He shook his head, bewildered. 'Please,' she whispered, her eyes filling with tears.

He held her and she didn't pull away. 'Don't cry. I'll do anything you want. Please, don't be upset,' he said.

'You won't tell Katya?'

'I won't tell Katya.'

'Thank you,' she whispered, ready to break down. Then she turned around and walked away, not allowing herself even the tiniest of glances at his broken face.

Nina lay with her eyes open in the dark, the sky a grey blanket above her. For a moment this morning, she didn't know where she was. A new airfield stretched before her, another dot on the map of their war journey that was taking them further and further west. A full moon shone its indifferent light on Nina, while somewhere nearby, the girls were cooking beans on a portable stove. Zhenya had some salt and Dasha had the most important thing – a spoon. The smell of beans was what had woken Nina up that morning, she realised. It had been a while since she had smelt something so delicious.

'Where did you get the beans?' Nina asked, her voice heavy with sleep.

'The villagers,' said Zhenya.

'And the salt?'

'The villagers.'

They had liberated the village from the Nazis the day before, and the locals were happy to give them what little they had. Unfortunately, it wasn't much. When the beans were ready, the girls had a teaspoon each. By the time the food was gone, Nina's stomach was still hurting.

Yulia said, 'Today is my birthday. How about a bet to make things interesting?'

'Happy birthday, Yulia,' said Nina. 'What kind of bet?'

'Whoever hits the most targets today gets the hardboiled sweets Mama sent me. And no lying in your journal, Katya.'

'I would never lie on an official document,' grumbled Katya.

Nina eyed the sweets with longing. 'You've got yourself a deal. But there is no way you girls can win. Katya and I have been hitting the most targets out of everyone for days.'

'We'll see about that. I'm feeling lucky this morning.'

'No chance,' said Katya. 'We might as well eat the sweets now.'

Yulia brought the bag of sweets to her face and inhaled. 'It smells like home. Smells of the soap Mama uses. I miss them all so much. I remember when I was a child, Mama always made the sweets on Saturdays. We would have some and then go to the village *banya* to wash. It was the best time. I can still see it now, the steam, the heat, my sisters hitting me with bunches of dried leaves, Mama singing. She has the best voice. Sometimes the only thing that gets me through the day is the thought of seeing them again.'

Masha said, 'I know what you mean. The only thing that gets me through the day is the thought of seeing my little boy. My parents died during the siege of Leningrad. Starved to death. My son is staying with my aunt in Omsk. His name is Danil. He's only eight but he writes the most amazing letters. He writes every day but I only got a few of them. I swear they are the only thing keeping me alive.'

'Danil must be so proud of his mama,' said Nina, smiling at Masha, who rarely revealed anything about her personal life.

'He is. And I am proud of him. He is the love of my life.'

Nina put her arms around Yulia. 'You are lucky, Siniza. You will see your parents soon.' Suddenly she felt so sad. She blinked. 'How about we have a couple of sweets now, to cheer us up?'

'Yes, let's,' said Yulia, opening the bag. The girls sat on the ground in a circle, taking turns putting their hands in the bag.

'They taste amazing. Of childhood and happiness and peace. I miss it. I miss waking up in the morning and not feeling afraid,' said Masha.

They continued to eat the sweets and reminisce about their families until they heard the bell summoning them to the airfield. As they walked to the planes, Yulia said, 'The bet is still on, girls. Let's see which one of us is the best.'

'But we ate all the sweets,' said Nina.

'It's not about the sweets. It's about pride.' Yulia winked and pumped her fist in the air in triumph, as if she had already won the bet.

Nina couldn't help but laugh at her enthusiasm as she climbed inside the cockpit. She watched the Yak fighters leave first, followed by the Pe-2s flown by the male pilots. Finally, it was their turn. She bit her lip to get her brain to focus as she sped down the runway.

It was a beautiful day, bright with not a cloud in the sky. The rain of the past few days seemed like a distant memory. As they flew, Nina tried to spot Anton's Yak; *For Katya* written in bright red on its wings. She couldn't see him but knowing that he was nearby somewhere, providing support for her and Katya, protecting them from the enemy, brought her comfort. It made her feel less alone.

Half an hour after they left, a giant storm cloud caught up with them, appearing as if by magic out of nowhere. It started to rain, lightly at first and then harder and harder, while the fog descended from the nearby mountains.

Fortunately, they were only ten minutes away from their airfield. Would they make it? Nina wondered if she should risk it or look for an emergency landing. The planes in front of her were going back to the airfield. Nina decided to follow.

A minute later, she could no longer tell where the other planes were, nor even where the airfield was. She could no longer see the wings of her Pe-2 and felt like she was flying inside a giant ball of cotton. Suddenly, the cockpit began to darken and she knew the land must be close. Then she saw a bright light. Someone had sent up a red flare to show them where the runway began. Thanking God for their foresight, Nina pulled the nose up and sank to the ground, praying she wouldn't collide with another aircraft. The first thing she did when she landed was look for Anton's Yak. There it was, safe and sound, and here was Anton, chatting to the other pilots, his eyes on her plane. She raised her hand and waved. He waved back. He was walking in their direction when they heard a loud noise.

Horrified, Nina turned around. She couldn't see anything in the mist but by terrified screams from the other crews and by Katya's sobbing nearby she knew something bad had happened.

In seconds Nina was out of the cockpit and running across the airfield. In front of her she could see two Pe-2s next to each other, engulfed in flames. When she got closer, she could hear cries for help. They were still alive! With a superhuman effort she propelled her exhausted body towards the wreckage. She was almost there when a heavy hand descended on her shoulder, stopping her in her tracks. Turning around, she saw Anton.

Moments later, an ear-shattering explosion was heard. She watched helplessly as the two planes disappeared inside a fiery ball. The cries for help stopped.

Nina felt her legs giving out under her. She would have collapsed to the ground if Anton wasn't holding her. He stroked her back, whispering sh-sh, like she was a child.

'Who?' she groaned. 'Do you know who it was?'

'Masha and Yulia's planes collided in poor visibility. I'm so sorry.'

'No,' she whispered, her gaze on the orange tongues licking what was left of the two aircraft, her hand clasping a wrapper from one of the sweets that Yulia's mother had prepared for her daughter with love as she counted the days until she would see her again.

Chapter 16

August 1943

The regiment was in mourning. The girls were grim like the clouds over their heads. Major Markov barely spoke and was it Nina's imagination or did his hair have more grey in it? Katya cried herself to sleep every night. She cried as they flew to their targets and when they released the bombs. 'That will show them,' she would mutter under her breath. Some days it was the only thing she said.

Nina didn't cry. She had no tears left, only a dull ache inside her heart.

It was a quiet day in the second week of August. It felt like the enemy were holding their breaths, as if waiting for something. For once, the air around Nina wasn't rumbling with the sound of battle. If it wasn't for the bomb craters under her wings, marring the countryside that had once been so beautiful, if it wasn't for the weight of the explosives making her plane heavy and difficult to control, Nina could trick herself into believing there was no war. She let her mind wander as she flew over the fields of gold.

Anton had once told her gold was his favourite colour. 'I love autumn. Love the burst of colour before everything dies.' Was that what their relationship had been? A burst of colour before real life intervened? A memory to treasure forever? She tried not to think about the future and what life would be like once the war ended. Life without him.

Nina was distracted and didn't see where the enemy fighter plane had come from. Suddenly she heard a terrible noise and felt a heavy impact, like a train slamming into her plane at full speed, splintering it in two. For a moment, her Pe-2 shuddered and froze in the air, and then it started gliding slowly towards the ground. Nina could hear screaming. For a fraction of a second, they continued to fall with the plane. Then instinct took over. Nina didn't want to die. Once she might have wanted to. But Anton had showed her that life was worth living. It took all her skill to straighten the plane but she could tell it wouldn't stay in the air for long. Nina didn't know where they had been hit but the aircraft felt irretrievably damaged.

The plane was engulfed in black smoke. The airframe and the starboard wing were burning.

'We don't have much time,' shouted Nina. 'We need to jump, now.'

'I second that,' said Igor, letting himself out of the hatch in the gunner's rear cabin and leaping out of the plane. Now it was the girls' turn but when they tried to open the canopy over the pilot and navigator's cockpit, the release catch broke off. 'Damn it,' cried Nina. 'What do we do now?'

'Quick,' cried Katya, her head twitching in panic, her shaking hand pointing towards the tail gunner's cabin. Choking on smoke, the two of them crawled to the back of the plane that was losing altitude fast, and climbed through the hatch.

Nina stood over the precipice, her heart in her throat. She had never jumped in combat before, only in training in Engels. She had never done it under German fire. And the Messerschmitt was still out there somewhere, sniffing around, not ready to let his prey go. She could hear its engine buzzing like an angry bee.

Nina could feel her body shutting down. She couldn't move a finger, couldn't take the step necessary to save her life, like there was an invisible wall between her and safety. She couldn't jump. *I won't think about it now*, she told herself. *I won't be afraid now. I will have plenty of time to be afraid, afterwards, when it's all behind me.*

'Are you ready?' asked Katya.

Nina shook her head. 'I can't.'

'You can. Now go.'

Katya pushed her. It wasn't a hard push but it was exactly what Nina needed to step into the nothingness. Her breath caught as she felt herself falling through the air at breakneck speed. Finally, the parachute opened, yanking her back, and she glided through the air, wondering where Katya was, twisting around to see if she was next to her, frantically calling her name and looking down to check how far she had to fall. All she wanted was to feel the firm ground under her feet. Then she would get her bearings and find Katya and Igor. Everything would be fine once they reached the ground safely and were reunited.

Suddenly, she heard gun shots and her heart nearly stopped. Aghast, she watched the German fighter, coming straight at her, almost clipping her parachute. She squeezed her eyes shut, preparing for impact, for a moment of sharp pain, for death. The fall took under a minute but it felt like an eternity. It was the longest minute of Nina's life. As if by magic, the clock had stopped and Nina remained suspended in time and place, gliding through the air in mortal danger. Wrapping the parachute straps around her hand to increase her speed, she rushed towards land. When her feet touched the ground, she could breathe again. All was quiet and the fields swayed in the breeze, while a small forest in the distance looked like a green oasis in the sea of gold. Nina was standing in a ravine full of bomb craters. She looked up. The plane with the dreadful swastikas was no longer there.

The fields seemed deserted. Where were Katya and Igor? The wind must have carried them away from her.

A sudden realisation hit Nina like an explosive wave and her blood ran cold. When their plane was shot down, they were flying over enemy territory. Her knees trembled and she sank to the ground, the overgrown wheat covering her completely. *It's going to be all right*, she told herself. She wondered how far into the enemy territory they had strayed. Katya would know. She wasn't one of their best navigators for nothing.

It took her a few seconds to get rid of the parachute. She tried to stay low, any moment expecting gun shots. Her hands were shaking so badly, it took her a long time to find her flask and a piece of stale bread.

Once she had a few bites to eat, she checked her pocket to make sure her identity card and party ticket were still there. Without her papers, she wouldn't get far. The documents were where they were supposed to be. Thank God. It was late afternoon and the sun was low in the sky.

Carefully, she peeked through the grass, hoping to see Katya or Igor. There was no sign of them but in the distance she spotted the downed plane, like a carcass of a large animal, broken and twisted. It brought tears to her eyes to see her Pe-2 helpless and destroyed. She felt naked without her plane, exposed and vulnerable. As the sun went down, she crawled through the grass to the crash site. Softly she called out, 'Katya!' When there was no response, she called louder. 'Katya, can you hear me? Igor!'

She crossed the field and turned around, looking for her friends. She didn't know where she was or if there were any German soldiers nearby. What she knew for sure was that she wasn't leaving until she found Katya and Igor. Not this time.

As she walked in circles around the plane, she stumbled on something dark lying in the grass. It looked like a rucksack but when she approached, she realised it was a body. She saw the familiar blond hair and paled. In a moment she was by his side.

'Igor, is that you?' she whispered urgently. She shook him but he didn't reply. Tears blinding her, she turned him around and looked into his unseeing eyes. 'Igor, oh no,' she cried. 'No, no, no!' She made a sign of the cross on him and then on herself, closing his eyes.

A terrible thought crossed her mind. What if around the next bend of the road she would find Katya's lifeless body?

She crouched by Igor and stared into the distance, at the trees and the grass and the peaceful landscape around her that was at odds with the horror she had just been through.

She thought she heard someone calling her name. 'Nina! Where are you?'

Jumping to her feet, she shouted as loudly as she could, 'Katya!'

'Nina, over here.'

The voice was faint, far away. Nina turned this way and that, not knowing where it had come from. All she could see was the green ocean of the fields stretching in every direction and a small forest nearby.

'Nina!'

Choking on her tears, Nina walked as fast as she could. All she wanted was to put her arms around Katya, to make sure she was still alive. It was all that mattered. Alone, Nina felt lost. But together, they could face anything. As long as they had each other, they would find their way back. They would walk east, cross the front line and rejoin their regiment. They would be safe.

Nina saw faint shadows moving by the trees. She stopped for a moment and covered her eyes from the sun. One of the shadows raised a hand and waved. 'Katya,' Nina whispered, her body quivering with exhaustion, her head spinning. She wished she could lean on something because any moment her legs would give out and she would slide into the dust. She wanted to cry out, to call her friend, but for a moment couldn't speak.

The shadows disappeared behind a bend in the road but now Nina knew where to find her friend. The thought gave her the strength she needed and she ran. She was almost there. Another minute, and she would hold Katya in her arms. Ignoring the branches lashing her face as she made her way through the forest, she shouted Katya's name again and again.

A cloud ran over the sun and thunder sounded. Or was it the noise of a distant battle?

Katya appeared from behind a large tree and Nina nearly knocked her off her feet. 'I can't believe I found you,' she whispered, pulling her into an embrace and trying to catch her breath. 'Thank God.'

For a moment, neither of them spoke. Katya's smile, the warmth of her in Nina's arms, made the horror of it all fade a little.

Suddenly, Nina heard a voice behind her. A loud German voice. 'Is that the pilot?'

It was so unexpected, Nina jumped and let go of Katya, spinning around to see two German officers stepping out from behind the canopy of trees and in large strides crossing the space separating them from the girls.

A hand descended on Nina's shoulder and held her in place. She couldn't understand what was happening. Why were the officers here, tapping her pockets, searching her, removing her weapon and documents? Why were they ignoring Katya? And why didn't Katya look at all surprised by the sudden appearance of the Nazis?

One of the Germans squeezed Nina's arm and she cried out. 'You are coming with us,' he said in broken Russian, pushing her in front of him. Next to them, the other officer approached Katya and twisted her hands behind her back.

'Wait,' cried Katya, her voice high-pitched, arms flailing. 'Where are you taking me?' The Germans didn't even look at her. Katya was suffocating and could barely speak. 'You promised me. You told me if I took you to the pilot, you would let me go. You gave me your word.'

'You led them to me to save your life?' exclaimed Nina, her breath catching. She couldn't believe what was happening. It felt like a terrible dream. Surely any moment now she would wake up in her dugout, with Katya stirring in the bunk next to her, grumbling about being tired and having to go out in the rain when she would rather stay in her warm bed.

When she closed her eyes, in her mind Nina saw the two of them braiding each other's hair in Nina's bedroom, in a different lifetime, before Mama died and before the war had broken them. Katya was saying, 'You are my best friend, did you know that?'

'Of course.'

'And we tell each other everything, don't we?'

'Always.'

'And we forgive each other for everything?'

Nina had nodded. 'Is there something you want to tell me?'

'I broke your favourite doll this morning. I'm so sorry. I wish I could replace it but I don't have a doll and we don't have any money to buy one. I know how much it meant to you.' Katya had looked like she was on the verge of tears.

Nina had hugged Katya and laughed. 'Don't cry, silly. I don't care about the stupid doll.' And she hadn't. She had a best friend, a sister, who would tell her everything and would forgive her for anything.

As she stood in front of Katya in the middle of the green sea, Nina wanted to pinch herself to make sure she wasn't dreaming. A sharp push from the officer hurried her along. Head down, eyes down because she couldn't bear catching Katya's gaze, Nina followed the officers through the small forest to a waiting car.

In the car, Katya was silent. She turned to the window and not once did she glance in Nina's direction, which was just as well because Nina couldn't look at her.

'Igor didn't make it,' Nina said quietly. 'In case you were wondering.'

Katya didn't reply but by a sharp intake of breath Nina knew she had heard her.

They were in the car for what seemed like forever. Nina watched as the same scenery she had seen from the plane now flashed in front of her through the car window at a speed of eighty kilometres an hour. She must have drifted off because, the next thing she knew, the car stopped and one of the officers was dragging her out and pushing her inside a large tent, where a monosyllabic man with angry eyes searched them, confiscating their watches and shoulder straps.

Finally, they were separated and Nina was taken to a room where another man questioned her in bad Russian. Where was she from? Where was she stationed? How many high-ranking officers in her battalion? How many soldiers? How many planes? How many missions did they fly every day? What was the location of their ammunition supplies?

Ask Katya, she wanted to say. *She'll tell you everything.*

She remained silent, turning her head away from the officer and closing her eyes, pretending she was somewhere else, on the lake with Anton perhaps, with his arms around her, during the happiest day of her life. How short-lived it had been, the happiness. She blinked once and it was gone. And now here she was, sitting at a table opposite an angry German man with Soviet blood on his hands, refusing to answer his questions, afraid to imagine what her future held.

Chapter 17

On a train making its slow way west, further and further away from the Soviet territories towards their unknown destiny, Nina tried to sleep. Having stood for ten hours, the entire journey, without a minute's rest, with not a morsel of food touching her lips, she drifted off as she leaned on the wooden wall of the carriage, while other bodies pushed and shoved, making her feel like she was about to suffocate. As the train chugged slowly through the countryside that had once belonged to her people but was now controlled by Hitler, Nina felt the earth underneath rumbling. Overhead, ear-splitting explosions were heard. She was grateful she was on a freight train without any windows. She didn't want to see the Soviet land devastated by the Nazis.

Next to Nina, by the small stove that coughed up putrid hot air, Katya curled up on the floor with her eyes closed. Nina wanted to move away from her but there was nowhere to go.

'Do you know where they are taking us?' she asked her neighbour, a skeletal man with sunken eyes and sallow skin, ravaged by war, not years.

'Does it matter?' asked the man, flashing a mouthful of golden teeth. 'Wherever it is, your life as you know it is over.'

Nina knew the man was right. The enemy had seen their identity papers and knew who they were. Whatever happened, Nina and Katya were not getting out of this alive. And it was all Katya's doing.

The man took pity on her. 'They are taking us to Bryansk, to a POW camp. I just escaped from there. Never thought I would see it again.' He shuddered. 'And here I am, on the Nazi death train again.'

'What was it like?' Nina didn't want to know, was afraid to ask but the question slipped off her tongue before she could stop herself.

The man stared right at her and smiled a sinister smile that sent shivers down Nina's spine. 'Eighty thousand people living in inhumane conditions under the open skies. Freezing cold, hungry, fearing for their lives. Day after day. Imagine your worst nightmare and multiply it a thousandfold.'

With a screech and a groan, the train stopped moving. The human mass quivered and began to stir. 'Are we there?' asked Nina, hiding her shaking hands behind her back.

'Not yet. They will probably move us to a different train,' said the man.

Nina heard loud German voices. Someone shouted words she didn't understand. She moved closer to Katya. 'Why, Katya?' she whispered. 'Why did you do a thing like that? Did you really believe they would let you go if you led them to me?'

'Why do you think?' Katya snapped, her face distorted in the eerie light coming through the beams of their wooden carriage.

Nina had never heard that tone in her voice before. It almost sounded like hatred. 'You are my best friend in the world. My sister. What happened?' she whispered.

'I could ask you the same question.'

Katya turned away without another word. The prisoners began

to move towards the exit, while the German guards continued to shout. As she stepped off the train under the German machine guns, Nina tried to catch Katya's eye but her friend wasn't looking at her.

Nina, Katya and a thousand prisoners just like them spent the next three days at an interim camp, sleeping on bunk beds made of hard wood with no mattresses and eating bread made of reserve flour – not bread but cardboard. They rose before dawn and toiled until the sun went down, chopping wood and placing it in neat piles, while the earth shook under their feet and the horizon lit up with streaks of red and purple. Nina's hands felt raw after hours of carrying heavy logs. She could barely put one foot in front of the other, but if she slowed down even for a second, the German guard would be there in a flash, his whip at the ready.

When they first arrived, Nina and Katya had been stripped of their uniforms and given prison clothes and a number plate to wear on their chests. They were no longer Nina Petrova and Katya Bogdanova, heroic women pilots flying for their country. They were number 3178 and 3183.

This is what my life is going to be like from now on, thought Nina bitterly. She was no longer human and didn't deserve a name or an identity. She was just a number on the Nazi conveyor of misery and doom.

Finally, they were taken to a train station to be transported further west, away from the front line. In the crowd, Nina spotted the man with golden teeth. She was glad to see a familiar face, until he beckoned her to him and said, 'You think this was hard? Wait till you get to Bryansk.'

Nina recoiled, and when the crowd pushed him away, she glared at Katya.

'Don't look at me like it's my fault,' cried Katya.

'I never said it was your fault.'

'I remember when I left the hospital to return to the front. I was so relieved to be out of there. All I wanted was to see you and Anton. My biggest fear was that I wouldn't find you alive. I prayed for both of you. Please God, let them live long enough so I can see them one more time. Not once did I think there was something else I should have worried about.' Katya looked dishevelled and slightly mad. Her hair was matted and her face had smudges of dirt on it. Her voice quivered.

Nina's heart stopped. 'I don't know what you are talking about,' Nina whispered.

Katya turned around to face her. 'Tell me, how long after I was gone did you wait before claiming my husband for yourself?'

'No,' Nina said, shaking her head. 'No, I never did that. You are wrong.'

'You think I'm stupid? Or blind? I saw straightaway that something was going on between you two. I know you both too well.'

'Nothing was going on.'

'Then why couldn't you look at him? Why couldn't you laugh at his jokes and talk to him like before, like you talk to me or Zhenya or Masha? You couldn't raise your eyes to him. Like seeing his face physically hurt you. Why is that?'

For a moment, Nina couldn't speak. Her throat was dry. It had been too long since she'd had a drink.

'I saw the two of you together, after the two planes collided. I saw the way he held you,' said Katya.

Nina bit her lips until they bled. Here, at the station controlled by the Nazis, awaiting a train that would take them to a fate worse than death, she didn't want to have this conversation. She whispered, 'We never meant to hurt you.'

Around them, the crowd ebbed like an ocean wave, pushing Katya away from Nina. Moments passed, minutes of painful silence while the German guards shouted and thunder clapped overhead.

'Then why did you?' demanded Katya when the two of them found themselves next to each other again. 'There was a whole regiment of men to choose from. Why Anton? Why my husband?'

Nina thought carefully about what to tell her best friend. How could she explain it to her when she couldn't understand it herself? She sighed, unable to look Katya in the eye, staring instead at the number plate on her chest. 'We were grieving. When we thought we lost you, our world shattered. And when Vlad died, I didn't want to go on. I didn't see the reason to. Anton gave me that reason. He saved my life, in so many ways.' Nina took Katya's hand. 'I'm so sorry, Katya. We thought you were gone. If we had one sliver of hope that you might come back, none of it would have happened. The moment you came back, it was over. I swear.'

'You love him, don't you?'

Nina hesitated before replying, 'We needed each other, that's all.'

Katya turned her twisted face away. 'This is too difficult for me. I don't want to talk anymore.'

A train rolled in, engine roaring. The human sea trembled, once again pushing Nina and Katya away from each other. Nina found herself next to two peasant women, who had forced their way onto the station. When the guard saw them, he threatened them with his rifle. 'Stay away,' he barked. 'You have no business being here.'

'We have some bread for the prisoners and a few potatoes,' said the shorter of the two, pulling her kerchief tighter around her face, as if trying to shield herself from the German rifle and the guard's anger.

'Not allowed,' he said, moving closer.

'Please, take pity on them. Look at them! I know you are a human being and not a monster. What would your mother say if she could see you now?'

To Nina's surprise, the guard shrugged and turned away, like he was bored with the whole thing and no longer cared. One of the women passed something wrapped in paper to Nina. 'There is a sharp knife in there,' she whispered urgently. 'Eat the food

and hide the knife. If the Nazi pigs find it, they will shoot you.'
Before Nina could thank the woman or ask her any questions,
she was gone.

They were loaded on the train like cattle. As she stepped
wearily inside the carriage, Nina pressed the precious package to
her chest. Once they were on the train and the sentries weren't
looking, she peered inside, finding some crackers wrapped in a
kerchief, a pot containing mashed potato and a knife with a long
blade. Nina had a few spoons of the potato and hid the knife
inside her prison overalls, thanking God for the kind peasant
women who were prepared to risk their lives to help the Soviet
prisoners, hoping perhaps that someone somewhere would help
their loved ones when they needed it.

Nina had no idea where they were. She couldn't tell if it was
day or night or how long they had spent on the train. It was
perpetually dark inside the carriage and all she heard hour after
hour was the chug-chug-chug of the wheels as they carried them
to hell on earth. Katya wasn't talking to her. When Nina offered
her some potatoes, she took a handful without saying a word.
The potatoes were gone hours ago and Nina felt lightheaded and
dizzy from hunger.

After a few hours on the train, she managed to find a small
space to sit down. Despite her exhaustion, she couldn't sleep. What
awaited them at their destination? Would they ever make it back
home again? Would she ever see Anton? She needed to lay her
eyes on him, if only for a moment. One glimpse of his wonderful
face and the turmoil inside her would melt away.

The train was alive with loud voices and miserable words.
Shouting, mad laughter, women crying, people shoving one
another and arguing over space. A fight broke out at the other
end of the carriage and someone screamed, a desperate howl in
the dark, like a coyote in pain. An old man sang Marina Raskova's
favourite song and Nina's heart filled to the brim with everything

she had been through, the bad and the good, the losses and the joy, and all her hopes and dreams that had been destroyed by war.

Night fell and little by little the voices faded, giving way to snoring and groaning and tears. Grateful for the darkness, Nina took the knife out, pressing it to her finger. When she brought her finger to her mouth, she could taste blood. She hoped the knife was sharp enough to cut through carriage walls that were made of plywood.

Inch by inch, Nina pushed her way through sleeping bodies, finally sitting with her back to the wall and pressing the knife into the wood as hard as she could. The result was a small incision, barely noticeable under her fingertips. Encouraged, she pressed the knife harder, using it as a saw. While others slept, she continued to work. Her progress was slow but it was progress nonetheless.

The next night, swaying from hunger, she cut through the wall a little bit more.

On the third night, she succeeded in making a trapdoor in the wall of the carriage, big enough for a small human to crawl through. She made her way to Katya and prodded her with her hand, whispering to her to wake up.

'What are you doing? Why are you shaking me?' cried Katya.

Nina brought her finger to her mouth, not that Katya could see her in the dark. 'Sh-sh. Not so loud. Follow me.'

'Follow you where? What is happening?'

Nina pulled Katya by the sleeve of her prison overalls. 'I'll explain later.'

The two of them inched their way across the train on their haunches, bumping into sleeping bodies, ignoring exclamations and curses. When Katya felt the opening with her fingers, she exclaimed, 'Where did this come from?'

'I made it. I'll tell you all about it once we are safe. We don't have much time. We need to jump.'

'Jump off the train while it's moving?'

'Would you prefer to stay?'

There was a moment of silence, a terrible moment during which it occurred to Nina that all Katya had to do was tell the guards and Nina would be shot. She had betrayed Nina once, hoping for preferential treatment. What was to stop her from doing it again?

Finally, she heard Katya's voice. 'You're right. Let's go.'

The girls waited till the train slowed down a little and took turns pushing through the opening. Holding her breath, Nina jumped into the unknown, in pitch dark, like she was parachuting from her plane, while the train moved through the Ukrainian countryside further and further west. A sharp pain shot through her shoulder when she hit the ground. She groaned. A moment later, she heard Katya land nearby with a thud. They lay in the grass in silence, watching the train of death as it sped away without them. The fields smelt of fresh grass, of rain and early morning dew. They smelt of freedom. The moon threw dim light over their tense faces.

After a long silence, Katya asked, 'Are you all right?'

Nina coughed and cleared her throat. 'I think I dislocated my shoulder.'

'I'm sure there are doctors at the prison camp who can fix it up for you. All we need to do is run after the train and wave, and the Nazis will stop it for us.' Katya's eyes twinkled. For a moment, it felt like the old Katya was back.

'What do we do now?' whispered Nina. In the far distance, she could see a forest. All around them was tall grass.

'We walk till we find a village. We have something to eat. We continue walking until we reach the Soviet territory. Then we rejoin our regiment.'

'You make it sound so easy. It could take weeks.' Nina tried not to sound discouraged. Yes, the road ahead would be a long and difficult one. But they were alive. They were free. It was a miracle.

'It takes as long as it takes. I have to make it back alive. Tonya and Anton are waiting for me.'

Disheartened, Nina turned away from Katya.

They had three crackers between them and drank some rainwater before setting out in the near dark. Every step made Katya wince as she limped on her one good foot. 'Why don't you lean on me?' offered Nina. Katya did. It became twice as hard for Nina to walk and soon her arm and shoulder were hurting. 'Are you sure we are going the right way?' She was shaking from the cold. The prospect of spending the night under the open sky didn't appeal to her at all.

'All we need to do is walk east. Sooner or later we'll reach the front line.' Katya pointed at the sky, where the clouds had parted and a few bright stars shone down at the girls.

After the camp of death and the cramped trains, having said goodbye to her freedom and her life, it was a dream come true to feel the breeze on her face and see the sky over her head. Nina had never felt more alive. She wanted to twirl under the night-time sky until she was dizzy, if only she had the energy, if only her breath didn't catch from fear of what lay ahead, of the dangers around every bend of the road, of the great distance between them and their regiment, between them and safety.

The girls walked in silence. Minutes passed. The wind picked up. Nina could barely hear Katya when she said, 'Why didn't you leave me on the train? Why didn't you run without me?'

Nina stopped. She needed a moment to rest, to catch her breath. She touched Katya's hand. 'You are my sister, my best friend. Nothing could ever change that.'

'I'm sorry for bringing the Nazi officers to you. For a moment, I let the worst of me get the better of me. You know how it happens? In a blink of an eye, you make a decision that you regret for the rest of your life.'

'I know what you mean. And it doesn't matter. Those Nazis would have found me eventually. I'm sorry too. For everything. I hope you can forgive me.'

'There is nothing to forgive. You thought I was dead. The two of you needed each other. I understand.'

'Thank you,' Nina whispered. 'That means the world to me, hearing you say that.'

'I understand why you did what you did,' Katya said, 'but it doesn't make it any easier.'

The first hint of silver appeared on the horizon. In the distance, Nina thought she saw something. Was it clouds or more trees? It looked like houses.

'A village!' exclaimed Katya. And then she added, quieter, 'We need to be careful. It will be under Nazi control.'

'The villagers are our people. They will help us,' said Nina.

Seeing the little settlement gave them strength. They walked like they had wings, like they hadn't just spent most of the night on their feet. When they reached the first house, a wooden lopsided structure with broken windows, they stopped on the porch and listened. Loud voices reached them. A man and woman were arguing in Russian. The girls knocked. The voices fell quiet.

It took a few minutes but finally the door flung open and they saw an old woman with worried eyes. She watched the newcomers in silence, staring fearfully at their prison attire, the dirt on their faces and their matted hair. In German-occupied Ukraine, a knock on the door first thing in the morning was indeed something to be afraid of.

'Don't be alarmed. We are from Raskova's dive bomber regiment. We escaped from the Nazi prison camp,' said Nina. She was speaking fast, worried the woman would slam the door in their faces.

The old woman smiled with relief. 'Come in, come in. You look exhausted.'

'Thank you. We walked all night,' said Katya.

The woman's hands flew to her face. 'All night in the rain. You poor girls. I might be able to find you something dry to wear.'

The girls followed the woman to the kitchen, where a grim-looking man with a crooked mouth and suspicious eyes sat at

281

the table. In front of him was a slice of stale bread and a bowl of oats soaked in water.

'Afanasi, look who's here. They are with the famous Raskova regiment. Remember, we read about it in the papers, before the German pigs came here?' asked the woman with joy.

The man grumbled something under his breath, his eyes darting this way and that.

'You girls are heroes. Anything you need, you let me know. I'm Alyona.'

The girls introduced themselves. 'We *are* a little hungry,' said Katya, eyeing the oats.

Turning away, Afanasi barked, 'Don't you dare give them any of our food. We don't have enough.'

Alyona smiled apologetically. 'The Nazis give us three hundred grams of bread a week. They took all our chickens and animals. We have nothing.'

'We don't want to impose,' said Nina, swaying on the spot. The soles of her feet were raw and she could barely stand. She was desperate to fall into one of the chairs and close her eyes. 'If we could sleep here for a few hours, we would be very grateful.'

Alyona whispered, glancing over her shoulder at her husband, who hid behind a newspaper, 'We don't have any tea but I can give you some hot water to drink, to warm you up. And some oats.'

'We are not giving our oats away,' cried Afanasi.

'Be quiet, you old fool. These girls risk their lives to protect people like us. They look like they've been through enough. We can spare a bit of food.'

Afanasi scoffed. 'What food? We have no food.'

Alyona ignored him, pushing a bowl of oats towards the girls. 'It's not much, we have no butter or milk or salt.'

'Thank you,' whispered Nina. She wanted to say no to the oats. She knew these people needed food as much as she did. But she couldn't. She felt if she didn't eat, she would not be able to continue walking. And she needed to continue walking if they were to make it back to safety.

After a few spoons of oats and some lukewarm water, Nina put her chin on her hands, struggling to keep her eyes open and nodding in agreement as Katya told their hosts where they had come from and what happened to them. Nina felt like she was about to fall asleep, right there at the kitchen table, in front of Alyona, who was hanging on Katya's every word with admiration, and Afanasi, who looked angry enough to throw them out on the street.

'My, my,' Alyona shook her head. 'After everything you've been through, you must be so tired. You can sleep in the shed. We can't have you in the house. The Germans come sniffing around almost every day. They are always asking for warm blankets, clothes, towels. Like we have any left.'

'They will shoot us for hiding them here,' said Afanasi quietly.

Alyona ignored him again. 'Let me find you something warm to wear.' In the bedroom, the girls changed into warm stockings, long skirts and blouses. Alyona lent them two of Afanasi's fleece coats and two woolly kerchiefs to tie around their heads for warmth at night. 'I knitted them myself. You'll never be cold in these,' said Alyona proudly. The clothes were old fashioned and fit poorly. When Nina and Katya saw each other, they burst into giggles.

'Better than what you had on before, isn't it?' asked Alyona, smiling.

'A thousand times better,' said Nina. 'Thank you for your kindness.'

Alyona picked up the prison uniforms with the tips of her fingers and wrinkled her nose in disgust. 'If they find these here, we'll be in big trouble. If you don't mind, I'm going to burn them.'

'Please do,' said Katya. 'I'll be happy if I never see them again in my life.'

'Now rest. I'll take you to the shed.' They crossed the yard and walked inside the empty shed, which was spacious and surprisingly clean. 'We had horses, cows, goats, a dog. Everything was taken away. It broke my heart,' said Alyona.

Nina could barely hear her. She fell on top of the hay and was asleep in an instant. Her last thought was of Anton, who had no idea what had happened to them. He must be beside himself, not knowing if he should be mourning them or looking for them. Nina doubted they would have found their downed plane or Igor's body because they were deep in the Nazi territory when they crashed.

She was dreaming of Anton's face when she was woken what seemed like minutes later by a scratching sound at the window. At first, she thought she had imagined it, that it had been part of her dream. She sat up and listened. For a moment, all was quiet. Late afternoon light was streaking through the shed, playing on the walls, on the ceiling, on Nina's mud-streaked face. She lay down again, desperate to go back to sleep, when suddenly there it was again, the noise. Scratch, scratch, scratch at the window, like metal on glass.

'Katya, are you awake? Can you hear this?' Nina whispered, crawling across the hay to where her friend was sleeping, only to find Katya's makeshift bed empty and her boots gone. Alarmed, Nina looked around the shed and checked behind the haystacks, in case Katya was hiding there for some reason. She didn't find her.

Someone knocked on the window, quietly but persistently. Nina climbed on one of the haystacks to see better.

'Nina, it's me.' She heard Katya's muffled whisper coming through the glass.

'What are you doing out there? I thought you were sound asleep next to me.'

'No time to explain. Walk out the door and join me. We have to go.'

'Where? And why?'

Katya sighed. 'I went back to the house because I wanted a glass of water. I overheard Afanasi telling Alyona he's called the Nazis on us.'

Nina gasped. Her hands began to shake. 'Why would he do that?'

'That's what Alyona wanted to know. She was furious with him. He said he could get some bread and even some real meat for delivering us to the Nazis. He said they haven't seen meat for over a year.'

'He sold us for a piece of meat?' Nina felt a panic rise inside her chest, choking her, making her voice sound shrill, like it belonged to a stranger.

'There's no time to waste. The quicker we get out of here, the better.'

Nina thought Katya made a very good point. Without further delay, she jumped off the haystack, hurting her knee. Grabbing what little belongings they had, she ran to the exit, towards freedom but, just as she was about to pull the handle, the door opened with a screech. A tall figure was standing outside, blocking the sun.

At first, Nina thought it was Afanasi. She opened her mouth to give him the piece of her mind about betraying army officers who were fighting for him at the front. When the man stepped inside and the sun was no longer in Nina's eyes, she saw the German uniform. Behind him was another officer and they looked at her through narrow eyes, like one would look at a fly or a rat. After a quick scan of the shed, they demanded to know where her friend was. Nina pretended she didn't understand, even though she understood perfectly, having studied German for ten years at school and, later, university. They gestured towards Katya's bed of hay. Nina shrugged. The officers swore.

One of them walked off, Nina assumed to search for Katya, while the other stayed in the shed, not taking his gaze off Nina. Her hands trembling, she sat down on the hay and closed her eyes.

She was cold and shivering and could sense the man watching her in silence. It made the hairs on the back of her neck stand up in horror. The two of them had been so close to freedom.

All they had to do was walk east, and sooner or later they would be reunited with their regiment. What was going to happen to them now? Would they find themselves back on the train of doom? Or worse, would they be killed?

The door opened, trickling sunlight all over the shed, blinding Nina, who for a moment couldn't see anything. She was about to jump to her feet when she heard a deafening popping sound. A gunshot. Whimpering in fear, wishing she could disappear inside the haystack never to be found again, she covered her face with her hands.

A moment later, she felt warm arms around her and a soft hand stroking her face. Katya's voice whispered in her ear, 'Get up and follow me. We have to be quick. One of them is still out there.'

'What about . . .' Nina's gaze fell on the Nazi officer, who was sprawled on the floor, his eyes still staring. Nina gulped. 'You shot him? Where did you get the gun?'

'Alyona. When Afanasi wasn't looking, she slipped it to me. It's her son's. He's a partisan and he was hiding it under some floorboards. She said I might need it and she was right.'

'Do you know what they are going to do to us for shooting an officer?'

'We shoot them every time we get inside our plane. This is no different. But let's not stick around any longer.'

And then they were outside, running as fast as they could across the garden, pushing through the overgrown grass, jumping over the gate into another garden and another, dogs barking and growling, their teeth snapping. The girls almost reached the road when they heard shouts.

'Halt!' cried the second Nazi officer. Nina turned around. There were maybe a hundred paces between him and the girls.

'Faster! Run!' exclaimed Katya. They ran faster but they were out in the open. The Nazi raised his hand and started shooting. Petrified, Nina slowed down a little, breathing heavily, raising her hands.

'What are you doing?' Katya shouted. 'Keep going, faster. We are almost there.'

'Maybe if we stop running, he will stop shooting.'

'If he catches us, he will kill us. Our only chance is that forest,' said Katya, stopping momentarily to shoot at the officer and then moving as fast as she could on her bad foot, crying out in pain with every step. *If she can do it, so can I*, Nina thought, increasing her speed. The forest beckoned, only a hundred steps away, thick foliage of branches welcoming them to safety. Nina's throat was burning and she was desperate for something to drink but she knew if she slowed down, she would pay for it with her life.

One more shot sounded and Katya cried out. When Nina looked up, she saw her friend face down in the grass. She saw red on green and screamed.

'Katya, no!' Rushing to her side, she turned her over, shook her slightly and searched for her pulse. Katya was still breathing, taking short wheezy gasps of air filled with pain.

Another shot, this time so close, it hit the ground by Nina's foot. To make herself smaller and less exposed, Nina threw herself next to Katya. She closed her eyes, listening to the officer's boots hitting the ground as he ran. Stomp-stomp-stomp, like hailstones pelting a roof.

Katya groaned and lifted her hand with great difficulty, taking aim. One shot, then another. Finally, she collapsed on the grass, as if the effort of it all had been too much.

There were no more heavy footsteps. The Nazi was on the ground, his arms and legs apart, making him look like an over-sized starfish.

Nina turned to Katya, unbuttoning her jacket, checking her all over, praying for a miracle. Katya groaned.

'Katya, can you hear me? Where were you shot?' Nina whispered urgently.

'My leg. It hurts so much. It feels like it's burning.'

'We need to get to the forest. We'll be safer there. Then I can look at your leg. Do you think you can make it?'

'I can't move.' Tears were running down Katya's face and her eyes were large and filled with terror. 'Go without me. I will only slow you down,' she whispered.

Nina shook her head, horrified. 'Leave you here to die? Why would I do that?'

'It would make everything easier for you.'

'I don't know what you are talking about,' said Nina. Katya watched her without saying a word, without moving. Her face was white like fresh snow. The pool of blood on the grass next to her was growing bigger, angry red blotches that made Nina's heart tremble.

Nina pulled Katya's hand. 'Come on, you can lean on me. I will help you to safety. Then we can decide what to do next. You can drag your leg behind you.'

Katya shook her head. 'No!'

'We can't stay here. It's too dangerous. Do it for Anton. He is waiting for you to come back to him.'

Katya shook her head, her distrustful eyes on Nina. 'Do you ever stop?' she whispered.

Nina ignored her. 'Do it for Tonya. She needs her mother.' With a superhuman effort, she lifted Katya and half-dragged, half-carried her to the forest. The weight of Katya's limp body was hurting her so much, she felt like screaming in agony. But she didn't. Katya needed her to stay strong. It took a few hundred steps to reach the forest, and every step was agony, and every step Nina repeated to herself, *Please God, don't let her die.*

All was quiet when they finally reached the cover of the trees. Hiding behind a thick oak, Nina placed Katya gently on the ground and stroked her face. 'Katya, can you hear me? Honey, are you all right?'

Katya opened her eyes. She looked unfocussed and confused. 'Where are we?'

'We made it to safety.'

'We are back at the regiment? Can a doctor take a look at me? I don't feel so good.'

'Not quite at the regiment yet. But at least we are not out in the open anymore.' Katya looked around her, groaned and closed her eyes.

Nina kissed Katya's cheek. 'Nice shot, by the way. You saved our lives.'

'All that training in Engels finally paid off. Remember our shooting practice? How we hated it.'

'I told you it would all be worth it in the end. Raskova would be impressed with you today.' She brushed long strands of hair out of her friend's eyes. 'You could have escaped. You could have left me in that shed and run. But you came back for me.'

'Of course, I came back for you. I couldn't leave you behind. Just like you couldn't leave me behind on that train.' Her voice was getting weaker. Nina could barely hear her.

'If you left me, you wouldn't be hurt now. You would be on your way to safety.'

'If I left you, how could I live with myself?'

Trying to ignore the nagging pain in her back, Nina exposed Katya's leg and examined the wound. The flesh near the kneecap was badly torn. Had the bullet exited or was it still lodged inside? And how to stop the bleeding? If only she had some water and sheets to clean the wound and bandage it.

Nina cleaned around the wound with rainwater but was unable to touch the damaged flesh because it hurt Katya too much. She wished she had something for the pain, thinking with longing of the medical kit on board her Pe-2. Unwrapping her scarf, she used it as a bandage, while Katya whimpered like a kitten. 'How bad is it?' she wanted to know.

'Not bad at all,' Nina lied.

'Then why does it hurt so much?'

'It's healing. Your body is healing.' She kissed Katya on her burning cheek. 'Are you hungry? Would you like a piece of bread?'

Katya shook her head. 'I'm not hungry. I want to sleep. I feel so tired. So weak.'

'Of course, you should sleep. Sleep is the best medicine. But eat first. You need your strength.'

Alyona had packed some bread and a boiled corn on the cob for the girls before she took them to the shed. Nina fed some corn to Katya, who started coughing. Then she collected more rainwater and gave some to Katya, who drank with desperation, like she needed every drop to live. When Katya fell into an uneasy sleep, every few seconds shuddering and crying out, Nina nibbled on the corn, thinking of Alyona. Was the old woman still alive? Was she going to pay for her kindness with her life? Nina couldn't bear that thought.

After finishing her food, she lay down next to Katya and closed her eyes.

When she woke up, it was getting dark. She checked Katya. Her breathing was heavy and the makeshift bandage was soaked with blood. Nina took off the cloth and gasped. The wound was angry and red, oozing blood.

Scrunching the useless soiled scarf into a ball in her fist, Nina cried with frustration. How could she help Katya when she had no medical supplies? What were they going to do? They couldn't move forward because Katya couldn't walk. But they couldn't stay in one place either. Sooner or later, the Nazis would stumble upon them. Nina remembered the stretcher Anton had built for a wounded man when they were searching for Katya, what felt like a lifetime ago. The thought of Anton warmed her heart and gave her strength. She leapt to her feet and looked around. A few steps away she found a piece of old bark that was large enough to fit a human body. She picked it up and carried it to Katya.

'What's happening?' Katya asked with a groan.

'We need to keep moving. Look, I found a sled. I'm going to pull you all the way home, just like I did when we were children.'

'It's a long way home from here,' whispered Katya, looking up at the grey sky above her head.

Pulling Katya through the rocky terrain covered in branches and roots was excruciatingly hard. After five minutes, Nina's arms were aching and her fingers started to bleed. Gritting her teeth, she continued walking, every now and again looking at the stars to make sure they were moving in the right direction.

Soon they came out of the forest. Walking became easier but now they were out in the open again. Luckily, they no longer had their prison uniforms on. Thanks to Alyona, they looked like two peasant women returning to their village. Even if they came across a Nazi patrol, they would not raise suspicion.

When it became completely dark, they found themselves outside an abandoned house that was missing its front door and some of its roof. Nina suggested they stop there for the night. Katya didn't even reply. She barely had the energy to nod.

'This is exactly what we need. We'll get some rest. In the morning, you'll feel so much better,' Nina told Katya as she made her comfortable. 'Look, a real bed. Isn't it wonderful?'

Katya stared without replying.

'Tomorrow we'll continue walking but tonight you'll sleep in real luxury.' Nina smiled but Katya didn't see. Her eyes were closed.

There was only one bed in the house and Nina gave it to Katya, happy to sleep on the floor or in a chair by Katya's side. As she walked from room to room, glancing at the photographs on the mantelpiece, at ghost-like silhouettes of people who had once lived inside these four walls, Nina wondered what had happened to them. With all her heart she hoped they had evacuated east and were safe. Other than the photographs, there were no personal belongings of any value. Either the inhabitants had taken them when they left or the Nazis had confiscated them.

In the cellar she found some old potatoes and the girls ate

them raw. Nina wrapped a dozen potatoes in a paper napkin to take with them. With luck, they would last a few days. Her stomach was no longer hurting and she felt a glimmer of hope. All they had to do was hold on long enough to reach the Soviet territory, then all their troubles would be behind them. A doctor would take a look at Katya. Once she was better, they would return to their regiment. They would see Anton.

When Nina checked Katya's leg, she felt her hope deflate a little. Even to her untrained eye it didn't look good. Katya's forehead felt hot to the touch. Nina cut up some old linen she had found in the cupboard, cleaned the wound as best she could and bandaged the leg.

'I feel so tired,' whispered Katya. 'If I close my eyes, I feel like I will never open them again. My eyelids feel so heavy.'

'We've been through a lot. Of course, you are tired. You need some rest. Have some sleep and you'll feel better tomorrow.'

'Please, don't go. Stay with me until I fall asleep.' Katya's voice was nothing but a whisper in the dark.

Nina perched next to Katya on the bed. 'I'm not going anywhere, honey.'

Katya slept, while Nina sat in a chair, watching her face, every now and then glancing out the window into the darkness outside. The sky wasn't rumbling with plane engines and explosions that night. It was quiet in the little village and all Nina could hear was Katya's laboured breath. The air smelled faintly of wet grass, conjuring images of autumns past, of untroubled evenings of her childhood, of happiness and adventure with not a care in the world.

Lost in Nazi-occupied territory, in a little house abandoned to the Germans, with danger lurking, next to her wounded friend, Nina made a promise to herself. If she survived the war, if she returned home safely, if she made it back in one piece, she would never take anything for granted. Every smile on a loved one's face, the rain hitting the roof and the sun on her face, the whisper of a river and the song of a nightingale, she would treasure it all.

'I don't want to die,' Katya said, opening her eyes and reaching for Nina's hand, her voice barely audible above the wind whispering outside. 'I have too much to live for. I want to see Tonya. I want to hold my little girl one more time before I die.'

Fighting tears, Nina said, 'You are not going to die.'

'How do you know? Are you a doctor?'

'I won't let anything happen to you. I'll take you to a hospital. You'll be just fine, I promise.' Nina stroked her friend's hand, slow reassuring circles to make Katya and herself feel better. 'We will return to the regiment. We will fly again. I will finish the newspaper for Markov. I was almost done with my article and the girls were contributing too. Soon, the war will be over and we will go back home. Imagine hugging Tonya again, how happy you will be. We have so much to look forward to. Everything will be all right.'

Katya touched Nina's face. Her fingers trembled. 'You are a good friend. The best friend I could ever wish for.'

The candle danced in the breeze, throwing shadows on Katya's face. One moment she looked animated and alive, the next like she was about to fall asleep. Nina said, 'Remember when we were ten and Vlad and I visited you in hospital?'

'I remember. I broke my leg climbing the neighbour's apple tree, trying to get some apples for my little brothers. When the neighbour came to see me at the hospital, he brought a basket of apples. He told me I should have just asked.'

'We were always at the hospital with you. The nurses were sick of the sight of us. Even after visiting hours, when the lights were out, we would climb back into your hospital room through the window. We played cards and chess, and read your favourite books. When the nurses came to see you, we hid in the closet. Then one evening Vlad sneezed and they found us.'

'I remember. They threw the two of you out but you were back the next day like nothing had happened.'

Nina threaded her fingers through Katya's. 'We didn't want you to feel alone at the hospital. We didn't want you to be sad.'

'Thank you for not leaving me alone. Then or now.' Katya's body tensed as she cried. Moments passed. The wind howled, blowing icy sharp breaths through the broken window. Outside, cars drove past, their headlights throwing light on Katya's pale face. Her eyes glistened in the near darkness. Finally, she whispered, her eyes staring, 'Promise me something.'

'Of course, anything.'

'When I'm gone, I want you to be there for Tonya and Anton.'

Nina shook her head. 'You are not going anywhere. I won't let you.'

Katya squeezed Nina's hand until it hurt. 'Listen to me. I don't want Tonya to grow up with a stranger. You lived with a stepmother, you know what it's like. You are going to make the best mother for her. Marry Anton if you want to. But don't ever leave Tonya.'

'Anton doesn't want me. He loves you.'

'No, he loves *you*. It's so obvious, every time he looks at you. Anton and I . . . we hadn't been happy for a while, and I was jealous that you made him happy. That's why I was upset at you. It broke my heart.' Nina raised her hand in protest. She opened her mouth to argue but Katya interrupted. 'You love him too. And you love Tonya. It means everything to me, knowing she won't be all alone in the world.'

'I promise to take care of Tonya like she is my own daughter if anything happens to you. But we don't have to worry about it because you are going to be fine. We'll make it. Remember what Raskova always said. We can do anything.'

Nina held Katya's burning hand as she slept. When the sun came up and Nina opened her eyes, Katya's hand inside hers was cold. She shook her gently and called her name. Katya didn't answer. Nina shook her once more, choking on her tears. 'Don't leave me,' she pleaded. 'Please, don't leave me here alone.' But it was too late. Katya was gone.

Nina didn't know how long she spent by her friend's side,

sobbing and praying and hoping for a miracle. Hoping her Katya would open her eyes and smile.

When the sun was high in the sky, Nina heard German voices. A motorcycle rode past. When she glanced out the window, she saw two Nazi officers talking across the road, pointing at the house and finally making a move towards her. She knew she couldn't stay there any longer. Covering Katya's body with a blanket because she didn't want her friend to be cold, she stepped outside and started walking, barely able to see the road in front of her from her tears.

She had never felt more alone.

Chapter 18

September 1943

The first day of autumn found Nina on the road. The Ukrainian countryside had donned a golden attire, its beauty at odds with the horror of the Nazi invasion, as if nature itself was defying Hitler and his Army Group South. In September 1943, as she made her slow and painful way east, seeing the gold and red hues of the trees and the yellow fields around her made Nina weep, because Katya would never see them again.

On and on she walked, day after excruciating day in the rain. She ate one potato a day, shuddering at the memory of Katya's twisted face as she tried to swallow her last potato and couldn't. Nina had seven potatoes when she left the little house, and when they ran out, she went two days without food. She looked for berries but couldn't find any. A couple of times she came across villages and the locals gave her a little to eat.

After what had happened with Afanasi, Nina didn't trust the villagers. She kept to herself and never disclosed who she really was, telling them she was a peasant woman, walking east to join her sister in Kuban. After a week, her clothes hung on her, her feet were sore and her skin felt greasy to the touch. But she knew she was getting close because the earth trembled under her feet and she could hear distant explosions.

For the first time in her life, she was not afraid of the sound of battle. Once she was on Soviet land again, all her hardships would be behind her. Finally, ten days after Katya died, Nina reached the front line and crossed a ravine covered with bodies, trying not to look at the horrifying scenes of death and devastation. Bullets whizzed above her head. She ignored them and continued walking, looking at her feet. All she could think about was getting to the other side, to her own people. That and Katya's face as she lay dying in her arms.

A sergeant grabbed her by the hand. 'Are you out of your mind? Get down right now or you are going to get killed!' He pulled her to the ground, cursing and muttering. Despite his harsh words, she wanted to hug and kiss him on both cheeks, overjoyed to hear Russian again and to see a Red Army uniform. She was no longer in the territories occupied by the Germans.

When it got quieter, he asked, 'What are you doing, walking across the battlefield? Are you insane? Where are you going?'

'I'm going home.'

'Well, if you want to get there in one piece, you need to be more careful. I'm Stanislav. What's your name?'

'Nina.'

She told him who she was and he took her to the headquarters of one of the regiments of the 21st Army, bringing her some water and sharing his ration with her – warm barley and a chunk of bread. After the last few weeks, it felt like she was having a feast. Who knew that barley could taste so good? If only Katya was here to see it. She hated barley, absolutely hated it.

As Nina ate, she had tears in her eyes, tears of joy and sorrow, because she had finally made it, because of this young stranger's kindness, because she was among Soviet soldiers eating familiar food. That night, for the first time since their plane had been shot down, she slept soundly because she was almost home.

* * *

In the morning, Nina had breakfast with Stanislav and his comrades. Their ration wasn't as good as a pilot's but they were happy to share it with her. They wanted to drink to her health and her happy escape from the Nazis. She raised a shot of vodka with them but barely touched it. She needed a clear head. The sooner she got back to her regiment, the better.

An alarm sounded. The Nazis were advancing.

'Are you going to join us in battle, soldier?' asked Stanislav, his eyes twinkling. 'Show those Nazis!'

'Gladly,' she replied, still wearing her peasant dress, a kerchief on her head, her hair the longest it had been in years.

But she didn't get a chance to join them. An officer came to see her, telling her to follow him. 'We need to ask you a few questions.' He smiled. He had a good smile and a broad Soviet face that inspired trust.

In a large room, three officers sat behind a desk, their guarded eyes watching her. Nina looked at their epaulettes and saw that they were a captain and two majors. They invited her to take a seat opposite them and she did so, happily. These people were here to help her return to her regiment. After everything she'd been through, her heart was bursting with gratitude.

'Why don't you start by telling us who you are,' asked the captain.

She told them.

'Very impressive. I knew Major Raskova personally. I have the greatest respect for what you girls have achieved.'

'Thank you, sir.' Nina beamed.

'And you are returning from enemy-occupied territories?'

'Yes, sir. We were flying a mission, bombing Nazi factories, when our plane was hit. We parachuted out . . .'

'Over enemy territory?' interrupted the taller of the two majors. He was older than the others and less friendly. His red-rimmed eyes watched Nina with suspicion. Feeling a little uneasy under his gaze, she wondered why he would be suspicious of her.

'Of course, since our mission was to inflict damage on the Nazi infrastructure.'

'I understand,' said the captain, smiling kindly. 'I was a fighter pilot myself at the start of the war. I flew in Stalingrad.'

She felt an instant warmth towards him and decided to address all her answers to him instead of the unfriendly major who scared her. 'Me too.'

'It was a bloodbath, wasn't it?'

'Absolute hell. You don't fly anymore?'

He shook his head, his eyes darkening with sadness. 'I was wounded. No more active combat for me. I miss it. As a former pilot, I can sympathise with your situation. What happened after you parachuted out?'

As she told them everything, she tried very hard not to cry. She would save her tears for later, when she was alone in the bunk bed that the soldiers had found for her. But when she got to Katya's death, she couldn't help it. She broke down in front of the three officers, who watched her in silence.

'You've been through a lot,' said the captain.

She took a deep breath and tried to calm her heart by counting to ten inside her head. Finally, she said, 'All I want is to return to my regiment and make the Nazis pay. I want to fly again. Can you help me?'

The three men hesitated. The captain said, 'Can you prove that you are who you say you are? Do you have any documents on you?'

She shook her head. 'The Nazis took them. They took everything before putting us on the train to Bryansk.'

'That's most unfortunate.'

'Anyone at the regiment will confirm who I am. Ask Zhenya Timofeeva, my squadron commander. Ask my regimental commander, Major Valentin Markov. Ask anyone.'

'We will do our best to help you but it will take some time.'

'Do you know where my regiment is fighting? Can I go there?'

'We will find out and get back to you.'

299

'Thank you, sir. I appreciate it!'

Back in her quarters, she lay down on her bunk bed and closed her eyes, tears of relief running down her cheeks. It was almost over. The unfortunate chain of events that started the day their plane had been hit was coming to an end. It was only a matter of time before she saw her regiment again. It was only a matter of time before she saw Anton again.

They came for her two days later. Two days filled with relief, at hearing the Russian language and seeing Soviet uniforms around her, at no longer having to hide, at having something to look forward to after so many days of bleak despair. She had spent the time helping the soldiers mend their clothes, cooking for them and serving their meals in the mess tent. And now here she was, sitting in the familiar chair opposite the same three officers, her heart trembling with hope. Was she about to be sent back to her regiment? She could hardly wait.

'It's not that simple,' said the captain. 'There are a few things we need to ascertain first.'

Nina's hands began to shake. For the first time since she had crossed the front line, she felt a slight trepidation, a vague fear she couldn't quite fathom. She squeezed her fists tight and sat up straight. Surely, she had nothing to be afraid of. These were her people and they were here to help her. She had left the horror behind once and for all in the German-occupied territories. 'Is it because I don't have my documents on me?'

'That's one of the reasons.'

'Have you been able to get in touch with Major Markov? With my regiment? They'll be overjoyed I'm still alive. They have no idea what's happened to us.'

'Not so fast. We have to ask you a few questions first.'

'More questions? I've already told you everything.'

'Yes, and we were very impressed with your tale,' said the captain. When he looked at Nina, he no longer seemed friendly or kind. 'Your escape from the Germans, especially. Not many have done it. It must have been hard.'

'It *was* hard. I lost my best friend. I barely made it back.' Nina shuddered as she thought of the nightmare she had been through.

'And yet, you made it. How extraordinary. Miraculous even. The stuff of fiction novels. Hard to believe,' said the unfriendly major. 'Did you really escape? Or did the Nazis let you go?'

Nina paled. 'Of course I escaped. Why would they let me go?'

'In exchange for some information, perhaps?'

'What information?'

'A lieutenant in an aviation regiment possesses a breadth of knowledge that could be extremely beneficial to the Nazis.' The officer's eyes narrowed.

Nina couldn't believe her ears. What were they accusing her of? 'Are you saying I betrayed my regiment?' She couldn't speak. Needing a moment to compose herself, she reached for her glass of water but found it empty. The officers didn't offer to refill it for her. She sat there, with the glass in her lap, tracing the pattern with her fingers. A minute later, she said in a calm voice, 'No, sir. Nothing like that happened.'

'And yet, you are free. Perhaps they let you go in exchange for a promise to spy for them and provide them with strategic information? Is that why you are so eager to return to your regiment?'

It felt like a terrible nightmare she couldn't wait to wake up from. 'No, sir. I want to return so that I can be with my comrades and fight the Nazis.'

The captain spread his hands and lowered his big round head. 'With the suspicion on you, we can't let you go back, I'm afraid.'

'What suspicion? I haven't done anything wrong.'

'But you have.' Three pairs of hostile eyes watched her.

'What do you mean?' None of it made sense. These people were meaner and more aggressive than the German who had interrogated her when she was first captured. How was it possible?

'Have you heard of Order 270?' asked the other major, a tall, stick-like figure with bulging eyes that bore into her with disconcerting intensity.

Her insides went cold. Of course, she had heard of Order 270. Everyone had. She just never thought it would apply to her. What happened was outside of her control. She didn't ask to crash in German territories. She didn't ask to be picked up by the Nazis and sent to a prison camp. She had done all in her power to escape and make her way back home. Why were they treating her like a criminal?

'In August 1941, Comrade Stalin made it treason to fall into enemy hands. We should resist the Nazis at all cost, even that of our lives,' said the captain. He spoke slowly, enunciating every syllable, like she was a child or a foreigner, like Russian wasn't her first language. 'By falling into enemy hands, you have committed treason. Do you know what the punishment for treason is?'

Nina shook her head.

'The punishment for treason is death.' He let the last word hang in the air for a few seconds, before continuing, 'But we are feeling lenient towards you. We sympathise with you and everything you've been through. If you are who you say you are, you have an impeccable record. You've done a lot for our country. And we understand everyone makes mistakes. Fighting a war is hard for everyone but for a woman especially.'

'You will let me go back and fight?' She looked up with hope.

'Ten years of hard labour. Or a penal battalion. Your choice.'

'What?' she whispered. Had she heard him right? It couldn't be. 'Ten years? That's not possible.' She shook. 'What about a hearing? A tribunal?'

'This was your tribunal.' The major cleared his throat. 'Your family will lose their rations.'

'Don't have any family left. They all gave their lives for the motherland.' She looked up, her eyes pleading with them. It was like pleading with a brick wall. There was not a trace of human emotion on their faces, no pity or compassion. She whispered, 'I have dedicated everything I have to fighting the Nazis. This is the thanks I get?'

'We all dedicate everything we have to fighting for our country. That's precisely why we can't abide traitors.'

'I'm not a traitor.'

'I'm afraid Comrade Stalin doesn't see it that way.'

The room was spinning, the walls moving closer, as if trying to crush her. She could barely hear their voices. Only disjointed phrases reached her. *There are no Soviet prisoners of war, only traitors. Deserters. We are fighting a war. Cowards must be liquidated. Not one step back.*

She wanted to scream.

'Cheer up, Comrade. You are lucky. Most people in your position would have been turned to the wall and shot,' said the captain, flashing his kind smile at her.

But Nina didn't feel lucky. She felt betrayed.

Nina returned to her quarters, lay down on her bunk and refused to get up. For three days she remained in bed, turned to the wall with her eyes closed, saying no to food, not responding to Stanislav and his attempts to cheer her up. She would have stayed like this forever, in her mind going over everything that had happened, the plane crash, her captivity and escape, Katya's death that broke her heart and the tribunal that broke her faith, but three days after she had stood in front of the officers and heard the terrible words – treason, death, labour camp – she was ordered to get up and was marched to a truck.

Nina and half a dozen others were moved to a camp, where they were to wait for transportation to Kolyma in the Far East, a frigid region embraced by the Arctic Ocean on one side and the East Siberian Sea on the other, behind the Arctic Circle, a bleak dot on the map with no sunlight or hope. In Kolyma, she would spend months every year plunged into darkness. She would toil from dawn to dusk until she could no longer move. In Kolyma, her life would be over.

The camp where Nina was to await her fate was no different from the German prison camp – same bunk beds, mournful faces, early starts and gruelling days of hard work, only the food was worse and the jailors spoke Russian. In the German camp, she felt hatred towards her captors and it got her through the day. It fired her up and gave her the strength she needed to escape. In the Soviet camp, all she felt was confusion. These were her people. Why were they doing this to her?

One evening in the first week of September, her cellmate Zina sidled up next to her on her bunk. 'What a waste!' she said. 'Hundreds of thousands of us could have gone back to the front and continued to fight this war for Stalin. Instead, here we are.' Zina was a heavy woman in her thirties with a mouth that pointed downwards, giving her face a perpetual frown. Nina supposed she had many reasons to frown. Zina had been an anti-aircraft gun operator when she was captured by the Nazis in Kursk. A few weeks later she was liberated by the Red Army. Just like Nina, she had been overjoyed. And just like Nina's, her joy had quickly turned to confusion and a deep sense of betrayal.

'How long have you been here?' asked Nina.

'Three months. Waiting to be sent to Kolyma for the next ten years of my life. More like the rest of my life. No one survives Kolyma.'

'Three months?' Nina couldn't imagine spending another day here. And yet, she knew she wasn't going anywhere other than further east, to a place a thousand times more horrifying. A place not many had come back from.

'I'd rather be in a penal battalion than wasting away here. I've done nothing wrong,' said Zina.

Nina shuddered. Penal battalions were used as cannon fodder for the Germans. Most soldiers didn't last there longer than a few days.

Zina continued, 'At least they haven't killed us yet. We had a commander, Major Solovyev. The kindest man and a great officer. He fell into German hands at Stalingrad, just before the Germans surrendered. He was liberated by the Soviets, just like me. Ten days later he was shot. He was a decorated officer, a Hero of the Soviet Union.'

'I don't understand it at all,' Nina said quietly. 'Do they think we wanted to be captured? That it was our fault?'

'Of course, they think it was our fault.'

'What could we have done differently?'

For a moment Zina remained quiet, as if she didn't want to answer Nina's question. Then she said, 'You know what Stalin says? Last bullet for yourself. To save our families from repression and ourselves from shame, we should have shot ourselves rather than allow the Nazis to take us.'

'It can't be,' whispered Nina.

Zina shook her head. 'Ten years of hard labour. I wish they'd killed me instead, like they did Major Solovyev. It would have been more humane.'

Nina wished she had never spoken to Zina at all. Over and over through sleepless nights she heard Zina's voice inside her head, telling her of the unspeakable horrors to come. For all the gruelling training in Engels, for hunger and exhaustion, for her frostbitten face, for her bleeding heart, for seeing her comrades die one after another, for seeing her brother die in front of her but flying on and on, day after day, against all odds, Kolyma was what she got. Kolyma was her thanks from the Soviet government for years of loyal service.

For the next few days, Nina moved in a daze, like her feet were caught in something sticky and she could only take small, careful, confused steps as she went about her day. She wanted to throw herself on the ground like a toddler and scream and kick her feet. *It's not fair, it's not fair, it's not fair.* But she didn't scream and she didn't kick her feet. There was little point because no one cared. All she did was retreat inside herself, into silence. The routine provided some solace. If she worked herself to the point where she almost passed out from exhaustion, she wouldn't have the energy for pain or tears or relentless thoughts whirring through her head. She wouldn't have any space for feeling. To preserve her sanity, she became an empty shell of the person she had once been.

'How can I send a letter to my regiment?' she asked Zina one morning, when the rain had stopped and the sun peeked from behind the cloud, playing on the leaves that were turning golden. *What a beautiful autumn it could have been*, thought Nina. If only Hitler hadn't come to the Soviet Union. If only Papa, Vlad and Katya were still alive. If only she wasn't a prisoner. If only . . .

'You can't. They won't allow it.'

'I have the right to contact my loved ones.' Her regiment was her family. The only family she had left.

'You were sentenced to hard labour. You have no rights. Soon you won't even have a name anymore. You'll be a number. After a couple of years, you won't remember who you are.' Zina stared at her grimly.

Nina's face fell.

Zina must have felt sorry for her because she smiled and said, 'Sometimes trucks come to collect and return the laundry. When you are working outside one day, why don't you ask a truck driver to take your letter? He could post it outside the camp.'

Nina thought it was a great idea. She wrote to her regiment and Major Markov, detailing everything that had happened to them, finally adding a short heartfelt note for Anton. 'I'm sorry to be the bearer of bad news,' she wrote. 'But Katya didn't make it. Sorry I couldn't keep her alive for you and Tonya. God knows I tried.' Tears fell on the paper, smudging the words, as she thought of Katya's feverish face and her twisted mouth begging Nina to look after Tonya. 'Before Katya died, I gave her my word. I promised to be the best mother I could possibly be for Tonya. I risked my life to return back to the regiment. To return to you. But it was impossible.'

On her walk the next day, she approached a truck driver and he agreed to take her letters. He shared his lunch with her and told her about his own daughter, fighting in a tank battalion somewhere. 'Since the day she was born, she was a tomboy. Never played with dolls. Never wore dresses. And as soon as the war started, she was off.' There were tears in his eyes as he spoke about his little girl. 'Where did you say your regiment was stationed?'

'I only know where it was before our last mission.' She leaned over the truck driver's map and pointed with a finger. 'Here, not far from Kursk.'

'We destroyed the Germans at Kursk a couple of weeks ago,' he told her.

'We did?' She was pleased to hear that. All the sacrifice, the deaths and the heartbreak had not been in vain.

'Raskova's regiment, did you say? I think they've been sent to Smolensk.' He pressed her hand reassuringly. 'I won't post your letter. The post is terrible. Even if it reaches the regiment, it will be months from now.'

'At least they will know what's happened to us.'

'Tell you what. I'm supposed to drop off some packages not far from Smolensk in the next week or so. I will do my best to find your regiment. I will deliver your letters personally.'

'Thank you.' She shook his hand, fighting tears. 'Thank you for your kindness.'

'You are most welcome. It's the least I can do. You remind me of my Rita. As determined and headstrong.'

Nina watched the driver leave on his truck, her letters safely in his pocket. He drove through the gates to freedom, leaving an unfamiliar feeling behind – hope.

* * *

Day after day in the camp, getting up at dawn, a meagre breakfast, chopping wood next to Zina, who looked like she was ready to fall down, a short break for lunch and more work, finally collapsing into bed, shaking with exhaustion. 'This is what the rest of our life is going to be like,' Nina said to Zina one day.

'Worse, much worse,' whispered Zina.

Night after sleepless night she was alone with her thoughts, listening to Zina in the bunk above, tossing and turning as she battled her own demons. It felt like the authorities had forgotten all about them and they would remain in this camp until the end of war and beyond. Then one day, three weeks after she had sent her letters, they were ordered outside and marched in the rain and wind to the nearest station. Nina trudged behind the others blindly. A few times she slipped and fell and the person behind her bumped into her, making her cry out. Zina was walking by her side. She hadn't said a word that morning. Everywhere Nina looked, she saw miserable faces. Some women were crying. Others were staring mutely into space, their eyes dark with grief. It was one thing hearing their sentence read out to them. It was quite another to be walking to a train that would take them to hell on earth from which there was no return. Until this morning, they still had hope, however small. Now this hope was disappearing with every step they took.

Nina didn't cry or complain. If only she concentrated on walking, on putting one foot in front of the other, eyes to the ground, hands clasped into fists, then she wouldn't have to think about what lay ahead.

A guard told them to line up in front of the train. He reminded Nina of the German guard at a different time, a different station, before Katya had died. Before Nina had learnt that her motherland could turn its back on her. Before she had lost her faith. This man had the same angry face, suspicious eyes and threatening manner as the German guard on the train bound for Bryansk. Nina had to remind herself that this was a

Soviet soldier, that until now they had been on the same side, fighting for the same principles.

The train was exactly the same too, a freight train without seats, not meant to transport people. Where was the peasant woman with her knife when Nina needed her? But even if she managed to escape, where would she go? Before, she had thought she could return home. She had fought tooth and nail to make her way back. She had raced through fields, trying to outrun the Germans bullets. She had walked through battle-fields, explosives bursting over her head. Hope had given her strength. What was left for her now that her country had betrayed her?

'What are they doing?' asked Nina, turning to Zina. 'Why did they tell us to line up?'

Zina stood on tiptoes to see better. 'They are searching everyone, I think.'

'After weeks at the camp, what are they hoping to find?' she whispered to Zina. 'Weapons?'

The woman who searched Nina looked her up and down with disdain, like she was someone to be despised, like she was a traitor to her country. With horror Nina realised that from this moment on, that was exactly what she had become, forever. It didn't matter that she had done nothing wrong. All that mattered was that she was tried and condemned.

The woman ordered Nina to take her boots off and stand barefoot in a puddle of water. Nina shook from the cold and the indignation of it all. Thankfully, the search didn't last long and soon she was putting her boots back on and moving along in the queue of prisoners waiting to board the train.

I only have these few minutes, she thought. *A few more minutes before I become a convict.*

She wanted to take it all in. The grey sky over her head. The trees dressed in their autumn best, groaning in the wind. Autumn had put on her best attire for Nina to enjoy on her last day.

She knew once she stepped on that train, her life would change forever. She would never look at things the same way again.

Before she turned away from the sky and the trees and faced the train, faced her bleak and uncertain future, Nina saw a car appear in the distance and speed down the road towards the station. In a few moments it stopped and the doors opened on either side. Out came one of the officers who had interrogated her, the unfriendly major who seemed to hate her, with his bulldog face and sour expression. In his hands he held a piece of paper. Nina shuddered, remembering the words treason and betrayal as they came out of that crooked mouth, directed at her. So focussed was she on the major, she didn't even look at the other man who stepped out of the driver's seat and walked as fast as he could towards the train. When Nina finally glanced at him, her heart stopped.

It was Anton.

Was she imagining it? Was Zina right? Did the labour camp drive her crazy? Here was Nina, seeing things that couldn't possibly be real. Was her imagination playing tricks on her? Giving her what she wanted the most because his was the face she saw every time she closed her eyes at night.

And yet, it didn't look like a figment of her imagination. Anton stopped for a moment and wiped his forehead with the back of his hand, glancing around as if searching for someone. Dazed, she watched as he started walking again, faster this time, as if afraid he would run out of time. Nina shouted, 'Anton,' then pushed the woman in front of her out of the way and began to run.

She heard Zina's voice behind her. 'What are you doing? They are going to shoot you.'

The guard made a move to go after her but the major rose his hand and ordered the man to remain where he was. Nina continued running, falling in the rain, getting up and running again, oblivious to everything and everyone around her. Except him. All she could see was him.

Moments later she was in his arms and he was spinning her in the air, holding her tight, whispering her name, kissing her cheeks that were damp with tears. 'Don't cry, why are you crying?' he whispered.

'Is it really you?' she asked. She felt dizzy, lightheaded from hunger, exhaustion and everything she was feeling. Suddenly, the noises faded and everything went dark. The last thing she saw before she fainted was his face close to hers.

She came to in the car. Anton was leaning over her. He looked worried. 'Are you all right? I'm going to find a doctor. I will be back in two minutes. Can you wait here for two minutes?'

'No, don't go. I don't need a doctor. I'm fine. I'm great, actually.'

'You fainted.' He pushed a loose strand of hair away from her face.

'Can you blame me? I didn't expect to see you here.'

He held her close and through his tunic she could feel his heart. They remained like this for a long time, holding each other, not saying a word. His face was unshaven and his hair had more grey in it than she remembered. But the smile and the twinkle in his eye was unmistakeably his. Finally, he asked, 'Are you sure you don't need a doctor? In that case, we better go. The sooner we get out of here, the better.'

When he was in the driver's seat and the car was moving away from the place of so much horror, she said, 'What are you doing here?'

'I'm taking you home.'

'Really?' She could hardly believe it. A part of her thought she was dreaming. Perhaps she was on the fateful train destined for Kolyma, with Zina and the other women around her, and she finally managed to doze off. None of this was real. She would soon wake up and realise she would never see Anton again. She shuddered.

'The girls are waiting for you. I think they are baking you a cake.'

'A cake? How? Where did they get the flour?'

'They spent weeks drinking their tea without sugar and saving their vodka, so they could exchange them for everything they needed. They can't wait to have their sister back.'

She pressed her face into his shoulder and cried. 'Are they letting me go?'

Anton nodded. 'We didn't know what happened to you. We didn't know what to think. When the Germans retreated, we found the plane wreckage and Igor's body. And still we didn't know what to think or where to look for you and Katya. Then your letters reached us. Major Markov became like a man possessed. I've never seen him that angry. He was like a raging bull. "What are they doing to one of my best pilots? Don't they know who she is and what she's done for our country? How dare they? Who do they think they are?"'

Nina laughed, feeling relieved, her heart full. 'Markov said I was one of his best pilots? I'm going to remind him of that next time he tells me off for a grease stain on my uniform.'

'He spent weeks going from general to general. He cajoled and threatened and told them all about you. He was unstoppable. According to Markov, if we had a thousand officers like you, we would have won this war a long time ago. "Shoot her or exile her," he said. "What a present for the Nazis." He didn't give up until he had your release papers in his hands. Now, why are you crying?'

'I'm crying because I'm grateful. And touched. And so happy. I've always known we had the best commander in the world.'

'Always?' Anton's eyes twinkled.

'He saved my life.'

'You girls are like family to him. He might be grouchy sometimes but he'll move mountains for you.'

They drove past the camp that had been her prison for the last few weeks. She felt her hands begin to tremble when she saw its silhouette in the sun. She knew that for as long as she lived, she would not forget this place. Not because of the hard work she'd had to endure within its walls. She had known hard work before, in Engels, at the front and escaping from the Nazis. And not because she didn't know what tomorrow would bring. Her future had been uncertain since the day the war had started. She would never forget this place because its grey walls symbolised the worst betrayal she had ever experienced.

'I'm so sorry about Katya,' she whispered. 'I tried to save her. I did my best to bring her home for you and Tonya.'

Anton's eyes filled with tears. He blinked. 'It breaks my heart that I couldn't protect her, that Tonya will never see her mother again. And I'm sorry you had to go through so much. This war hasn't been kind to you.'

'Has it been kind to anyone?' Nina smiled sadly, sitting upright in her seat, forcing her eyes open, forcing herself to stay awake, so she could see his face. All she wanted was to see his wonderful face. 'I'm so happy you came to get me. So relieved. It was . . . Everything seemed so bleak. Hopeless, like my life was over.'

'The last couple of months have been hell. I didn't know if you were dead or alive.'

'I'm alive. I'm right here.'

'Thank God.' He looked at her with such warmth, her heart fluttered like a butterfly inside her chest, while the ravaged countryside whizzed past them, while the earth rumbled in the distance.

'What else have I missed? What's happening at the front?' she asked.

'Italy surrendered to the Allies. We are slowly pushing the Germans back.'

'That's good news.'

'Yes, it is. It took the Germans a few weeks to occupy all this land. It's taking us years to claim it back. But we are not giving up. We'll take as long as we need.' His eyes on the road, he added, 'Oh, and there was a letter for you.' He reached inside his pocket and gave Nina an envelope folded in two. She recognised her stepmother's handwriting.

'I missed you, Anton. Like a part of me was missing.'

'A small part? A finger? A tip of your nose?'

'Like my heart was missing.'

He looked away from the road, took her hand and smiled. 'I know the feeling.'

Nina had no idea what the future would bring. She didn't even know if they had a future, with the war that had already taken her father, brother and Katya still raging with no end in sight. All they had was this moment. But it was a moment together and she knew she would treasure it forever.

Dear Nina,

I haven't been the best stepmother for you and I'm sorry. I wish I could change it all and start over. Losing your father made me realise that family is everything. And you are the only family, other than myself, that my children have left in this world.

It broke my heart to learn about Vlad. I hope you are keeping well and staying safe, wherever you are. I worry about you. Every time I see something about Marina Raskova's regiment in the paper, I cut the article out and paste it in my notebook. I have quite a collection.

Leo asks about you every day. We settled in Krasnoyarsk, and although there's hardly any food, we are doing fine. I am enclosing our address. I hope you can come and visit. I don't want Leo and Lena to grow up without knowing their big sister.

With love,

Anna

Epilogue

May 1945

In a small Lithuanian town of Gruzdžiai, east of the Baltic Sea, under the topaz spring sky, Nina was ready for take off, the controls under her hands shaking in anticipation, the Pe-2 trembling impatiently, herself trembling impatiently, when suddenly she heard voices. Popping her head out of the cockpit, she spotted Inna, her mechanic, and Lada, her armourer. Seeing their faces always made her smile. They had gone through the war together. They were family. Every time she was upset or afraid, one look at their calm smiles and she felt the stress and the fear leave her body. Except, this morning their faces were anything but calm. Lada had tears running down her face. Inna was gesticulating widely. Their eyes were round and glistening. Nina waited, her heart beating in trepidation. Did something bad happen? Had they lost another a plane? But when the two of them approached, Nina saw that they were smiling. She relaxed a little.

'What's happening?' asked Dasha, Nina's navigator.

'I know as much as you do,' replied Nina, watching as the girls ran up to the plane and without explanation proceeded to take the bombs down.

'Is there something wrong with the plane?' Nina shouted to Inna.

Inna stood up straight and waved to Nina. 'Everything is fine with the plane, Lieutenant,' she replied. 'But we were told to unload the bombs.' The same enigmatic smile and a quiet chuckle as they continued working.

Nina jumped out of the cockpit and stood next to Inna. 'Private Pechkina. That's quite enough. This instant tell us what is going on.'

Inna looked like she was about to burst. The smile was wide on her face. It was Lada who jumped up and said, 'Haven't you heard? The war is over!'

Nina thought she had misheard. Either that or Lada was messing with her. 'What?' she whispered.

'Hitler surrendered. It's over.' Lada bounced up and down like a ball. 'Can you believe it? It's all over!'

'I can't believe it,' muttered Nina, her hand on her heart, her breath catching.

Dasha joined the girls on the ground, followed by their tail gunner, Maksim. 'The war is over?' they kept repeating.

And soon they were jumping around, dancing a mad tango in circles, holding each other's hands, hugging and shouting, 'The war is over! The war is over!' While all around them the bombs lay innocently at their feet, like felled pigeons.

Instead of flying that day, the regiment celebrated. With tears in his eyes, Major Valentin Markov toasted those who didn't live to see this happy day. He toasted those who had made this day possible, with their hard work and sacrifice. 'I have to admit, when I came here and learnt I was to lead a regiment of women, I felt furious. I didn't know what I had done to deserve this. I was going to refuse, only I wasn't given much choice. Little did I know, you girls were the best thing that had ever happened to me. Side by side, we learnt and we grew as soldiers and human beings. We inspired each other. We risked our lives, mourned and rejoiced. Through the years, you have become my family. You are the most talented pilots I had the pleasure of working with, dedicated and fearless warriors. You are an inspiration to me, an example to all of the Soviet Union, to generations of men and women that will come after you. Together, you have achieved the impossible. You are selfless and brave. You are heroes.' The man who had led them and cried with them, who had saved so many lives, who had shared everything with them through ups and downs, who had drunk from the same cup and eaten form the same bowl with them over the years, took off his cap and bowed. 'Many years ago, Major Marina Raskova had a vision. A vision no one believed in. You lived this vision. You made it a reality. If she could see you now, she would take her cap off to you too. Women of Raskova's Dive Bomber Regiment, I salute you. It was an honour and a privilege to have served as your commander.'

There was not a dry eye as far as Nina could see. The girls rushed to Major Markov, the man who they called *Batya* and came to think of as their father, and took turns to hug him. Zhenya picked up her guitar, her face beaming. She had been an older sister to the girls and their best friend. She had carried them through war, as a regimental commander, a comrade and later a squadron commander. She had done her job, holding their hands through adversity to safety, all the way to the end of war.

Her voice thick with emotion, Zhenya sang Yulia Siniza's favourite song. Strumming her guitar lovingly, she sang the way Yulia had once sung, every word filled with hope.

Wait for me, and I'll return.
Only surely wait.
Wait, when yellow autumn rains
Bring on long regret.

The wait was finally over for the women of Raskova's regiment. They could go home and, after four long years, embrace their loved ones.

But not all of them could go home. Nina blinked and saw their faces. Marina, Katya, Yulia, Masha, Vlad, Papa. They were still among them. They watched over them and their hearts were full.

It wasn't a jubilant celebration. They had lost too much for that. Too many people they loved were not there to share their joy. But it was a celebration nonetheless because they had persevered and made it, through blood and tears, through joy and sorrow, day after backbreaking day, night after restless night.

When it got dark, Nina and Anton sat side by side on the grass, next to their trusted planes that had got them through the war, their airfield behind them. It was one of many hundreds of wartime airfields they had known over the years but it was special. This was where they had become victorious. The sky was studded with diamonds, thousands of them twinkling their joy at Nina and Anton.

'What do you think of it? The peaceful sky. The sky that doesn't rain deadly explosives,' said Anton, looking up in wonder.

'It will take some getting used to. It will take some time to stop waking up in the middle of the night, afraid.' Nina wiped the tears off her face. 'I wish my father and brother were here to see this. I wish Katya was here to see this.' Anton moved closer and pulled her to him. She relaxed in his arms, closing her eyes. The war was over. Now real life could begin. She threaded her fingers through his. 'Can I ask you a question?'

'Of course.'

'Promise to tell me the truth.'

'Ask me first and then I'll decide whether I can make you that promise.'

'All right.' She watched his face for a moment, beaming. The stubble on his chin and around his mouth made him look like a pirate. She stroked it with her fingers. It felt rough to the touch. 'When did you first know you loved me?'

He was silent for a moment, as if lost in the past. 'On the day your brother was killed. I remember holding you in my arms and wishing I could give my life for you. It broke my heart to see you so distraught. That's when I knew I would do anything for you.' He kissed her fingers, the palm of her hand, her wrist. 'What about you?'

'At the hospital. I was so afraid of losing you. I had already lost so many. I realised if I lost you, I would have nothing left. That's when I knew you were everything to me.' She moved closer, placed her head on his chest and listened for his heart. 'I think I knew long before then but I refused to admit it, even to myself. You were Katya's. Who was I to take her place?'

As if he could read her mind, he said, 'You have nothing to feel guilty about. We didn't ask for any of it. We didn't ask to be the only two left standing. We didn't ask to fall in love.' He turned her slightly so she could see his face. There was a smile but his eyes were serious. 'Katya was right, you know. You are going to make a wonderful mother for Tonya. And a wonderful wife for me. What do you say, Lieutenant Petrova?'

'Why, are you asking me to marry you, Captain Bogdanov?'

'Indeed I am.'

'I have to think about it. I will let you know.' She laughed and pinched him. 'Yes!'

'Is that a yes?' He lifted her in his arms and spun her around, while she squealed in delight, in long circles and small circles around the airfield that had seen too much, into the rest of their lives.

As Anton held her and the sun went down, Nina thought of Katya, her father and brother. She thought of Zina in the arctic wilderness somewhere, lost and afraid. She thought of Major Marina Raskova, a young woman with a vision, and of her sisters-in-arms and everything they had achieved, at the cost of so many lives, of death and hopeless despair, of flying off to war every morning, even when their hearts were breaking. After two and a half years at the front, they had made their beloved commander proud. Day after day, they had proven that they could indeed do anything. Just like Major Raskova knew they would.

A Letter from Lana Kortchik

Dear Reader,

Thank you for choosing *Sisters of the Sky*. I hope you enjoyed reading it as much as I enjoyed writing it. As soon as I began my research into Major Marina Raskova's regiments, I knew I had to write this book. This story has captured my imagination and I'm so excited to be able to share it with you.

When Hitler attacked the Soviet Union in June 1941, thousands of women rushed to conscription points across the country to volunteer for the front. Not content to sit back and wait, they joined active service as nurses, pilots, snipers, machine gunners, artillery operators. It is estimated that 800,000 Soviet women served in the military between 1941 and 1945.

Shortly after the war had started, the world famous pilot and navigator Marina Raskova approached Joseph Stalin, offering to create, train and lead three bomber and fighter aviation regiments comprised entirely of women. Although Raskova died in a plane crash on her way to the front in January 1943, her vision lived on. A thousand women, who had been trained by her to become the best aviators they could possibly be, fought combat missions against the Nazi invaders until the end of the war. At the time, the Soviet Union was the only country in the world to allow women to fly in combat.

Although Nina and Katya are fictional, there were many women just like them who had left their families behind to fight at the front, risking their lives every day for their motherland, with little thought of personal safety. Besides Raskova, three real people make an appearance in *Sisters of the Sky*.

Militsa Kazarinova served as Raskovas's chief-of-staff. Despite her reputation as a strict commander who never forgave a transgression, she loved her aviators dearly and protected them as much as she could. She survived the war, achieved the rank of colonel and retired from the military in 1956.

Valentin Markov served as regimental commander for the 587th Dive Bomber Regiment from February 1943. Despite his reluctance to accept this post and the women's initial distrust, he soon became like a father to his pilots and navigators, taking to the sky and sharing the realities of war with them, leading by example and saving many lives.

Evgeniya 'Zhenya' Timofeeva was like a sister to the women of the 587th, even though she was their squadron and deputy regimental commander. For her heroic actions during the war, she was awarded two Orders of the Red Banner and two Orders of the Patriotic War.

While researching Raskova's regiments, I came across many fascinating diaries, memoirs and letters, such as those written by Nataliya Kravzova, Raisa Aronova, Klava Blinova, Nina Ivakina, Galya Dokutovich, Lilya Litvyak, Lera Homyakova and Zhenya Rudneva. These fearless women wrote about hard work at the front, their daily routine, the pain of losing comrades they had grown to love, their longing for home and not knowing if they would live long enough to see their families. They were often afraid but ignored their fear, performing acts of bravery every single day. And that's what made them true heroes.

If this story touched your heart like it did mine and you would like to learn more about Raskova's regiments, *A Thousand Sisters* by Elizabeth Wein is a wonderful resource in English.

I'm always happy to hear from my readers and would love to know what you thought about the book. Please feel free to reach out by leaving a review or contacting me via my website or social media.

Thanks,

Lana

Twitter: https://twitter.com/lanakortchik
Facebook: https://www.facebook.com/lanakortchik/
Website: http://www.lanakortchik.com/

Sisters of War

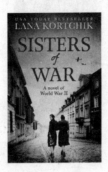

Can their bond survive under the shadow of occupation?

For fans of *The Tattooist of Auschwitz* and *The German Midwife* comes this unforgettable tale of love, loss, family, and the power of hope.

Kiev, 1941: Watching the Red Army withdraw from Ukraine in the face of Hitler's relentless advance, sisters **Natasha** and **Lisa Smirnova** realise their lives are about to change forever.

As the German army occupies their beloved city, the sisters are tested in ways they never thought possible. Lisa's fiancé **Alexei** is taken by the invading army, whilst Natasha falls in love with **Mark** – a Hungarian soldier, enlisted against all his principles on the side of the Nazis.

But as Natasha and Lisa fight to protect the friends and family they hold dear, they must face up to the dark horrors of war and the pain of betrayal.

Will they be strong enough to overcome the forces which threaten to tear their family apart?

Daughters of the Resistance

Ukraine, 1943

On a train from Ukraine to Germany, **Lisa Smirnova** is terrified for her life. The train is under Nazi command, heading for
one of Hitler's rumoured labour camps. As she is taken away
from everything she holds dear, Lisa wonders if she will ever
see her family again.

In Nazi-occupied Kiev, **Irina Antonova** knows she could be
arrested at any moment. Trapped in a job registering the
endless deaths of the people of Kiev, she risks her life every
day by secretly helping her neighbours, while her husband has
joined the Soviet partisans, who are carrying out life-threat-
ening work to frustrate the German efforts.

When Lisa's train is intercepted by the partisans, Irina's
husband among them, these women's lives will take an unim-
aginable turn. As Irina fights to protect her family and Lisa is
forced to confront the horrors of war, together they must make
an impossible decision: **what would they be willing to lose to
save the people they love?**

**Be swept away by this heart-wrenching novel of love, resil-
ience and courage in World War II, from the author of *Sisters
of War* – perfect for readers who loved *The Tattooist of
Auschwitz* and *The German Midwife*.**

The Countess of the Revolution

March, 1917

Petrograd is on the eve of revolution. For **Countess Sophia Orlova**, the city of her childhood – the only home she has ever known – has become her deadly enemy. The mob are ready to get rid of anyone connected to the old regime, including Sophia. When rebels threaten to shoot Sophia and her husband, they are saved by **Nikolai**, a fervent supporter of the revolution. Determined to help Nikolai's cause, Sophia sets up a hospital wing in the house, nursing injured victims by his side.
Her kindness has captured Nikolai's heart, but their burgeoning romance is forbidden. With battle lines drawn between the new and the old, both their lives are in danger . . .
Will their love be strong enough to overcome the horrors of war? From the bestselling author of *Sisters of War* comes a heart-wrenching novel of lovers trapped on the opposite sides of a terrifying political conflict, loss, and sacrifice.

Acknowledgements

Researching and writing *Sisters of the Sky* has been an incredible experience and being able to share it with the readers worldwide is a dream come true. I am forever grateful to all those who have made it possible.

Thank you to my rockstar agent, Mark Gottlieb, for believing in me and always being there for me.

Thank you to my fantastic editor, Audrey Linton, whose vision for this book made it the best it could possibly be, to Charlotte Phillips for my beautiful cover, and to the talented teams at HQ and HarperCollins360 for working so hard to bring this book to readers.

As ever, I would like to thank my family for allowing me to lock myself away for hours to write this book and supporting me every step of the way. Thank you to my mum for her kindness and wisdom. Thank you to my husband Joel for all his help, from watching the children to making sure I eat. And to the children for the cuddles and unconditional love. You are my everything!

Finally, I would like to thank my readers around the world for buying my books, reading and reviewing, especially those who reached out to let me know how much they enjoyed my stories. Your words mean the world to me.

Dear Reader,

We hope you enjoyed reading this book. If you did, we'd be so appreciative if you left a review. It really helps us and the author to bring more books like this to you.

Here at HQ Digital we are dedicated to publishing fiction that will keep you turning the pages into the early hours. Don't want to miss a thing? To find out more about our books, promotions, discover exclusive content and enter competitions you can keep in touch in the following ways:

JOIN OUR COMMUNITY:

Sign up to our new email newsletter: http://smarturl.it/SignUpHQ

Read our new blog www.hqstories.co.uk

https://twitter.com/HQStories

www.facebook.com/HQStories

BUDDING WRITER?

We're also looking for authors to join the HQ Digital family!
Find out more here:

https://www.hqstories.co.uk/want-to-write-for-us/

Thanks for reading, from the HQ Digital team